C.A. Dawson

C.A. Dawson was born in Montreal, Canada and raised in the small Quebec town of Rawdon. She has been writing since she was eight years old.

Dawson has written seven SF novels. Her first novel, *Alien Stalker*, appeared in 2000. She currently lives in Victoria, British Columbia.

www.cadawsonsf.com

This novel is entirely a work of fiction. The names characters and places portrayed in it are the work of the author's imagination or are used fictitiously. Any resemblance to actual persons living or dead, events or locales is entirely coincidental.

CACIN

Babora Books
Victoria, British Columbia, Canada
www.baborabooks.com

Copyright 2010 C.A. Dawson
Cover illustration by Duncan Long

C.A. Dawson asserts the moral right to be identified as the author
of this book.

ISBN: 978-0-9866443-0-6

All rights reserved. No part of this publication may be reproduced, stored in a retrieval system or transmitted in any form, or by any means, electronic or otherwise without the prior permission of the authors.

Second Printing

This book is set in Palatino Linotype and Century Gothic.
The original MS was written in Microsoft Word. Text and cover layout were created with using Adobe InDesign CS5.

For Paul, who knows all about mountains.

C.A. Dawson
Cacin

Chapter 1
Flight of the Lemming

"I'm going to kill her!" Kagoule roared, his black mane glistening in the overhead light. "I've had enough, Gradspin! Enough! She can't do this to me."

He paced the length of the council hall, slamming a fist repeatedly into the palm of his other hand. Gradspin jumped with every smack of flesh on flesh.

Outside the huge windows – beyond the door that led to the garden – a day as dark and grey as Kagoule's mood was evolving. A storm gathered outside - and in, Gradspin thought. Could he keep her alive? It didn't look good.

"Wasn't she your best choice?" Gradspin asked calmly.

"She challenges me at every turn," Kagoule shrieked. "She refuses to answer my questions. Refuses!" He hammered his fist on the cold stone table top. Then, turning back to his pacing, he shoved a chair out of his way so forcefully it upended and skittered across the tiled floor, slamming into the wall and splintering.

"She persists in believing I will go away if she ignores me. So she does. Me!" he screamed, pounding his massive chest, and disregarding the shattered chair almost as well as Hill'carn spurned him. "She ignores ME! The King of the Gron'dalin Empire. She thinks I'm a figment of her imagination! How dare she!"

Light from the ceiling lamps danced off the complex shell-like pattern on his face. Sweat beaded there and ran through the design like a small river meandering through a field. His flat nose flared, his black eyes flashed menacingly. "I will kill her and choose another," he said resolutely, brushing aside any potential dissent with the flick of a wrist.

"She is the best of the breed," Gradspin insisted. A breeze played at the hem of the old gron's floor-length cape, moving it slightly, just a whisper. "You must be patient with her, Lord. It must be hard for her, hearing but not seeing you."

Kagoule looked to Cacin for sympathy. His young cousin stood silently at the head of the table, one hand firmly planted on a hip, his silver cape thrown carelessly back over one shoulder to accommodate his stance. Instead of sympathy, the young gron lifted his shoulders signing indifference.

"Why are you shrugging?" Kagoule demanded, turning his fury on the teenager. "Do you wish to anger me further?"

"Gods no," Cacin replied boldly. "No one dare do that."

Gradspin stiffened and held his breath, fear coursing over his weathered features along well worn paths carved by time.

"Only YOU can speak to me thus," Kagoule replied after a brief pause, his annoyance subsiding a little.

Gradspin breathed again.

Cacin sighed audibly, not trying to disguise his displeasure with the King. He forged on. "Don't they always think ill of us at first?"

"She thinks of me as a THING," Kagoule complained, vexation riding his voice. But the crisis passed quickly. "When she thinks of me at all."

Gradspin relaxed.

The King moaned loudly. "When she's not thinking she's lost her mind, that is," he added contemptuously. "She doubts her own sanity from time to time."

"That is a normal reaction," Gradspin declared.

The long stone table where the Elders gathered daily to hear the King's Assessment of his future bride lay between Kagoule and Gradspin.

"Think of it from her perspective," Gradspin ventured, seeing that Kagoule would now listen. "She doesn't use her mind. None of them do. None of them ever have."

"Which is just as well for us," Cacin interjected. "We would have a terrible battle if they did."

"Suddenly, you're in her mind." Gradspin pressed on. "Telling her what to do, demanding answers from her, assessing her. She knows nothing of Assessment!"

Kagoule grunted and continued pacing the length of the room, working off his fit of temper. His back to the old gron, he snorted.

"You must be patient with her," Gradspin reiterated. "If you are patient, I believe you can win this female. She is very intelligent.

More so than any we have encountered before. Just the fact that she speaks so many of her people's languages attests to that."

Kagoule turned and paced back toward the Lord Elder, then turned abruptly and strode away towards the wall again.

"Think of it," Gradspin continued. "Think what it would be like to actually win them, instead of just dominating them. Give her a few more hours. Give yourself a rest first. Put a mind grid around her. Ensure she goes nowhere, speaks to no one. Then go back into her mind when both you and she have had a break from the Assessment."

"Another waste of time," Kagoule complained drawing a hand through his curly mane. He hooked his hand in the thick hair and kicked at the bits of broken chair. "I should go there physically," he blurted suddenly, rounding on them.

"Patience," Gradspin admonished.

Kagoule released the breath he had just captured and nodded at the Elder. "Alright," he said slowly. He closed his eyes and rolled his broad shoulders. On opening his eyes he added, "I can use some sleep. And you can be sure I'll build a mind block for her or the little fool will flee while I'm indisposed." He snorted with disgust at the thought of the female attempting an escape. "If she resists me when I go back into her mind, I'll kill her."

* * * *

Outside the open windows, people chatted, car horns beeped, engines revved. A breeze hot as the blast from a furnace swept through pine trees, making a soft swishing sound as it grazed the long needles. Faintly, the Venetian blind rattled against the window frame. Hillary looked at it nervously as she slammed the old alligator suitcase shut.

"I have to go," she whispered, pulling herself away from that seductive pit, that crater of inaction that seemed to hover always nearby. With cold black fingers it beckoned, promising to re-immerse her in inertia. Her mind kept falling back into it, residing there for minutes at a time. She couldn't let it happen again.

"They're coming, dear," Martha whispered as though trying to sooth a deranged person.

The fragrance of flowers in bloom mingled with car exhaust and floated through the open window. Children, their voices, muted by traffic, called to friends on the street below.

"I've been a prisoner here," Hillary murmured. "I've been a hostage. Violated!" Raising her head she shot a fearful glance around the room. "It did it with its mind."

Martha looked away briefly, down at the floor; at the overturned plant pot, the dirt that unfolded from the dying plant in little mashed down heaps; at the broken glass strewn through it. "With . . . its mind?" she said hesitantly, still looking at the mess, scowling.

"Yes. Its mind."

After a long awkward pause, the apartment manager's wife suddenly turned back to Hillary, grabbing her shoulders and shaking her slightly. "You're hallucinating, dear!" Martha blurted.

She jerked Hillary again more forcefully. "Whatever happened in here these past few days has unhinged you." There, she'd finally said it, or something approaching what she was thinking

Letting Hillary go, Martha inhaled through her nostrils. "Maybe you'd better lie down! Help is on the way!"

In spite of the heat, Hillary shuddered. "I've been trapped here. My mind has been defiled by . . . something. That's all I know. I'll figure the rest out later."

She hauled the old suitcase off the couch. The action inadvertently knocked away Martha's hand. Not caring, Hillary rushed to the door.

Martha followed at her heels, holding hands to her head as though her brains would spill out if she let go. The older woman kept in step, nattering about Hillary being ill; about the importance of not doing anything rash.

If Hillary heard the word 'rash' one more time, she knew she would scream.

"I don't think you should be leaving like this, dear. Help is on the way," Martha repeated.

"They can't help, Martha. Please try to understand. No one can help. Look around this room."

Hillary stopped abruptly. Martha slammed into her. She gestured at the debris in her apartment. In addition to the mashed plant, the sweep of her arm took in an overturned chair, thrown seat cushions and strewn knickknacks. "Just think for a minute about what I'm saying. It did this with its mind. It can do anything with its mind. The operative word here is 'mind' not man, Martha. No man has abused me in here." Then to herself she added, "But it CAN be beaten if I can only analyze what happened, learn about it from what it did to me."

"Dear, I think you're suffering an awful shock of some kind," Martha said as Hillary turned and fled the apartment. "Why don't you come and hide from it in my apartment," she insisted, still searching for some way to detain Hillary.

Hillary ignored her and ran for the elevator.

"Come with me, dear."

"You don't understand," Hillary yelled, turning on the woman suddenly, frightening her, her dark eyes wide with fear. "Something has kept me prisoner in that damned apartment with its mind! Get it? Going to your apartment in this bloody building isn't going to help! Walls don't stop it! I know it sounds crazy, Martha. But it happened. I've been a captive in that flat for nine days!"

Hillary said this as though speaking to someone dull of wit. "Look at the mess in there!" Hillary motioned toward the apartment door Martha had closed on the way out. "Look at me! I'm a wreck. How do you think I got this way?" She strode quickly to the fire door that separated this stretch of corridor from the next and heaved it open, urgency propelling her on.

Martha watched as the disheveled, dirty, frightened woman stumbled, thrown off balance by that funny old alligator suitcase.

Hillary had told Martha on renting the apartment earlier that month that her father had loaned her the suitcase when she persisted with plans to attend the University of Toronto. The case banged against metal as she pushed through the fire door.

Oh how Martha had liked the young Aussie girl. From the moment they met, Martha had warmed to her. She'd told Gus something was wrong when Hillary didn't come for tea. She always dropped by for tea in the afternoon on Wednesdays and Fridays.

Had done since she moved in. And she'd enriched Martha's lonely life.

When Hillary didn't turn up two tea times in a row Martha knew something was wrong. Felt it in her bones.

If there was anything Martha could do to save Hillary now, she would.

Martha followed. She had lowered her hands from her head and now pressed the knuckles of one hand firmly against her lips while holding the other to her throat.

Hillary's small purse, expertly tucked under one arm, slipped slightly. Out of habit, Martha jumped forward to assist but failed. Hillary wedged the purse against her body and continued her rush toward the elevator.

"There's no hope for you if you go off alone," Martha declared, fighting tears. Hillary ignored her and hurried toward the elevator.

"Oh dear, whatever am I to do?" Martha moaned under her breath.

"Go home, Martha!" Hillary blurted, stopping at the elevator. "Just go home!" she said unkindly. These brisk words were so out of character that Martha gasped.

Seeing Martha's discomfort Hillary added, "I'm running for my life. You can't help me. No one can." She said this last bit through clenched teeth, then quickly added, "I have to get away before it comes back."

"Listen to me!" Martha yelled summoning a commanding, almost angry voice. "You're ill." Hillary turned back to look at her. "You're probably running a fever." She threw a weathered hand up to Hillary's temple. The wrinkled white skin stood out against Hillary's golden brown. "Yes. Most likely," she said lowering her hand. "Help's coming. Just hold on and don't do anything silly."

As the elevator door slid open with a grinding sound that did not inspire confidence, one of the latches on the suitcase popped with a noise equally as distressing.

"Oh sure," Hillary whispered, stepping into the elevator car. Stooping she fought to close the clasp and then rose and pressed 'Lobby' once, firmly. Leaning against the elevator wall she slipped her purse strap over one shoulder and stared at Martha who stayed behind in the corridor.

"It's coming for me," she whispered, brushing hair from her face with one hand. The doors ground shut and the last thing Hillary heard from Martha was a soft moan.

As the elevator settled to the ground floor with a jolt, she snatched the suitcase off the floor and bolted for the glass doors that led to the street.

"Hey! Where you goin'?" the apartment manager called. Gus was a big man with greasy grey hair and a beer belly that hung over his soiled green work pants. "I thought you was dyin'. Where's Martha? The police are comin'. And an ambulance."

Chapter 2
The Coming Storm

The light from Ranat's suns danced on Cacin's mahogany skin, skipping over the delicate loops around his eyes. Beside him, Gradspin held his breath again and tried to straighten. Age had welded him into a stooped posture and the attempt was wasted.

I must speak, Gradspin thought. I at least do not face the possibility of a Challenge at my advanced age. Leaving Cacin exposed alone to absorb Kagoule's outburst would be cowardly.

"The youngster's right," Gradspin said, steeling himself against Kagoule's fury.

"I'll not be called that again," Cacin said abruptly, spinning to face the Elder. "I am no longer a youngster."

Suddenly the parameters of the argument had changed. Though Gradspin knew it was unintentional, he was grateful for the new direction the dispute took.

"Indeed," Gradspin said admiringly. "You are right again, My Lord." The Lord Elder bowed slightly to Cacin, then turned back to Kagoule. "This gron is right about the female, my King. While it is hard to accept she has fled your mind grid, think of the sons she will bear you."

Kagoule scowled at them. "The sons," he said contemptuously. "She angers me too much to have around. You expect I can mate with this one? I have been angry for days now because of her," he said like a spoiled youth, neither of which he was. "She resists me at every turn. And now this."

"You will locate her," Cacin said.

"Of course I will locate her," Kagoule snapped back viciously. "And when I do, I will kill her." He adjusted his silver dressing gown at the neck, an action of irritation, not necessity.

"The ship will be ready to leave in another two weeks, Lord," Gradspin said. "The Elite are ready to mate. It would be unwise to detain them."

Kagoule sighed loudly. "I will have a mate ready before they leave Ranat," he promised. "I will kill this one and choose another. I will assess the new one quickly."

"What if they're all like this one?" Cacin asked. "What if they all resist you as this one has?"

Kagoule laughed bitterly. "None could resist me like this one has."

"Then she is a prize," Cacin stated.

Leave it there, Gradspin prayed. Say no more, young gron.

Kagoule looked at his youthful cousin with an intensity that could have killed one less strong than Cacin. "You go too far," he whispered.

Please be silent, Cacin, Gradspin thought to the youth.

Locked in a battle of wills, Cacin ignored the warning.

"Have you assessed them all?" Cacin continued.

Gradspin cringed, and not for the first time since this Bride Quest had begun. If the young Lord would just keep quiet!

"Your tongue will get you in trouble if you continue, Cacin," Kagoule warned, casting a wicked look at the young gron.

"I mean no offence, Lord," Cacin answered. "You have asked me to be blunt with you when, in your words, I feel your composure is vanishing."

"That I have," Kagoule admitted, finding the excuse he needed not to accept the young gron's tone as a Challenge. "And it does get away from me, doesn't it?" Kagoule admitted, glancing at the wastepaper basket he had kicked into the corner.

He drew in a deep breath and moaned. "Why? Why? Why can't she just accept her fate?"

Gradspin realized he'd been holding his breath during their discourse. His old hearts couldn't take many more encounters like this.

* * * *

Hillary woke with a start, surprised she had slept so long, surprised she was still alive.

She rolled over and looked at her travel clock. Birds chirped early morning songs outside her open window. She yawned and picked up the clock, tried to focus on the small hands and squinted. Six o'clock.

She groaned and slapped the clock back down on the night table. Where was she? Oh. Spring Arbor.

She yawned and stretched.

Sitting up in bed she looked toward the window. Beyond the glass, morning dawned with fingers of mist that crept out from the horizon so naturally that, in this quiet pre-dawn light, it sang to her of safety. Everything was, as the poet said, unfolding as it should.

She yawned and wiped away tears as her brown eyes watered. The smell of growing things filled the room. She could almost forget why she'd come to this distant land. Toronto and all that had happened there was surreal. It was far away in time and space.

She was safe. Nestled here in this warm morning bed with the breeze carrying the early morning songs of birds, she was safe. Nothing could touch her; certainly nothing as unreal as a mind probe.

Throwing off the lethargy, she arose quickly; showered for the third time since checking in the night before; hit the road within half an hour.

Turning the dirty little Toyota onto the Interstate at precisely seven-o-three she told herself not to let down her guard. Something had kept her prisoner for over a week. This wasn't over yet.

Then her thoughts turned to home.

What was she going to tell her father when she arrived back in Australia? Would he think she had just come to her senses? Couldn't last a month without him? She shrugged. What did it matter after what had happened in Toronto? She would be safe at home; safe in the arid Outback she knew like the palm of her own hand; like her own reflection in the mirror.

Suddenly fear coursed through her afresh.

What if it followed her home? She shuddered and forced the thought from her mind. Then again, what if she had lost her sanity and none of this had even happened? Martha had certainly thought she was crazy.

Focus, she told herself. You know what happened.

The countryside slipped past. Cows grazed in the fields. The smell of cow dung occasionally hung on the air as she drove south along the circuitous path she had planned. Tidy red barns dotted the landscape, distracting her from her fears. Farmhouses surrounded by white picket fences and kitchen gardens blossomed everywhere, speaking to order in the world, calling her away from the darkness that threatened to consume her.

The little car sped toward freedom. Looking out at a farmer driving a giant mower across his field, she sighed. How long would it take to drive to New York? The delectable smell of freshly cut hay drifted in through the open vents. She breathed it in and drove on, leaving the farmer far behind.

As she drove in silence, farms whizzed by. The morning came alive with children and dogs and more farmers in their fields. The day brightened, taking on a more permanent air; a solid 'here I am', daytime quality that early morning seemed to lack. This was real time. This was what life was all about.

When she was a child in India, Hillary had thought in the delicate light of early morning that the day was tentative. It was a funny thing for a child to think, perhaps, but then again she had been a funny child.

Day might change its mind, she had reasoned, and not become a full fledged day at all. The sun might decide not to rise; might slip back behind the horizon and night might recapture the land, dreaded night. Night seemed like it belonged in the world more than day.

The events of the past week confirmed that view.

But that was when she was little, when she knew nothing of the laws of nature, how things worked in the larger scheme of things. Now as an adult she knew day might refuse to rise for other reasons; for reasons connected to the will of OTHERS; others who had control of your destiny or who sought it.

She gazed at the passing farms full of living things as daylight took a firm hold and thanked God for the laws of nature.

"It's not from Earth!" she suddenly proclaimed, the understanding flooding in from somewhere she could not identify.

The sound of her words in the empty car terrified her. "Oh my God!" She threw both hands up to cover her mouth. The car swerved onto the shoulder. She grabbed the steering wheel, jerked the car back onto the pavement just in time to keep it from the ditch.

"Dear Lord! Please let me get home," she begged, struggling to maintain self-control. She pressed her lips together, choking back debilitating tears. She had to bone up, as Martha had said! She had to stay in control, but in ways different than Martha had envisioned!

A sign on the side of the highway read 'Welcome to Kinderhook.'

She took the exit lane for town to search for a breakfast she did not want to eat. She had to stay healthy and strong.

Unable to stop her hands from shaking she drew the car up in front of a small restaurant much like the one she had dined in last night just before crossing the border.

* * * *

"She can't evade me! I won't allow it!" Kagoule roared. "I will crush those who protect her!"

Gradspin pressed his lips together, the wrinkles around his mouth taut with anger. "Let Orgone find her, Lord. He will have her in a matter of hours."

"Never!" Kagoule screamed. "Get out, Orgone. I will handle this female myself."

"Orgone is the best mind scanner we have. We are up against something special here, Lord," Gradspin insisted. "You have found us a rare prize with this species. Let Orgone track her."

"NEVER! Get out," Kagoule waved a dismissing hand at Orgone. "When I find her, I'll kill her. And I'll kill any who give her shelter! Get out!"

Orgone bowed slightly and left. Outside the room, Cacin waited.

"Well?"

"He won't let me. I knew he wouldn't let me. He's a fool."

"He's a great warrior but not much of a mind scanner."

"He is a great fool," Orgone insisted contemptuously. "He will make a grave mistake on this Bride Quest. Mark my word."

Chapter 3
Before Sunrise

The stifling and humid July night wrapped around Hillary like a sauna. She slept fitfully atop the covers, her bare back glistening with sweat, her bikini underwear stuck to her rump. The motel room's air conditioner labored relentlessly to no avail.

Lying on her stomach in the sparsely decorated room, Hillary groaned and fought to wake from a bad dream. A slight breeze picked up outside the motel window. Half asleep, she heard the branches of a nearby tree rustle and worked it into her dream.

The branches swayed to a gentle easy rhythm, their leaves sporadically blocking the light from a street lamp across the cracked concrete parking lot. Moving back and forth, the leaves allowed light to spill carelessly across Hillary's naked back. In alternating light and shadow she lay with her dreams of monsters, trying to awaken.

A low whistling sound, like wind through telephone wires, began rising on the night air around two o'clock. The wind picked up gradually, twisting the tree branches sharply, thrashing them against the lamp standard.

Suddenly Hillary was wide awake. Bolting from the disorderly bed, she stood in the center of the room, fearfully analyzing the sounds that had registered in her subconscious mind. Wind in the wires? Where had she heard that noise before?

When it first came to her in Toronto she'd heard that sound in her mind!

Heart pounding, she quickly pulled on jeans. A moan escaped her lips as the zipper stuck stubbornly under her fumbling fingers.

"Come on! Come on!" she gasped.

Certain it intended to kill her for this 'act of treason' she yanked on a tee-shirt, not bothering with her bra.

Suddenly she knew what had brought it to her in Toronto. The revelation shocked her. That first fleeting contact had caused her to reach out with curiosity.

Her own curiosity had helped it find her then! How could she forget something as fundamental as that? Reaching out with her mind, this time she threw back a challenge!

She thought an insult at it, a focused burst of hostility.

Coward! she taunted, even as she pulled on her shoes, grabbed her keys and purse from their bureau perch and ran from the room where she had taken refuge the evening before. Out into a rapidly rising wind that seemed to be blowing from all directions at once, Hillary rushed.

Name calling; the only defense she could think to throw against the powerful mind that now confronted her in rage. She goaded it again. Coward!

Rushing down the poorly lit concrete stairs, a low moan of fear escaped her lips. She burst into the courtyard, panting. "I'm not even twenty-three yet!" she screamed irrationally. "I don't even know what's going to kill me!" Sprinting toward her car, her hair streamed out behind her in the mounting gale.

As she reached the parking lot, the building imploded; pulverized by a funnel of wind. A rush of air tugged at her back, pulling the tee shirt tight across her chest as she fled across the dusty concrete.

Groping for the car door handle, her hands shook uncontrollably.

"Shit! Open you stupid thing! Open!" she screamed. The keys rattled against the car. Finally connecting, she yanked the door open and dove into the driver's seat, slamming the door behind her.

In the dark she fumbled for the ignition switch. Pieces of debris hurtled through the night air around her.

Finally ramming the key in the ignition she cranked the starter.

The engine caught, coughed and died.

Taking a deep breath she tried again. Fighting hysteria as the car was battered by flying objects that crashed down on the hood and struck the windows hard enough to crack the safety glass, she cursed out loud.

Suddenly, an explosion rocked the darkness and a wall of flame expanded toward her from where the motel had stood.

"Come on!" she screamed, turning the key in the ignition, battling the panic that promised to consume her as thoroughly as the flames would if she remained any longer.

The engine caught again. Stalled.

"Oh God NO!" she screamed.

Burning debris rained down on the hood of the car. "Please! Dear God! Please!" she screeched. "Let it start!" She turned the key again, keeping her foot away from the gas pedal with enormous effort. The engine turned over and roared to life. Hillary gasped, and a string of swear words flooded the car in several languages. Then tears of relief streamed down her face.

She stepped hard on the gas pedal and the car lurched forward toward the flames. Shrieking, she braked hard and the car skidded sideways.

Ramming the gearshift into reverse, she backed out of the parking lot and across the street, bumping hard against the opposite curb.

She cranked the steering wheel around and slammed the car into first gear, then peeled away as gravel and rocks from the verge sprayed up behind her, raining down on the trunk.

As she sped from the blazing inferno, Hillary challenged it again, more out of spite than good judgment.

"Coward! You just killed dozens of people in their beds to get at me! Do you hear that? You bloody coward!" she screamed. "Innocent people!"

Her heart pounded furiously. Anger now replaced fear. Show your face, she thought over and over as the car sped down the road. Then, more from frustration than good sense, she dared it to meet her face-to-face in her own physical world.

I know what you are! I know you're not from Earth! Come here and face me! I dare you!

Time seemed to stand still. The roaring gale held its breath. In the deepening silence that surrounded her, Hillary sensed shock. Puzzlement. What was it she felt from it? Disbelief. Yes. Disbelief.

Abruptly, it replied. Its tone measured. Calm.

I will come, Hill'carn. I will be there within the week. You must not hide from me, though. You must be honorable.

"Honorable?" she screamed back. "You talk of honor? You haven't exhibited decency or honor once. You have no idea what the word HONOR means!" she yelled her outrage. "You violated my mind." Spittle flew from her taut lips.

Hillary gripped the steering wheel with both hands as though it would get away from her if she didn't. "You kept me captive! You tortured me for attempting to resist you! Now you stalk me! Honor is not a word that belongs to you," she screamed, putting all her will to projecting her thoughts outward like throwing a ball as she yelled the words into the confines of the small car.

She realized she had felt its displeasure building with the first sentence she uttered. Now she could feel its anger far surpassing her own. But she couldn't stop, couldn't force her lips and mind to silence.

A loud hissing noise assailed her ears like some giant steam boiler building towards an explosion. Instinct told her not to drive a straight course. She zigzagged through the dead of night to avoid its wrath, manifested in bursts of something akin to wind, slamming into trees, houses and even the road itself beside, ahead and behind her.

For upwards of five minutes, it took aim and missed her moving target while its fury built.

Finally it caught her.

When it seized her, lifting the small car high into the night air, its punishment was swift and decisive. Hillary's car, hoisted like a toy, was thrown brutally into a nearby ditch.

As darkness closed in on her broken body, she saw the image of a huge and merciless beast, standing erect; a full seven feet tall on scaled legs. Clothed in a skirt of shining silver mail that fell within inches of its knees, her captor wore a breastplate of gilded armor. Large black eyes penetrated her soul.

A scaled brown and green covering of something - not skin, scales perhaps but never skin – covered its face and hands. It had a small, almost flattened nose. Curly black strands of something that wasn't hair, hung in tidy ringlets from the top of its head. This extended down its back, leaving the sides of its head bare, as the creature turned so she could see all of it. The rest of its head, around where its ears were, was covered in small delicate scales; scales that reflected hues of red, purple, green and blue like an intricate crystal.

I will come, the creature thought to her coldly.

"No. Please," Hillary begged, drifting into unconsciousness. "Dear God, help me!"

"God cannot help you. I am Kagoule. I am King."

Letting herself sink down into darkness, she let the well known abyss where she had hidden from this creature before claim her.

Chapter 4
No Patience

"I didn't kill her," Kagoule stated, launching himself from his work chair like a mighty war craft thrusting off the tarmac.

Gradspin lowered himself into a chair that was, of course less ornate and physically lower than Kagoule's. Beyond the open doors of the King's chamber, birds flitted through the garden, chirping spring songs with chatter reminiscent of children at play. Their happy prattle drifted on the morning air in stark contrast to the mood that built within the room.

The old gron sighed and folded his tired arms in his lap. "My Lord, you are making this very difficult for everyone," he ventured, throwing caution to the birds in the garden.

What could this impetuous king do to him anyway? Gradspin was Lord Elder. There was no post higher on the planet except the King's, and the King would never lightly Challenge one just under his station, especially when that person was as old as Gradspin. It was unthinkable. Age proved a protection of sorts.

If Gradspin didn't counsel him, then who would? Everyone else put themselves at risk. Cacin had tread dangerously close a number of times because he recognized Kagoule's need; Orgone likewise. Gradspin didn't want Cacin's or Orgone's blood on his head. A selfish motive for action but better that than no action at all.

"I will do as I please," Kagoule snapped.

"You will be the cause of a disaster if you do." Gradspin threw the words at him more boldly than anything he'd said to Kagoule before. They were out of his mouth and glancing off the walls like tiny daggers before he realized what effect his words would have.

No expectant silence filled the room as one might have envisioned after words so strong, so sharp. With terrifying spontaneity, Kagoule struck out with his mind. Before his old reflexes could respond to block the attack, Gradspin felt Kagoule's mind slam into him; felt himself launched into midair like an old tired battleship. Equally as suddenly, he felt himself snatched from Kagoule's clutch and held aloft, protected in a mind grid.

"GET A HOLD OF YOURSELF!" Cacin yelled from the doorway.

The old gron's tired hearts beat violently. His hands trembled. Slowly lowered toward the floor by Cacin, Gradspin saw the King turn his fury on the teenager.

"How dare you interfere?" Kagoule shouted, his face a twisted mask of hate. Light glanced off the shell shaped pattern around his eyes and sent splashes of red around the room that seemed to reflect his wrath.

With his eyes locked on the King's, Cacin seemed to swallow some remark that fought for liberation. "I would be remiss not to," he replied. Unflinchingly, Cacin held his ground.

Gradspin felt the grid lowered. His feet landed firmly on the floor. The old gron adjusted his cape and tried to steady his racing hearts. "I'm too old for this sort of thing," he said aloud, resentment hanging in his voice much as he had hung helplessly in mid-air only moments earlier.

"I'll rip your hearts out for this!" Kagoule hissed at Cacin, his chest heaving with each rapid breath. His nostrils flared as he spoke. The words he'd said were so barbaric, so obviously out of place that Kagoule visibly flushed. Blood rushed around the shell pattern on his cheeks, making them glow slightly.

Was he realizing the dishonor rage had driven him to?

Cacin took a step forward, challenging Kagoule with his silence, daring him to proceed with the threat or apologize. The young gron said nothing, his eyes steadily fixed on the King's, unmoving, unblinking, his face a study in strength.

Slowly, the fire died in Kagoule's eyes and a look of deep shame replaced it. "I apologize, Lord Elder," he whispered, his voice trembling.

Now silence embraced the room like a morning fog. Cacin and Kagoule continued to stare at each other without flinching, as though the first to stir would prove the weaker of the two. The King and the heir to his throne, locked in a silent battle of wills, dared not move. Neither dared break the stare. Cold silence filled the space between them.

"It has been a hard Assessment," Gradspin offered. "Perhaps the longest and hardest in our history." There, he had done it for them. Now it didn't matter who spoke. No one lost face.

As the opportunity presented itself, Cacin spoke. "I am here to assist in any way I can." He did not bow, however, when he spoke. It was customary to bow in situations where Challenge had almost been issued if a retraction was offered, but Cacin wasn't recanting, exactly.

Kagoule gestured with a sharp snap of his head. With his eyes still fixed on Cacin's, he said, "She taunted me." He shifted his gaze to Gradspin. "I took it out on you, Lord Elder." His voice was little more than a whisper now.

Kagoule shook his head in disgust at his own actions, dismissing them as he always did. He accepted his anger and the things he did when consumed by it more easily than he accepted anything else. His short-lived shame faded before he turned back to Cacin.

"I came this close to killing her." He indicated how close with the index finger and thumb of one of his huge, six-fingered hands. "This close!" he repeated through clenched teeth. The words hissed out around him like angry bees, ill humor fastened firmly. "But I didn't kill her," he said, looking into Cacin's emerald eyes for approval.

Cacin nodded but said nothing.

"I told her I would come. I am going to Earth ahead of the Bride Quest to secure her," he said calmly, almost too calmly.

"Do you think that's wise?" Cacin asked. His voice was level, steady; as steady as everything else about Cacin.

There was so much insight in his voice that Gradspin flushed with pride. Oh, if only Cacin were King. How different things would be.

"Wisdom may not enter into it," Kagoule replied, noting Gradspin's reaction to Cacin's words. "She challenged me to meet her in her world. She called me a coward. And not once, but repeatedly."

Both Cacin and Gradspin nodded at this. Yes. That was a compelling dare indeed. Would either of them be able to resist such a challenge?

Kagoule noted their understanding; their approval.

"I hope I controlled my temper enough to ensure her safety. I tried to immobilize her, not kill her. It's hard to judge your own strength when you're piqued, though. And I was upset." He turned away toward the palace garden beyond the courtyard doors. Birds still fluttered among the Tala blossoms, singing their playful songs.

* * * *

A heavy chemical smell permeated the air around her. Voices floated in it like helium balloons. Hillary stirred, tried to move her arms. One arm was heavy, too heavy to lift. Pain shot up through her shoulder as she tried to move her arm, stabbed at her mercilessly. She fell rapidly back to darkness to escape, back to soothing darkness. Let time take her where it would.

* * * *

Kagoule strode across the floor of the council hall, his huge frame casting a shadow that seemed to see-saw back and forth as he went. The long silver cape of the Zi ancestry flowed out around him and caught the light, snapping back and forth with each determined step. Beneath the cape, the armor his father had worn when capturing his mother hundreds of years earlier glistened where the light caught it. It was tradition on Bride Quests to wear the armor of your sire.

Kagoule's mother's race was not as desirable to mate with as the Humans were. The King considered his tiny mother briefly, her hands folded at her waist, head bowed. He despised her servitude. It made him cringe inside. He looked away in disgust and continued to pace.

Humans were diversified. Many of them were tall. His female stood almost six feet in height. Some were even taller. Cacin's father had been luckier than his own. He had mated with a Tranterian who was over five feet and not the servant class that his own mother came from. Kagoule shot an envious glance at his taller cousin.

The doors to the hall suddenly swung open and Gradspin entered. "I am sorry to keep you waiting, Lord," Gradspin said breathlessly, bowing. He took his place among the Elders.

"No matter," Kagoule replied. "Well, we are all here now. I can go." Matters of state were a hindrance to him and he concealed his irritation with them poorly. "I will stop on Sanit-ba briefly overnight to obtain food and rest. I will be on her planet in two weeks time. I will contact the Elders by mind transfer, both at Sanit-ba and when I have secured the female on Earth."

His mother cringed slightly, though her eyes remained downcast. Kagoule noted this and looked at her. Was she worried for him? Did she care? She said so little it made it hard to know. Not being allowed inside her mind posed a distinct disadvantage. Only the King could read her mind, but not when he was her son.

"Will you wish me well?" he asked, stepping towards her.

Bopack looked up from the floor she had been studying. "Of course," she replied meekly, but no feeling accompanied the words. No warmth. He nodded at her but made no attempt to embrace her. It was not his way. It was not her way.

Turning, Kagoule wrapped himself in a mind grid and willed himself away. He faded from the room like an evening shadow on a summer breeze.

Cacin felt the wind of Kagoule's exit rake over him and stepped up beside Bopack. Putting his arm around the old woman's shoulders he whispered, "Don't worry. He'll be alright. He'll return to us safely."

"It would be better for you Gron'dalins if he did not return," Bopack confided in the same whispered tone.

* * * *

Again Hillary smelled that chemical odor. She lay on her back with one leg extended above her at an uncomfortable angle. What a stupid way to sleep.

A loud thump startled her. She tried to open her eyes. Around her, voices buzzed in a hive of activity. She caught snatches of conversations without understanding, and more noises, shuffling, clinking, metal against metal. Where was she? What were these noises?

The ethereal air hung like syrup, sticky and hard to breathe. Oh for peace! Blessed darkness welled up and enfolded her again. It sucked her down to safety and she went with it willingly.

Chapter 5
Awakenings

"Can you hear me, Hillary?"

A male voice called through the shadows that flowed over her. Would he never stop? What an annoying man!

Hillary moved her unbroken arm and opened her eyes.

"Well. Nice to see you back in the land of the living, Miss Bopal," the voice said warmly.

Hillary groaned. It wasn't nice to be here. Pain coursed through her body, her legs, one arm. Someone - that awful nagging man - flashed a light in her eyes. Would he never go away and let her be? He bent over her, his breath warm and sweet on her cheek. Her eyes were heavy. Too heavy to keep open. She closed them and drifted away to darkness, glorious pain-free darkness, again.

* * * *

"Hillary? Can you hear me? Come on Hillary," he coaxed.

Oh! Not him again. It was him. Wasn't it? "Go away," Hillary murmured weakly.

"I think she's trying to talk," a woman's voice said. Someone patted her hand roughly, not a soft touch. She tried to pull away; tried to slip down into darkness again. That patting, that awful annoying patting just kept on and on.

"Buzz off," Hillary croaked.

"She IS trying to speak," the woman said.

Of course she was trying to speak, fool woman! Hillary tried to open her eyes again. Shadows embraced her but she could make out the two intruders, hanging over her. Didn't they have anything better to do?

"That's it. Come on. Wake up." The man's voice softened.

She groaned.

"She's nearly come around a dozen times, doctor. Just slides back into unconsciousness."

"She'll wake up when she's ready." His steady voice resonated with certainty.

Hillary stirred again and tried to move her legs. They felt like they were tied down. Oh what a silly thing to think! How could they be tied down? Actually, one of them seemed to be tied UP! She breathed deeply and tried to reposition herself.

"Will you be needing anything else, Doctor?"

Doctor? What was she talking about? Was this another of those silly dreams? Hillary had been dreaming such silly things all night. As she tried to recall the dreams, they tumbled away, just out of reach.

"I don't think so."

"I'll be going then, Doctor. Just call if you need me."

Doctor? What kind of dream was this? She groaned again.

"That's it Hillary. Come on," the male voice called. "You can do it." He patted her hand roughly again.

The sound of a door softly closing registered in the distance, far from the sea of mist that rose and fell over Hillary. She sucked in another breath and with it awareness washed over her.

"Good. That's it. Come on. Wake up."

A light flashed in her eyes again. Hillary frowned and grimaced. "Go away," she croaked.

"No. Sorry. I'm here to stay."

"Where am I?" she heard herself say. Was that her voice? So frail? It couldn't be.

"In the hospital. You were brought in by ambulance two weeks ago. You've been in a coma since." The doctor hovered over her. "Nice to finally have you back."

Was he smiling at her? She tried to focus on him. He drifted in a thick fog, or several of him drifted there, sometimes two, sometimes three smiling faces.

"You've had quite a bad bang on the head. That's why you're having trouble focusing," he said, as though reading her mind. The thought inexplicably frightened her.

Hillary moaned and tried to focus on him again, blinking repeatedly. She drifted in a sea of confusion. Light and shadow danced across her line of vision like Irish fairies.

"I was beginning to think you Aussies were a lazy lot," he chided good-naturedly.

Was he smiling? There was laughter in his voice. He donned his bedside manner like most people put on a pair of gloves. "Do you mind if I call you Hillary?"

"No," Hillary croaked. Her throat, sore from disuse, pained her. And something else. Had she had a tube down her throat at some time? She could remember something gagging her. Or maybe it was one of those dreams. She swallowed and drew in another deep breath. Her chest hurt. Breathing hurt. She struggled to focus on him again. Her head pounded but her vision slowly cleared.

The doctor hovered over her. A strong, tall blonde approaching middle age, late thirties, he adjusted an intravenous drip. Hillary watched with interest as two of him performed the task. Her eyes finally focused properly and the ghost image vanished. With a broad smile, he quickly walked to the foot of the bed.

"Where am I?" She cleared her throat. Her voice sounded stronger, more like it should.

"South Bend."

She moaned as she tried to move.

"Are you in pain?" The doctor looked up from a chart he now held.

"You have to be kidding!" Hillary responded. She laughed quietly and motioned to the casts that encased her limbs.

"As well as the concussion, you have two broken legs; broken in six places all told," he said casually. "One broken arm. It's only fractured in two spots. A fractured collar bone; six broken ribs; a punctured lung," he looked up from reading her chart. "That's just for starters," he said, raising his eyebrows. "And a partridge in a pear tree," he added, scribbling something on her chart.

"What happened?" Hillary asked in amazement.

"I was hoping you could tell me."

Hillary sighed. "Well, I can't. I can't remember a thing. Where in the world IS South Bend?"

The doctor smiled again. "Indiana," he said. "In the good ole U.S. of A."

"What am I doing in Indiana?" she asked incredulously.

"That's a good question. And one that's been asked repeatedly. Apparently you're supposed to be in Toronto, Canada, studying at college."

"University," she corrected. "They call them universities up there. Their colleges are very different institutions." She sighed. "And yes, I am supposed to be in Toronto. So why am I here? Last I remember I was in Toronto."

"Well, you're here now. My name is Paul Muntz," the doctor said, dropping her file to fill a syringe. "I'm your doctor, as you've probably guessed."

A grin swept across his face, lighting it with a friendly glow. She smiled in response, her head clearing, the cobwebs flaking away like dead skin.

"Lucky you," he added. His smile broadened in answer to the weak attempt at congeniality she mustered through the pain. Soft age lines around his eyes creased. They fanned out to his hairline where the slightest hint of grey was starting at the temples.

Tapping the syringe, he approached the bed. Throwing back the covers he donned his bedside manner again. Hillary flushed, knowing what he was going to do.

"What are you doing?" she asked anyway, buying time, preparing to be embarrassed.

"Two guesses," he answered. "Just lean to one side please," he instructed.

Oh that infuriating bedside manner was back. She closed her eyes and obeyed. Lifting her hospital gown he gently helped her lean away from him by pushing her slightly on one hip. With cold wet gauze, he quickly cleaned the area he was going to inject.

In his bedside voice he said, "Take a deep breath."

He gave this last instruction in a cold, indifferent tone of voice, as if speaking to a piece of meat. Hillary felt the needle prick her hip.

"You've had a very bad accident, Ms. Bopal," he continued, as the vial emptied. "You shouldn't be alive today to tell about it."

"It seems I CAN'T tell about it."

He withdrew the needle and rubbed the area with sterile gauze. "Often patients have some memory loss after a trauma like you've experienced. It will all come back." He straightened her gown and the blankets as he spoke. Gone was the bedside manner she found annoying. "You just concentrate on getting well," he said.

"I feel like I'm forgetting something important," Hillary replied hesitantly, frowning.

"Well, you are. You're forgetting a chunk of your life. That's important."

"No. I think it's more significant than just that," she declared, adjusting herself in the bed. "I don't know what I'm doing in the United States either. I was writing a paper for one of my classes," she continued by way of bringing the thought that tickled her mind to light.

"Wrong direction for dropping off a paper," he teased. "Look, don't be anxious about the loss of memory. Like I said, it's quite normal. It will return in time."

He reached for a plastic needle disposal jar that sat on a side table. A sharp click echoed in the room as the needle snapped off in the dispenser. The plastic syringe landed in the metal garbage pail with a loud clunk.

She looked away from him, out the window, trying to recall what had happened. She'd been driving along a straight stretch of road. No. She'd been speeding over the road, trying to get away from something! But what? Or was that all a dream?

As the doctor walked to the foot of the bed, she looked back at him, following him with her eyes. He was a shockingly handsome man. His thick blonde hair gleamed in the overhead light. The thought that he was too old for her crossed her mind and she looked away, afraid he would know what she was thinking. But why would she be afraid he would know what she thought? What a silly thing to think.

Suddenly a chill ran through her.

Lifting the chart that rested at the foot of her bed, he made a note. She looked back at him, drawn by the movement of his large hands.

"Tell me," he said, looking up into Hillary's brown eyes.

Another shudder rippled through her with those words, someone had said that to her recently. 'Tell me!'

"What do linguistic students study?"

She fixed him with a blank stare. Her mouth fell slightly open. The words 'tell me' spun through her brain like a child's top. Unable to make sense of the rest of his words, she squinted, wrestling with fear that irrationally swelled to consume her after those simple words that now ricocheted through her mind.

Tell me!

"Are you alright?" he asked, pondering her sudden mood flux.

She quivered again. Gooseflesh danced across her neck and down her arms. "Some sort of wind storm hit the area," she said. "Did that have anything to do with it?" Her eyes were no longer focused on him. "I was driving along a long dark stretch of road. No. I was speeding. Had to get away from..."

She stiffened as he touched her arm.

"You're starting to remember what happened," he said. "Now, don't rush the memories. They'll come back on their own."

The memory took flight, leaving behind that 'just on the tip of your tongue' sensation.

"Yes." She snapped her head, as though shaking off dust. "I nearly had it!"

Abruptly the pieces fell into place as if someone were reading a list of past events. Hillary saw herself sitting in the driver's seat of the small car, fear etched on her face. Then the events leading up to the crash came into focus. She gasped again, drawing her good hand up to her face as the memory of that night and her imprisonment resurfaced.

"Is there anything I can do?" Paul asked stepping toward her.

Struggling with the bedding, she tried to gain her feet. "Oh God! I have to go," she mumbled. Her suspended leg dangled precariously in the sling as she tried to get up. Again that feeling of desperate panic; that feeling that had engulfed her as she sat in her car at the motel trying to start the engine; again it swamped her. Run! Get to the door and run for your life! her mind screamed.

"Hey, hey, hey! Take it easy!" Paul asserted, rushing to stabilize her. "What are you trying to do, finish the job? You won't be going anywhere for a long time."

He easily forced her back onto the bed, and while her body succumbed to his superior strength and insistent manner, that nagging urgent desire to run, to flee, to simply throw the covers off and dash from the room in wild abandon continued to engulf her.

"I have to go!" she stuttered, ardently repeating the irrational words like they were some kind of incantation, some peculiar sort of mantra that would save her from death. "Please, let me up," she begged.

Paul Muntz regarded her with incredulity. His friendly face became stern before looking puzzled.

"You can't be serious? You can't even be moved, let alone walk out of here. What's the rush?" he snorted. "What happened to provoke this sudden compulsion to be mobile? Did you remember something you'd rather not?"

She looked at the casts that had cemented her in place for as long as the creature had said it would take to reach Earth and find her. "Yes."

"Well, just take it easy, Hillary," he said in a softer tone. "Whatever you've remembered, I'm sure we can work through it in time."

Hillary sniggered scornfully and fell back on the sterile sheets. Filled with self-pity, her situation crystallized. She was alone with her knowledge. By breaking her legs, the creature had ensured she could not escape. In its usual 'honorable' way it had guaranteed its own victory.

It was cunning, she would give it that. In any event, you can't run with broken legs. And who would believe her story? No one would help. With her good hand she clumsily wiped tears from her cheeks.

"Look. Whatever is bothering you..." Paul began in a soft, compassionate voice, not the bedside one he reserved for medical purposes.

Hillary snapped. "There isn't anything you could do, even if you believed me. And I can almost guarantee you wouldn't." Hillary turned away to conceal tears that were in free-fall now.

"Try me," Paul said sympathetically, sitting down on the edge of the hospital bed.

She sniffled and looked at him, drying her eyes awkwardly on the back of her one good hand.

"Let me help you, Hillary."

"Doctor, trust me," she said gently. Then she laughed cynically, shaking her head at him. "You wouldn't believe my story if I told you what happened. And I'm not about to do that and have you think I'm crazy into the bargain." She looked away again, out the window into the flawless blue sky that would soon open to admit the creature that had projected its image to her on the highway two weeks earlier.

"Okay. If you don't want to talk about it..."

She heard the offended tone in his voice and laughed to herself. Yes. Some people employed that tactic to oblige others to confide in them. And it worked on some people. She chuckled to herself again and glanced up at him.

Standing up, he pretended to change the topic. "I contacted your father in Australia when you were brought in."

"You did what?" she blurted in disbelief, as though he had said something that was totally outlandish, something completely inappropriate and out of place. Hillary scowled at him.

Paul frowned and threw up his hands in frustration, palms outstretched beseechingly. "Well?" he asked, as though awaiting an explanation. When none came, he added, "I had to tell your next of kin you were brought in."

"I'm an adult! I don't want my father interfering." Even as she said it she recalled how she had been flying back to her father's house to hide.

"You were an unconscious adult very near death," Paul said, genuinely offended this time. "We aren't going to keep your admittance to hospital a secret from family members."

"Why did you have to involve my father?" Hillary asked accusingly, wiping at tears that still lingered on her face.

"Why NOT involve your father?" Paul retorted. "Do you two detest each other or something?"

"Pretty close. Besides, it will kill him too," she said more to herself than to him. She threw her head to one side as a statement of disapproval, unable to easily move any other part of her body. "You'll have to send him back to Australia," she said resolutely.

Paul gaped at her in amazement. "I can't do that! You don't have to see him but I can't force him to go home."

"Even if I don't get along with him, I do love him very much. He's the only family I have," she said, as though Paul should have known better than to involve her only family member in something this sordid. "I don't want him dead."

"Who's going to kill him?"

Paul sat down on the bed, determined to have the facts. His bedside manner, abandoned some time back, never resurfaced again.

"What are you afraid of, Hillary?" he asked in a tone that demanded an answer. "Are you involved in something illegal?" No reply. She glared out the window, her lips pressed together rebelliously. "It's easy enough to fall into things we eventually regret," he continued. "Look, I even know the son of a Mafia Don for crying out loud. I can't say I'm proud of it, but I know him. Went to college with him."

She looked at him searchingly. "You're an odd doctor," she said, smiling despite herself.

Paul shrugged. She was already thinking of him by his first name. She'd never done that with a doctor before. "Doctors don't confide things like that in patients," she said.

He passed off the remark with another hoisting of those strong shoulders.

"You really want to know?" she asked.

"You got it!" Paul asserted.

"Well, you're going to be sorry you asked," Hillary said slowly, almost maliciously. "First, you're going to think I'm nuts." She murmured a few words to herself suggesting that didn't matter. "Then, when I'm torn limb from limb," she continued, "I won't even be around to tell you I told you so. So just remember, I told you so."

Chapter 6
Room at the End of the Hall

"Why am I doing this?" Paul asked. Silence descended in the car as the powder blue Porsche skimmed the streets. "Do I have a death wish or something?" Still no reply.

Brendon sat like a lump in the seat beside him, a worried look on his lined face.

"The old man is going to think I'm nuts," Paul continued.

"You are nuts!" Brendon finally said.

"I have to do this."

"Face it, Paul, you're infatuated with her. She's young. She's beautiful." Brendon paused. "She's also East Indian," he added in a funny sort of tone.

"I'll ignore that."

"Well, she is."

"You're not going racist on me are you, Brendon?" Paul asked, turning to look at his friend as they sped toward the garage.

"Keep your eyes on the road," Brendon cautioned.

Paul looked back at the crowded road ahead of him. A car passed him and cut in front.

"She's beautiful, but what a can of worms," Brendon warned.

"Yes, she is beautiful," Paul retorted, deciding to ignore the message Brendon was framing for him. "Did I tell you she speaks seven languages fluently – another one well enough to fool me?"

Brendon snorted in disgust as Paul guided the car through traffic. "Only about ten times," the geneticist replied.

"She moved to Toronto to do a masters degree in linguistics."

"Where's Toronto?"

"Canada," Paul announced.

Brendon guffawed contemptuously.

"Brendon, this woman is special."

"Ya, she's a fruit loop. I'd say that makes her special. Someone you specially want to avoid."

"Brendon?" Paul frowned. "She's had a terrible accident, a serious concussion."

"Turn here. It's just around that corner." Brendon pointed and cleared his throat.

"Why do you always have your car fixed in the most out of the way places?" Paul complained.

"I told you I'd take a cab."

Paul smiled at him. "Ya, sure. You know I always drive you."

"I know. But I did say I'd take a cab." Brendon grinned mischievously.

Paul slowed to thirty miles an hour. "She's a special woman, Brendon," he said, returning to the topic dearest to his heart.

"You just be careful, old bud. Tread lightly. I've got a bad feeling about this. I hear wedding bells ringing and you know what mixed marriages can be like. Look at Sam. Mixed marriages are hell. You're in limbo. Don't belong here, don't belong there. And the kids."

"Don't worry about marriage. I've held out this long." He laughed. "Fact is no one will have me."

"That isn't true. You've made a conscious choice to stay single. The fact REALLY is, you're afraid to make a commitment."

"Just haven't found the right woman. Maybe this is her."

Brendon shot him a glance. "You really mean that?" he asked. He frowned at his friend.

Paul squinted in the bright light that streamed through the windshield.

"This is the place here," Brendon said, turning his attention to the road. "Pull up here." He pointed to where he wanted Paul to stop. "I don't think there's too much to worry about anyway," he said, comforting himself. "They're as racist as we are. She'll never marry you. Besides..." he wrinkled his brow and his mouth fell open in feigned shock, "you've just met her this morning, Paul. She's been unconscious until today. Boy, this must be some lady!" He shook his head.

Paul pulled over to the curb. "She is," he replied.

"You know what kind of prejudice you'll run into? And think of your kids, man."

"I know there's prejudice out there. I might also be hit by a car crossing the doctors' parking lot when I get to the hospital tomorrow morning. I'm not putting my life on hold because there are bad drivers, OR small minded people, Caucasian OR East Indian."

"Well, I hope you know what you're doing."

"Brendon, does it look like I know what I'm doing? I'm just about to tell an old man he should go half way around the world, back to Australia without seeing his only child because she's had a bump on the head and thinks she's being hunted by a huge green scaly thing from Mars. I ask you, does it look like I know what I'm doing?"

Brendon laughed. "Don't tell him about scaly green monsters, for God's sake." Brendon shook his head in disgust. "He'll think you're mad."

"HE'LL think I'm mad? I think I'm mad."

"So do I," Brendon laughed again. "No, you're just thinking with your genitals, Paul." Brendon patted him on the shoulder.

"Get out!" Paul chided.

Brendon reached for the door handle. "You'll have to think up something more believable than monsters from space, Doctor Muntz."

"Like what? What am I going to tell him? She doesn't like the color of his eyes?"

"Your problem."

"Thanks a lot."

He opened the car door. "Thanks for the lift."

"Any time."

"Well, good luck with it."

"Thanks."

Stepping onto the curb, Brendon turned and leaned back into the car. "Your attraction to this woman is very unusual, Paul."

"Can it."

"Okay, consider it canned. Are you SURE you want to go through with this request to her father?"

"No. I'm not sure."

"It's going to look very bad in light of your intentions toward his daughter."

"God, I hadn't thought of that!"

"Then think about it, my friend," Brendon said in a pleading tone. "Think about all of it. Go back to the hospital. You're a doctor, not a sucker."

"I'm a sucker of a doctor. I'm not booked in at the hospital right now. This is time out of my practice. I've got patients waiting in my office."

"Well, go back to your practice and forget about this hare-brained request. Forget about this woman. Get Sam to take over for you."

"I said I would try to get him to go home and I'm going to," Paul answered, ignoring Brendon's admonishment.

"Pig headed. You'll get yourself in trouble one of these days, Paul." He slammed the door. "See ya," he called as he walked away.

"Not if I see you first," Paul called after him. Brendon turned and waved.

He put the car in gear and pulled away from the curb. Brendon waved again as Paul sped off, a streak of light blue in the dirty surroundings.

* * * *

All the way to the father's hotel he tried unsuccessfully to talk himself out of telling the old man his daughter wanted him to go home. Through hectic traffic he guided the Porsche expertly. He turned onto McKinley Avenue where the elder Bopal was staying, pulled into the parking lot and motored into the first available space.

Jerking the parking brake, he turned the key in the ignition. The engine fell silent in the oppressive heat. Paul wiped his brow. Though his air conditioning worked perfectly, he left it off and kept the windows open.

"God. I'm thirty-eight and look at me." He shook his head. "Pulling a stupid maneuver like this. What on Earth am I going to say to this man?" He opened the car door and swung his feet out. Standing up, he pocketed the keys and slammed the door.

He crossed the lot, winding in and out of parked cars and bounded up four steps that introduced massive plate glass doors with brass handles. As the front door of the hotel shut behind him, he hesitated, scanning for the registration desk.

Plush carpet; tropical plants; to one side several comfortable lounge chairs were filled with people waiting for luggage. People came and went, carrying suitcases, attachés. Hotel staff bustled about with purpose. An odd smell he couldn't identify cleaved the air, out of place in the opulent surroundings. He shuddered.

"Better get this over with," he muttered under his breath.

Maybe he'd know what to say when he reached Bopal's room, he reasoned. Frowning hard, Paul glanced over one shoulder and searched the hotel lobby behind him. What was he looking for? Finding nothing, he glanced over the other shoulder and performed the same task. Weird, he thought! What exactly was he expecting to find behind him? That odd odor sent shivers down his spine again. He shuddered and shook off a feeling of foreboding.

Paul walked around the corner to the bank of elevators. A bell chimed and a door slid open before he could press the call button. Stepping inside he glanced at the note Bopal had given him with his room number. He pressed the floor button and the doors slid shut. The elevator rose rapidly. Then, at the second floor it quivered in a decidedly unhealthy manner and jerked to an abrupt stop!

Paul stumbled forward, throwing his hands out to break an impending impact with the elevator door, just as the lights went out.

"Oh Great!" He slapped the doors with one hand. "Now what?" he said into the pitch black that engulfed him. "Maybe this is a sign I should forget the whole stupid thing," he said contemptuously.

Standing in complete darkness for some minutes, he finally started groping around the panel beside him for an alarm button.

"Aren't there supposed to be emergency lights on these things?" he complained aloud. He stood a while longer, groping at the control panel for an alarm, pressing various buttons. The lights suddenly came on, blinding him.

The elevator jolted. He threw one hand up to his eyes and thrust the other out to steady himself. The elevator began moving, jerkily at first, then the ride smoothed out. He adjusted his suit coat indignantly. The car rose steadily, finally snapping to a stop at the sixth floor. The door slid open.

Stepping out of the elevator, he took the note Bopal had given him from his suit-coat pocket where he'd shoved it in the darkness. The elevator door slowly closed behind him.

Squinting, he read the number on the crumpled sheet, not that he'd forgotten it. Reading it gave him time to think.

The peculiar stench Paul had noticed in the lobby saturated the air on the sixth floor. He fought off more shivers as he walked in the direction of Bopal's room. His muscles tensed. The flesh crawled at the back of his neck.

"This is ridiculous!" he chided.

That awful smell, something like stale aftershave, rolled over him in ever increasing intensity. He gagged and a rush of raw unexplainable terror surged through him. A tingling in the pit of his stomach followed; then a tightening of his genitals. He lowered his head. The muscles in his shoulders taut, he drew his arms into a ready position. Taking slow, shallow breaths, he stepped forward, forcing his feet to move.

One of the doors on his left stood slightly ajar, at the end of the hall. A slender stream of light shone from the room onto the thick carpet. He shuddered and stepped up to the door. Slowly he pushed it open. Hair stood on the back of his neck. He fought to control the trembling in his hands.

The smell of old aftershave in Bopal's room overpowered him. He gagged. Then another more familiar smell swept over him. Blood.

"Oh God!"

Blood bathed the walls. Stepping over the threshold, Paul gagged. The bloody corpse of Hillary's father lay half on, half off the bed. The bulk of his torso hung onto the floor. Dismembered, the senior Bopal was unrecognizable in death.

"Butchered!" Paul heard himself whisper, as he instinctively fell into a crouching position. His movements became rapid, jerky.

Nothing moved in the death vault but Paul. Listening, he ran his gaze through the shadows, over the bloody night table, dresser, and bed. Perspiration formed in tiny beads on his forehead and his breath came in short quiet gasps.

With the curtains in the room drawn, the lamp from the night table, which lay on the floor, tried to blaze out a small beacon from under bloodied clothing. He could see little.

The sound of his own heartbeat pounded in Paul's ears. He rose slowly, ready for anything. Senses honed to a fine edge, he stepped into the room, gathering himself for a physical encounter. He flattened against in the short hallway outside bathroom wall and quickly lunged into the main part of the room.

Empty.

His heart ripped at his chest. The muscles in his arms ached from keeping them tight and ready.

The bathroom!

He whirled back into the hall outside the bathroom and thrust himself through the door into that small room.

No one.

Gone.

His mind raced. He returned to the bedroom.

Who or what had done this? he asked himself silently. He panted now, staring at the dismembered corpse, recalling Hillary's description of the thing she said stalked her.

No.

He wasn't going to believe a space creature actually dismembered the father of one of his patients. He just wasn't going to be that paranoid; that insane.

Accustomed to death in its many forms, but horrified by the scene that confronted him in Bopal's room, Paul retched.

"This just happened."

He breathed rapidly, trying to settle his stomach.

Time passed; crept away from him silently. Unnoticed, it glided off as Bopal's assailant had skulked away. He stood in shock, frozen to the spot. The soles of his shoes, soaked with sticky dark blood, fused with the carpet.

"Get out!" he finally whispered, as though waking from a dream. "If they catch me in this room there's no telling how long I'll be detained." Questions would be asked, like what was he doing there; why had he come?

"Have to get to her," he murmured. "Hillary. Oh God!"

Fear gripped him anew.

Paul ran from the room. He practically flew down the emergency exit stairs. His blood soaked shoes stuck to every concrete step; leaving prints that joined another set of blood soaked prints on the steps, larger ones.

His escape echoed through the stairwell as he steadied himself around corners by grasping the cold metal handrail. Stopping to compose himself at the ground floor exit, he walked slowly through the lobby, glancing carefully toward the reception desk. The desk clerk absent, Paul heaved a sigh of relief and hurried out the doors.

* * * *

Paul ran a red light, missing an oncoming car by inches. The driver swore, shaking his fist out the window of an old beater. His words, drowned out in the screech of brakes from both cars, died quickly on the hot air.

Paul laid rubber and the powder-blue Porsche raced frantically on, swerving around a car stopped at one busy intersection; barely missing a bus loaded with passengers at another. The driver of the bus laid on the horn as Paul's tires screeched across the pavement in front of him, barely holding the road.

"Scaly monsters from space! I must be crazy," he yelled as he cut off an elderly woman in a boxy brown car. "More like a psychopath from Earth!"

He could believe in psychopathic killers from Earth. That was possible! That was sane!

He steered his car into the Doctors Only parking area at the hospital, almost hitting Brendon.

"Hey!" Brendon yelled, jumping back from his modest BMW as Paul slammed the Porsche into the parking space beside Brendon's and jumped from the car.

"Took it that badly, did he?" Brendon yelled.

Ignoring his friend, Paul dashed among the parked cars toward the doctors' entrance. His suit coat flapped as he ran.

"Hey. What about your practice? What are you doing back here?"

Again Paul did not answer as he stormed into the building, fourth floor, south wing his destination.

The doors to the south wing stood closed. They always did. But through the window he could see the wreckage that lay beyond.

"Dear God!" He pushed through; the heavy doors sweeping bloodied debris aside. It piled behind them, creating resistance, making them hard to open on the devastation that lay beyond.

Total destruction embraced the ward. Stretching out before him like the aftermath of a tornado, every cart overturned and demolished, the contents strewn across the floor. Blood soaked the refuse, coating walls, floor and ceiling.

He gazed on the chaos and death with horror. Directly ahead, the nurse's station, obliterated, a pile of rubble amid blood, bodies and parts of bodies.

"Dear God in heaven!"

He tried to close his gaping mouth; tried to force his brain to work.

Paul stepped slowly down the hall, warily moving toward Hillary's room at the end, unable to hurry, immobilized by fear. "Dear Lord!" he uttered.

Patients called from their rooms.

"What's going on?" someone yelled. From somewhere on the floor someone else screamed incessantly. From behind one of the closed doors another patient moaned continually. Behind another, a woman cried hysterically. Some doorways were full of gaping patients, alive like Paul and, like Paul, in shock.

"What happened here?" Paul demanded of a middle-aged man who stared from his doorway with wide eyes. The man made no reply. "When did this happen?" Paul asked, grabbing him roughly by a shoulder.

"Ugh?" The man shook his head slightly. "Few minutes ago, maybe five or ten. No. Not ten."

"How many were there?"

"One," the patient stated hesitantly, suddenly focusing on the doctor, staring at Paul as though what he'd said was impossible. "One guy!" He looked into Paul's eyes in disbelief. "I uh, didn't hear any shots fired, just screaming. And," he shrugged, "Tearing metal. Everywhere. Things were flying around out here." He gestured toward the nurse's station. "The nurses were screaming. They're dead! Everything went quiet all of a sudden. I came to the door. Saw him from behind. Just one guy was all. One big guy. Bloody Rambo! Long black hair. Shaved on the sides I think."

Paul let go of the man's shoulder. "One person couldn't have done this," he replied as he stepped cautiously but quickly toward Hillary's room.

"One guy," the patient reiterated behind him. "Ask Henry" he called after Paul as the doctor gained speed down the hall. "I swear ta God! Ask Henry."

"One guy!" Henry yelled after him.

"Not likely a man. Smart man not to say it was some sort of creature," Paul stated to himself. "Get security," he called back over one shoulder, finally forcing his mind to work, forcing the reality of the devastation to register.

He propelled himself through the debris toward Hillary's room. One THING maybe. Nothing human could have done this. Nothing short of a small human army could have done this!

How could he fight it? He tried to recall everything Hillary had said about the creature that hunted her; its size; its shape; the way it behaved when it held her captive; how it held her captive.

"With the use of its mind," he heard himself say. "It did this with the use of its mind?" He mumbled this as gooseflesh kissed the nape of his neck. He shuddered as fear gripped him, tightening around his gut.

What if, whatever it was hadn't left Hillary's room? What did he think he was going to do to a creature that could do this with just its mind?

The body of the little black-haired nurse, who had flirted with him only this morning as Hillary regained consciousness, lay to one side, her limbs unnaturally twisted in death. The smell of old aftershave drifted in the hospital corridor, a sickly sweet smell that mingled with death to turn his stomach. He retched and suppressed the urge to turn aside and vomit.

Outside the room he gathered himself then flung the door open. To his relief, the creature was gone.

But Hillary was gone too.

Chapter 7
The King's Arrival

Hillary opened her eyes and tried to look straight at the creature that had arrived in her world. It had made no attempt to communicate with her over the course of the three hours she had been its captive. She had said nothing, thought nothing, her fear evident only by the width of her nostrils and the dilation of her pupils.

She rubbed her right arm, no longer in the heavy cast and remarkably healed but still sore, and gazed on the creature.

It had resumed its own shape and form on entering the house.

A shape changer?

That was impossible. But it was not of this world. Who knew what was possible on other worlds?

Other worlds? How could she believe in other worlds? That was so impossible.

She continued to rub her arm and tried to think; to make sense of what she was seeing.

Again the image of the human form it had taken in the hospital filled her mind. She shuddered as she recalled her recognition of it. Even in human form it could not fool her. She knew it after all; had been in close personal contact with it for over a week. And somewhere in the depths of her mind she had recognized it. It was practically part of her.

The creature stirred as she thought this, and Hillary thought it looked pleased. The thought that it was part of her coursed through her mind once more, revolting her. She felt nauseous and fought off an urge to vomit.

The creature drew in a slow deep breath and glared at her; its eyes oddly expressive.

It was reading her mind! Of course! That's exactly what it would do.

She closed her eyes again, grappling with her terror. When she opened them, it hadn't moved. She looked down at her right arm. Even the itching had stopped. It was red where she had been rubbing at it, but there was no swelling or pain.

How did it heal her broken bones? The power of its mind. It must have used its mind. What else could it have used? Hillary had been there. She'd seen no instruments, no drugs administered. It had touched her legs and arm briefly, not taking its eyes from hers. She felt a tingling sensation. Then it had run its hand over her collar bone, over her hospital gown, over her breasts. Then it had torn away the casts like they were tissue paper.

She shivered at the thought of it touching her breasts, fought back a wave of nausea. It still stared at her.

The fractures were completely and impossibly healed. Hillary closed her hand into a fist, trying out her repaired arm, tensing the muscles.

Why hadn't it just killed her?

"I want you alive."

She jumped.

"You belong to me," it replied in answer to her unspoken thought.

The sound of its voice grated down her spine like metal over concrete.

She swallowed hard. "What do you mean? I belong to you?" her voice quaked uncontrollably. "On Earth people don't BELONG to anyone but themselves."

It threw back its head and peals of course laughter raped the air. "Don't tell me that. I've been studying your Earth," it said contemptuously.

"Well, here in America..." Hillary began.

"I am Kagoule. I have chosen you as a mate. You will adapt to being my property," it said.

Hillary gaped at it. For one split second she could not breathe. The air, suddenly too heavy, simply refused to enter her lungs. Abruptly she drew it in with a gulp. Her mind swam with images of her homeland, images that had stayed with her from childhood. The dust, the poverty, her mother's shack, her mother's bondage, danced through her mind.

How could this be happening to Hillary? She wasn't her mother. She was free. Only a few weeks ago she had been studying in a new country, in a new city. No! She wouldn't accept this. She had a life ahead of her. No! She wouldn't be something's property. This couldn't be happening.

"Of course it is happening." The creature smiled. "You Humans are odd." It chuckled then continued more severely. "I will provide for you," it said. "You will want for nothing."

Again changing its tone, it added, "You are intelligent, soft and beautiful in your way. We have had many like you over the centuries." It paused to fill its huge lungs. "You will fulfill my needs," it added nonchalantly. "You will be my mate."

Hillary shuddered. Surely this was an awful nightmare. "You must need one of your own kind to mate with," she whispered with apprehension and disgust. Her voice faltered, betraying her fear.

"There are no females of my own kind," it snapped. Continuing, it adjusted the armor around its scaled neck. "There have been no females in my race for over six hundred epochs. We travel the universe in search of receptive females when a mate becomes necessary. We find mates quite successfully, I might add."

"I bet," Hillary said, trying to get her breathing under control.

It shifted positions in the armchair it more than filled.

Hillary glanced at the bodies of the couple that owned the house. The man of the house lay in the doorway to the kitchen, facedown. His wife, a woman in her sixties, sprawled in the living room. Kagoule rose and, taking the woman's body by one arm, slung her over one shoulder. He turned to look at Hillary.

"Sit where you are. I will tolerate no attempts at escape." As he whirled around, the ringlets that hung down his back brushed against the corpse. Hillary's eyes bulged as he stooped and lifted the man's body, piling it over his wife's like so much meat in a butcher shop.

As he left the room she felt that familiar prickling sensation at the nape of her neck. She slowly rose. The vice tightened until pain brought her to her knees, gasping for air.

Footsteps descended the basement stairs. She slowly re-seated herself in the chair and the pinching lessened, returning to the prickly feeling.

From downstairs she heard the sound of door open. Not a door. A freezer. Then muffled thuds as the bodies tumbled in. The freezer door closed and Kagoule's steps ascended the stairs. Hillary's heart raced as its massive form crossed the living room. It sat back down in the chair across from her.

"We always locate a planet with intelligent life," it continued. "Then we assess the suitability of the females using the manner in which I assessed you." It said this as if nothing had just happened; it hadn't carried two dead bodies to the basement; she hadn't disobeyed its direct order not to undertake an escape.

"That was assessment?"

It frowned at her and continued. "We take what we want. We are warriors. We seek strong aggressive females in order that the strength of our species will not be diluted." It regarded Hillary closely as, overcome by the image that had entered her mind, she retched.

"You will become accustomed to my looks."

A chill ran down Hillary's spine. She attempted to regain her self-control.

"If you obey me," it continued, "You will be comfortable, protected and cared for. Nothing can harm you. No member of any race is powerful enough to challenge us."

Hillary sat stunned, as though drugged. This couldn't be happening. She would wake up and laugh about this later; all of it; the days in Toronto; this. She didn't believe in life on other planets, had never believed in flying saucers. She wasn't going to believe in strange ugly alien creatures kidnapping her for the purpose of procreation. She swallowed hard again.

"You are not dreaming," it said flatly. "A strange ugly creature has kidnapped you for that very purpose." Its sarcasm assailed her.

"You said your people locate a planet and take what they want. Does that mean there will be other women taken from Earth?"

"We will take all the females from this planet."

"But wouldn't the children born of such a union be different?" She gestured wildly with her hands. "In appearance I mean."

"Are you trying to talk me out of this?" It smiled at her, then chuckled.

She breathed unsteadily. Hoping not to upset it with her questions, she strained to hide her thoughts from it. That took a great deal of energy. She relaxed visibly when it laughed; happy it wasn't angered by her queries.

"Like all other races we have used, your genes are recessive. You will contribute to the disposition of the child only. That is why it is important for us to find the right females."

"That's not possible."

"What? To procreate with a different race?"

She nodded.

"Within whose framework of knowledge?" it replied. "Who's science are you relying on to make that judgment?"

It stood now, turning its back to her as though putting itself on display. Slowly it walked around behind the chair it had been sitting in. From behind, it looked not unlike a giant man with a kind of glistening green/black hair that draped in ringlets down its back. Its torso remarkably resembled the human torso in design, only larger. Clothed in a silver garment covered by armor that emphasized its hair (if you could call it that) and broad scaly shoulders, it stood arrogantly.

It was trying to show itself in the best light! It was narcissistic. As ugly as it was, it was vain. She involuntarily gagged again at the thought of having intercourse with this creature. It turned abruptly and looked at her.

"As I said, you will become accustomed to my looks," it said calmly, aware of her revulsion. "In time my looks will please you. Everything about me will please you." It said this threateningly. "I will be your loved one," it said contemptuously.

"What are you going to do with me now?" she ventured, trying to keep herself calm.

"I will take you back to my planet when the exodus is arranged."

NO! NO! She wouldn't go.

"Oh, you will go. You cannot be removed from this place for many weeks," it continued, "as you would perish in transit over so long a distance without the protection of a vessel. We are arranging a star ship to transport all of you. Your species is very frail," it added. "It is fortunate your genes are recessive. We would never mate with you otherwise. It would be awful to be so restricted. So merely physical."

It strolled around the room as it talked now, picking objects up, examining them, putting them down.

"I would not have come this soon if you hadn't angered me," it said, examining a Royal Doulton figurine. It held the china doll in a massive hand and turned it slightly. "You annoyed me so much," it paused and turned to look at her, "that I almost killed you. You will not do that again. Will you?"

Hillary's heart sank. She was again this creature's captive. This was no nightmare. It looked away again, not waiting for a reply.

"I would have arrived here in another three weeks, your time, with my warriors and a mighty Bride Ship to take what we want, had you not provoked me." It cast a quick resentful glance at her and placed the figurine back on the mantel.

"I am pleased I did not kill you, though. Your looks delight me." It drew in a deep breath and straightened. "My warriors will arrive at the allotted time. You, my bride, and I, will await their coming."

How could she escape? Dear Lord! How could she escape? She was frantic to be free, to return to the old way of life she had known and loved; to elude this nightmare.

"You cannot escape me." Smiling, it added, "You know that. I can locate you anywhere on the planet's surface within seconds now that I have Marked you."

Marked? MARKED?

"But even if you were unmarked, being this close I could find you in a matter of hours as you keep time."

Hillary gasped. Marked? Like a dog marks its territory?

"Do not insult me, female!" it bellowed, covering the distance between them in a stride. It raised its hand to strike her. Hillary cringed and it restrained itself at the last minute. It chose instead to lower its hand to her face, gently tapping her in warning.

"This is Marking," it said, running the edge of its hand down the side of her face as it had done in the hospital when it came for her. Hillary felt a tingling - like pins and needles.

She retched and fought to conceal her thoughts. It could have disciplined her more forcefully. She knew it was being lenient, showing its gentler side; the side she could see on a regular basis if she obeyed it. An involuntary shudder went through her.

"I do not wish to be your mate," she said boldly, astonished she had said it.

It stepped away from her. Peals of harsh sarcastic laughter shook the room. "Do you think your wishes are my command? I am a warrior." Its voice rose. "No one commands me but ME." It was making an effort not to lose its temper; a temper that Hillary knew from experience was substantial.

"You will indeed be a most suitable mate, bold and outspoken. But you will hold your tongue," it hissed in warning. "I will not often tolerate such outbursts, and never in public. You will bear me many fine sons. But do not rankle me. Learn your place quickly. Whatever else you do, do not irritate me."

It stepped back toward her and stroked her face with the side of its hand again.

"I am inclined to take you now," it breathed, its nostrils flaring. "But I will not dishonor you. Chief Commander's bride should be untouched before the union. You will be my consort before I bed you." It gazed at her softly, as softly as a creature of its harsh nature and appearance could.

"You are a rare and priceless gem, female. From this time onward your name will be Hill'carn. Carn in my tongue means lovely jewel." Again it stroked her face. Hillary sat rigidly. Unable to move for fear of punishment, she tried not to be sick.

"Few mates have owned this name," it continued, walking away from her. "It can be the name of Chief Commander's consort only. Even so," it turned suddenly, "only three females have ever born the name Carn and all of those were Gron'dalin. You are the first alien to bear this name."

Gron'dalin. Her mind raced. Presumably there were females once. Well, of course there must have been.

It lowered its head to look at her from the tops of its eyes. The whites of its eyes were clearly visible below.

"You are inquisitive. That is what I liked most about you when we first met. I liked how you drew my mind to you."

Hillary cringed.

"Yes, once there were Gron'dalin females. They are gone now. You may call me, Kagoule," it continued. "Chief Commander's mate alone may call him by his name. You are in a very privileged position, Hill'carn," it said, drawing in a slow proud breath as it raised its head. It squared its shoulders. "You will come to realize this, my Queen."

Hillary tried desperately to remember how she had planned to block its access to her mind. Did she have a plan?

It smiled but said nothing.

* * * *

Days passed with no promise of escape. Hillary sat in the living room or prepared their meals as directed. She read or watched television. As evening approached on the fourth night of captivity, the creature stood and disappeared to the upper rooms without comment. Hillary ran for the door, still reading her book, not allowing any thoughts in.

Locked! The thought forced its way into her mind. "The door was indeed locked," she read, although the words did not appear in the mystery she was reading. She returned to her seat, working the words. "What about the windows?" Frank asked in the story. She ran to the window, shoving with one hand as she held the book aloft in the other and read frantically. "Stuck," Frank said. "Wouldn't you know it?"

The sound of the creature's return forced her, still reading, back into her seat. Her face flushed.

On re-entering the room, it went to its customary seat.

"None the wiser," Hillary read.

It looked at her in a puzzled manner, possibly because her face was red, her breathing labored. Conceivably, it thought she was excited about the book she was reading?

Dear Lord let it be only that!

"Only what?" it asked.

She cleared her mind. "Only what?" she asked innocently, or as guiltlessly as a guilty person could ask.

"Are you planning escape again?"

"You know every thought I have," she said.

It nodded. It hadn't understood what she'd done!

Reading is good for me, she thought. Keeps me busy, meaning she had found a way of concealing her thoughts, of wrapping the renegade ones into a story.

The creature looked puzzled and a little suspicious. It sighed but appeared to accept the innocence of her activity.

She looked at it. It had left her unattended to don a tight fitting shirt and slacks that she was sure were intended to reveal its massive body, its armor gone. Was it still trying to attract her? Gooseflesh coursed down her spine. The scale that passed for its skin was more exposed than usual in this outfit.

The tight fit of the garment necessitated that the keys be placed somewhere other than on its person. It dropped them on the coffee table at its elbow.

Instead of thinking about the keys being set on the coffee table, which might have alerted it to the fact she had taken note of them, Hillary thought about doors. The word association was weak but the only one she could create on a moment's notice. She scanned its face for tell-tale signs that it had unraveled her thoughts.

Horrified that this scrutiny would draw its attention, she deceptively thought how nice it looked in the clothes it had just donned and to her surprise, saw a look of satisfaction cross its face.

She was learning to conceal her thoughts. It believed it was making headway with her.

Lies. Did it know anything about lying? She suppressed thinking about lying now, let the thought graze her mind like thoughts had earlier.

She returned immediately to her book for protection, reading the words more rapidly than ever to keep from thinking.

The evening proceeded as all others, hopelessly, until ten o'clock when the creature rose and left the room abruptly.

Without the keys. Hillary read the words onto the pages of the book, heard the shower turn on and continued to read.

It had never left her alone before this evening for any activity, and now it had left her alone a second time in as many hours. There was hope.

Now she tried not to think that it was gambling that she would not attempt escape while it was indisposed. Was it ever indisposed? Perhaps it had simply forgotten it had left the keys behind.

She struggled not to think these thoughts, filtering images of camping trips with her father on the west coast of the United States through her mind. She tried to force the thoughts to skim her mind, stay at the edges only.

She rose, thinking of herself camping in Washington State, thinking she should return to the book she was reading. Pulling the book up to her face, she crossed the floor to the coffee table.

Agitation blinded her to the words on the page. She couldn't focus so she improvised on the story she had been reading, carrying it on in her imagination.

She concentrated hard on letting the words flow through her mind, fill her mind entirely. She could feel a tight prickling feeling at the base of her neck and knew it carefully monitored her.

Lifting the keys from the table, she composed a sentence. "The road was darker than he'd imagined it would be on this moonless night." Her improvised sentence fit in perfectly with the story.

The sound of the keys coming off the table caused her to think 'keys' so she ad-libbed again, continuing the thought, weaving it through the story. "Keys could not be found for the summer house on so dark a road, so as he walked he searched his pocket for his lighter."

She heard Kagoule in the shower. The sound of the water altered as it hit its body and an image of Kagoule in the shower, naked, filled her mind.

She knew it had read the thought! She had never considered what caused thoughts to enter a person's mind before - sounds, smells, sights perhaps. That thought would not upset it, though. It would be pleased she thought about its naked form. She did nothing further with the thought, just let it hang there.

Another thought suddenly crossed her mind; that the last sentence she had thought about the story was a stupid one. He should have carried a flashlight, not a lighter on so dark a road.

To cover any incongruity the sentence might present, and to account for her thinking the sentence stupid, she thought the book was equally as stupid and she should get another book from the library if this one did not improve soon. She thought this as she crossed to the front door.

The tightness at the back of her neck still pressed as she fumbled with the keys. Holding the book in her left hand, she read, "He turned off the main road toward the house." She tried one key.

Didn't fit. Again she let the thought slide off her mind, not holding onto it.

Breathing hard she read part of another sentence from the book. "The lights of the car flashed on empty fields."

Suddenly she felt her brain pricked by a thousand pins! Fire ripped at her mind, tearing it apart! She screamed in pain and frustration, knowing she had blundered by returning to the real story. Thinking about the protagonist walking and driving at the same time undid her. It hadn't missed the incongruity. Even without its physical presence, it controlled her. That was why it had left the keys on the table. It wanted to teach her there was no hope of escape. Perhaps she hadn't fooled it at all.

Hillary fell to the floor in agony, releasing the precious keys as she went down in favor of holding her head, an activity that did not relieve the pain.

As unconsciousness filtered in, her only hope lay in someone outside rescuing her.

But no one even knew she was a prisoner in this house. She'd told no one about Kagoule but Paul Muntz, and he didn't believe her. With no hope in sight she writhed in agony for what seemed a lifetime as Kagoule continued his shower uninterrupted.

Finally, mercifully, she fell unconscious.

Chapter 8
Attack

Paul slipped the .38 revolver he ordinarily kept in the night stand into his belt. Likely not enough against a beast like the one Hillary had described, it never-the-less felt reassuring to have it lodged there. Funny how the mind works, what makes us feel safe, he thought. He patted it lovingly.

Picking the micro-Uzi up off the kitchen table, he said a silent thank you to Heraldo Bennize. The snub-nose Colt might feel right somehow, tucked securely in his belt, but the old gray matter told him the boxy looking machine pistol was his only real chance – slim but better than nothing.

Heraldo's words ran hopefully through his mind. "Hitting something with an Uzi demands a level of marksmanship commensurate with watering a lawn." Warming to his subject, Heraldo had gone on to wax about civilian and military variants, muzzle velocities and rates of fire. Paul had tuned out most of it, but now he added a second silent thanks to his old college buddy.

Nothing could happen without the Uzi and without Heraldo there would be no Uzi. Of course even with the weapon, nothing might happen, or at least, nothing positive from Paul's perspective.

He clenched his teeth, straightened, and drew in a deep breath, trying to seal his resolve. With the Uzi carefully stashed under one arm, he turned and strode into the garage, securing the kitchen door behind him.

He set the weapon carefully on the front passenger seat of the Porsche, covered it with a blanket and closed the door. He strode determinedly around to the driver's side, intent on not losing his nerve. He had to do this. If not him, then who? He drew in another deep breath and pursed his lips as he opened the driver's door. Who else would do it, indeed? Who else was stupid enough?

Well, at least he wasn't foolish enough to believe he could convince police there was a huge scaly monster - one he'd never seen, but which had been described by a patient who'd experienced severe head trauma - holding his patient captive on Hilltop Drive. He chuckled cynically to himself.

The real clincher was that a well respected physician was on his way right now, with a highly illegal firearm, to blow this thing away.

Paul laughed aloud, sat behind the wheel and slammed the car door. He rammed the key into the ignition and let the house keys dangle there. He pressed the automatic garage door opener. It started sliding up, grinding behind him in the evening heat.

What if he was wrong? What if he burst into some middle-class home, ranting about space aliens and captive patients with an Uzi in hand, to find nothing? He looked down at the keys that hung from the ignition. How would he explain it to the home owner? Good Lord! How would he explain it to the authorities if the home owner, probably armed himself, didn't kill him first?

The keys stopped swaying. No, it was there. It had to be. He couldn't get any closer than half a block from that house without retching because of the smell. That same smell he'd first encountered in the lobby of the elder Bopal's hotel, then again in the south wing, drew him on.

Six days of tracking, sniffing it out like a bloodhound, hadn't been for nothing. He looked over at the heap on the seat beside him and started the engine.

* * * *

"Mary, I think he's going off the deep end."

"Well, you have to admit, Brendon, he's been through a lot these past few months. He lost his mother when he was only three. His father died in January, then your closest friend in June. That's pretty stressful for anyone. It must be even harder for Paul because he was an only child of two only children so there's no extended family out there to rely on. And he's never married. The poor guy has no one. You would be a little unhinged too if, after all that..."

She blew on her coffee, and then sipped at it as Brendon waited for her to finish the sentence. "If you had a patient snatched from a ward that was totally destroyed by some whack-o."

She sat back in the comfortable leather reclining chair and placed her glass coffee mug on the side table. Putting her feet on the leather stool she shrugged at her husband.

"I know. I know," Brendon sighed. "But honestly, Honey, this is getting out of hand. He really believes this Martian story. You should have heard him going on about being able to smell it all the way up Hilltop Drive. He's obsessed with finding this imaginary thing. He's been looking for it." Brendon paused, astounded at even the thought of a doctor searching for a Martian. "I think he wants to find a Martian more than he wants to find his patient."

"As soon as the police find her, he'll come around," Mary said. "You'll see."

"If they find her alive, maybe. Who knows what he'll do if they find her dead. And there's more likelihood they'll find her dead."

Brendon ran his fingers through his hair and exhaled loudly. He sat on the edge of the leather couch in his living room, his fingers tangled in the sandy-colored mess he called hair. "I'm really worried about him." He wrinkled his brow and the freckles on his face almost seemed to stretch as he did it.

"I know," Mary said, smiling gently at him. "Why don't we have him over for dinner tomorrow night?"

Brendon smiled at his beautiful wife and stood up. Stepping around the coffee table he leaned over and kissed her solidly on the lips. "You're a doll," he said. "I don't know if that's all he needs, but Paul loves your cooking. Don't be too freaked if he goes on about ugly scaly Martians though."

Mary pushed straight black hair behind one ear. "I won't be." Her blue eyes sparkled. "Who knows? Maybe there IS a Martian involved in this girl's disappearance."

Brendon groaned.

* * * *

Nearing the house, Paul turned the car lights off and cut the engine.

He rubbed his watering eyes. As the smell of the creature overwhelmed him, he fought back a wave of nausea. Slowly, he took several deep breaths as the car drifted to a stop. He gently set the parking brake and sat in the gathering darkness to acclimatize to the smell. The retching finally subsided.

That familiar prickling sensation started in his nostrils, bringing another flood of tears. Saliva filled his mouth. He dabbed it away with tissues. His heart pounded. Finally, when his heart slowed to something more like normal and the allergic reaction passed, he wiped his eyes, blinked repeatedly to clear his vision and blew his nose.

Uncovering the Uzi, he slid silently out the door, leaving it slightly ajar behind him. With the dome light disconnected, no informant winked on in the blackness behind as he crept past the homes of sleeping neighbors.

The memory of Bopal's mangled corpse filled his mind for one frightening moment. He pushed the image away and prowled on through the night.

The last tinge of light hung stubbornly in the western sky, dispatching faded rays of red and orange.

With agile steps, he crossed the perfect weed-free lawn, the Uzi, concealed under his light summer jacket, its weight pressing against his body. Stopping beside the attached garage, he slung the weapon over one shoulder (ever-thoughtful Heraldo had thrown in a shoulder strap); scaled the structure to its roof with a boost from a cedar fence and, hoping the house alarm wasn't engaged, he pushed open a window that was already slightly ajar.

He strained to hear noises from within. A television newscast droned away from the living room below but nothing else. He swung his leg over the sill and stepped onto plush carpet.

Drops of sweat ran into the corners of his eyes, stinging. He ignored them. Concentrating on his breathing, Paul gently closed the window to where it had been.

He stood motionless in the tidy room for several seconds, gathering his bearings, listening, thinking thoughts that he hoped would not disturb the creature if it scanned its surroundings. No noise but the murmur of the evening news disturbed him.

Holding the Uzi out in front, he cautiously stole toward the open bedroom door, never taking his eyes from it. The carpet silently crushed underfoot. With each careful step, whatever calm he might earlier have self-imposed, fled. Now, his heart worked painfully like a giant hammer in his chest. Sweat broke and ran in streamlets down his cheeks, along his hairline. He blinked it from his eyes and clutched the Uzi with slippery hands.

For one terrifying minute, his heartbeat became the only sound. Then his senses sharpened. He crept down the hall toward the stairs.

Focus.

Night sounds came to him. A cough from the living room echoed through his mind. A shuffle. A sigh. He glided on automatic pilot. Instinct took over. The Uzi moved with his body like an extension, welded to him.

At the top of the stairs, he stopped. The gun jutted ahead, egging him on. He started down the stairs. His fluid movements brought him to the landing without notice.

Paul froze when he saw it.

Aware of him at last, the creature stood.

Fear gripped him.

Somehow he lifted the weapon. Up and up forever it travelled.

The beast turned.

On the weapon's upward journey, he pressed the safety and fire selectors just as instructed. His finger tightened on the trigger and, miraculously, flame shot from the barrel. A blood curdling cry left his lips as bullets streamed from the gun. Hillary sat welded to the spot, staring, unmoving as Paul screamed a primeval battle cry.

Bullets struck the creature's body in a steady stream of fire.

Blood splattered the walls and furniture.

The creature fell.

Paul continued firing short bursts, continued to shriek that bloody cry. Then words spilled with the scream. "Die you bastard! Die!"

Was that his voice? Did those words come from him?

And the creature struck out with its mind. Chairs and tables splintered, coffee tables overturned, disintegrated. Ornaments shattered and exploded. Plaster burst from the walls.

Paul continued to empty the contents of the Uzi into the creature, continued to scream as the creature writhed on the floor.

Roaring in pain and fury, the creature rose up to its full height and slashed the sofa to shreds with the power of its mind; then suddenly the stairs themselves exploded out from under Paul.

He fell, tumbling head over foot. The stairs splintered around him.

"Shit!" he yelled.

The Uzi, welded to his hands by fear, continued to discharge as he plunged into the debris of the living room. Bullets flew around Hillary, missing her by inches.

Having emptied the Uzi, he discarded it in favor of the trusted Colt. Ripping the small handgun from his belt he shot off another round.

The creature pulverized the wall at the top of the stairs where moments earlier Paul had stood, then collapsed to the floor for the last time.

Paul lay in a heap of rubble, struggling to re-gain his feet as the creature's screams ceased to rend the air.

* * * *

Hillary sat immobile amidst the devastation of the house where she had been held captive for so long. How long had it been, a week, a month? Time stood still for her. She stared ahead, unblinking, vaguely aware of Paul's presence. Was that handsome doctor really here or was she dreaming? Was it all a dream? This awful imprisonment couldn't really be happening.

The destruction of her jail cell went largely unnoticed. She stared ahead blankly as Kagoule's huge frame hit the floor; chairs overturned, tore to bits; the stairs fell in splinters; great holes punched into the walls; light fixtures shattered; the rattle of gunfire punctuated the mayhem. She saw it all but saw nothing.

Oh, what a silly dream. A nightmare, really. She would wake from it soon. Darkness flowed back in. She welcomed it as an old friend.

* * * *

"Hillary, are you okay?" Paul's trembling voice filled the silence that had fallen over the house. His hands shook violently. Blood streamed from a gash in his forehead. Mingling with sweat it snaked down to his shirt collar.

Not waiting for a response, Paul moved cautiously toward the fallen alien, pointing the empty weapon at it. His feet crunched through broken glass and china, making a loud unpleasant noise as he stepped forward. He stepped over splintered tables and around a demolished floor lamp, melted like some of the carts in the ward had been. Before him, the shattered body of an enormous, six fingered, scaled creature, its mouth grotesquely twisted in death, loomed like a silent harbinger. A shiver ran through him as he gazed at its corpse.

"Hillary?"

* * * *

Hillary made no reply. Her name echoed in the distance through a long tunnel of fog that protected her. It reverberated down to where she hid in shadows. She pulled the darkness tightly around her and shut out the noise.

"Hillary?" His voice demanded she reply. Undaunted by her silence he repeated it again. "Are you alright?"

Such an annoying man. Why wouldn't he leave her alone?

Go away! Leave me in peace! She thought.

* * * *

The sound of a siren wailing toward them in the night filled the room and Paul glanced toward the window.

"Well, the neighbors might have no olfactory senses but their hearing is intact," he murmured.

He stood over the body of the beast. The smell of its corpse nauseated him in the extreme, the more so for the blood that spattered the walls and the blood that flowed from it onto the floor.

The siren stopped outside and he breathed a sigh of relief, not thinking he still held the Colt, thinking simply that someone else could take over. Let the authorities take control. They knew how to handle this sort of thing, surely.

The front door burst open.

"Freeze!" A man's voice screamed. "Drop it!" the police officer bellowed.

Paul didn't turn, suddenly aware of the weapon he held, abruptly cognizant of his own stupidity. The sound of the man's voice descended as he swiftly crouched behind Paul. Paul could feel the cop's trepidation. He was in trouble! Without turning he spoke slowly, as though the officer might be jolted by his words if he spoke too quickly. He might end this evening shot by mistake.

"Okay officer. I'm going to drop this thing on the floor now. Don't shoot, okay?"

"Just drop it, NOW!" the cop yelled. "Just drop it, no fast movements or I'll shoot."

Paul complied, dropping the Colt beside the creature's body while holding his arms out, away from his own body. He heard the officer straightening behind him. The stress level in the room dropped but only slightly.

"Hands behind your head!"

Paul obeyed instantly. Without hesitation his hands flew up behind his head.

"Take two steps back. Don't turn," the cop yelled as Paul started turning around. Paul tried to back up through the debris.

"What the hell?" another voice blared, apparently taking in the destruction in the room.

Paul looked at the officer who had just entered from the direction of the dining room, his gun held in a two-handed grip. He stared at Paul while Paul backed awkwardly through the rubble of the living room furniture, with his hands behind his head. His eyes never left Paul's for that whole trip. Then suddenly the cop caught sight of the creature. His eyes settled on it. Now, mouth agape, he stared at the creature on the floor.

"On your knees!" the first officer commanded. Paul knelt.

On your stomach, face down!" Paul lay down in the rubble, his arms stretched out ahead of him. Blue and red strobe lights throbbed against the far wall and the sound of more sirens approaching filled the air.

"Stay where you are, buddy. Don't move!" the first officer admonished. The stress in his voice had subsided somewhat.

The creature, directly in the second cop's line of vision, continued to distract that officer, as the first cop came forward and started frisking Paul, turning him over slightly.

It wasn't every day you responded to reports of shots fired and found a creature the like of what lay on the floor in front of this cop.

"Don't move. Don't even breathe," the first cop warned.

Paul obeyed. Holding his breath until the first cop stood up, Paul finally breathed again.

"Back up on your knees. Hands over your head," the first cop said.

Hadn't he looked around yet? Hadn't he seen the body of the alien on the floor? If he had he wouldn't be doing his job as usual, surely.

"Any other weapons?" he asked.

"No," Paul replied.

"What IS that?" the second cop finally asked, still gaping at Kagoule's massive body.

"Are you asking me what this creature is?" Paul asked from his kneeling position. "Do you want a reply to that question?" His hands were still behind his head as he spoke.

Suddenly the other cop saw the alien corpse.

"Madre de Dios!" he whispered.

The sound gushed from his lungs like the rush of wind through pine needles.

The second cop now looked in disbelief from Paul to Hillary, and then to his partner who was moving away after collecting the weapons. Both officers stood rigidly, backs stiff. The second officer, the younger of the two, closed his mouth finally as he looked from Paul to Hillary.

"You can stand up now. Real slow," the older officer said. But he had no heart for it now. Paul could hear that in his deadpan voice. "No sudden moves."

Paul stood up awkwardly with his hands behind his head.

"Can I lower my hands?"

"Ya. But don't try anything funny," he said this more from rote than with any emotion. He stared at the alien on the floor.

"You got it officer. Nothing funny," Paul said soothingly.

"I see it," the first cop said to his partner. "But I don't believe it." The second cop shrugged and blinked at the first. "What is it?" the first cop asked.

Static filled the air as a message came across a radio. The officer took the radio from his belt and announced the scene was secure.

"Jesus!" the first cop exclaimed. "What the hell is it?"

"I don't know," Paul answered. "It kidnapped her," he jerked his head toward Hillary who still occupied the armchair in utter silence, "about a week ago from the hospital."

"From the hospital? This doesn't have anything to do with that ward being trashed. Does it?"

"Yes. I tracked it here and killed it."

"I'll say you killed it!" the older cop remarked, looking at the bullet-riddled alien corpse in disbelief.

"You almost shredded it!" the younger cop added.

The two officers lowered their weapons in unison. "You her husband?" the older one asked, holstering his gun.

"Just her doctor."

The younger officer addressed Hillary from across the room. "Miss? Miss? Are you alright?"

Hillary did not move or give any indication she was alive. Her eyes, vacant and wide, stared past them to another plane of existence. In the darkness she heard her voice being called. She drew the blanket of fog more securely around her and sank lower into the safe pit that had come up to embrace her the day she had tried to escape.

"She's in shock," Paul said. "May I?" He inclined his head toward Hillary.

"Sure. Sure. Go ahead," the older cop replied, stooping to pick up the Uzi. He moved closer to the dead creature, poked it tentatively with his foot. "Her doctor?"

"I suppose this is a house call then?" the younger officer remarked, watching his partner prod the body of the dead alien. "I'm not surprised the lady's in shock."

The young man stepped through the debris to look down at the creature's shattered body. Cautiously he towered over it, as though half expecting it to rise up off the floor and devour him.

"I would be in shock too if something like this held me captive," he said. "What did it want with her?"

"I don't know," Paul answered. A silence fell over them. The two men briefly exchanged looks before Paul tilted Hillary's head back and looked into her eyes.

"Hillary can you hear me?" Paul called. "Hillary?"

Paul's voice drifted down to her. She reached for it at first but withdrew, pulling herself back down to safety.

Sirens died outside the house. More policemen poured in through the open front door. One of the new arrivals joined the two already staring at Kagoule's body.

"The doc here just came to collect a patient," the young cop said to an even more youthful recruit. "Remind me never to stand between him and his patients."

"Holy Shit!" the new cop replied. "What is it, Jack?"

"What WAS it is more like it," Jack said. "You're not the first one to ask that, Henry."

Chapter 9
Disclosures

"It's good to have you back."

"It's good to be back, Brendon."

Nervously, Brendon glanced over one shoulder. Glaring into Paul's blue eyes, he asked, "What is going on here?" His voice, laced with fear, trembled. "Staff and patients are butchered," he glanced over his shoulder again, "the nursing station on the fourth floor is trashed. NO! The whole ward is trashed! Your patient disappears." He lowered his voice to a forced whisper. "The one that was seeing aliens. Remember?"

"How can I forget?"

"Then YOU vanish before I can invite you for supper and your patient turns up accompanied by a bunch of weird looking interns that don't know the first thing about medicine. Interns my ass! And the military is guarding her door twenty-four hours a day."

"Let's walk," Paul said, gently taking Brendon by the elbow and turning him. Allowing himself to be guided, the other man straightened his tie and adjusted his white coat as they started down the hospital corridor. Over the PA system, Doctor Morris was paged to emergency.

"I hope they aren't letting them handle cases," Paul whispered.

"WE are not letting them handle cases," Brendon replied calmly, more calmly than he felt. "The administration is just expecting them to stay out of trouble." They're some kind of undercover cops, right? CIA or something?"

"I guess. I know about as much as you do about them. Less. I didn't know until now they were here."

"Where have you been? I've been calling your house, the office. Your receptionist wouldn't tell me a thing. Expected me to believe you'd taken a trip somewhere. As if you'd go away without telling Mary and me."

"I've been on vacation with what I expect are the bosses of the men posing as interns. Frankly Brendon, I didn't think I would ever see the light of day again."

"What is going on?" Brendon whispered, smiling and nodding to a passing nurse as though nothing was wrong. "I didn't believe that bit about your going on holiday any more than I believed your patient's story about alien monsters."

"Well, start believing the alien monster part. I've seen it now with my own eyes."

"You're kidding! Come on Paul." Brendon stopped abruptly and grabbed Paul by the arm, halting him. "This is too big to fool with me about."

"Just keep walking," Paul admonished. "Don't look like anything is wrong."

"Stop clowning around," Brendon answered as he started moving again. "You're scaring me."

"I was a guest of the government, Brendon." Paul peered over his shoulder. "Underwent every sort of 'user friendly' interrogation possible. All because I killed that alien thing Hillary described."

"God!" Brendon muttered.

"I was treated like a criminal for killing a greenish brown – no – a HUGE greenish brown scaly thing that couldn't possibly have been spawned on Earth."

"You're being serious?" Brendon said.

"Deadly serious."

Brendon fell silent. They stopped beside the elevator and Brendon feigned a calm exterior as he pressed for the lift.

"I got an Uzi from that old college bud of mine."

"You got what?" Brendon asked incredulously.

"You remember Heraldo? The guy who came to me in the dead of night once with a gunshot wound?

"Ya. I remember." Brendon looked around at a group of nurses on their way for a coffee break.

"Him. And they weren't even concerned about where I got the weapon from." Paul cleared his throat. "I'm telling you, it was like something straight out of a sci-fi movie, Brendon."

Paul nervously scanned the corridor as the elevator door slid open. They stepped in. "I tracked the thing to Hilltop Drive. Remember I told you it was up there?"

"Ya."

"Well, it was." Paul shook his head at Brendon. "And you didn't believe me."

Brendon shrugged.

"Smelled like a sewer. Did you see that trashed nursing station?"

"Who didn't?"

"You must have smelled something there?"

Brendon shrugged. "Not a thing. You've already asked me that. I couldn't smell anything."

"Well, I could smell it. That's how I found it. That one creature did all that destruction, Brendon. You know, I only half believed it myself. But I saw it in action this time. The thing was incredible!"

Brendon pressed their floor number. "Good Lord!"

"It was just like Hillary said. A huge scaly thing. Must have been seven feet tall, broad shoulders. Uses its mind." He tapped his head. "Ripped the living room of that house apart with its mind. It's MIND, Brendon!" He shook his finger in Brendon's face as he stressed the word.

"I don't want to believe this."

"Me neither. But it happened. It was real."

Brendon sighed.

"It looked just like a man except it was covered in scales and didn't have hair like ours. Ringlets, kind of. From the middle of its head." Paul patted the top of his own head as he spoke to illustrate where the creature's hair grew from.

"I'd say that was a pretty big difference. Scales and ringlets," Brendon replied.

"Same torso though. Anyway, I broke into the house it was hiding in and nailed it."

"Brother!" Brendon looked astonished. The elevator door slid open and they stepped out. "You're always pulling my leg, Paul. If this is another one of your jokes, it isn't funny."

"It's not a joke." They walked side-by-side down the hall. "Wish it was. By the way, I'm not supposed to tell anyone about this so you didn't hear it from me. Okay?"

"Didn't hear a word. Not that I could repeat any of this story without looking like I'd flipped out."

"No kidding. Now you know how I felt. Just don't forget, I tried to tell you about it then, and you thought I was nuts."

"Well, what did you think I was going to think? It isn't every day a space monster lands on Earth."

"How is Hillary?" Paul asked as they walked on.

"She's still unconscious." They arrived at the nursing station on the third floor, north block. "Hillary Bopal has undergone a battery of tests as you'll see," Brendon handed him her chart. He took a stethoscope from the pocket of his white cotton coat and put it around his neck.

"I see that," Paul said, flipping through the test results. "Is there anything you didn't do?"

"Nothing. Still, she hasn't moved since the evening of July thirtieth when she was brought in. We turn her every hour, irrigate her eyes."

"You mean she isn't even blinking?" Paul closed the file and they stepped into a room behind the nursing station.

"NO."

"Brain dead?"

"No way. Lot of activity there. More than normal really. None of it's going anywhere though."

"Why did they put you on it?"

"Needed some DNA testing."

"What for?"

"She seems to be changing."

"How!"

"Subtle things. Texture of her skin mostly."

"Well, what did you find?"

"Skin on her face is a bit grainy all right but that could just be the way she is. I haven't found anything. She looks perfectly normal to me, although the test results aren't all back yet. You know how long it takes to analyze someone's DNA for crying out loud. And they've just put me on it. I think they're spooked, frankly. Now that I know the story, I think they're running scared. She was in contact with an alien and they're waiting for her to turn into one, or explode, or something." He shook his head in disgust. "You know what we humans are like."

Paul nodded and scanned the medical records as Brendon pulled x-rays out of a long brown manila envelope.

"The fractures to her legs and arm are beautifully and impossibly healed," Brendon said, snapping the films one-by-one into the clips that held them against an illuminated viewer. He pointed to one of the images. "You'd never know she'd broken a bone." Paul hooked one hand behind his neck and stared at the x-rays.

"Terrifies me," Brendon remarked. "What kind of technology could do that?"

Paul sat on the edge of a desk. He set Hillary's medical records down on the desktop beside him while he studied the x-rays for a moment in silence.

"What kind of technology could have done that?" Brendon repeated, wanting an answer. Any answer would do right about now. His world had been turned upside down.

"Damned if I know," Paul replied shaking his head. Standing, he removed the x-rays in silence and stuffed them back in their envelopes. Brendon switched off the light as Paul swept Hillary's medical file off the desk and tucked everything under his arm.

"You've done an excellent job, Brendon."

"Oh I wasn't alone. There were eight of us working on her."

"Well, there isn't another test I can order."

"So why isn't she reactive?"

"Beats me," Paul answered, shrugging.

"It didn't rape her, thank God."

"Christ!"

"It's like she's keeping herself unconscious," Brendon suggested.

Paul sighed. "I'd better get in to see her."

"Good luck," Brendon said. "Oh. Did you know they pulled all of us off the case?"

"No I didn't."

"Ya. You're back. Lunch later?"

"If I'm allowed," Paul answered. "They're keeping me on a short leash. They don't want me talking with anyone."

"You? Talk? Never." Brendon chuckled. "Why didn't they attach someone to you?"

"They did." Paul winked.

Brendon chuckled. "What did you do to him?"

"No one gets IN or OUT of my car if I don't want them to."

"You locked the sucker in the car?" Brendon slapped his leg. "That's classic. I hope you parked in the shade. It's hot out there."

Paul cuffed Brendon on the shoulder. "I think of everything," he said. "Besides, he won't be in there long. They'll get him out and he'll be right back on my heels. I'm surprised I'm still alone and they haven't clued in to what I pulled, yet."

* * * *

Entering Hillary's room Paul spoke in an authoritative voice to the nurse beside her bed. "You can take a break, nurse." No one made an effort to stop him from entering the chamber. No one questioned where his escort was. The woman rose and left the room, walking briskly past the guards stationed at Hillary's door. Paul closed the door behind her and crossed the floor to Hillary's bed.

Sunlight poured in through the open window. Paul slipped around the side of the bed and closed the curtains, then turned back to his patient. Lifting her eyelids one at a time with his thumb and index fingers he flashed a light across her pupils. They dilated normally. That didn't surprise him. According to the tests they had run, her brain was functioning better than normal.

"What did it do to you? You poor kid."

* * * *

The sound of Paul's voice reached Hillary through the fog that silted her mind. She stirred. Like sound heard at the bottom of a deep well, his voice echoed in the distance. She reached for it and moaned.

"Hillary? Can you hear me?"

For the first time since the incident, Hillary took a deep breath and moaned again. Was that Paul calling her? Or was it Kagoule? Was Kagoule real? Would it still be there when she opened her eyes? She thrust her hands over her ears like a frightened child who doesn't want to hear some part of a horror film.

"No. Please, let me go. Please." Her voice was a low whine that surely couldn't have come from her.

"It's gone Hillary. You're all right. You're safe. It's gone." He took her by the shoulders. Come on now," he said, coaxing her. "It's over."

She opened her eyes. Paul stood before her. She focused on him. Hospital smells registered in her mind for the first time. She sat up slowly, tears coursing down her cheeks. Grasping his arm she pulled him to her, her eyes wide with fear.

"You killed it," she said softly. "I saw you. You killed it." She clung to him, crushing her thin body into his. She cried softly, clinging like one of those skinny little famine victims on television.

"It's over now," he repeated, trying to pry her off. "You're safe."

Her body quaked uncontrollably against his. "Paul," she whispered, letting him push her away. "It has just begun."

The fan in the room hummed. A message came over the PA. "Doctor Brice to O.R. six. Doctor Brice."

"What did you say, Hillary?" He inclined his ear toward her. "I didn't hear you."

"It's just begun," she repeated in the same whisper. "They're coming."

"Who's coming?" he asked.

He looked at her strangely, as if he knew what she was going to say. His thick blond hair, longer than she remembered it, brushed his shoulders as he turned his head.

How long had she been lying in this hospital bed? How long had she been hiding, waiting for Paul to come?

"The Gron'dalins," she said, clearing her throat. "That's what they're called." She wiped her eyes on the backs of her hands.

"I was afraid of this," Paul answered. He dropped his hands on the hospital bed and looked into her eyes. "Why did I think it wouldn't end with this one creature?" he asked, then added, "why are they coming Hillary?"

"They want wives." She shuddered visibly.

The same shudder appeared to run through him and he drew in a sharp breath.

"Something primitive in me knew that," he confided. "Some dark shadow that was clinging in some unknown pit somewhere knew that. In a primitive area of my mind I knew what this thing wanted you for," he said. "And so did those cops at the house when they saw you sitting there with it lying on the floor dead. I sensed their horror in more than the fact that a creature lay dead on the floor."

* * * *

"This goes straight to the President," Simon Cahill said to his partner. A group of seven intelligence agents gathered at the one-way glass installed between Hillary Bopal's room and this one. They stood in shock.

"If we didn't have a body I would be reluctant to believe any of this," Cahill added.

"No kidding!" Anderson Manning answered.

No one else in the room spoke as Hillary continued.

* * * *

"They will take every female," she said.

"They can't mate with human beings," Paul protested.

"They're from the same genetic base."

"Hillary, as a medical doctor I find it hard to believe they can successfully mate with humans. It's just not genetically possible, same genetic base or not. They're a totally different species." He snorted. "It's like..." He searched for a comparison. "Men mating with monkeys," he finally said for want of a better comparison.

After seeing the x-rays of her arm and legs he knew who the monkeys were in his analogy. "It can't be done."

"Well, believe it," she said. "They've been doing this for a very long time, Paul. They've done it to countless species."

"Okay." Paul answered, throwing up his hands. "Until a few weeks ago I wouldn't have believed that large scaly creatures from space were possible either. Okay. Every adult woman is going to be taken?"

"I think it meant every female who'd ever be able to bear children, even if they weren't of child-bearing age right now."

"What makes you think that?"

In the next room Cahill nodded. "Ya! Good question Doc. What makes you think that?" The tension in the room hung like an ice fog. "I've got a daughter, he finally added. Sit down men."

He took a seat himself. They had all jumped to their feet when Hillary started coming around. He leaned forward in his chair staring at Hillary through the one-way glass.

Hillary paused to consider her response. "It said the little ones always die for some reason the Gron'dalins can't understand. I suspect they're dying for reasons they won't understand. They're so close-minded."

"Shit!" Paul said. "So we're not just looking at the loss of a generation if these things are successful."

"Loss of a generation?" Hillary snapped. "Can you imagine what the lives of women who were taken would be like? How dare you talk about losing a generation?"

"Okay, okay," Paul said, holding up his hands in supplication. "Sorry. I was just thinking about the overall effect of this thing on our civilization."

"Me too," Cahill said quietly. The men around him all nodded agreement.

"This creature…," Paul continued.

"Kagoule," she said, regaining her composure as she wiped tears on tissue Paul handed her. She only half listened, lost in thoughts that raced through her mind.

"Kagoule," he repeated. "Was it alone?"

"Yes. A flagship is on its way. It was the head guy."

"A flagship?" Paul repeated as though he were talking to himself. "How many are aboard this ship?"

"I don't know. The flagship carries their elite. They get first choice." She sounded resigned and about an inch away from tears.

"Hillary, we've got to tell the authorities about this," Paul suddenly announced. "Is there any way of stopping them?"

"There has to be, Paul." Hillary looked up into his blue eyes. "If there isn't…"

Cahill sat back in his swivel chair. "Ya, if there isn't," he repeated. "I knew they'd cooperate, Manning." He said serenely. "No one is going to hold anything back on these bastards. It was pretty obvious Muntz wasn't fond of the creature. How many rounds did he put into it?"

"Thirty-four. Parabellum."

"Ya, I'd say that was dislike." Simon Cahill reached for his coffee mug. Paul was speaking again and the back room boys fell silent.

"When are they getting here? Have you got any idea? "She looked uncertain. "Think back to anything it might have said."

"Uh hum, think back," Manning said from the hinterland, looking intently at Hillary Bopal over the top of his glasses. He stood and leaned against the table. Folding his arms across his chest and added, "But don't take too long thinking, Hillary. They're on their way."

"Well," she looked down at her hands resting in her lap, and sniffled loudly. "It spoke about an exodus."

"Taking all the bloody women," Paul snapped, placing his hands on his hips in a challenging manner.

"In several weeks. It said 'we' - us humans had to travel in vessels."

"You mean THEY don't!" Paul said incredulously.

"They travel in ships only when they want to arrive in a group."

"NO WAY!" he said with skepticism. "Jesus Christ!" His pupils fully dilated with fear.

All seven men in the back room mimicked his amazement with various words of disbelief.

"Oh." Hillary continued, trying to concentrate, trying to force herself to remember. "It said it would have arrived here in three Earth weeks if it hadn't been for my angering it."

"You were angering it?"

"I refused to answer all sorts of questions it put to me, but it got really angry when I wouldn't tell it about political structures. Then I ran away. Remember."

"Yes, yes that's right," Paul answered. "You ran away." The look of fear in his eyes intensified. "Rather belligerent of you wasn't it?" he remarked sarcastically, his jaw set defiantly. "I'll bet it wanted to know about political structures so it could plan its attack. Hillary, do you realize you've been," he chose his words carefully. "Comatose for close to three weeks?"

Dead silence fell over the surveillance room. Cahill looked at Manning with searching eyes. "We've probably got less than a week to prepare for this," he said.

Manning pushed his glasses up his nose. His eyes bulged in utter amazement. "Maybe hours," he said.

"These fuckers are almost here," Cahill continued, calmly but intensely. "They're coming here to take our bloody women."

Manning launched himself from the chair he'd been sitting in. "I'll notify the President."

Bedlam ensued as men darted from their chairs and rushed out the door.

Chapter 10
Cacin

Cacin stroked his neck and stared at the star studded sky. The ship sped toward the ninth quadrant. Behind it – in front – all around – an ever changing sea of bright lights that faded to pinpricks dotted the heavens, then vanished to be replaced by more bright lights as the liner raced on.

He loved travelling by vessel. There was something quaint about it. It spoke of earlier times, times when the pressures of life hadn't been so great.

He caught the reflection of his comely emerald green and mahogany face shining back at him in the banit'ye barrier of the observatory window. His massive shoulders covered by the silver cape of his ancestry, he commanded an impressive physique. He nodded at his likeness, deep in thought.

How could they think him ugly, these 'women' of Earth? Kagoule's reports revealed that the future Queen thought the Gron'dalin form totally repugnant.

Repugnant! Were they so limited in their exposure to other life forms that they had no appreciation of strength, of variety? He sighed, recalling his father's account of his first contact with Cacin's mother. She too had held this same view. It was hard to believe. His father was a fine specimen of gron'hood, tall and stately.

Cacin breathed in deeply, filling his huge lungs. He raised his head and squared his shoulders defiantly. He clenched his jaw obstinately. Well, they would see. Like all others, nothing these females on Earth could do would avoid their fate. Like it or not, the Gron'dalins were coming.

Although it was always like this, Cacin had never believed for a minute he would be rejected by his mate. Now that his coupling drew near, he still couldn't accept he would be seen as 'repulsive.' The word vexed him.

Kagoule had informed the Elders by mind link that these females were very desirable, larger than many of the species their race mated with, and more intelligent. Their appearance apparently pleased his cousin and Cacin's own curiosity prickled with anticipation. He pined to see the female who had excited his cousin so, the female he would bed.

"My Lord?"

Cacin jumped. "You startled me."

"I don't wish to intrude on your thoughts."

"I didn't hear you enter, Gradspin." He turned to face the old Elder.

"I have come to discuss the Zadanin situation as you requested."

"Yes. It's unfortunate it has to be an issue. I can't tolerate backbiting."

"You are young for this governing, Lord. He thought to take advantage of your youth. I believe he has reconsidered."

"I am prepared to kill Zadanin if he continues with this disharmony. I won't be tested."

"He has said nothing further since my conversation with him."

"Fortunately for Zadanin. I'm glad my cousin has stopped this treasonous behavior. I'm stronger and far more determined to have the throne than he is. I would easily succeed in combat against him. I don't like the idea of killing a Zi, Lord Elder, but I'm not going to allow him to undermine my position."

"You can rest easy, Lord. He is no longer on the attack. It's sometimes hard for the brother of a childless former King to see the throne passed to the next in line, out of the immediate family."

Cacin nodded. "I'm glad things are settling down." He turned back to the stars. "It gives me the freedom to do what I talked to you earlier about."

"I hope you have given it a lot of thought. We've already lost one King."

"Gradspin, Kagoule was always impetuous. He paid for it with his life. I will be careful."

Gradspin bowed. "If there is nothing more, My Lord."

"You may go, Gradspin," he said, looking over his shoulder at the stooped old gron.

Cacin turned to the stars again as Orgone Butanie Zad entered. Passing Gradspin at the door, he nodded to the Elder and muttered a respectful greeting.

"You called for me, Zi," Orgone said when Gradspin was gone. He bowed as he spoke.

Cacin glanced back at him. Orgone's long pale green/brown mane fell to one side in glistening ringlets as he lifted his head.

"Dispense with that nonsense, Orgone. You don't need to bow in my presence. You're my friend."

"It's custom."

"Yes, yes. Custom. I'm sick to death of our mores. They get us in more trouble than enough." Cacin looked at the Zad over his shoulder, then returned his attention to the star clusters that dotted the dark sky. He sighed. "I have decided to leave the vessel, Orgone, and travel to Earth ahead of the Elite." He looked back at the Zad to observe his reaction. "To assess my bride."

"If you can't find her to assess her from here, what makes you think you will there?"

"I will." Cacin sighed again. "And you will take command of the *Gazadeback Emperor* in my absence, Orgone." He paused briefly, looking into his friend's eyes. Then he turned back again to star gaze. "One advantage of travelling this way is the view."

"One disadvantage is the time it takes," Orgone said.

"I am expected to accept Kagoule's choice of mates and concentrate solely on acquisition of appropriate females for the rest of the Elite."

"I know."

"That stinks. I don't like it. I'd rather find my own mate."

"I know."

"What if I don't like her?"

"You will. Your cousin was very demanding and he had impeccable taste."

"Yes. He had that if he had nothing else." Cacin folded his arms across his chest. "There will be prolonged warfare on this Bride Quest, Orgone. These beings are not only smart, they are determined."

"All races are bent on keeping their females. None are as determined as we are to take them."

Cacin smirked into the banit'ye viewing screen at his friend. His reflection was crisp. Orgone stood just behind him smirking back. "No. No one is as stubborn as we are. We expend everything we have on these Bride Quests. I sometimes wish it was not so."

A silence fell over them briefly.

"She may have died in the attack on Kagoule. If she did, I will have to choose another quickly." Orgone shifted his weight as Cacin continued. "I want you to establish a colony on the fourth planet as soon as you arrive. I'm sorry I won't be there to oversee the project."

"No trouble. I'm honored," the tall youth replied.

Cacin squared his shoulders and straightened to his full eight feet. "Make sure the receiving bay is built immediately on your arrival. I'll have to bring the female there through body latch."

He turned to look at his friend again. "If Hill'carn has lived through the attack on Kagoule, I will bring her," he added, decisively. "I don't know what strengthening effect, if any, the Marking will have on her mind. I don't want her to perish in transit, so have that bay ready."

"Yes, Zi. May I speak freely?"

Cacin had returned to his inspection of the stars outside the vessel as he finished speaking. Now with this candid request he turned around to face the Zad. The long silver cape of the Zi lineage swept out around him, creating a slight breeze.

"Go ahead," he invited.

"Before you do this, I need to bring to your attention that we have already lost a King on this Quest."

"I know that. Gradspin has also mentioned it to me."

"An older and more experienced Zi than yourself."

"Don't YOU start," Cacin stated, pointing a finger at his friend accusingly.

"You know what I mean," Orgone said.

"Perhaps it's for the better that Kagoule is dead," Cacin mused, knowing Orgone meant no harm. He looked down at the floor for a moment and, on raising his eyes, added, "Where our culture is concerned, I mean. Kagoule was feared by the Elite."

"He wasn't a thinking gron," Orgone admitted.

"That is putting it kindly. Are you becoming diplomatic as you get older?"

Orgone chuckled. "But my point IS that he fell to these Humans. In his death message he warned us of these beings, my friend. Kagoule the warrior fell to them. You are not as experienced a warrior as he was." Orgone cleared his throat.

"I studied with him, Orgone. Perhaps this and the fact that I'm a 'thinking gron,' as you call it, will ensure my safety. I won't be nearly as rash as Kagoule was."

"I realize your urgency but..."

"I am GOING, Orgone. Nothing you can say will change that."

"Will you consider taking one of the Sentry with you then?"

Cacin squeezed Orgone's shoulder. "If I took anyone, it couldn't be a Sentry. It would have to be a Zad or another Zi. With the exception of Cruchton." He turned back to the window. "And I wouldn't leave the ship handicapped by removing his expertise." Orgone stepped up to the window beside him as Cacin continued. "With the exception of Cruchton there is no Sentry capable of rapid group conversion assimilation."

"Then take a Zad, or a Zi," Orgone responded.

"No. I'll do this alone. I've decided to accept the challenge this female presents, unaided. If she's alive, she must be very clever to have hidden herself from me."

"She may only be unconscious, Lord."

"If she's keeping herself unconscious my point is made."

"Your cousin was a demanding Zi. If she displeased him, it's my guess he would have been quick to punish. And I believe he would have used the harshest punishment we have at our disposal. She may not be keeping herself thus."

"That's possible," Cacin conceded. "But close to three weeks?"

Orgone shrugged. "No way of knowing. It wasn't the female who destroyed Kagoule's life, Zi." Orgone pressed on. "It was a male. We may be facing unknown peril where these Humans are concerned."

"That may be. But I'm still going. I won't be dissuaded. No matter what way you look at it she's a powerful and versatile conquest; perhaps the like of which we've never seen before. It's paramount that I understand this life form before we commence the Bride Quest. Going there will avail me of the opportunity to more thoroughly assess them."

He looked at the Zad. "Besides, honor demands that I go alone." Then he turned his scrutiny back to the viewing screen. "She's eluded me all this time. I hope she is as much the challenge I think she is. I want to take her alone, as my cousin did."

"Your cousin died trying to take her."

"I know. I won't."

"Well, it's obvious your mind is made up. Good speed then, Zi. Be careful, my friend," he added. They embraced briefly and Orgone stepped back, bowed as he had on entry, and walked toward the door.

"Stop that bowing, by the way," Cacin demanded.

"It's tradition."

"Well, hang tradition when we're alone at least."

"Very well." Orgone smiled at him. "Be careful."

"Yes. I know this species is dangerous, Orgone. I will be careful."

"It's unfortunate Kagoule was killed on planet," Orgone said, stopping at the exit.

"They know what we look like and they'll be prepared," Cacin added, nodding.

"Yes. There will be no element of surprise in this Quest," Orgone replied.

"Assume command immediately."

"At your will," Orgone replied. He turned and the door swished open.

Chapter 11
The Gathering

"I left them an hour ago. She's pretty scared. Thinks they can take on human form," Simon Cahill said. "Thinks they're shape changers."

"Christ!"

"That's what Bopal said. And after hearing the rest of her story, I'm inclined to believe her, sir."

"Well, you said this thing just walked right into a hospital in broad daylight and trashed the place. You'd think someone would have noticed a seven-foot, green/brown, scaly thing with black ringlets doing something like that," the President replied, sitting back in his chair. "I believe her too, Simon."

Turning to his chief of staff he continued, "Jonathan, this is in our ball court now. I'm meeting with Drzycimski, Hunter and LeBlanc this afternoon. Hopefully we'll set up some more meetings with other heads of state tonight. I'm going to take them over for a viewing. That's what did it for me, seeing that thing lying there." He drew in a sharp breath.

"We need world support on this operation." He sat forward and put his arms on the desk. "Keep me informed," he added, dismissing them.

A series of 'Mister Presidents' resounded through the room as the group dispersed. The stream of men pouring from the Oval Office was lead by Jonathan Mires. Simon Cahill was located somewhere in the middle of the eleven-man entourage, all top-ranking military officials and advisers.

Chapter 12
Discovery

Cacin materialized in a grove of trees at the edge of a park, easily drawing his molecules around him with the power of his mind. On a nearby footpath, several Humans walked, oblivious of his presence. He felt them nearby, sensed their ignorance of him, their calm. Rounding a corner they went out of view, their minds still easily accessible.

He straightened and stepped from the shadows, covering himself with a likeness of a Human male of just above average height and projecting it for a large audience. This form would please the Humans that had just passed him. Yes. This species admired males, especially tall well-muscled ones. And one with this pale skin color would not be challenged in this society.

He browsed the minds around him. Unexceptional, though possessing a certain odd quality that suggested they could be more than what they were. He scanned for sophisticated minds, alert and informed.

As in most social orders, he found some members far better educated than others. He searched these minds for knowledge of any alien life form. After a few moments he fell on what he probed for. One individual had complete knowledge of Kagoule.

He detected a preparation against the Gron'dalins. His worst fears were realized. But Hill'carn must be alive, he reasoned, for them to know the name of his race. That at least was good.

"They will make excellent breeding stock," he transferred to Orgone as he walked toward a road in the distance. "But not without a battle. I will contact you again in a half span."

Cacin continued to inspect the mind of the male he'd found that knew of Gron'dalins. The mind he probed belonged to Simon Cahill. Simon Cahill. What an odd name? A two-part name, neither of which denoted standing in the social order.

What facts could he glean from Simon Cahill?

They were preparing to take the females underground! So, they knew something of the limits of the Gron'dalin mind. This was more knowledge than Cacin was comfortable with them having. He stood silently, searching the creature's mind as his eyes scrutinized the park around him.

Cacin sighed and disengaged his mind probe, satisfied he had obtained all the information of the Gron'dalins the Human carried.

Not having searched for Hill'carn's mind pattern for a long time, as long as he had been in transit, suspended in the universe by the power of his own mind and thereby unable to search for her, Cacin stopped briefly at the edge of the road to survey the area before attending to business.

Beautiful. Exquisite. Green trees with broad leaves dotted the landscape interspersed with slopes of grass, ponds filled with water birds and pathways meandering throughout.

When he finished that brief inspection he turned to searching for Hill'carn.

And instantly he found her.

* * * *

Hillary felt a slight prickling at her mind. Had she imagined it? She stiffened and glanced at the door where two soldiers had been positioned by the man called Cahill. Perhaps she should get up and open the door so she could see them. She drew in a deep breath and smiled to herself.

"Just nerves."

Sitting on the edge of the bed toweling her hair dry, she shrugged off the feeling of foreboding that descended like drifting autumn leaves.

The shower had felt good. It revitalized her.

Suddenly she lurched forward. Her face twisted in a mask of terror.

"NO. Please NO," she begged in a hushed whisper. The probing, like in Toronto in the beginning, barely registered. A general sweeping perception touched her mind, gently fading in and out, rolling through her brain like moist, warm cotton wool, gently dabbing at her thoughts.

"No!" she screamed, instantly jumping from the bed. "No!"

Bolting for the door Hillary shrieked for the guards that stood outside. Her heart hammered. "Guard!" Fear raked over her as she ran toward the closed door. Oh why hadn't she left it open? "Guard!"

No reply came. Her voice echoed as though she stood inside a tunnel, everything around her fogged up. Wrapped in a blanket of mist, no sound came in to her. Could no one hear her?

No one came!

She would run. She would hide. She must hide! She would go to the basement. She should have gone there earlier, before it came. She screamed again.

"Dear God help me!"

The sound came back to her, as the earlier pleas for help had, in echoes, as though she were yelling into a canyon.

She must get to the basement; must get to safety. She must not lose her freedom again.

What was happening to her? She felt an invisible weight descend, gently gripping her mind, her body. She froze where she stood, gasped and fell toward the floor.

* * * *

Cacin stood erect, portraying the likeness of a Human male on a sidewalk several miles from Hill'carn's location. Behind him, Earth's lush greenery fanned out in a sea of trees and ponds. In front, a city stretched away in concrete and brick. Discerning the strong desire for escape that flooded Hill'carn's mind, Cacin was saddened.

Kagoule did not relate this aspect of your character to me, he thought to her. But then, that was consistent with Kagoule's nature. Your desires and needs would not have mattered to him. They matter to me. I am sorry. He sighed as he took his first step toward his bride.

Hillary's facial expression hardened in terror but she actually felt more shocked that terrified now. Locked inside her own mind she heard it as though it spoke from beside her.

If my needs matter to you, then let me go free, she thought back, from where she kneeled on the floor

I can't. I'm sorry.

Hillary forced herself to her feet again, forced her feet to move. Like a person just learning to walk again after a debilitating accident, one foot came awkwardly off the floor and slammed down a few inches ahead of the other.

With the first step she took toward freedom, her body came to a grinding halt. Her mind was gripped more forcefully; she was gently forced to the floor again, aware that she was moving but unable to stop. Her mind was betraying her! Her own mind was not her own. It responded to orders she herself did not give; overrode orders she gave.

There was no pain in her mind, only paralysis of a sort. Unable even to breath, Hillary passed out, slipping into a forced unconsciousness.

* * * *

Paul hurried along the hospital corridor past the nurses' station to Hillary's door with a sandwich in one hand and a paper cup of coffee in the other. He nodded to the guards at Hillary's door, their stiff demeanor reminding him of toy soldiers.

"How's it going?" he smiled at the stern men who stood like statues, thinking how unnecessary it was for them to look so stern, yet how reassuring their posture was after the events of the past few weeks. No one could defeat these men. Nothing could touch them. They were strong and determined.

"Fine, Sir," they responded in unison without moving.

Then he pushed the door open with his left elbow and entered the room and that thought took flight like a flock of startled pigeons. He stopped dead in his tracks. There, lying on the floor immediately in front of him, Hillary's limp body was immersed in some kind of fog.

"Guard!" he yelled, tossing the sandwich and coffee at the sink beside the door. He rushed to Hillary and knelt beside her, carefully keeping his head above the fog. "Get in here!" He felt for a pulse. Behind him, the heavy door crashed open and the sound of combat boots beating across linoleum resounded though the room.

"What's the matter, Doc?"

"What do you mean what's the matter?" Paul snapped. "My patient is on the floor in some kind of fog and you ask what's wrong? Get a grip man!"

The two soldiers gawked at him. "She's asleep on the bed, Sir," one of them stammered.

Paul looked over his shoulder at the man, then at the hospital bed. "You see her on the bed?" he asked. To Paul's mind the only thing on the bed was a shimmering mound of towels and blankets.

"Of course I see Miss Bopal on the bed," one of the soldiers said. The other man nodded confirming his comrade's opinion.

"Come here." Paul ordered.

The soldier stepped over to him.

"Stoop down, carefully."

The soldier stooped. The rifle now slung over his shoulder slipped and its butt clanked on the floor beside Hillary's shoulder.

He lowered the rifle to the floor as a frown creased his youthful brow. "What is this?"

"Feel here." Paul guided the soldier's hand to Hillary's face.

"What is that?"

"It's Miss Bopal's face!" Paul blurted.

"That can't be! She's on the bed!" the shocked soldier insisted.

"Go and touch the person on the bed," Paul said as the second man shifted feet and looked uneasy.

The soldier rose, picked up his rifle and crossed the floor. His hand extended to the shimmering on the bed and passed through it to the towels and blankets below. He spun around, gasping. "There's no one here! There's only blankets and a wet towel! It's just an optical illusion or something that I'm seeing. A projection," he stuttered."

The other soldier ran to the bed and thrust his hand out to confirm his friend's report.

"That's what they do," Paul stated, realization dawning. "They don't take on other forms. They aren't shape changers at all. They project a likeness of what they want you to see!"

"What?" both men said in unison.

"Never mind. Help me get her to safety."

* * * *

Looking up from his timepiece at the structure he thought housed Hill'carn, Cacin sighed. He lowered his massive hands to his sides and read the large English words emblazoned on the building.

So, he thought. They took her to a hospital. Obviously she was injured in the attack that claimed Kagoule's life. Why else a hospital? Unconscious? Was she unconscious for a period of time? Yes, that was it, wasn't it? He inhaled sharply, expanding his chest against the armor plate that encircled him. The vision he portrayed did not move.

A sudden chill gripped him. Had she forced this state on herself? He shrugged off a feeling of dread that descended like an iron fist.

"Orgone, you are right about this female. I think she willed herself into a state of unconsciousness. I scanned her body on finding her and she was well, yet I've found her in a hospital."

"Zi," Orgone transferred back. "Be careful. If she has done this herself her mind is very powerful indeed."

Drawing in another deep breath, Cacin straightened. The facsimile of the Human form he depicted remained the same, unmoving.

A young female smiled at the image he portrayed. The reproduction nodded and smiled back as would be expected.

The buzz of relaxed Human activity around him saddened him, threw him into a melancholy.

It would be good to be accepted by these creatures. Just for once to have friends in the universe, to arrive somewhere and be welcomed. Greetings were not something that could ever be extended to the Gron'dalins. They were the enemy - everyone's enemy. The Gron'dalin race had become everyone's nightmare, with the loss of their females. Sighing he turned back to the Quest at hand.

He adjusted his armor making ready for combat, at the same time maintaining the projection of a Human standing on a sidewalk outside a hospital. A soft breeze wafted over him. Unlike the beings he was about to plunder, the breeze knew of his presence. It touched him softly, almost tentatively.

Where was she? He scanned for Hill'carn's mind, confident in the fact that no one had overheard her cries for help. The curtain had lowered before the gripping. It would absorb all sound. If one of her guards opened the door for some reason, her likeness on the bed would satisfy his curiosity.

Cacin scanned for her mind again, turning his head as though listening for something. Finding no trace of her, a sudden chill went through him. Fear clutched at him with jagged claws! Surely no one here had the ability to decipher his projection of her on the bed.

They couldn't be THAT advanced. No. In all their travels, the Gron'dalins had never encountered a species with the ability to pierce the camouflage his race used to hide themselves.

She should have re-gained consciousness by now, though. The flesh on the back of Cacin's neck tightened and one nasty little word with big repercussions filled his mind. Trouble.

"I won't 'storm the fortress' the way Kagoule would have done," he whispered to himself. "His rashness got him killed."

He stood tall, squaring his shoulders, readying for the sortie, then walked briskly to the front entrance. He passed uniformed guards without incident. Unable to decipher the projected reproduction that surrounded him, they stared ahead, looking powerful and in control.

He took the primitive lift up to the third floor with a number of Humans. None of them saw his real form. Another female smiled at the image that surrounded him. He made it smile back, then disembarked, just one of the crowd. Hesitating at the elevator door to skim the minds of the guards at her door, he stood quietly to one side, out of the way.

The guards didn't know his abilities. He had discovered this earlier when scanning for Hill'carn. Incredibly the Human guards didn't know what he was capable of. How could their leadership put warriors up against him without arming them with knowledge?

He shrugged and shook his head but the likeness he rendered stood quietly beside the elevator.

He scanned for her mind but failed to find it. Could she now hide her mind from him?

Hoping he knew all the skills possessed by the warriors at her door, Cacin drew in a deep breath. He could smell her. The Marking was well advanced. He felt his genitals tighten; his hearts suddenly began thumping wildly. What a wonderful fragrance.

"Have to keep a clear head," he reminded himself under his breath as he walked toward her room.

He browsed minds around him for an appropriate reason to enter her room.

Housekeeping.

At one end of the corridor an older dark-skinned female slowly pushed a wheeled cart filled with cleaning supplies. Cacin stepped into a storage room across from the elevator and found it contained a similar cart. He changed the visage he mimicked to that of a middle-aged female with dust rags. He stepped from the storage room and pushed the cart to Hill'carn's door and through it as though he had a right to be there.

The room was empty. That couldn't be. Only the image he devised of Hill'carn asleep on the bed was left to him. Tricked. He had been tricked.

"Here. You're not allowed in there," a guard yelled.

"I'm just cleaning," Cacin replied in a female voice as he crossed to the bathroom and pushed the door open.

Empty. She had escaped.

"Look. Get the hell out of here! This room doesn't need cleaning. Get out," the guard ordered sharply, making to grab the arm of the little female he saw. What a shock he would get if instead of the thin arm of a small woman, he felt the powerful biceps of a fully grown Gron'dalin male. Cacin smirked at this but wisely turned and rushed from the room.

"Very well," Cacin said in a female's voice. He left the room quickly, dodging the soldier, not daring to bump into him.

"We aren't standing here for no reason, lady," the other guard complained. "No one comes or goes through this door unless authorized. Understand?"

"I'm so sorry," Cacin said in the raspy little sound he had chosen for the female's voice.

He could smell their fear. He scanned them as he pushed the cart toward the elevator. They had no knowledge of him. None! They were told to allow no one entry. That was all that had been divulged. They knew someone was coming for Hill'carn, but nothing more. Then he gasped. They knew about the deception he had created on the bed. They knew this and he had missed these thoughts because he'd been looking for specific information only. He was getting sloppy. Like Kagoule he was getting sloppy.

They'd been informed by other guards, who in turn were told by a Doctor Muntz. Was this his cousin's killer? Yes, probably. The minds of both soldiers held great respect for this Muntz Human.

It was this Paul Muntz who had seen Hill'carn on the floor. Great Gods! How could he have seen her in the shroud Cacin erected?

Doctor Muntz was a menace.

And what had he done with Hill'carn? He scanned the guards' minds again, probing deeper. They knew nothing. He scanned for Cahill, found him easily. Hill'carn had been taken somewhere below ground. He sighed.

Great!

Wonderful!

Now he had to physically search for her. A feeling of irritation swept over him. More aggravation than wrath, but mingled with a small measure of fear, it pricked at him mercilessly.

"Where?" he said aloud as he continued to scan Cahill's mind. Cahill had no knowledge of where she was. But information about Doctor Paul Muntz came flowing to him like iron filings to a magnet.

This trophy, this future bride of his, was proving perilous; not only a mind of unprecedented quality but a person wanted by this Doctor Muntz; this being with the ability to penetrate his shroud; see through likenesses; kill his cousin.

That alone was no small feat.

Pausing for one moment outside the elevator he transferred to Orgone, telling him all that had transpired.

"Be careful," was the only admonishment that came back.

As the mechanism settled to the ground floor, with time to think about everything that had occurred since his arrival, the Zi thrilled at the challenge this female presented.

Excitement coursed through him, but with it jealousy, until now an unknown element. Fear, a little known factor, also travelled. There was something here Gron'dalins had never before experienced, some unknown quantity existed in these Humans.

As the doors slid open, he said, "So it's this doctor I'm up against." Resentment swept over him like a malignant tide for the first time in his life. But accompanying resentment was that all-pervasive excitement for the hunt.

He walked smoothly past the small glassed-in stall where old females sold flowers and gifts for the sick. The summer sun beat down on the pavement as Cacin stepped toward the sliding doors.

"These Humans will be admirable opponents," he transferred, eyeing the guards at the door. "Perhaps too admirable." His nostrils flared at the prospect of mating with such exceptional stock. He crossed the entry area and stepped calmly out into the late afternoon sun, marshalling mixed feelings without any reply from Orgone.

Chapter 13
Adjustments

"I'm sick to death of sitting here with nothing to do," one guard whispered. "Four hours, for crying out loud!"

"Stop bellyaching. I think the guy's bonkers but orders are orders. Deal the cards, Mac." Then as an afterthought, "What's he doing now?"

The other guard pivoted to look through the kind of brass-rimmed spy hole normally found in apartment doors. "Sitting beside her on the couch," he whispered, turning back to his partner and picking up the cards that landed one-by-one in front of him on the wobbly card table. He arranged them in suits. The card table swayed as his knee hit one flimsy leg. "He picked a magazine up off the coffee table. Looks like they're gonna read instead, Keith."

"Why doesn't he just kiss her and get it over with?" Keith asked.

"Already has," a third guard hissed in a hoarse whisper as he crept from an adjoining room. "They were pretty close to going all the way last night." He motioned toward the door. "That's the only real entertainment you'll get around here. And if you think four hours of playing cards is boring, just wait. You're in for a real treat." He pointed awkwardly over one shoulder from his crouched position at the television mounted on a make-shift shelf high overhead. "Don't lose the remote for that thing. You're going to think that TELEVISION is made of gold in a few days. You'll tire of watching them. Believe me."

"Why aren't you asleep?" Keith asked.

"How the hell can I sleep with the two of you chattering away like a couple 'a old hens out here?" he hissed back.

"Sorry," Mac replied. "How long ya been down here?"

"Five days! Longest five days of my life. That's why you two were called in. We're about worn out. We were sleeping at intervals and sitting alone most of the time. No one to even talk to. You guys think you have it tough? Try sitting here alone."

"Mac here thinks he has it tough."

"Why are we here anyway?" Mac asked, ignoring his partner's jab.

"Ya. And why can't we stand up?"

"Ya mean ya don't know?"

The two guards at the card table looked at each other then shrugged at him. "We were told we were guarding the lady."

"You were told what?" the squatting guard asked with surprise. He didn't wait for a reply. In the same whisper he'd been using all along, he said, "Well, you're not gonna believe this. Cahill told me himself that some kind'a alien creature..." Mac scowled at him as he spoke. "Ya that's right. You're not gonna believe this." He pointed a finger at the disbelieving guard. "Some kind'a alien thing with mind reading abilities is huntin' the lady." He gestured toward the adjoining room. "I told ya you weren't going to believe me," he added as Mac rolled his eyes to emphasize his skepticism.

"Aw, get real!"

"I know it's far out. But that's what Cahill told me. Honest ta God. You're not supposed to stand up 'cause this basement isn't entirely below ground. This alien thing can read your mind above ground. Didn't they tell ya any of this?"

Mac snorted. "Not about the alien thing."

"I don't know if standing up would be a problem for Mac," his partner said in a teasing voice. "He's got his brains stored at the other end."

The third guard chuckled under his breath.

"Knock it off," Mac replied. "I don't believe a word you're saying," he continued, looking back at the third guard.

"Hey! It's true. I'm not stringin' ya."

"So what are they doing about this alien thing then? We're just gonna go on hiding from it like this? Can't just hide forever."

"They're linking us up to some kind'a underground command post."

"Oh SURE!" Mac chided.

"That's what I was told," the third guard insisted. "Think about it. The Pentagon is giving this doctor guy a lot'a freedom to decide OUR movements. Cahill told me it was coming right down from the top. From the President. Did they tell you to do whatever Muntz said?"

"Ya."

"Muntz says jump, we say how high?" the third guard continued. "That's what we were told."

"Just not as high as above ground," Keith chided.

"And just how do you come to be so thick with Cahill that you get all this inside info?" Mac asked with a hint of resentment in his voice.

"He's married to my sister," the guard replied. "But it isn't inside information. Jack was told too." He jerked his head toward the closed laundry room door where Jack slept.

"Oh." Mac shrugged. "Well, it sounds pretty far out to me."

"WHATever," Keith said. "So you guys been cooped up down here for almost a week?"

"Once you're in, you're in," the other guard replied. He gripped one feeble leg of the card table for balance and shifted his weight onto his other leg. "Even when they link us up we're not going home."

"GREAT!" Mac replied. "We have to go home sometime."

The door to the laundry room cum barracks, suddenly opened, startling them all. Jack, creeping in a stooped posture toward the bathroom, frowned at the three of them.

Turning back to the two card players, the third guard asked, "Did Cahill tell you he'd allow you to phone out tomorrow as long as you don't tell anyone where you are or what you're doing?"

"No. I wouldn't tell anyone what I was doing anyway, if that wild story about aliens is the only one we're going to be told," Mac replied.

"He'll tell you about the phone calls later, I guess. I call my wife every night and talk for about an hour. We'll have to draw straws for the best times to call, now that you guys are here."

Behind the bathroom door the toilet flushed. The door opened and Jack crept out.

"Come on, let's get some shut-eye," he said as he crept away. "Bad enough I have to sleep on a cot in this guy's laundry room. I shouldn't have to listen to the three of you jabber on all night."

"Aw," Mac said in a taunting voice. "Poor boy."

"You just wait 'til you want'a sleep, wise guy."

* * * *

Hillary sat beside Paul, close enough that she could feel the warmth radiating from his left thigh. The clock on the wall over the pine television cabinet read ten after midnight. Setting the book aside, she looked at him. He turned another page of the medical journal as alertly as he would have at six in the morning. Hillary yawned, thinking as she did that he was tireless, one of those people with boundless energy. Well, she wasn't. Stifling another yawn, Hillary stretched.

"You getting tired?" he asked.

"Aren't you?"

"I'm a night owl."

The comfortable couch they sat on was in earth tones, khaki, beige and light browns. Desert cactus they called it. She'd seen similar fabrics on couches back home in Australia. It suited him somehow, this earthy room with its earth-tone couch and love seat, its beige and brown wool rug, its warm pine coffee and end tables. This room reflected the causal person who sat beside her with an ease and comfort that bespoke good nature.

In the far corner, the television sat neatly in a closed pine cabinet. Atop the cabinet, riding like the waves they were accustomed to, two killer whale figurines shone black and wet in carved stone, reflecting the light on streamlined bodies.

She closed her eyes.

"Is something wrong or are you just tired?"

Opening her eyes Hillary replied, "I'm tired. But I was thinking about my father." She blinked back tears. "He used to practically live in the family room."

"I'm sorry, Hillary. I feel responsible somehow. If I'd arrived sooner."

"If you'd arrived sooner you would have died too." Hillary sighed. "No. It's not your fault, Paul. It's Kagoule's fault."

"You must have been very close to your father, being an only child."

"I was. He was a tyrant really. But I loved him. I had no choice but to love him. He was all I had." She drew in a deep breath. "Did I tell you he was a prince?"

"No. You never mentioned that."

"Well, he was. He was the youngest of seven sons. I guess they threw some money at him and shipped him off to keep him out of their hair. I never met any of them and he refused to talk about them. I can only speculate. I think he was a bit of a rebel." She leaned back in the cushions. "Only a bit of one though. Didn't marry my mother; just fell in love with her. She was a commoner. The class system over there is everything."

She laughed bitterly. "I feel like I've been robbed of the chance to tell him he had no right to do what he did to my mother and me. Unfinished business in a way. I would have told him if this 'thing' hadn't attacked me. Probably at Christmas. I was planning on going home for Christmas."

"I've seen a lot of death," Paul confided. "Unfinished business is always connected with it. The most common phrase I hear is, 'I didn't say good-bye'."

"Ya. I didn't do that either. I feel an emptiness inside when I think of him. Even if we had our differences, I loved him." She laughed softly. "I don't think either of us ever said 'I love you'. I don't even know that he did love me. Maybe I was just a possession."

"Oh, I doubt that."

Silence slipped in for a moment and Hillary stared down at the beige strip that snaked through the wool rug. "What about you, Paul? You never talk about your parents."

"There's nothing to say. I loved them. They're dead."

"There must be more to it than that. When did they die?"

"While back. I don't harp on it. My father died in January. My mother died when I was a child."

"I'm sorry. That's not that long ago to have lost your father, Paul. You make it sound like it was a long time ago. That's barely seven months."

"Seems like forever. Anyway, my mum died of a heart attack when I was three. I can barely remember her. She didn't have a history of heart problems either," he mused. "She's probably the reason I went into medicine." He sighed and pursed his lips.

"You're being very brave," he said.

She smiled warmly. The wall clock ticked loudly for a few minutes. Then taking Hillary in a warm embrace, he kissed her.

"You know, the first time I laid eyes on you, I told a colleague of mine that you were the one for me. I won't let anything happen to you Hillary. I promise you."

A shudder ran through her. She tried to dismiss a feeling of unease that settled on her like smoke.

Paul cleared his throat and sat back. "Hillary, I have to talk with you about something." He retched. His eyes watered.

"About that retching?" Hillary shrugged at him, looking baffled.

"Sorry. Yes, about this retching."

Hillary looked at him, frowning. "What Paul?" she said. "Why are you gagging when you kiss me? That's the third or fourth time you've done that."

"Now, I don't want you to take offence at what I'm about to say. And I don't want you getting scared. Alright?" He held his hands up pleadingly and suppressed the urge to vomit. "Promise?"

"What do you mean?" Hillary laughed nervously. "What could be so terrible that you would retch when you kiss me?"

"Well, I think the creature that captured you did something to you." He paused, not knowing how to continue.

"I'll say it did something to me," she laughed anxiously again. "A lot of things. It controlled my mind; imprisoned me; hit me."

"I don't mean like that. I mean something different."

"Different? Different like what? What do you mean, Paul? What are you getting at?"

"There's a smell that I've noticed."

"A smell? On me?" Her face twisted into a mask of disbelief, a mask of revolted skepticism.

"Ya. I noticed it first when I arrived at your father's hotel."

"The smell on me? You noticed the smell on me when you arrived at my father's hotel room?" Her voice elevated slightly.

"No. I noticed a smell like the one on you when I arrived at your father's hotel room. Remember I said there was a smell in the lobby? It was worse in his room? Remember I said I tracked the creature to find you by smelling it?"

Hillary nodded slowly. "Sure. But that was the creature. Not me." The mask of doubt she wore slowly transformed into one of terror. Although her voice trembled, she lowered it now, controlling it. She shrugged as if to say 'get on with it'. He only blushed.

"Are you saying I smell?" she asked with disgust.

"Now don't panic." He said it so flatly, so totally devoid of emotion that he shocked even himself.

"Oh my God! That IS what you're saying." Her deep brown eyes grew as large as crab apples, bulging with fear. She drew a hand to her throat with revulsion. "What do I smell like?" She quickly sniffed at one of her arms. Tightness developed in the pit of her stomach. "I can't smell myself. My God! This is too much!"

"Now don't lose it," Paul said, lowering his voice and casting a furtive glance toward the door where the guards sometimes peeped. "It's a sweet, syrupy sort of smell."

"And it makes you feel sick?" Hillary said in a whiny tone. "You've been gagging harder every time you kiss me. It's getting worse, Paul." She stiffened and drew in a sharp breath. "Isn't it." She blinked back tears. "It said it marked me. Remember? I told you it said it marked me." Her breathing grew rapid now as she sat trembling on the edge of the sofa.

"Ya. You said that. I remember you said that."

She shrugged. "I thought it was a figure of speech or something." Hyper-ventilating she shuddered. "Oh God help me!" She groaned as the memory of the creature rubbing its huge hand along her face resurfaced. "Can you see anything wrong with my face?" she suddenly asked, turning her cheek toward him.

"I don't see anything. Why?"

"It came over, the first night it captured me, and stroked my face like this." She ran her hand down his cheekbone – grappling with her emotions.

What else could happen to her? She'd been through hell and back – now she smelled. Would it never end?

Paul looked at her face carefully. "Nothing. Oh wait a minute. What's this?"

Hillary gasped.

A flash of color caught his eye as he turned her face into the lamplight that spilled from the far coffee table.

"Oh no!" she moaned.

"Don't panic," he reiterated. "It's probably nothing. Maybe it's just a bit of dirt." He licked a thumb and rubbed at something on her face. "Won't come off."

"Please God!" Hillary closed her eyes tightly for a moment to regain her composure. Tears squeezed from between her closed lids. "I have to see," she said suddenly, opening her eyes.

Holding her face gently in his strong hands, Paul turned her face in the light, this way and that.

"I have to see," she whispered again, desperation clinging to the edges of her voice.

"Just a minute. Be patient. Just hold still," he ordered, continuing to pivot her head.

"Well?"

"Okay," Paul said. He looked for a dark green splash of color. "Oh my God!" he blurted as his eyes focused on the delicate emerald green and mahogany scale, just under the skin.

"What is it?" Hillary gasped in horror. "Dear Lord! What is it?"

"Now it's nothing to get worried about Hillary," Paul said, glancing at the door the guards sat behind. "It's just a line of color."

"What do you mean a line of color? Where?" Hillary screamed, jumping to her feet.

"Sit down! Sit down!" he said pulling her down on the sofa. "You have to stay below ground, remember?" The door opened and a soldier, bending so he wouldn't break the surface of the ground, peered in.

"Everything alright?"

"Fine, fine. We were just having a conversation and she forgot and stood up," Paul answered, concealing Hillary from his view. The soldier nodded and closed the door again.

"I bet they were just having a conversation," Mac said. "She's getting cold feet. Ten to one."

"I don't believe in this mixed racial stuff," Keith, replied. "Know what I mean?" The other men took in his dark skin, red hair and delicately tilted green eyes, and shrugged in unison.

Paul lowered his voice. "Look, I'm going to get you a mirror and you can have a look at it for yourself, but remember we already knew there was a change in you. Brendon's tests are coming back and your blood has things happening that we can't explain. Your DNA is altered slightly. We've been expecting something to happen – some outward sign. I thought the smell was the only thing," he added, more to himself than to her.

Exhaling, he cleared his mind of all thoughts pertaining to Hillary and rose to get the mirror. "Think of apple pie," he said aloud. The muscles on his back rippled through his T-shirt as he concentrated on apple pie. He crossed the floor to the television cabinet, opened it, picked a hand mirror up off the top of the T.V. and returned to the couch.

"One of these days that isn't going to work for you," Hillary said.

"Thinking other thoughts?"

"Ya."

"Hasn't failed yet. Besides, someone has to leave this place to get food and things we need. The military delivery service does a rather poor job, constantly forgetting things. So far I've been blocking it. My father always said my concentration was unparalleled."

Taking the mirror in both hands, she stared with terror at her face. She saw it easily now that she knew what to look for. On either side of her jaw, a band of delicate emerald green, intermingled with reddish brown scales, slipped down to her neck. It began with a fine point of color beside her eyes and expanded to about an inch in width by the time it reached her cheekbone. She tore her blouse open at the top, ripping the buttons from the cloth. It continued down her neck. She ripped the blouse open all the way, gaping at herself with disgust. The bands came together and ended in a lacy U shape just above her breasts.

"Oh my God!" Hillary whispered.

"Now Hillary, we've discussed the possibility of changes in you," Paul whispered back.

"In my blood! Not in my face and body," she gasped.

"In your DNA."

"Not my body!" she said determinedly. She stared up at him, a look of horror in her eyes. Still holding her blouse open as the shock subsided, she began to cry. "My face! Not my face," she begged.

Paul hugged her. "Hillary, we have to analyze this carefully," he said in his most pragmatic tone; his best bedside manner. "We have to understand what is happening here." He held her close, as though holding her thus would chase her fears away. Breaking the grip he said, "Think back to that first night. What did it say?"

Looking into Paul's deep blue eyes, Hillary said, "It just said it marked me."

"Son-of-a-bitch!" Paul whispered, clenching his jaw. Anger unveiled a quality of perseverance in his handsome face that Hillary hadn't seen before.

"I thought about a dog marking its territory," she said. "That outraged it. Remember I told you it got angry with me for things I thought?"

Paul nodded, gritting his teeth.

"I never thought it did this to me!" She lapsed into a wailing fit, covering her eyes and crying softly so she wouldn't be heard on the other side of the door.

"You said it stroked your face?" Paul asked. He placed his hand on her shoulder comfortingly.

"Yes," she lowered her hands and thought back. "It ran the edge of its hand." She showed him the side of her own small hand. "Down my face." Tears glistened on her smooth cheek next to the scaled skin. "I felt a tingling, like when your leg goes to sleep."

"Pins and needles."

She nodded. "It did it twice on both sides of my face during the course of the evening."

"A chemical? Did it excrete some sort of chemical from the side of its hand?" He frowned, thinking hard. "This could be some kind of gene altering chemical the thing carries in its hands? I mean, how do you alter someone's DNA with the stroke of a hand for God's sake? But that's what it did. Or at least that's what it looks like. How do you do that?"

"I don't know." Hillary shrugged. She stopped crying.

Frowning hard, Paul looked down at the wool rug, his eyes darting over its surface. "I don't know either. It exuded SOMETHING from the side of its hand that penetrated the skin on your face and altered your DNA where it touched you. But what was it?"

"We'll never know. But it didn't touch me here," she indicated her breasts which were still uncovered. The ripped blouse lay open at her chest. Realizing this she gathered it around her.

"Ya. Your DNA is altered. To have spread like that, it has to have changed your DNA," he said with a kind of resignation in his voice. "But we knew it altered your DNA. We just didn't know what changes would happen in you as a result. God! What are we dealing with here?"

"Does that mean it's going to spread?"

"I don't know." He sighed.

"Why didn't we see anything before today?"

He shrugged. "Probably took time to develop.

"This is too way out for me." Hillary wiped away tears that were starting to dry. She folded her hands in her lap, letting the blouse fall open again. "I can't hide here forever with this scale stuff growing all over my face."

"If we're going to beat them, we have to use our minds," Paul said, out of the blue.

"We're no match for them, Paul." She hesitated, then went on. "But I may be, soon."

"What do you mean?"

Hillary looked across the room, fixed on a book on the small bookcase beside the television cabinet. Lifting it with her mind she brought it to them.

"How long have you been doing that?" Paul looked at her steadily.

"Couple of days now."

He nodded and bit his bottom lip.

"Paul? Am I one of them now?"

"No! Don't even think that Hillary," he ordered. "You're a human being just like me."

"He said I belonged to him."

"It's not a 'he' Hillary. It's an IT. It lied and it's dead." He made it sound as though the lie had caused its death.

"It's dead but what has come to replace it?"

"We'll deal with it," Paul said, his voice sounding confident. But inside, Hillary knew he was afraid. She sensed his fear, could practically taste it. His face was a facade of self confidence but his stomach twisted in knots. She could almost hear his thoughts.

"Now that my face is like this, how will they feel toward me?" She gestured toward the door, toward the guards.

"I won't let them see you."

"I'm scared, Paul," she leaned close to him and he put his arms around her.

"I won't let anyone hurt you. I promise that." He pulled her away from him to look into her brown eyes. "I love you, Hillary," he closed his mouth over hers, then drew away and retched.

"I'm sorry," she said, suppressing her anguish.

"It's not your fault. I'll get used to it."

"Not only am I afraid of it finding me now," she looked up into those soft eyes of his. "I have to worry about what will happen to me if it doesn't."

"Don't think that," Paul admonished. "Nothing is going to happen to you. You're one of us. I won't let anything happen to you." He pulled her back into his embrace.

"Maybe I should just go with it," Hillary sobbed. "Maybe I'm one of them now."

"No way! Why?" Paul asked. "Because you have a few scales on the side of your face?" he said, as though it was nothing to have a scaled face.

"A few scales?" Hillary chastised, pulling from his grip again. "A few scales? It's not as though I can just shave them off Paul. This isn't a small thing."

Paul nodded. "Maybe they'll fall off in time."

"Not likely," Hillary said. "You said it yourself. My DNA is altered. My DNA is who I am. My DNA isn't just going to fall off!"

* * * *

Cacin sat on the edge of the bed, his hands resting on the pale pink chenille bedspread. "Where has he taken you? Clever Human. Kagoule was right about them. They are smart. Didn't have time to take you far, though," he whispered as a breeze wafted in through the open window and grazed his patterned face.

"You're nearby," he whispered. "I feel you ever so slightly at times."

This doctor's abode was close to the hospital. In this area. Cahill thought that before he too disappeared underground. Damn! And his friend? Brendon? He had been to Paul Muntz's house but didn't know the number on the door.

Feeling trapped, Cacin shuffled his feet impatiently. Perhaps he should go to this Brendon Andrews person and force him to take him to Paul's house. Brendon didn't know the number, but like most Humans he could find his way there. They had photographic minds, although for some reason Cacin couldn't access this Brendon man's 'mind map' through mind transfer.

She probably stowed herself away in Paul Muntz's basement. Brendon Andrews thought Paul hid her there. Cacin knew the layout of every room in Paul Muntz's house from Brendon's memory but not the way there.

What if he was wrong though? Careful! He warned himself, not wanting to make the same errors in judgment the former King had made. Don't get too sure of yourself, he admonished silently. Look what happened to Kagoule.

With a sigh, Cacin flopped onto the bed.

Chapter 14
Taking Chances

"Get down!" He easily pulled her slight frame to the floor.

"I forgot! I'm sorry! Oh God! I'm sorry," she said from under his considerable weight. He rolled off her. Tears suddenly burst from her eyes, streaking into her hair. Days of imprisonment; mind probe; punishment; torture, then a flight from her new home and the life she was trying to build for herself in Toronto, had drained her. Even the creature's death didn't end it.

Tears of self-pity streamed down her face as she sat up. "It's going to come for me now."

An invisible enemy, worse than face-to-face contact with a flesh and blood foe in some ways, hovered always ready to spring. Its presence made her question her sanity. Even the sound of its voice in her mind in Toronto, even on that last day, was better in some ways than what she was going through now. Knowing something lurked, waiting for her to make the simple mistake of standing up, suddenly became too much to endure.

"Don't worry. It won't come," Paul said softly, kissing her forehead, holding her in an awkward embrace as they sat on the floor. "I won't let it hurt you, Hillary."

The knowledge that a seven-foot, fierce thing from God only knew where in the universe - with a mind that could manipulate matter - hid somewhere in the city waiting for her to stand above ground, defied his bravado. Too much to bear, Hillary gave herself over to anguish at the thought that she might have alerted it to her location.

"Now it will come for me," she wailed repeatedly, crying freely.

"No, Hillary. No. You weren't standing long enough." He pulled her into his arms and hugged her. "Radar couldn't get a fix on you that quickly. No harm done." The door opened behind them. Hillary quickly wiped at her eyes, averting her face, her now considerably altered face, from the soldier.

"Anything wrong?"

"No. It's okay," Paul replied. "She just forgot and stood up again."

The young man nodded. The door closed with a soft click.

"How can you be sure it won't come?" Hillary asked beseechingly, wanting to believe him.

"Common sense," Paul said gently, pushing her hair from her face. "You weren't standing long enough." He shrugged and smiled reassuringly.

"I can't go on like this Paul. I'm not the kind of person to hide. I can run! I'll fight it, but I just can't hide any longer. I can't sit and do nothing." She clung to him.

"You won't win against this thing, Hillary. Running from it won't do you any good. You've tried that already. You tried to run from one of them and it found you. It found you from a very long distance away."

She had to do something, anything. Running, so primitive a response, beckoned to her as the only thing she wanted - no - needed to do. She pictured herself running from the basement, past those two strange guards; up the stairs to the kitchen and out the back door. An immediate action, it called to her more strongly than she dared admit. Fleeing would be to seize control of her life.

"Besides, we won't have to conceal you much longer."

Paul's voice broke through the barrier her thoughts were erecting, grounding her, tumbling her back into reality, back into focus.

"The tunnel will be finished soon," he said. "They're working round the clock to link us up." He looked affectionately into her eyes. "They'll be here in another day; two at the outside, sweetheart. Just hang on. Then you'll have the freedom to move around the whole lower level of a shopping complex at will. Think what it will be like to walk upright again." He laughed good-naturedly.

"Ya. With make-up plastered all over my face."

"Can't be helped."

She nodded. "I'm looking forward to it, Paul. Really I am. They must be looking forward to it too." She gestured toward the door the guards sat outside, day-in, day-out.

"Ya. It will give them something better to do than peek in at us through a spy hole," Paul said resentfully. Rising from the floor he sat on the edge of the couch. "Come here, Hill. I have something

I want to talk with you about." He spoke softly and reached for a small package lying on the coffee table.

"Oh not again. Last time you had something to talk with me about it was disastrous," she remarked, recalling the revelation about the scale on her face.

Hillary slid over to him along the floor. "What is it this time?" She slipped onto the couch beside him and pushed her long dark hair behind one ear.

"I've decided to inject myself with your blood," he confided in a lower tone.

"PAUL!"

"Shuuu," he admonished, placing a finger to his lips and glancing at the door.

"I told you I don't think that's a smart idea," Hillary whispered. "What if YOU start to change? What if you get scales on your face? No. I can't let you do it."

"Well," he smiled softly. "I'm willing to take that chance. The fact is I want to change. I want to be able to move things with my mind."

"That may not be all you get," she said.

"If I get a little part of you, I'll treasure it."

Hillary flushed and looked down at her hands. "You won't treasure scales, believe me. Look. I think you would be better off finding someone else altogether; someone who isn't half-human."

"I don't want someone else. And you're not half-human." He gently ran his fingers through her hair. She looked away, across the room. Then she glanced through the bedroom door.

Paul lowered his hand to his lap. "Please Hillary. Don't deny me this. It may be the only chance humans have against these things."

"I don't want you dead."

"It won't kill me. Might make me sick for a few days but I'm sure it won't kill me."

She could see he wasn't sure it wouldn't kill him. Even without the ability to pick thoughts from his mind, which she now had, she knew he was lying.

"I've thought it all out," Paul continued. "The way your mind is expanding, we might have a fighting chance against these things. If our minds can operate as well as theirs, we'll win this coming war."

Well, he had a point there, didn't he? "But you don't know if my blood will give you that," she protested, looking back at him pleadingly with her eyes. "Maybe it would just change you physically or..." She paused and frowned at him. "Or kill you. I don't want you to die, Paul."

"I'm willing to take that chance, Hillary. I'm not willing to just stand by while that thing comes for you. And there'll be more of them coming. This is a question of preservation. And I don't think there's much of a chance that your blood will kill me. I love you Hillary."

She smiled at him. That wasn't the first time he'd said it. Had anyone ever said that to her before? Had her mother said she loved her? Hillary couldn't remember. Her father certainly hadn't.

"I want to spend the rest of my life with you," Paul said. "And what better way to do it than by making this commitment. We'll be blood brothers." He smiled and winked, leaned over and kissed her. Then he tried to keep from vomiting.

Hillary chuckled. "We make the classic odd couple." She touched his lips softly with her fingers. "I know how stubborn you are, Paul Muntz. You're not going to be happy until you try this, are you?"

"You won't have a minute's peace," he replied, wiping his teary eyes now that the retching had stopped. He smiled at her with one of those unique Paul smiles that lit his face from within.

"I'll always remember you like this," Hillary whispered, "with your face aglow with that smile of yours." He literally beamed at her now. "Okay. But I'll never forgive myself if you die, Paul. I'll never forgive my weakness. I should insist you forget this stupid idea."

"I won't die. But I'm embarking on a new career, Hillary. I'm going to be the first scaled doctor."

"You're launching on more than that." She held out her right arm and looked sharply away toward the bedroom door again, it being the easiest place to look.

"You aren't weak, Hillary. I want this. And I won't die." Paul swabbed the skin on Hillary's arm with disinfectant as he spoke. "Now this is going to pinch a little."

"Yes, Doctor," she said, shaking her head. There was that awful bedside manner again. What would she do if she lost him? Paul, with all his little traits and flaws, would be gone, dead, no longer a part of her life. What would she do? Had she ever been this close with anyone?

He smiled and turned her face toward him. Sweat was gathering in tiny droplets on his forehead. "It's going to be alright," he said reassuringly.

She knew his confidence was an act, a bluff. She could feel his fear. If she wanted to, she could pick the very thoughts of fear from his mind.

He plunged the needle into her arm and Hillary looked around to see the barrel fill. He took the needle out and placed a bit of cotton over the spot.

"Press on this."

"I hate this stuff," she said, pushing her finger down on the spot where the needle had taken her altered blood.

"What? Cotton wool?" he asked.

"Ya. That's what it feels like when he's in your mind."

"IT. Not he," Paul reminded, pointing a finger at her as he always did when she called it 'he'. He looked stern.

She nodded at him and couldn't resist a smile. "It's so out of character for you to look stern, Paul."

He winked at her and cleaned the skin over a bulging vein on his left arm with the same antiseptic.

The smell was sharp, prickling her nose. "Are you sure you want to do this?" Hillary asked, shaking her head slowly as she spoke.

"I'm sure."

"Stubborn man. Please think about it, Paul. You have no idea what is going to happen."

"We've talked about it for days, Hillary. I've thought it through from a medical perspective. I'm through thinking. I'm through talking. We won't know until I do it." He shrugged. "Our blood types are the same."

"They WERE the same."

"Well, there are a few small differences now." He winked at her and looked at the needle, drove it into the soft flesh of his arm. He slowly pressed on the plunger with his thumb. "Don't worry." He looked up as the syringe emptied. "Maybe I won't get scales. Maybe I'll just smell like cheap aftershave." He winked again and smiled one of those unique smiles.

"Or maybe you'll die," Hillary replied, resisting his charm.

"I won't. Stop worrying." He sat perched on the edge of the couch, holding the needle that protruded from his arm as though it were part of him. Slowly its contents emptied into his bloodstream.

They sat quietly watching Hillary's blood drain from the syringe, listening to their own thoughts and the sound of the clock on the mantel.

"This is like my first dive off the eight-foot board when I was nine," he said in the thickening silence. "You know, when I'm scared Hill, you'll never guess where I get this funny tingling feeling."

"Where?" She smiled, despite a feeling of foreboding that embraced her. The sound of the ticking clock filled the silence between their words, accentuating the tension, highlighting their mutual fear.

"In my nose."

She laughed nervously. "Your nose? You must be kidding."

"No. My nose. Crazy, eh? Can you rub it for me?"

She laughed again. One of her knees touched his. She leaned over, resting the palm of one hand on his knee and rubbed his nose with her fingers, smiling at him tenderly.

"Thanks."

"Anytime," she said, lowering her hand. She left the other hand on his knee. It felt so right there, so comfortable. She loved being close to him, touching him. He was so vital. So alive. A shiver ran through her as she realized he might not be alive in a few minutes.

He removed the needle, pressed a wad of cotton over the point of entry and drew his arm up, fist balled.

"Now, if my guess is right, in about three weeks I won't mind your body odor at all." She smiled weakly. "Then look out." He leaned forward and kissed her lightly on the lips.

She smiled. "So, welcome to the club," Hillary said sarcastically. "Now you are 'flesh of my flesh', Paul Muntz," she said. Paul nodded and chuckled. "How do you feel?" she asked.

"Fine."

He put the needle into the jar he'd brought for that purpose, sealed it and dropped it into a wastebasket beside the couch. The glass jar struck the wooden pail hard, sounding so final. There, it was done. He had finally injected her blood. Inevitable really, wasn't it? From the moment he'd first thought of doing it, she knew he had to do it.

"Have you ever thought there might be someone else out there who can smell this cheap sweaty aftershave smell you're always talking about?" she asked. "You may be getting more than you bargained for," she teased.

"So be it," Paul said, shrugging at her playfully.

"If you can gain the ability to read their minds from injecting my blood, maybe it will be worth it. Maybe we'll have a chance against these things. How many men would need to be injected do you think?"

"I don't know. But they've got quantities of your blood frozen, so don't worry. They won't be coming around to drain you daily. I think Cahill has already thought of this, you know."

"There. If it were going to kill me it would have done it by now," he added with relief.

"Good! Because I don't want to be alone in a sea of human faces, none of them knowing my true identity. It's not just that I'd lose the man I love." There, she'd said it now too. Now it was sealed in time. Nothing would ever change the fact that she loved him.

"You won't lose me," he said leaning forward again and kissing her. "Don't worry. I'm here to stay."

Yes, he was. But what of her, she thought as he retched.

"What's the matter?"

"I just feel a little sick to my stomach."

"Oh Paul! You're turning really pale."

"Don't worry." He put his hands over his face. Lowering his hands he retched again. "I have to go to the bathroom."

"Oh God!"

"I'm not going to die, Hillary. I just feel sick to my stomach. This is going to be a bumpy ride." He started toward the door. "Morning sickness," he said, trying at humor as he dashed for the bathroom in the hall.

"Use the one in here," she said in a hoarse whisper.

"And stink up this room? No way. I'll use the laundry room john. All I need is a toilet. Besides, I don't know how long I'm going to be. This might take some time." He choked. "Be right back."

Closing the door behind him, he slipped from the room and past the guards. She heard the bathroom door slam followed by the sound of Paul vomiting into the toilet.

Chapter 15
Capture

Cacin sat bolt upright out of a sound slumber. Shadows danced across the room and the smell of night air drifted through the open window. His sharp mind, tuned to Hill'carn's, was never completely somnolent. He burst awake!

"You're closer than I expected. I'm very near you," he whispered scornfully. This knowledge pricked his anger. Brendon's recollection of the neighborhood had been accurate to within three blocks. Only three short blocks separated them all this time.

He fought back his wrath, battling to control it. There were things to do that resentment would only impede.

He arose calmly - a forced calm - but calmly nevertheless, from the bed he occupied in the comfortable home he'd taken by force. Placing a mind grid around the area she resided in, he rubbed sleep from his eyes, yawned then stripped.

"You're going nowhere now, Hill'carn," he said, somewhat spitefully.

He crossed to the bathroom and showered at his leisure. Lathering himself generously with scented soap, he tried to control his mood, tried to reason it away with rational thinking. She had a right to hide from him. If it were him in the same position, he would hide. But she had been so good at it, so nearly successful at it. His temper flared.

Sliding the glass partition back, he stepped from the shower and went to the sink to groom himself for their first encounter. Carefully brushing his mane, he ran his fingers through it to draw it into ringlets.

His face set in rage. His eyes, normally round and smiling, sang with fury. How dare she? Everyone waited to commence the Bride Quest for this one female.

On finishing, he left the bathroom, nude, and strode out into the hall with a confident gait. A long mirror stood at one end of the hall. His naked reflection glistened back at him. He admired himself, trying to conquer the feelings of anger that teased his mind.

Nine days! She had consumed nine days! He could have assessed another bride three times over in that time.

The muscles in his chest and shoulders bulged as he tensed and relaxed them. The overhead light played on the green and mahogany shell-shaped design that covered his body. He nodded with satisfaction at his image but did not smile.

So, this Earth female, this Human, would find him repulsive. Well, he was ready for her scorn. Prepared for tearful entreaties, self-pity, accusations and bursts of temper, Cacin sucked in a deep breath and squared his shoulders. He had heard all about it. He had been groomed for this day all his life.

"At last we will meet, Hill'carn. You have caused me a lot of trouble. In time, you'll come to appreciate my beauty as Kagoule appreciated yours," he said sternly to the reflection that stared back at him.

Spinning abruptly on his heel, he strode into the bedroom, ducking under the door frame. Finally dressed again in his father's armor, he descended the stairs. As he walked he transferred a message to Orgone.

"I have located the whereabouts of my Queen, Orgone. Prepare a team for our arrival. We will be there within an hour."

"You sound angry, Lord," Orgone replied.

"I am. I've been waiting here for more than a week for her to commit one small slip." Cacin's mouth tightened. His eyes glared. His controlled and deliberate movements screamed of his wrath as he stepped off the last stair out into the night.

"Don't do anything rash, my friend. Remember the desire for freedom you told me she had. She has as much right to resist you as you would have to resist her."

"Yes, I know. I won't do anything rash."

"I'm sorry you haven't had a chance to assess her."

"So am I. This is going to be an ordeal."

"To my knowledge, no bride has ever been bedded without Assessment," Orgone thought.

Cacin stood on the front lawn in the cool night air. His pulse pounded in his temples.

"There's no protocol to say it can't be done," Orgone continued, sensing Cacin's need for him to go on. "Kagoule would have done as he pleased. Has he bedded her?"

"No. There wasn't anything about it in her mind. I need my concentration Orgone. I must go. Prepare the Zad team," he thought abruptly.

Cacin drew in a deep breath. An image of a Human male, six feet in height walked off the lawn for the journey to her hiding place.

In the darkness, stars flickered in the night sky. How he longed to travel through them, to be free again, not tied to this planet as he had been for nine days. Suddenly he felt sorry for Hill'carn again. She longed for freedom too. But she had caused him so much trouble.

A cool breeze that had leached away the day's heat rolled over him. The fragrance of flowers drifted lightly on the air and insects hummed in the long grass.

Cacin's rancor simmered under the thin veneer he tried to impose as he thought of the wasted time. He took in several slow deep breaths, trying to dispel his temper, trying to force it away from him. It had never been difficult to throw off anger before. He had always wondered why Kagoule could not do it.

She had the right to defy him after all, he kept reminding himself. Defy as she might, he would prevail. Her resistance was an inconvenience to him only. If she knew how futile resistance was, perhaps she wouldn't be so stubborn.

Irritation adhered like syrup, refusing to drip off. He took some more deep breaths to cleanse himself of it, and found malice building instead. It was one thing to know something. It was another to accept it.

Ignoring Orgone's warning - his jaw set, nostrils flaring - Cacin thrust himself onto the footpath, stalked down the street to the intersection that led to Hill'carn and rushed into the black night.

"Perhaps she needs to see the other side of me. The side she should learn to respect!" he said as he strode toward her, indulging his dark mood.

* * * *

Hillary sat alone in the recreation room of the large house. Paul still occupied the bathroom. The sounds of his pitiful vomiting continued to reach her ears.

Suddenly, the sound of splintering wood cleaved the air! The front door crashed in above her. Startled, she drew her hands to her mouth and stood up.

"Please no," she whispered into her cupped hands. "Dear God, protect me?"

One of the guards yelled, "What the HELL?"

Hillary moaned, knowing only too well what they faced beyond the closed door.

Pandemonium broke out. Shots, then shouts and bedlam ensued. Screams rent the summer air. The body of one of the guards slammed through the wall into her room. Hillary gasped and lowered her hands to her sides, stiffening. Another guard lay on the floor just outside the room in a pool of blood.

From a side room, gunfire erupted. She heard the other two guards lunge into the hall to their deaths. Both were crushed against the wall in moments. The sound of Paul vomiting violently in the bathroom remained in the eerie calm that followed. And oh, how Paul vomited.

Hillary stood very still in the center of the room, trembling and waiting. "Please let it kill me," she whispered. "Please let it kill me."

Through the hole in the wall she saw the creature advancing, obviously enraged. It flung the door open and stooped, fixed its gaze on her and, from outside the room, spoke.

"I am NOT an IT! My name is Cacin."

She shuddered as the sound of its voice resonated through the room like thunder. It ducked and slowly stepped over a body into the room, eyes still fixed on hers, its head brushing the ceiling.

Paul's vomiting was the only other sound in the house besides the creature's voice. All that Hillary could focus on was the sound of the creature's voice that echoed through her mind though it had stopped speaking moments earlier. Then the pounding of her heart was all she heard.

It straightened. Its head touched the ceiling and she shuddered again. Her body trembled uncontrollably. Taking a step backward she clutched at her throat and stared wide-eyed at it. One of her legs pressed against the sofa. Head held high, defiant, Hillary locked eyes with it.

"Please let it kill me," she whispered under her breath. The tendons in her neck tensed as her body quaked with fear.

"I haven't come to kill you," the creature said. "I would hardly travel hundreds of light-years to do that. I could accomplish something that simple from Ranat," it snapped.

Then its voice softened and the anger drained from its face. Its scales glistened like gems under the light.

The thought crossed her mind that she was glad she wasn't dressing when it came. In the distance she heard Paul struggling with the bathroom door. Had it jammed the door?

"Yes, it's jammed. That's my adversary no doubt. Paul Muntz." It stared steadily at her. The scales around its eyes shimmered in the overhead light.

Hillary could say nothing. The shock of hearing Paul's name from its lips stunned her. How did it know about him?

"Come here," it demanded ignoring her thought.

"No!" Hillary breathed, her voice barely audible, her back stiff. She stood with a defiant bearing. Perhaps outraging it would end this nightmare. Perhaps then it would kill her. Her nostrils flared with fear. She had promised herself that when it came she would goad it into killing her. She would rather DIE than live a life of horror with this beast. She would kill herself if it didn't kill her.

"Very melodramatic. You won't kill yourself," it said, drawing in a deep breath. It seemed to relax slightly and the look in its eyes softened. "You are brave."

Without another word it drew her across the floor. Unable to withstand the power of its mind, she placed one treacherous foot in front of the other until she was face-to-face with it. She could smell a mild, sweet smell coming from it, not at all unpleasant.

In the distance Paul challenged it to combat, all the while alternating between pulling at the jammed door knob and stopping to vomit.

"And you prefer that over me?" it asked, jerking its head toward the bathroom door. It looked down at her and slowly shook its head. "Why is he sick?"

She said nothing, choosing to concentrate on keeping herself from passing out, just letting go and fainting away. It took all her willpower not to drift away to darkness, her old friend, as she blocked it from reading her mind.

"You are worth the wait, my Queen," it said, stroking her face.

"NO!" Hillary moaned through clenched teeth, knowing what it was doing. "I hate you," she stammered.

"You don't even know me," it replied coldly, drawing its hand down the other side of her face. "You were wise to conceal the colors with this paste. A novel concept."

Hillary shook violently as it touched her.

"You're the only person, outside of my mother, who is officially allowed to call me Cacin. You belong to me now, Hill'carn. And I belong to you." It stroked the side of her face again and stared down into her eyes, towering more than two feet above her.

"I belong to myself. You mean nothing to me! You never will." She spat the words despite the hold it had just placed on her mind to draw her to it. It looked at her incredulously.

"What do you expect?" Hillary challenged. Her heartbeat throbbed in her ears, interrupting her concentration, ruining her ability to word things properly. She had wanted to say appropriate things when it came. "Do you think I'll come with you happily?" Had she wanted to say happily? No. She wanted to say willingly. She cursed her racing heart. "You are forcing me against my will. If you touch me, you'll be raping me. I don't consent to this," she blurted, completely out of control at last.

"Oh, I will touch you. I have no choice in that," it replied solemnly.

"You're an animal!" she screamed.

It shrugged. "Yes, possibly. That unfortunately is the way things are." It physically gripped one of her arms.

"Let me go," she demanded.

"I understand your sense of frustration."

"No you don't. You couldn't possibly understand. You have whatever you want. All your life you've had what you wanted." She was babbling now, raving. Again she cursed herself. "You are a despicable slime," Hillary hissed, gathering courage if not composure.

It gripped her mind. "Don't press my patience," Cacin hissed back, pulling her off the ground until they faced each other.

"I'll never let you touch me," Hillary continued.

"How can you speak when I've got you in a total mind grip?" it asked, its displeasure abating again, replaced by admiration. It applied more force to control her mind. She felt a pinching at the base of neck that spread up and over the surface of her skull.

"You're a real prize, Hill'carn. I hope I can be as much of a prize for you. You have a very powerful mind."

"I'm not a prize. I'm not a belonging. I'm a person. My name isn't Hill'carn and you can't do this to me."

"You have the right to resist me."

"Well THANK YOU!" Hillary spat sarcastically, hating herself for the lack of composure she exhibited.

"Why shouldn't you? It's just that no one has ever succeeded against one of us. It's a waste of effort."

The thought flitted through her mind that Paul had succeeded against Kagoule. She buried it deep in her subconscious, masked it with other thoughts. It looked slightly irritated with her, then puzzled.

His voice sounded different than Kagoule's, softer, almost human. His voice wasn't raucous like Kagoule's was. She realized she was thinking of it as a him again. That dismayed her.

"You approve of me," it said, smiling broadly.

"You've just killed four men and you're taking me captive for the purpose of raping me. I would hardly say I approve of you." Her voice trembled.

"I'm sorry I must do this. Soon all this will be behind us. We'll have many fine sons and we'll be happy."

"I've heard that before," she uttered with difficulty through the hold it had on her mind. "From Kagoule. And IT was absolutely wrong! It's dead now."

"I won't make the same mistakes Kagoule made."

"I despise you. I'll get away from you. Like I got away from Kagoule. I'll have no fine sons for you. Not a one."

It looked intensely at her and shook its head slowly. "No. You will not escape me. Kagoule was an idiot. I am not." Behind him, Paul ripped at the bathroom door, challenging it to fight him.

"You have no right."

"I have every right!" it yelled.

Hillary cringed.

"I have the right, the MIGHT, and I will take you. What is it you Humans say? Might makes right?"

"You can be proud of that, I'm sure."

It adjusted its hold on her arm and lowered her to the floor.

"There is no point in talking with you now." It turned and started guiding her from the room.

Its touch was commanding but not rough. Unlike Kagoule, this creature would allow her to speak. But it wanted to hit her, she sensed that. More than anything it wanted to strike her.

Self control, she thought.

I pride myself in self control. I would never strike a female.

"Get out of my mind."

"NO. I will never do that either. That is the essence of what we are, Hill'carn. We control matter with our minds. We communicate with our minds. Asking me not to read your mind is like asking me not to breath."

Oh gladly, Hillary thought.

This thought it ignored. They left the small room, the creature still firmly holding Hillary's arm though she knew there was no need for it to make physical contact. In the hallway, the crushed bodies of three of the soldiers lay in pools of blood. Hillary looked at them as it stepped over them. She retched.

Self control, she thought, looking at them.

I'm not a saint, it thought back.

Paul hammered at the bathroom door; his hammering unceasing. He challenged it to a contest. "Come on you coward! Face-to-face. Come on!"

"Paul, there's nothing you can do," Hillary called to him, suppressing the urge to tell him one last time she loved him. What would it do to him if she admitted she loved Paul? She hid the thought. She was getting better at doing that.

"Hillary? Oh God! I'm sorry!"

"Let me go," she demanded, hitting the thing with a closed fist.

"You can move when I hold your mind thus?" it said incredulously. "NO. I will not let you go."

"Your life will be hell from this day forward if you take me."

"You'll adapt."

"Never!"

"You will."

"You're a bully and a coward."

"You're not going to anger me."

"I detest you!"

"I can imagine what it must be like to be physically captured like this. And for the purpose I intend for you? I understand how you must feel." It was starting up the stairs.

"Then let me go," she pleaded.

Paul had stopped smashing at the bathroom door. It sounded now like he was shouldering it. A repeated loud thud grunt, thud grunt was the only noise in the house.

"Please let me go?"

"I can't do that. This is something we have to do. That's all there is to it."

Paul's efforts were finally rewarded. He burst into the hall as Cacin reached the top of the first set of stairs.

"Let her go you bastard!"

Hillary looked over her shoulder. Empty handed, naked from the waist up, still retching, he closed on them, running with reckless abandon up the first steps, his strong muscular shoulders covered with sweat.

"Get back Paul!" Hillary called. "It will kill you."

"I'm not an IT," the creature said coldly, turning on the landing to face Paul. "This is what you prefer over me?"

"Don't kill him," Hillary begged, bursting into tears. The creature looked gently at her. Paul lunged up the steps toward the thing that was holding her aloft, entirely with its mind now. Both its hands were firmly planted on its hips. "Don't kill him, Cacin," Hillary begged again.

"Cacin?" the creature said. It smiled scornfully. "When you want something you know how to say my name. It drew in a deep breath. "You will adapt."

Before Paul could touch it, he flew backward against what remained of the wall the soldier had been thrown through. His body fell to the floor.

"NO!" Hillary cried.

It turned to look at her. "He's not dead. He's the one who killed Kagoule, isn't he? I saw it in his mind and in the minds of his friends. That is what you were hiding from me earlier, isn't it. I also saw that he wants you."

"Please let him live."

"I've already done that."

It turned and continued up the next set of stairs to the kitchen. Hillary floated behind it, straining to see Paul for the last time, her motor functions paralyzed now. Impossible to rotate her head she opened her eyes wider to no avail.

Let me go, she thought.

No. I will not. And you are able to use your mind to voluntarily think to me. Now you are thinking to me. Only minutes ago you were demanding I not read your thoughts. Now you are in mine? You will certainly adapt.

It crossed the kitchen in a few steps, opened the back door and walked out into the night. Hillary floated behind it. The pungent smell of marigolds drifted as effortlessly as Hillary did on the night air. Would she ever smell marigolds again?

Down the steps, onto the back lawn, it transported her. Past the flower bed and several large trees to the front of the house, it drew her.

"I'm surprised you're able to communicate with your mind," it said. "We've never encountered this ability in another life form."

"There is a lot you haven't encountered yet and a lot you will regret you ever got involved with if you take me. Let me go!" Hillary demanded.

"No," it said abruptly. "I won't let you go. I will try to give you everything else you desire but not that." It released her and she stumbled on her feet.

Hillary stood on her own now, motor functions restored. She half turned to run. It gripped her again.

"Let me go!" she demanded.

It turned her around. "I'm sorry. I have to take you."

In a lowered tone it said, "I really am sorry. I'm not my cousin."

"Kagoule was your cousin?"

"Yes. I am to be your husband and I would appreciate it if you would stop thinking of me as 'it' or, the 'creature', or the 'thing' or the 'beast'."

"I don't want to marry you."

"I know."

"How can you just say that as if it's unimportant?"

"Until now it has been. I didn't know just how opposed females were to being captured. Oh I've read about it; been told about it, but until today I'd never experienced it."

"Then let me go!" she begged.

"I can't. I would only have to choose another female and she would not want me either. I would then be faced with the same request."

With that comment the creature straightened. "I've brought you outside so I can safely transport you to the colony we're preparing on the planet you call Mars."

Hillary closed her eyes, wrestling with emotions that threatened to ravage her. I don't want this, she thought.

"I'm sorry. I have to," Cacin replied "I haven't said I'm sorry so many times in my life before this," it remarked, apparently to itself. "This..." It paused momentarily, "is the way we reproduce our species. I have to take you."

"You must have females," Hillary blurted, grasping at straws. None of this made sense. It was impossible. All of it was impossible.

"We did. They're dead. Kagoule told you that."

"Let me go," she pleaded.

"I can't," Cacin stated flatly. It continued after another fleeting silence in which a look of genuine sadness swept briefly over its face. "I'm going to transport you to Mars."

"Oh my God!"

"With the use of a practice we call Gaylant."

It glanced around, turning its head this way and that as if listening for something. Then it started removing its armor vest, exposing a massive scaled chest.

"What are you doing?" Hillary stared in disbelief.

"I can't take you as easily in body with my clothes on."

"What do you mean, in body? Oh my God!"

"It will be painless. Although..." It grunted as it pulled the armor from its shoulders and dropped it to the ground.

The thought that Paul would find the armor there when she was gone, crossed her mind. He would find it in a heap. Would he cry over it?

"You'll experience some very odd sensations."

"Please let me go." How many times had she said that? Shame welled up in her but she knew she would beg again.

"I'm going to take your physical body inside my own, through a method of absorption we call body latch. Gaylant in my tongue. It's a simple process that requires me to use mind over matter, that's all." He gazed intently into her eyes.

She stared at him in amazement, mouth ajar.

"Don't look so scared. I know what I'm doing."

"Please? Please let me go," she begged again.

Hillary stood motionless on the grass, unable to move as the creature began removing the rest of its armor, fastened on with large clamps that folded out over yet another layer of armor.

Her mind raced as she attempted to contrive some means of escape. The sound of the clamps clicking open snapped through her mind. Seeing no way of escape she averted her eyes, not wanting to see it undressing.

"I can't live the way you're going to make me," she pleaded.

"You'll adapt."

"That's what you keep saying but I'll die. I have to be free. You don't know what humans are like."

"Yes I do. We have studied Humans very carefully for this Quest."

"We have to be free. I can't be a slave."

"Humans have enslaved other Humans since before recorded history," it said, continuing to unbuckle its armor skirt. "Today, there are millions on your planet who are enslaved, in Africa, India, in the Sudan." It spoke calmly, in a sedate tone. "In nineteen ninety-one, on your calendar," it hesitated, calculating something in his mind. "What?" It shrugged. "Thirty years ago? When the Kuwait war forced the King of that country to flee to England, it was found that there were numerous slaves in his sister's household. Thirty years isn't a long time, even by your standards. Don't talk to me about freedom or slavery. You'll be treated much better than those poor unfortunates. You won't be a slave. You will be a queen. You'll adapt."

It was naked now. She heard the last of the armor fall to the grass. It drew close to her.

"Freedom is relative. It's never absolute."

She felt the warmth of its body.

"I'm sorry but I need to remove your clothes to do this as safely as possible," it said.

She cringed as it stepped away again but said nothing.

"It's extremely difficult to body latch a person who has limited mind function when they're wearing clothes. Even more trouble to travel with them any distance. It's more difficult still when they don't cooperate. I know your aversion to my seeing you naked but it can't be helped."

"Oh God," Hillary whispered, shuddering.

It stripped off her clothing, averting its eyes. She felt the warmth of its body press against her. A sweet delicate smell arose around her. Was this the smell of its flesh? Was this the smell Paul thought so repugnant?

"You'll be perfectly safe if you don't oppose me. I'm taking every precaution. If you cooperate it will be that much safer. Try to relax. Don't fight."

"Oh please let me go." Hillary wailed, still held fast by its mind. She fought in vain for control of her motor functions.

"I can maintain your life systems for approximately fifteen minutes within my body even with you fighting me. The trip to Mars will take less than four."

"Help!" Hillary screamed frantically. "Help!"

"Don't struggle, Hill'carn. It's futile."

"Look, if you're not an 'IT' I'm not Hill'carn. My name is Hillary."

"No one outside the grid I've placed around this house can hear you. No one is going to rescue you," it said, ignoring her request.

It took her shoulders and pressed her against itself. She felt its hard body, warm and alien against her. She closed her eyes and wished for death.

"You're going to feel a very odd sensation. In a moment your blood is going to flow with mine. I'm sorry things have to be like this, Hill'carn. I'd like nothing better than the opportunity to court you. But you would never have me."

"Please don't," she begged.

The creature stiffened and drew in a deep breath, pressing her against its massive naked form in a smothering embrace. She felt herself melt through the walls of its body. In her mind she gasped, feeling the flow of its blood through her. Before her mind seemed to dissolve she was inside it, could hear its heart beating, as though they were hers! Did it have two hearts? A loud thud, mild thud, punctuated by the sound of it taking air into its lungs, filled her mind. She felt warm and wet, indistinct. She wanted to scream as she became insubstantial.

Can't be happening.

Just relax.

Want to go home. Want my old life back.

Relax.

Thinking of it as 'he' again, she struggled to stop thinking at all. All she wanted was death. She lost consciousness and propelled off into a deep black void that waited to claim her. Her dear friend darkness came up to greet her.

Chapter 16
The Mars Connection

Four Zad shifted restlessly as they stood waiting, their massive bodies swaying in random motion. Immediately behind them, four more Zad doctors waited, and behind them, the crowded room vibrated with excitement. Conversation ricocheted off the high metal ceiling like tiny bullets. Thoughts transferred quickly between communicants and slipped silently around spoken words. Docking Bay One glowed with anticipation.

"Here he is!" Beau'nad announced, abandoning his usual calm in light of the events that unfolded. "Cran, get over to the other side. Ha'gral, move that bed closer to him. Orgone, step out of my way! You aren't needed here."

Orgone stepped back abruptly, bumping into Gradspin. "Sorry, Lord Elder," he whispered to the old gron, offense at Beau'nad's treatment of him crackling in his voice. The wind of Cacin's arrival swept his cape back.

"Let's move further back," Gradspin volunteered. "The doctors need their space. We don't want to impede them."

Arriving with his bride in body, Cacin materialized slowly. Just a dull shadow, his form took on a more solid shape as the congregation watched. A hush fell over the thousands gathered as a slight breeze moved around his almost imperceptible image and fanned out to touch those closest to the arrival grid, then built as he became more discernible.

"This is going to be rough," Beau'nad said to Cran. "We don't want her to die, so move quickly once he takes form."

"Gaylant is tricky with aliens," Cran said, shaking his head doubtfully.

"She's not alien anymore," Beau'nad remarked, "Foreign but not alien. Remember that. She's been Marked for some time."

Cacin's head thrust back sharply as he materialized, his eyes closed hard against the well-lit docking bay. Pain etched his comely face. The reflective force erected around his body to deflect the vacuum of space fell away suddenly. With its disappearance the wind that howled through Docking Bay One fell off.

"Cran, move in to catch him if he falls!" Beau'nad instructed the young physician. Turning abruptly, he spoke to his brother. "She's going to be very physically ill from this, Ha'gral, if she fought him. Get ready to assist me with suction."

He stepped forward calmly, his usual composure restored by the necessity of taking charge. "Come on," he whispered in a coaxing voice. "Unfold."

Ha'gral frowned and shook his head. "He's having a hard time of this Gaylant."

Cacin's form faded, then sharpened, then faded again. Anxious muttering rose and fell in small pockets as the assembly watched the King struggling to materialize.

A sea of troubled faces looked on from the crowded docking bay. Groupings of silver, red and blue capes, depicting the three segments of the Elite, dotted the huge docking bay and spilled into the corridors that fed it. Massive interior doors were open to Colony, allowing as many as possible to be in attendance.

"He's having trouble with this Gaylant, Gradspin," Orgone said in a trembling voice, motioning with his head to the image of Cacin that struggled to take form.

Stepping forward, Gradspin whispered to Beau'nad. "Should Orgone go in to help?"

"Give him another minute," Beau'nad answered, a slight disquiet barely perceptible in his otherwise rock-steady voice.

Suddenly Cacin stumbled, his body dimmed. When he solidified again, Pain carved deep lines through the youthful shell-shaped motif around his eyes.

This female has resisted him strongly, Gradspin quickly thought to Beau'nad. Look at his face! Look at how long it's taking him to materialize!

"Orgone is going in to help him," Gradspin announced aloud. "OR we can lose another King!" he said, challenging Beau'nad, whose authority extended over all medical decisions.

"Yes. He's slightly off the landing area too," Beau'nad remarked. "Go in, Orgone!" A mumbled concern rose around them from the thousands gathered.

Just as Beau'nad finished speaking, Cacin snapped into solid form, stumbling into a group of Sentry who stood to one side of the landing area. A gasp went up from all assembled and, caught in the supportive arms of the Chief of Sentry, Cacin was quickly re-directed toward the waiting Zad doctors.

Orgone, who had been tensing, preparing to assist with the Gaylant, relaxed as Cruchton guided Cacin.

"None too soon," Gradspin remarked to Beau'nad with a sigh. He shot Orgone a look of relief. "I will wait with the Elders."

Gradspin motioned toward a group of elder Zi who were assembled a few yards away, then walked toward the sea of silver capes they formed.

A flurry of activity now exploded in the bay as Cacin staggered forward on the smooth stone surface, supported by Cruchton.

Dismissing the Chief of Sentry, Cran gripped the King's arm, steadying him. Cacin grimaced with pain and moaned as he allowed himself to be guided to a treatment bed and laid down. Trembling with cold and exhaustion, his naked body vibrated on the white sheets.

"I hope I never have to do this again," he said to Cran. Grasping the edge of the bed he steadied himself.

"Turn on your side, My Lord," Beau'nad said.

Cacin groaned as he obeyed the chief surgeon.

"We're ready," Beau'nad announced. He held a large, curved metal instrument in his hand. "Discharge her now, Lord."

Cacin slowly excreted Hill'carn's body, encased in a transparent sack, onto the cold sterile sheets. As Hill'carn filled the space beside him, he was half pulled, half slid off the mattress to stand unsurely on shaky feet.

"Can you stand on your own?" Beau'nad enquired as he pushed past Cacin, scoring the membrane with the instrument he held.

"Yes."

"Cran will look after you. Orgone, help him stand," Beau'nad instructed as he went to work reviving Hill'carn. "Give me suction, Ha'gral."

Orgone stepped up to Cacin's side, supporting him firmly by clutching one elbow.

"Are you alright?" he whispered anxiously.

"A little dizzy," Cacin replied, smiling weakly at his friend. "She was unconscious when we started but regained consciousness and fought me all the rest of the way."

"It took you a long time to materialize," Orgone noted in a worried voice.

"How long?" Cacin whispered.

"Minutes."

Cacin shook his head. "Gods, I hope she is still alive."

"You've got her," Orgone said, smiling at him. "She will live, Zi. Have no worries. She will live."

"Let's hope so, Orgone. If it took me minutes to materialize she could be dead."

"She'll be fine," he said by way of encouragement.

The medics busied themselves around Hill'carn while Cran pressed and prodded Cacin like a pestering insect. Cacin tried unconsciously to brush him away. The doctor clung like a fly on sticky paper, cleared his throat and placed a cold stethoscope on the King's huge chest.

"Breathe in," he said in a determined voice.

"Attend to her," Cacin snapped.

"They are for her. I am for you. Breathe in," Cran demanded.

Cacin obeyed.

"Do you want me to get you some clothes?" Orgone asked in a whisper.

"No. I need you here, holding me up."

"That bad?"

"That bad."

Around them, activity bustled in a steady flow of smooth and articulate movements from the team of Zad doctors.

"Look at the pattern on her face," Beau'nad remarked to his immediate assistant. The assistant made no reply, he only nodded in amazement.

Metal instruments clashed against trays scattered around the bedside. Demands for new instruments peppered the air in the expectant docking bay. Voices arose and fell like the buzz of a dozen bees around a single flower. Glances darted between the doctors as thoughts transferred between sentences.

"Another deep breath," Cran instructed, placing the cold stethoscope firmly on Cacin's back.

"Perhaps you should lie down?" Orgone asked in a whisper.

"No."

"You should lie down," Cran stated, taking Cacin's pulse. He motioned to the second bed that stood to one side. "Cruchton," he called, waving the Chief of Sentry over.

"No. I must be standing when she comes around, Cran. You don't know how powerful she is. How able she is to resist me. She must not see me lying down."

Cruchton grunted from beside the King. Automatically his hand came up to grip Cacin's elbow, but he dropped it back to his side now and stepped over to the gaggle of long flowing blue capes he'd been a part of before Cran's request. His mouth fell ajar as he took his place. The mutter that increased from those around him confirmed his own astonishment. The King's statement was rapidly whispered through the bay. When the whisper died, an expectant silence fell.

"She resisted him in Gaylant?" Cruchton asked the gron beside him in a faint whisper.

"That's what he said," the startled gron replied. They looked at each other in disbelief. Glances were exchanged all over the docking bay as the news travelled.

Standing just off the arrival grid, Cruchton turned back toward the King and the Zad doctors beyond him. His blue cape lapped at the stone floor beneath his feet.

"Breathe in," Cran demanded of the King.

Cacin obeyed, watching the assembly of doctors working on Hill'carn, ignoring Cran. Aware of the shock that rolled through

Docking Bay One only moments earlier, he concentrated on Hill'carn.

"Live, Hill'carn. Please live," he thought to her in private transfer.

"Out again," The young doctor demanded. He had been holding his breath all this time? Cacin released the breath he held.

"She was able to resist your mind grip?" Cran asked. A strong hint of skepticism rode his voice. The doctor, a Zad Cacin knew well, said this with wonderment, his face lighting up. His blue eyes sparkled under the soft florescent glow from the overhead lights and sparks of light sprinkled off the dark blue and beige shell-shaped motif around his ears. His black mane fell in tidy ringlets to the top of his shoulders. Staring at Cacin, the stethoscope attached to his ears as though it were part of him, he raised his curly black eyebrows waiting for an answer.

Cacin looked at him, wondering how many times he'd seen Cran like this, with that thing hanging from his ears. He remembered the first time he'd seen him with it.

Cran's question fell from his lips like polished stones and, like polished stones, his amazement scattered across the stone floor before Cacin could reply. Everyone within hearing distance waited for Cacin's response.

Cacin replied, "They have incredible minds. Kagoule found us a wonderful prize."

A loud murmur went up around him and the news passed enthusiastically by thought transfer and word of mouth to those at the back of the docking bay and through the massive doors into the interior of Colony where others crowded in to greet the Queen.

"You'll be fine in a moment," the doctor said, lowering the stethoscope. He filled a syringe and jabbed the King's upper arm. "This will help." He glanced at the team working over the Queen. "Don't worry. She'll be alright."

Cacin just nodded and glanced at Orgone. "Attend to the Queen," he said to Cran.

"I can stand on my own now, Orgone. But stay close."

Orgone freed his elbow and took the cape Gradspin handed to him for Cacin.

"Congratulations," Gradspin whispered. He slapped Cacin on the shoulder, almost dislodging him from his unsteady stance. "I will be with the Elders if you need me." He returned to his post as Orgone helped Cacin don the silver cape. The assembly watched the doctors working over the Queen's naked body.

"She's so modest," Cacin told Orgone. "I loathe seeing her laying there naked for all to see, knowing that she is shy."

"There's nothing that can be done about it. It's custom that everyone greet a new queen and the doctors have to work on her."

"Oh stuff custom!" Cacin mumbled. "We have too much custom," he whispered. "Besides she's not supposed to arrive naked."

"I agree we have too many mores. I'm only charged with knowing them and reminding the Elite of them."

"Well, I charge you to shut up about them now."

Orgone snickered. "You know I can't do that."

"Well, you told me. So be quiet."

"She has really upset you, hasn't she?"

"Orgone, if the rest are like her we're in for it. What are they doing now?"

"Still removing the mucus sack from around her face."

"What's taking them so long?"

"It only seems like a long time because you're anxious. They're being meticulous. You know Beau'nad."

Hill'carn's body had been swiftly moved into the center of the bed by assistants. The membrane now removed, a hush fell on the doctors assembled as Beau'nad's voice alone instructed the others.

"Cran, pass me that syringe. I need suction here." A tube was instantly inserted in Hill'carn's mouth. One slipped up her nose. "Two cc's ralivat."

Cacin stepped back, giving them more room to maneuver.

"Did I embarrass myself when I arrived?"

"NO. Never!"

Standing by helplessly, Cacin rubbed the palms of his sweaty hands together. The silver cape Gradspin had brought him hung from his shoulders, covering his nakedness.

"She won't die," Orgone said, seeing his distress.

"It would sadden me. I like her. I tried to direct as much oxygen to her as possible."

"Relax. She'll be fine. It was a short trip."

"Orgone, I never realized how it would feel to have her inside me." He smiled at his friend. "She's a part of me now. I'm a part of her. She will never be able to resist me. I don't want her to die, my friend."

"She won't, Lord," Orgone said confidently. "And the Gaylant will speed her acceptance of you, as you say."

"Well, Orgone, something had better work in my favor where this female is concerned. I've never read of such resistance."

"We've never mated," Orgone stated. "Perhaps those who have just haven't written about the experience extensively."

Beau'nad threw them a glance. You can be heard by everyone around you, he thought to them jointly.

Orgone finished by private thought transfer. Perhaps all females are this resistant. We don't resort to Xingat on occasion for no reason, Zi.

Yes. That's true. Travelling in my body will heighten Hill'carn's senses and draw her closer to me psychologically, though. The Xingat will not be necessary for her. I abhor the thought of resorting to drugs. There's nothing more disgusting to me. What is keeping them?

Hill'carn's body trembled violently as he thought this to Orgone.

"She's coming around," Orgone stated.

Still wet with mucus, she stirred. Tubes hung from holders high above her head, running into her nose. At the sight of movement, the crowd sent up a cheer and Cacin started breathing again. He smiled broadly.

Hill'carn coughed and choked, ripping at the tubing in her nose. The tubes scraped against the back of her throat as she tore them out. Ha'gral stepped forward to stop her and was motioned back by Beau'nad.

"Leave her, brother," the chief surgeon thought to him. "They aren't necessary any longer.

* * * *

Hillary looked up at Beau'nad with bloodshot eyes, then, leaning over the edge of the bed she threw up into a basin that rapidly appeared under her mouth, shoved there by one of the things around her. Her head pounded.

The sound of cheering went up like the crush of flapping wings.

This wasn't home. Where was she? What had happened? She looked up from the basin full of vomit, trying to focus on the huge red and green blob that had ordered the other thing away from her. Something stepped around the bed and took her hand.

Do you see how welcome you are here, my Queen? A voice filled her mind.

Suddenly she remembered! She'd been captured by that awful creature.

I'm not a creature, Cacin thought to her, its thoughts filling her mind like a warm sweet liquid.

Crammed into its body! Oh Lord! She tore her hand away from it and attempted to wipe the vomit from her mouth. One of the creatures who were relentlessly forcing her back to life aided her.

She remembered it all now. The darkness she had been ripped from was her only hope. She tried to slip down into it again but found it gone. She pushed the creature away roughly as she directed a thought to it.

Welcome? You've kidnapped me from my home. You plan to rape me. I scorn you! I will never be happy here. You must let me go.

I can't believe you have this ability, it thought back. But you must be careful with it. You are directing your thoughts to everyone. We have never encountered a race that can project a thought like this.

"Zi, will you bed her this evening?" Orgone asked.

Hillary cringed. She would fight it! She would never allow it to rape her!

Another creature stood behind the one who had taken her, a little to his right. "This is a customary question to ask a King on his return with his bride," it whispered to no one in particular, or so it seemed to Hillary. It handed Cacin a blanket. "The customary answer is yes."

Oh hang custom, Orgone, was the though she heard in evident reply.

Hillary held her breath. She took the blanket that was handed to her gratefully, pulling it up around her neck, concealing herself from the thousands gathered in the cold hall. Was this a hall? She quickly glanced around at the assembly then back at Cacin.

Cacin drew in a deep breath. I know what's expected of me Orgone but to force this female now will seal my fate with her forever.

Hillary knew she was not supposed to hear that thought. It was directed to someone else. She understood at least that much about mind transfers. She lay motionless, trying not to think about having heard it in case it might be scrutinizing her thoughts and know she had this ability.

"I've had no time for Assessment, Orgone," it continued aloud. "I've only found her today." It turned to look at the things gathered around Hillary. "I know it's convention but..." it looked at the other again, "If we may break with custom on this one occasion," it confided in a lowered tone. "Ask Gradspin."

As chief Zi you have the right to change most customs, the other one thought back.

But politically it might be wiser to approach the question this way. I don't think they'll deny me this request.

Hillary swallowed. They were making decisions about her future with no input from her. It was worse than living in her father's house. Disgusted, maddened, she drew in several potent steadying breaths. Then she lost it. She felt her conviction to be silent dissolve, just melt like so much snow in the sun's hot rays.

"You are the most sickening race I've ever had the misfortune to encounter," she suddenly blurted.

Had she said it? Had she said what was on her mind after promising herself she wouldn't? She spoke quickly and got the whole sentence out before Cacin gripped her mind and silenced her. It did grip her, and brutally because of the suddenness of her statement and the necessity of speed on its part. But not before she was able to throw out one loud thought. You're all revolting, she yelled in her mind.

A sound of astonishment went up from those gathered. It was obvious by the murmur that she had been heard by everyone. She noticed it glance around, perhaps apologizing. Being much more careful with its mind than it had been before, she could no longer pick up its thoughts. She tried to see more of what was happening around her but couldn't move her head. Oh why had she thought that? Why had she reacted so impulsively? Now she was held like a dead fish on a plate.

The one Cacin had called Orgone crossed the floor. Hillary watched in dismay as a small gathering of floor-length silver capes tightened at the far end of the platform to decide her immediate fate. She abhorred herself for being rash. Now she was blocked from their thoughts.

Cacin waited in silence. What would happen to her? Hillary knew it would abide by whatever they decided. Her heart sank.

I am asking the Elders to give me the opportunity to win your trust.

I hate you. I will never trust you, she thought instantly, without thinking what would be appropriate to think. Again she chastised herself. This would get her nowhere.

The assembly was hushed as the Elders deliberated on their decision, nodding silently to each other. Hillary saw one of the creatures, clearly bent by age, step forward from the group. Fear leapt in her, replacing the outrage that had consumed her moments earlier.

This is Gradspin, Cacin thought to Hillary. He is the oldest and wisest of the Elders. He is spokesman for the Elders. He is not an 'it' either.

The old thing nodded to Cacin, its face a maze of cracked scales, its eyelids sagging over gray eyes dulled with age. It appeared to Hillary that they were thinking to each other. It looked strange to see two creatures nodding and shrugging, gesturing but not speaking. Then Hillary felt Cacin unbind her mind.

The old creature approached her.

"My name is Gradspin," it said. "I am honored to meet you." It bowed slightly.

"I want to go home," she said limply, trying to control her feelings of rage and fear.

Gradspin bowed slightly to Cacin and then to Hillary again. "We know. That is the way it always is. We will try to make you comfortable here." Then it spoke to Cacin. "We have considered your wish, Lord," the old creature said. It smiled at Hillary as though taking her needs into consideration too. "Under the circumstances we are in agreement with you. You have both inherited a difficult path," it said. "And you, Lord, have handled it well thus far. You need time to master this female."

MASTER THIS FEMALE? Had it said that? Antagonism flared in her. Around her, a throng of creatures stretched as far as she could see. Running was impossible. And where was there to run to? Hillary spat in the old thing's face.

Cacin grimaced, then frowned at her.

The old creature continued as though nothing had happened. There was not even a slight change in its demeanor, no stiffening or any indication that she had defiled it. It didn't even wipe the spittle from its face.

"The Zi are proud of your conduct, Lord."

Odd morality you people have. Hillary thought to Cacin.

Cacin cleared his throat. At least we don't spit on the old ones. Hillary flushed with embarrassment.

A moment passed before the old thing spoke again and Hillary suspected that a private communication had passed between the two creatures.

He says I will have a difficult time with you, Cacin thought to her, smiling.

That's right. Your life will be hell from this moment forward. Perhaps you should send me back.

I can't do that.

"We are aware of the control you exerted over yourself on the planet's surface, My Lord," Gradspin continued. "The circumstances you waited in were abominable," the old thing went on.

Oh get real! Hillary thought to Cacin.

Be silent, Cacin ordered sharply.

Send me home and you will never have to hear from me again. I will be silent forever.

"We would do nothing to restrict your influence over this female, Lord," Gradspin continued.

How dare you! Hillary thought to Gradspin. The old creature turned and stared at her in amazement. Then at Cacin she yelled in her mind, I detest you! You're all despicable chauvinist pigs.

Gradspin pivoted away from her, his eyes bulging. Then he turned back to her. "This Bride Quest will be difficult indeed if all Earth's females are like you, Hill'carn. The former King would not have tolerated this from you. You're lucky this gron is to be your mate."

"I find it hard to believe that luck plays any part of my being here," she snapped back defiantly.

Turning back to the King, Gradspin continued. "If three days is what you need you shall have it."

Three days! Three days! Hillary thought to Cacin.

"The Nationals are approaching," the old thing said. "And as you know, the Elite must be satisfied before they commence. They can be held off for awhile but I wouldn't recommend doing it for too long."

The Elite must be satisfied? What of the women of my race? Is their satisfaction of no importance? You can't do this to us, Hillary thought to both of them. Cacin ignored her but Gradspin flinched.

The old thing paused, smiling at Cacin, his stooped countenance reducing his height considerably. He was shorter than Cacin anyway, as Kagoule had been.

You are wise beyond age, Cacin, he thought. To have put this decision to the Elders reveals that.

She is able to hear your thoughts on this wave, Lord Elder.

Let her hear, Gradspin remarked smiling at her. She needs to know what a prize she is getting in you.

Cacin nodded and smiled appreciatively at him. He bowed his head slightly. "Thank you, Lord Elder. And thank you for the three days. We will retire now," he said, referring to Hillary and himself. The old creature genuflected.

WE will retire? I don't want to retire. Send me home, Cacin. I don't want to be here. I don't belong here.

Cacin smiled, shot a glance at Gradspin before turning his attention on her. You do belong here, Hill'carn. And I see you can use my name when it suits you, he thought.

My name is not Hill'carn. It's Hillary.

It was Hillary. When females on your planet marry they change their names, don't they?

That's different.

Is it? It has the same effect as what we're trying to accomplish with your name change.

Standing clothed only in a silver-colored cape, her captor turned abruptly.

I will grip your mind until you are in your quarters so you can't embarrass yourself again. It gripped her mind firmly.

"Orgone, you will house the Queen in separate quarters," he said loudly enough for all around him to hear. "This is Orgone," Cacin said to her. Orgone glanced briefly at Hillary then bowed slightly to Cacin who continued to talk.

"I will prepare for Assessment immediately," Cacin announced for all to hear.

It left the room quickly.

Chapter 17
Assessment

Not wanting Cacin to see her naked, Hillary dressed quickly in the undergarments that had been provided.

"Why are you so averse to having him see you naked?" the Old One asked, with a truly puzzled look on her small white face. "He's seen you naked already, at Gaylant. Everyone has." She turned away from the open wardrobe with a long red silk gown hanging over her arm. "He will never touch you before the time has passed."

"I don't want to wear that," Hillary snapped.

"What then?"

"Oh, that will do," she sighed.

Bopack, assigned to help her dress; to brush her hair; to bath her, gaped at her. As if Hillary wasn't capable of dressing herself.

"Never mind why I don't want it to see me naked," Hillary replied rudely. "I just don't want it to see me that way."

How many times had she explained the reasons why? How many times had she asked the old woman to leave the room, to leave her alone? Besides, what did it matter why she didn't want it to see her naked?

"Very well." The old one rushed across the floor taking tiny rapid steps. Across her small arm the red silk gown neatly draped.

"Why does it have to come so often?"

"He is assessing you, Hill'carn. I have told you this many times today." Exasperation laced her words.

"Hillary. My name is Hillary," Hillary protested, slipping quickly and nervously into the gown.

"Not any longer, my dear," Bopack replied, almost sadly.

"What does assessing mean anyway?"

"Oh it's something they do with brides to better understand them, get to know them."

"I don't want to be better understood. When will I be let out of this room?"

"After you are bedded. If all goes well."

"Oh God help me!" she said, adjusting the sleeves of the gown. "I want to go home."

"Turn around and I'll do you up."

Hillary turned. "I want to go home," she repeated, desperation sweeping over her, not for the first time since awakening in the docking bay.

"We all wanted to go home. There is no going home now, Hill'carn."

"Stop calling me that!" She turned on the old woman in a threatening manner.

"I can't. Turn around!" Hillary obeyed. The old woman hurried to button the back of the garment. "I have been instructed to call you Hill'carn. Those are the King's wishes."

"I loathe that name! And I don't like wearing these stupid clothes. Why can't they wear jeans or slacks around here? Why the stupid formal clothing?"

"You will be Queen. Cacin is doing everything properly. The Assessment of a queen should be done formally whenever possible and it is possible now."

"God help me!"

"You have made that request may times today and he has not responded."

"You are calling it Cacin," Hillary noted. Both Kagoule and Cacin told me no one but a wife could call the King by its first name. Cacin said no one could officially call it Cacin but its mother and I."

"Cacin is not formal in all things. He is part of a new wave of leaders." Hillary felt small cold hands on her back as the little woman fastened the buttons. "He allows me to call him by his name in private and has told me I may call him by his name to you," she continued. "Unless you object."

"Of course not. I couldn't care less what you call it. They have some pretty stupid customs. What difference does it make if people call it by its name?"

"There is a lot in a name." The old woman reached for the top buttons. "The use of a given name, instead of a title, is familiar. It gives the user a certain power over the person whose name they use. Bend down a little, child."

"Oh God! I'm trapped in this weird world. There's no way out." Hillary groaned, complying with the old woman's request to bend down.

"Yes that is so."

"If we were still on Earth there would be some glimmer of hope," she said despondently.

"There's none here." Bopack smiled but her eyes were sad. The red sands of Mars blew against the glass-like barrier in front of Hillary, reminding her where she was.

"How can you just accept that you were kidnapped?"

"Oh I don't JUST accept it. It was with great difficulty that I accepted it. Even when you appear to accept it, I will know the turmoil you feel. I don't think about it at all now, though. Nothing can be done, and besides, I've lived my life with these gron'ie."

"If I could only mind travel. Or if I could figure out how to use one of their spacecraft," Hillary remarked hopelessly. "I saw spaceships in the other landing docks last night."

"You couldn't fly one of those things, dear. Besides, it's the King who wants you. He would be obliged to follow. He's the King. A king can't have any weaknesses. Losing a bride would be viewed as a definite weakness. If it was one of the others, I would say there might be some small hope. There is none where the King is concerned.

"Paul is never going to save me this time," she said to herself.

"Paul? Was he to be your Human husband?"

"NO. He was just a friend," Hillary lied.

Bopack nodded knowingly and finished the last few buttons.

"I'll never see Paul again."

"No. You'll never see him again, child." The old woman looked whimsical. "There, you're done up. Oh wait. I've missed one." Her little fingers moved rapidly over the cloth. "Bend down again."

"Did they take you away from someone you cared for?"

"Yes."

A feeling of despair washed over Hillary and she choked back tears of self-pity. The barren red wasteland beyond the windows mocked her. After a few desperate moments where her resolve not to cry almost failed her, the self-pity subsided, replaced with resentment.

"It has no right to do this to me."

"I suggest you stop calling him it. His patience has been admirable but I fear it's coming to an end in that regard. There. All done." She patted Hillary on one shoulder and Hillary stood up straight.

"It has no right! I want to be free," she said emphatically through clenched teeth, ignoring the warning. "I want to go home."

"You won't be going home, Hill'carn."

"Where is home anyway?" Hillary said contemplatively, looking past the banit'ye barrier at the blowing red sand. "I can't really expect people to accept me with these scales on my face." Again tears threatened to fall. "They're spreading, too. These damn scales are spreading." She looked at the backs of her hands where faint scaling appeared.

"Oh wait," Bopack remarked. "I've missed another button." She reached for an unfastened button.

"A zipper would be more useful."

"He knows that. He wants to keep you busy with trivial things. To keep your mind off your plight. There. All done."

"Well, that won't do it. Then it sends you to do it for me anyway." Hillary snorted and crossed the floor. She looked at her reflection in the mirror.

Taking the nail of her right index finger, pushing her cheek out with her tongue, she lightly picked at her flesh where the scale first became visible next to the skin. Her nail skimmed over the surface of her face, leaving the scale unaltered.

Were they really scales? Actually, they were more like patterned skin than scales. Scales would have flipped off when she dug at them. Although they weren't exactly smooth. They were grainy but they weren't scales either. This was the first time she'd had an opportunity to really examine them, with the make-up washed off her face. And oh how they had darkened since she first laid eyes on them.

When she stood away from the mirror, which she did now, they looked just like scales. When she came very close (she moved closer again) they looked like a pattern just under her skin. Well, what was the difference? She didn't want them there whatever they were.

"Bopack, why don't you look like this?"

"My race didn't take the colors well," Bopack answered from where she watched Hill'carn perform this task of self-examination. "No race has ever taken the colors as well as yours. You will easily accept Cacin."

"Don't count on it."

"And certainly no race has ever been able to transfer thoughts like you can. Some races have learned a few techniques. Not many."

Hillary drew in a deep breath. "Who am I now?"

"Hill'carn." Bopack remarked flatly, shrugging.

"What am I?" she asked, ignoring Bopack. She'd given no thought to that question before, just taking it for granted that she was a person, a human being. She belonged somewhere before, or thought she did. Where did she belong now? She gazed longingly at her reflection. Knowing where you wanted to be didn't mean you belonged there. Despair gripped her.

"Cacin will be coming directly. I must go," Bopack announced, turning to leave.

"I don't want him to come," she said, looking over her shoulder at the small woman who quickly retreated from the room.

"That's better. You call him, 'him'. Everything will be alright. And Hill'carn? You could have done much worse." Bopack remarked, turning to look back at the young woman. "Kagoule would have been a terrible mate."

"Kagoule was a beast," Hillary remarked. "And I thought no one was allowed to say its name."

"After his death we may all say his name. Cacin is at least kind. There's something truly noble about him."

"I still don't want to be here." Hillary swirled around to better see the old woman. The red silk gown rustled with the movement. "But every time it comes I feel odd. I feel different toward it than I expect to feel," she confided, resisting tears of self-doubt and guilt.

"Him not it. That's the Marking. You're accepting him. The Marking will cause you to desire him. It eventually works on everyone. It even worked on me and I didn't take the colors at all. No. I didn't take the colors and I hated my mate but I lusted after him." She turned hastily to leave. "You'll let him bed you."

"I'll never accept him into my bed," Hillary blurted, hurt by even the suggestion she would.

"You sometimes refer to him as 'him' now," Bopack pointed out, gathering some things from the table by the door and saying no more. "I must go. Try not to fret so much, child."

The odd-looking old woman scurried from the room, her huge eyes and low forehead looking almost primitive in the dim light. Tiny by any standards, Hill'carn wondered how this little mortal could possibly have given birth to children for these giants. She had mothered one of Cacin's cousins, she said, and was also one of the few women in the Mars Colony.

The door closed behind her.

Hillary wandered around the room nervously waiting for Cacin.

"Everything I could possibly need or want," she said as she looked around. "My favorite music." She leafed through the lists of classical music reproductions. "Contemporary furnishings." Hillary had seen the different Gron'dalin taste in decor in the outer rooms as she was ushered in last evening. He's attempting to make me comfortable. Win me over. Well, he said he would try to do that. She was uncertain whether his motives for providing familiar surroundings were strictly selfish or whether he truly wanted her to feel secure.

"The only way I can be comfortable here would be to leave." But I don't find him offensive any longer. Perhaps the trip from Earth was too intimate. Surely making love couldn't be more so. And his aroma. She closed her eyes and recalled the sweet smell of him. Still, I'll never allow this Neanderthal to kidnap and rape me.

"I'm not a Neanderthal," Cacin asserted.

She spun to face him, her face burning. The gown rustled with the sudden motion. He had entered without her knowledge, while she thought about him. She could tell when he probed her mind on Earth and expected it to be the same here. She hadn't felt his presence in her mind since her arrival, but perhaps that was because she concentrated on other things. How much had he overheard?

His huge form filled the entrance which had betrayed her by opening silently to admit him. The silk gown flew out around her in another flash of red as she turned away from him. She was afraid again, and ashamed; ashamed he had slipped into her thoughts undetected and must know of her morose attraction to him.

"Where I come from," Hillary responded, turning her back to him, "Men don't steal women for brides. Those stone age practices are over. In my estimate that makes you a Neanderthal." She glanced over one shoulder to gauge his response.

"Come now, Hill'carn," Cacin said, entering the room with two glasses of wine in his enormous hands. She slowly turned back to face him. "That isn't how you feel."

He knew then! Mortified, Hillary flushed.

"Besides," he continued, "Where you come from women have been known to be blinded to keep them from running away from husbands that have purchased them from their parents."

"In some countries maybe. Centuries ago. Not now."

"Oh. NOW."

"I don't believe that. You're just making it up to influence me."

"I'm not." He stepped further into the room.

"Where? Where do they do this?" she challenged.

"In China at the end of the last century."

"NO. I don't believe you."

"Well, I'm telling you the truth. You'll find that we have no need to lie, Hill'carn. And we have no choices in the way we must reproduce. It's this," he raised one glass of wine in her direction, "Or perish as a race. But we have no need to lie. Would you like a glass of wine?" The glass, still held aloft, glistened in the overhead light. He slowly drew closer to her with the glass still outstretched as he spoke.

Hillary made no attempt to close the distance between them.

"I don't want to be your wife."

"We would be delighted to mate with women of our own kind. But as Kagoule told you, there are no women of our kind."

He kept his distance on other visits, she thought. His approach frightened her now and her heartbeat quickened. His voice droned on.

"To be able to stop the Bride Quest. To stop roaming the universe in search of women." He pressed his lips together in contemplation of the idea. "That would be most desirable."

"Well, I don't like being forced to do anything," Hill'carn blurted.

"I know that. No one does. But I must have a mate."

Still, the wineglass was in front of her in his outstretched hand. She took it, her face set in stone. To her amazement she just reached out and took the glass from him.

He smiled softly. "Be careful," Cacin warned. "You're starting to like me." His smile spread.

"I am not," she answered defiantly.

His eyes flashed and he continued smiling warmly at her. "I fear it's only my DNA introduced into your blood that makes you accept me, and not me at all. You Humans are very receptive to the colors," he continued. "More receptive than any other women we have captured."

"So Bopack tells me. You're using the word women a lot more instead of females." She sipped at the wine, watching him carefully.

"You told me you didn't like the use of the word female. As I mentioned on Earth, freedom is relative. By using this word 'women', I give you a measure of respect, and by giving you respect you have the freedom to make requests of me."

"I ask you to return me to my home."

"Not that request."

She stepped over to the window that looked out on the strange Martian landscape.

"I am giving up some of my freedom to call you what I will. Even a king must bend to the will of others."

"My freedom is being taken away in the larger sense, Cacin."

"Yes, I'm sorry it has to be. Perhaps at some point I can give you back some freedom."

"I don't believe that will ever happen." She stared out at the foreign landscape. With her back to him she asked, "Why are all your women dead?"

"Disease. The same disease affected the males of our species. The chemical that we carry in our blood which genetically allows us to pass our DNA through the sides of our hands and alter women of other races is an adaptation the males made to the disease that killed the women of Ranat. I won't tell you how they died except to say it was at the hands of disease."

"You couldn't always do this then." She gestured to herself, to the scales on her face.

"No." He stepped closer to her.

"I've been here only a day and already this incessant blowing sand tires me," he said, looking out the banit'ye barrier she gazed through. His closeness sent a chill through her.

In the reflection his black mane hung in neat ringlets from the crown of his head. Hillary had the sudden urge to reach back and touch it. She turned and looked into his eyes. The urge to touch it, to see if it felt like hair or something else was almost overpowering. It was beautiful, shiny. She didn't know if it was an urge she actually had, or if it was planted there by him. She resisted.

"The women died from the disease," he finally said, filling the silence that crashed in on them with her inspection. "We lived on in this hell."

Hillary's heart pounded.

He solemnly looked back at the shifting red sands. The overhead light danced off the scales around his eyes, making them shimmer. "We were left to live out this curse. These Bride Quests have become everything to us."

"Where did this disease come from? Was it something you brought back from some part of the universe?"

"The Gron'dalins have many enemies." He laughed cynically. "More now than ever."

"Since you've been taking women from other races?"

"Yes. Oh I may as well tell you," he said, reconsidering his earlier decision not to speak of the tragedy. "I would want to know if I were in your place."

"There was a race called the Golapians who bore us malice." He sipped his wine. "We traded with them. They were impossible liars and didn't like being caught up in their lies. They manufactured the disease to wipe us out after one of their leaders, a male named Jig Zopict, was caught up in a lie about the availability of a certain product." He sipped his wine again.

"The disease was shipped to us through another race that we habitually dealt with. They knew nothing of the true contents of the cargo." He turned to look at her again. "If the Golapians had attempted to poison us themselves, we would have read it in their minds. They hadn't been counting on the disease having the sort of effect it had on the males of Ranat," he said, looking briefly into her brown eyes.

He turned back to viewing the planet. He was so close. The mild sweet smell she had noticed on him before intoxicated her. "Theirs was the first planet we plundered of females and, believe me, it was the only one we've felt no remorse over." The room fell silent for a moment before he spoke again.

"Certain male hormones protected us against dying from the disease. All adult women died immediately. Female children died shortly after reaching puberty. We believe the disease is still virulent on the planet. It continues to kill any juvenile females we bring to Ranat as soon as they reach that critical juncture." He shifted feet. The long ceremonial cape he wore swayed slightly.

"Ranat is the name of your planet?" Hillary asked, sipping at the wine he'd brought.

"Yes. We generally call it Ranat. Like Humans, we're lazy. It's really called Ranatchit'had." He smiled and sipped his wine again.

Hill'carn smiled back then suddenly realized she had smiled. Why was she smiling at him? Why was she enjoying his company? The realization that she was enjoying his company alarmed her but she pressed on with her questions. "Why have there been no births of female children since all this began?" she asked.

"We don't know. Medical examination suggests we are capable of fathering female children but none are ever born."

"And you continue to bring juvenile females to Ranat in spite of the fact that they die at puberty?"

"Kagoule told you this?"

"Yes. And you have said as much just now."

"I did indeed. That upsets you?"

"Of course it upsets me. It's foolish and cruel."

Cacin laughed. "You're outspoken, Hill'carn."

"Where I come from, women are respected for their opinions."

"In some places they are. I wouldn't like to see how you would fare in what you call the Middle East."

"You haven't answered my question."

"You haven't asked one."

"I think you're avoiding answering it."

"Will you re-state it please?"

"Why do you continue to bring young women to your planet when you know they will die there once they reach puberty?"

"I don't know."

She looked at him, startled. "You are being honest, aren't you?"

"I have no need to lie. Lying isn't something we do."

"You are honest," she said, wrinkling her brow and looking at him with shock.

"You are outspoken." He tipped his glass to her and smiled, then sipped at his wine.

"I like to be."

"I will extend that privilege to you here, in private." He gestured around them. "And I will attempt to give you as much freedom as I'm allowed outside these rooms," he said touching her shoulder tenderly. His touch was soft. "And in private your opinions will be very welcome."

"You talked earlier of the Middle East. In one of the religions there, women are given the same sorts of freedoms that you have just described. They are compelled to wear certain clothes in public but are free to dress as they like within their home. You are proposing to control me in certain settings and trying to make me believe that's alright because I'm allowed to speak freely in private."

Cacin sighed.

"You will not be able to stop me from doing as I please soon, Cacin."

"Is that a threat?"

"That depends on your point of view. And I will not remain here," Hill'carn snapped, suddenly realizing she was thinking of him as 'he' again, realizing she wanted to be there with him. She breathed rapidly. Confusion flooded through her with his hand on her shoulder, with the sweet smell of him rolling over her in waves. If he would only take his hand away she could think more clearly.

"I must go home."

"I doubt you will develop your mind so much you will be able to do whatever you want. And you will not be allowed to leave me," Cacin said flatly. "The only choices I can advance you," he took his hand away and sipped at his wine again, dropping the hand that had touched her, "Will be the 'way' in which you stay."

She looked down at his hand and a shiver ran through her.

"My people will come for me!" Hill'carn blurted, knowing they couldn't.

Cacin did not laugh. "I see in you a great dignity and a respect for your people. I believe it's very hard to be female in any race," he said. "I suspect that being subject to my will now compounds that. Your people are very intelligent, very resourceful and determined," he answered. "But they do not yet possess the ability to travel in space. We are millions of miles from your planet. They cannot save you here."

The urge to cry swept over Hill'carn. She knew this feeling was her own but she would not give him the satisfaction of seeing her in an emotional state.

"I was prepared for crying," Cacin said, walking away from the window. He picked up the sheets of music Hill'carn had been examining earlier. He looked back at her. "I was prepared for screaming, fighting, hitting, biting, cursing. But you are truly a gem, my dear Hill'carn." He looked away from her, giving her the opportunity to compose herself. His voice was soft.

"I can't stay with you, Cacin." She felt an odd and inexplicable pang of remorse with this declaration. "I must be free! That is the way I am. Freedom is what my people want more than anything."

He turned to face her again. "Your people? You are no longer Human, Hill'carn. You've been Marked. You've been changed."

Hill'carn gasped. How long had she been thinking of herself as Hill'carn? "I will always be human," she answered, tears teasing the corners of her eyes. His statement terrified her, despite her affirmation. It was the truth, after all. She'd known it for more than a day. Hadn't she told Paul only yesterday that she was half-human?

"Let's not try to fool ourselves," he said calmly. "This is one of the most important issues you must face. You are no longer Human and you know as well as I that you wouldn't be accepted by them any longer."

"That's not true."

"You know it is. Why were you wearing make-up when I came for you? Why were you trying to conceal your colors?"

"You're trying to trick me, to influence me."

"I need to influence you, Hill'carn? You've passed through my body. You bear my colors. I need to influence you?" He set the glass down beside the sheet music.

"Forced on me. It was all forced on me!" she shouted.

"That's true," he acknowledged. "And I apologize for the necessity. But how do you feel about me now?" he asked.

"You had no right," she said in an angry tone. With this accusation she stepped forward and threw the wine she had not drunk in his face. It dripped off to the floor. He didn't move. He stood motionless, looking saddened.

"I had every right," he finally said, the wine still dripping from his face. "And what's more, I had the obligation that comes of being king, to act quickly. It's this or extinction for my people."

He paused while his sorrow subsided.

"Do you think we like this?" Finally, he took a handkerchief from a pocket under his cape and mopped his face. His voice had returned to a normal pitch, the sadness gone. "That we derive some perverse pleasure from the Bride Quest? We lose our lives in Bride

Quest. It consumes a great deal of our energy as a people. Our entire social structure revolves around it to the exclusion of everything else." He dropped the handkerchief on the tabletop beside where he'd placed his wineglass when she drenched him.

"There have been no real advances in any of the sciences since the commencement of Bride Quest." In almost a whisper he added, "We are as trapped as you are."

Hill'carn stood dumbfounded, surprised at his candor, his calm. She hadn't thought what a reality like this would have on a species.

Sensing her mood he offered her his hand. "WILL you come to me, Hill'carn?"

Hill'carn wanted to. Beyond all logic, she wanted to go to him. Was it her own desire or one planted in her mind by him? She hadn't felt him in her mind but she couldn't trust that sensation in his rooms. Or was it the Marking that made her want to be near him? She resisted.

"No. You cannot force me to love you," she said.

"I haven't asked for your love," he said, lowering his hand. "Love is not a concept we easily embrace. There is no Gron'dalin alive who has ever experienced love from a mate," he said.

It took every ounce of strength she had to resist him when he admitted this. To keep her distance she thought about Earth and the life she had lost, and Paul, who loved her.

Chapter 18
If Only Time

"I've allowed Hill'carn all the time I can to adjust to the fact she must be my bride." He stared out at the snaking crimson tide and sighed loudly.

"You've been admirably patient," Gradspin remarked, sadness in his old voice.

"I've tried with considerable success to understand her feelings." Cacin folded his arms and spread his legs as he watched the sand blow around outside the barrier. It piled up against the sides of the dome and crept up the banit'ye.

"Sometimes understanding them doesn't help them, Lord. Don't regret what you have to do. Xingat has been used for generations. It's a reliable drug. She will feel nothing, be aware of nothing."

"I know, Gradspin. That doesn't make me any happier about using it. It won't change how she feels about me after I've done it."

Cacin still stared through the barrier at the sand as they spoke. "Gods I hate this. Does it never stop blowing? Why did Orgone have to do this to us? And did we need all these cursed windows? We'll never be able to lower the barrier. We won't be here when the atmosphere is breathable and we have to put up with this raging gale now.

Anyway, make preparations for the ceremony, Lord Elder. I'm expecting Orgone any minute. As my confidant, he must inject the drug."

The bitterness in his voice rang on the afternoon air like tin bells. He turned away from the barrier. His silver cape flowed out around him with the sudden movement, brushing against a brass table with a circular glass insert.

"I've summoned him to my chambers to instruct him to administer the Xingat. I will not do it."

"The celebration will commence when you are done, Lord." He gripped Cacin's shoulder, a gesture not uncommon for Gradspin. "I am sorry it has to be this way." Releasing Cacin's shoulder, Gradspin bowed.

"So am I, Gradspin. So am I."

The door into the hall opened with a swishing sound. "You called for me, Zi," Orgone bowed as he entered.

"I did, Orgone."

Gradspin stepped carefully down the two steps from the observation platform and patted Orgone's shoulder in greeting as he passed. He left the room quickly.

"That's odd for him," Orgone remarked. "He doesn't usually touch me. He's not very friendly to me," Orgone said after the door closed behind him.

"He's duty bound," Cacin remarked. "He's always training you to take over from him. Perhaps he concentrates too much on that aspect of your relationship. But he does care for you, Orgone."

Cacin sighed. "Hill'carn still won't consent of her own will to bed me."

"I'm sorry, Cacin." Orgone's eyes were soft and sad as he spoke. "What can I do for you, Zi?"

"Orgone, you know what you must do."

"The drugging?"

"Yes."

"She's a powerful female, Zi."

"Woman, Orgone, call her a woman. She deplores being called a female. And she's more than just powerful."

"Our future Queen doesn't wish to be forced to do anything," Orgone remarked. There was an edge to his voice that sounded a little like irritation.

"I've not forced her to bed. I could have done that immediately."

"But you've forcibly removed her from the life she believed she would lead. The life she wanted to lead."

"And what could I have done? Wooed her, courted her like any other suitor on her planet?" he said with resentment.

"I know all this. I know you have no choice. I'm not faulting you, Lord."

"Stop calling me Lord." He turned again to look at the Martian sands that swirled beyond the barrier, before continuing. "I'm cursed. Especially after Kagoule's antagonistic approach earlier."

He turned back suddenly and kicked the leg of the table beside him lightly, a gesture only. Then he stepped off the observation platform to look into his friend's face.

"And when I force her to bed, Orgone, as I must, will she forgive me for it? Gods, I resent this curse. If only we could live like other species."

"You're not your cousin, Zi, for which you have my friendship. I know it goes against your precepts to do this. Kagoule would have enjoyed it. He loved the Bride Quest. He loved being more powerful than those around him. Forcing others to do his will intoxicated him. He was drunk with the power he had over others and that would have extended to Hill'carn. He would have enjoyed drugging her." He took Cacin by the shoulders. "But I think at this time you have no alternative but to drug her. You MUST bed her. It's my opinion she's attracted to you, if that makes the drugging any less offensive."

"I agree with you. She is attracted to me. But you know it doesn't make this any easier. In fact it makes it harder. If only I had time," he said with exasperation. He walked away from Orgone and sat down on a long hardwood bench that stretched out under a potted fig tree at the foot of the observation stairs.

"I know I could win her if I only had time. Maybe it's only the Marking, but I could win her." The hem of his cape heaped tidily on the floor. He rose abruptly, inhaled noisily, then breathed out in a loud gush.

"The Marking has attracted her to you but your gentle nature also attracts her," Orgone stated. "She would have fared far worse with your cousin."

"I know. Still, the thought of drugging and raping her makes me ill."

Orgone frowned. "Rape is not in your nature. It's my opinion, Zi, that the female," he corrected himself, "the woman, wants to bed you. I postulate that she can't yet accept her desire for you. She has been Marked for a long time and the passion is on her. She views it as treason. Her loyalties to the Humans are still strong. She hasn't fully accepted she's no longer one of them. That's crucial to your winning her."

"I wish I could believe that. So you're saying it's just a matter of time, which is what I believe too."

"She's able to conceal feeling from you now, are you aware of that?" Orgone turned and slowly walked toward Cacin's desk.

"I knew she could conceal thought. But feeling?"

Orgone stopped at the desk and turned toward Cacin. He nodded.

"Well, that's why I gave you permission to enter her mind, Orgone. So I could learn things like this, this I would miss. You're the best mind we have. I wish I possessed your abilities."

"Don't let Gradspin know I've been in the Queen's mind," Orgone warned. "He would never accept it, Lord. It's too unconventional."

"These are unconventional times. And stop calling me, Lord, Orgone. Call me Cacin. At least when we're alone."

"Cacin then. It would grieve Gradspin to know of our break with custom in this matter. A queen's privacy is paramount."

"Very well. I won't tell him. I was unaware that she was able to mask feelings from me, though. Something as fundamental as feelings should be easily read? I'm glad you have scanned her mind."

Striding across the floor to the desk where he often wrote, the desk Orgone was standing in front of, Cacin fell into the seat, sighing loudly. So much resignation hung in that sigh that he seemed older than his years. "Prepare the dosage then," he said.

Picking up a pen that lay on the top of the desk, he turned it idly in a six fingered hand then tapped it on the desk.

"Before you administer it I have to talk with her, though."

"It will only take a few minutes for Beau'nad to prepare it. You should go to her now."

Cacin paused and looked down sadly at the blotter on the desk as if it held answers for him.

"I will," he replied finally. "When you enter with the drug Orgone, I'll leave. You have to administer it alone. I'll only do what no one else can do in this foul deed," he added, throwing the pen onto the desk.

"If that's what you want, Zi."

"What I want is for her to willingly sleep with me!" Cacin snapped irritably.

Orgone turned and quickly left the room.

Cacin rose slowly and crossed the floor to Hill'carn's suites.

"Being Gron'dalin is not always pleasant," he muttered to himself outside the door. "Being King is sometimes worse."

* * * *

He willed the door open. It stayed closed. He demanded it to open. With that it slammed violently against the wall.

"You astound me!" he said to her. "Are you blocking my entry now? No woman has ever been able to do that. The Marking is expanding your mental capacity beyond anything we have ever seen."

"No woman has blocked any Gron'dalin before?"

"No."

"Weren't Gron'dalin women, when there were any, able to block you?"

"Well, yes," Cacin replied hesitantly. "Gron'dalin women could. They were better at mind controls than men are." He broke off, looking at her strangely. "Yes. Gron'dalin women could indeed." He entered the room. "And you're now a Gron'dalin woman?" he asked hopefully.

"I'm human." Hill'carn answered defiantly. "I will always be human."

"I think you're really one of us now. Look at you. You're exquisitely beautiful, covered with what you call scales and able to use your mind like this."

"I'm scaly. And that pleases you?" Hill'carn smiled at him. Her smile faded as she scanned his mind. "Have you come to rape me, Cacin?" Her eyes widened with apprehension. "I guess I was coming to believe you would never do that to me."

"I've come." He sighed audibly. "First to say I care for you."

"You love me?" Hill'carn snapped.

"I've told you, I don't comprehend that feeling. I care for you and don't wish to coerce you in anything more. If I were a National, or even one of the other Elite; if I had more time; if my cousin hadn't put me in so difficult a position at his death; I could wait for you." He put his hand on his forehead and drew his fingers through his black mane. Clutching his mane before letting his hand fall to his side, he frowned. "But those are wishes," he said quietly. He stepped forward. Looking into her eyes he added in an elevated voice, "Yes, I have come to rape you."

He closed his eyes tightly and turned away. "Three days ago that wouldn't have bothered me nearly as much as it does today. It DOES bother me today!" He drew in a deep breath before continuing, trying to steady himself. "Unlike many men on Earth, I'll accomplish it as painlessly as possible. You'll be drugged."

Hill'carn swallowed hard. "Why don't you just control my mind," she uttered. "Make me believe I want to bed you?"

"You do!" Cacin answered forcefully, turning to face her. "You do want to bed me, but you won't admit that to yourself."

She gasped.

"Believe me," he continued. "If I could do this any other way, Hill'carn, I would. You resist me more effectively than any woman has ever resisted a Gron'dalin. Of course, it's never been necessary before to have a woman's approval in this matter."

"And it is now?"

"It is to me."

He looked down at the floor. "I could apply a mind seize instead of using the drug." He looked back up. "I'm capable of maintaining control of your mind throughout." He paused. "And you would be totally aware of the act." Again he looked away. "You would experience pain and humiliation.

"I'm going to be humiliated, Cacin. You can't do this to me and not expect me to be humiliated."

He was so young. She stared into his eyes now as he looked back at her, wondering how young he was. He looked hurt at these words, torn between what he should do and what he obviously was going to do. In some things he acted like a boy. A teenage boy, unsure of himself, would have acted no differently.

"The drug is harmless and will afford you some removal from the process. I don't want to hurt you - physically or emotionally - but I MUST do this," he said with exasperation. Silence fell like an iron mallet, embracing them for minutes before he spoke again.

Her heart raced. He really was going to do this despicable thing to her. How could he? How could anyone?

"Hill'carn, I'm sorry it has to be this way. I have a kingdom to rule and no more time can be spent on this issue."

"I beg you. Don't do this to me." Hill'carn felt tears burning at the edges of her eyes but battled to control them.

"I'm sorry, I must do it. I'll make you one promise," he said, drawing close to her, taking her shoulders in the same manner he had grasped them at Gaylant. "I will not invade your mind as you so often put it. You may have complete privacy always."

Orgone cleared his throat behind them. "I'm here."

"I know." Cacin responded, straightening and drawing in another deep breath. Releasing her shoulders he turned and left the room abruptly.

As he left, Hill'carn thought of the life she would never have on Earth. She wondered how Paul or Cahill would view her tomorrow this time if they knew. Knowing Cacin was not reading her mind she wished Paul would come for her like he had before.

The thought drove a dagger into Cacin's hearts before he remembered he'd promised he would never read her mind again.

Chapter 19
Disclosure

Where was the benefit to the world if he kept it a secret? Paul hadn't injected her blood for fun. So he told Cahill as he walked into the living room from his kitchen. Just like that, he blurted it out while Simon Cahill leafed through some notes he'd brought about the underground bunkers.

Making no attempt to hide the scales on his face, he strode into the room as boldly as any human. Cahill's mouth fell open. He stared first at Paul's face and then at the pages in front of him for some time before speaking.

"I was wondering if you'd done it," he finally said, looking up and clearing his throat. Again silence enveloped them while both men thought their individual thoughts.

"I did it the night it came for her, just before it came."

"That's why you were in the bathroom throwing up. It was a reaction to injecting her blood wasn't it."

"That's right," Paul nodded, placing the coffee tray on the dining room table on top of some of Cahill's notes.

"Without the advantage Hillary's blood can give us, Paul, I'm convinced the Earth will be ravaged by these creatures."

Paul sighed. "Thank God you aren't upset."

"Upset?" he snorted. "I'm relieved. I couldn't ask anyone to inject her blood. Not knowing what it might do. It could have killed you."

Paul nodded.

"Finding that armor laying there in your yard the way we did, and her clothing laying there beside it, didn't inspire me with confidence one little bit. I can deal with the dead soldiers - even with the knowledge that it didn't use a weapon against them - more easily than I can deal with the implication of that armor and those clothes. Somehow, that bastard transported her without the use of any kind of vehicle. Just with its mind."

"Ya, but why did it have to remove her clothes?"

Cahill shrugged. "I don't know. The damn thing transported her without the use of a spaceship right off this planet. That's all that interests me. Honest to God! That's what it did." He stared into Paul's blue eyes.

"I think you're right," Paul answered, hanging his head.

"No." Cahill shook his head. "Civilization will perish at the hands of these things if Hillary's account of them, and what we saw in your basement, at the hospital when she was taken, and on your lawn, is accurate. If we aren't just going crazy, I mean."

"My abilities since injecting her blood are staggering," Paul confided. "And I've just begun. I can move myself across the room." He demonstrated. Simon gasped. "Move things around the room." He brought a book from the top of the coffee table to Cahill.

"My God!"

"It all makes sense to me," Paul said. He smiled. "It's only matter after all. Maybe in time I'll be able to travel in space like they can. And if I can, I'll get her back."

"We have to get some other men on line," Cahill said, closing the file he had opened to show Paul.

Paul sat down in the chair opposite Cahill. "Tell them what they can expect, Simon."

Cahill pointed at Paul's face and said, "Are those, ugh, scales. I mean really. Or are they just a pattern?"

"They're rough but they don't flake off. They're a pattern. You can touch them if you want."

Simon nodded, looking uncomfortable with the whole topic. "Naw. I'll take your word for it."

"Don't just inject them with her blood, Simon," Paul insisted, returning to the topic he had originally broached. "They'll resent you for the rest of their lives if you do. And remember, they'll have the minds to get even."

"Good point," Cahill replied. "Good point!" He laughed nervously. He looked uncomfortable. "Are you willing to meet with them? Show them what they can expect?"

"Sure."

"Well, I'll arrange something," Cahill said. "What are you going to do in the meantime?"

"I'm going to try to contact Hillary."

"Concentrate on Mars."

"Why Mars?"

Cahill looked down at the dining room table briefly. Was he considering withholding something? Well, he couldn't. If Paul wanted it badly enough he'd just take it from his mind now.

"There's been some activity on the planet's surface."

"You're kidding!"

"Afraid not."

"Well, it makes sense. If we were going to plunder a species of its most valuable resource, we would set up a base of operations as close as possible."

Cahill chuckled. "We've already done that time and again. Look at Africa. We took people then. Other places we've taken gold or other precious metals. Whatever we wanted. Hell, if they don't suspect what you're doing you can set up camp right in their midst."

"It's not really safe for them on Earth. We know about them. We'd be looking for them. And they certainly couldn't colonize Venus."

"There are places on Earth that would have been safe enough. They could have gone to any of the unpopulated areas."

"For a short time. Until we ferreted them out. They don't want to be the hunted, Simon. They want to do the hunting. They don't want to always be watching their backs. And that's what they'd be doing if they stayed on Earth."

"With THEIR minds? You have to be kidding. They'd know what we were up to before we did."

"Kagoule didn't. Besides, from what Hillary said, there are a lot of them coming. You can't hide hundreds of thousands of seven-foot aliens in any of our wilderness areas. No, it's easier to set up camp where your enemy can't physically go; where you can relax after a hard day's work." Sarcasm sat heavily in his voice. "Without even setting up guards they can keep us at bay. And with their technology, they can travel here in minutes. It's just down the street for them.

So Mars is where I can expect to find her," Paul said. "I should have guessed," he repeated.

"Paul, for all we know she could be dead. Don't get your hopes up. Even if you were able to contact her, she's out of reach. Face it. You're not going to get Hillary back. I wish I didn't have to be the one to break it to you, but she's gone for good."

"I'm going to get her back, Simon. It is not going to have her. I felt her presence this afternoon. I didn't know where she was but I could feel the stress in her mind. I still can't read her thoughts. Her mind is too sharp. Maybe it has something to do with the change in her DNA." He shrugged. "I don't know. I only picked up feelings."

"Paul you're expecting too much of yourself."

"I have to get her back. I failed her once. I'm not going to fail her again."

"You can't keep on blaming yourself. You were locked in the bathroom. Remember? And when you got out you almost met the same fate as the four guards."

"I failed her, Simon. I should have been able to do something."

Chapter 20
Turmoil

Hot dry air rolled over her. Hillary crouched in the dirt with three younger cousins flanking her, cheering her on. Squatting on the dusty ground with a handful of some sort of wooden objects, she concentrated on winning. Was it jacks she shook so furiously in her small clenched fists?

She usually won against her cousins. The air smelled of dust and cow dung and heat, always of heat. She shook her small fists, laughing, her eyes wide, the jacks – if that's what they were – pressing into her palms.

Suddenly a tall man in fine clothes appeared, looming over them, blocking out the sunlight like a black cloud. Silence fell over them. She looked up. She knew him from a photo her mother kept on the eating table. Hillary stood. His shadow, abruptly cast over the play area, frightened her three young cousins more than it frightened her. They ran crying for their mothers, leaving her alone with the tall stranger. He stood looking down at her for a moment in his fine looking clothes, saying nothing.

"Come," he said at last, extending a hand in an authoritative manner.

Hillary rose, dropping the playthings in the dust. She took his hand and walked away with him. The sound of a car engine idling in the heat disturbed the peace of the small dusty village. He lifted her into the back seat of the car and got in beside her.

Standing on the seat, she could see out through the small back window. "Mother's coming! Wait!" she cried. There, rushing toward the car, her mother, spearheading the onslaught of curious neighbors that followed along behind, waved and cried frantically. Dust rose around them in a great lazy cloud.

Her mother's eyes, a study in fear, fixed on Hillary's. Pleading and crying the woman ran closer. Hillary started crying too.

"Go man. What's keeping you?" her father said, tapping the window between the front and back seats.

Her mother tripped. Regaining her stride she broke into a full run, leaving the others behind, her sari flying out in the breeze of her passage. The car pulled away. Dust billowed in its wake. Mother fell behind now, stumbling, losing ground, hardly visible in the dust the car threw up.

"Don't go without my mother!" Hillary cried.

"Sit down child," her father said calmly.

"Don't leave my mother behind!" Hillary pleaded.

Her father said nothing to her but instructed the chauffeur to drive faster.

* * * *

As Hill'carn awoke in Cacin's bed, a feeling of violation swept through her, almost nauseating her. She opened her eyes and gazed up through the banit'ye barrier above the bed at the Martian sky. Two moons blinked down on her from their celestial orbits. A million stars dotted the blackness of space, sparkling like gems in a dark sea. She turned her head and searched for him, moving her thick tongue in its dry case and trying to swallow.

Sitting in a large wingback chair, a book open in those massive hands of his, Cacin read quietly. A curved floor lamp hung over his head, the only light in the room, shedding a soft glow around him. Beyond, only the darkness of the Martian landscape at night stretched out past the barrier, accentuating her isolation.

Hill'carn instantly swelled with hate. With his full profile to her, she glared at him.

He read on.

He had a delicate nose, where Kagoule's had been flat. He wore spectacles to read, spectacles! She drew the blankets up around her neck. Spectacles seemed so Earthly a necessity. She tried to swallow again. Her tongue grated along the roof of her mouth like sandpaper over dry wood.

She looked away, trying to clear her foggy brain. Around her, a massive odd-looking wooden bed adorned with books on shelves that jutted out around the bed, stretched away. She pulled the blankets tightly around her and gazed back at him.

There he sat, reading. What did she know about him? Very little, and she cared to know even less. Vowing she would never forgive him for what he'd done – that she would not spend her life with him – she struggled to combat tears. Knowing she could not bear a life that was not her own free choice, she pushed herself up on one elbow.

Sitting, she demanded with contempt and fury, "Did you do it?"

Cacin removed his glasses. Tilting his head and raising an eyebrow he looked over at her. "By your thoughts you obviously believe I have," he answered coldly.

Was he trying to impale her heart on an iron spike?

"My thoughts should be my own business," she snapped. "Answer me!" she demanded. "This is not a game! Did you rape me?" she asked this hatefully, not knowing what else to say, or how else to phrase it. Perhaps telling him she hated him was a better approach. "I hate you! I hate you!" she screamed, fighting tears.

Hill'carn had never really noted Cacin's eyebrows before. Like his mane, they were a jet black, orderly kind of curl, although not ringlets as his mane was, because of their length. She had seen them before, every time she looked at him, but hadn't assimilated the information. He raised them now as he wrinkled his brow.

Around his eyes the shell-shaped designs were tinier and more delicate than elsewhere. They glistened and stretched with this action, reflecting the light of the lamp, accenting the penetrating green color of his irises. He looked so young in this light. How old was he anyway? Was she dealing with a boy here?

"No. I did not," he answered, laying the book aside, obviously hurt by her thoughts.

The statement buffeted her senses. Shocked and disarmed, she gasped and looked down at the bed. Ready to do battle, she couldn't immediately understand what he'd said. Was this some sort of sick joke? With these simple words her hatred melted. Left defenseless and confused, she floundered for a reply.

He stood up. In her peripheral vision she saw his massive body gracefully rise from the chair. Still she stared down at the blankets, clutching them to her chest, trembling.

"I've deceived my people for the love of you," Cacin said. "Now we've both given up something. You, your freedom. Me, my honor." His voice fell like raindrops on parched land, pattering quietly around her. He stood looking at her for one inordinately long moment. Time seemed to halt, suspending them like pictures on a postcard.

Had he said 'for the love of her'? Unable to believe what she'd heard him say, she continued to stare at the blankets as though they held some answers.

What did he mean? Had he set aside some – what – some crazy kind of oath of office because he loved her? Is that what he meant? Of the little she knew of Cacin, she knew how important tradition was to him. So he would have her believe he had set aside tradition – broken with custom – and lied to his people while he broke it?

"Yes, that's what I've done. The worst part is that I've lied to them."

She drew in a deep breath and her heart started beating again. With a sudden jerk, time started passing again. The fog in Hill'carn's mind cleared a little. Was it the drug or the shock of what he'd said that dazed her?

She couldn't endure any more. Tired, mentally exhausted, she felt stunned. How could he love her? They weren't even the same species! She battled tears. No! Trying to get a fix on how she felt, trying to resist his psychological tricks, she shook her head sharply to clear it. Was this a trick? Her mind reeled.

"It's not a trick," he said calmly. "I love you. And because I do, I can't rape you."

Apart from her mother, had anyone ever really loved her? Had her mother loved her? Paul loved her. Yes. He said he did. She had been a possession to her father, something beautiful to command and display. That was what Cacin had wanted of her too, wasn't it? He wanted to own her.

"I don't own you anymore than you own me. But you do own me now," he said. He laughed cynically. "You've stolen my hearts as the Humans would say."

NO! She wouldn't believe him. Paul loved her. He said he loved her. He kissed her. He held her in his arms. She loved him too. She and Paul were the same. They were the same species. "Oh God help me," Hill'carn whispered. She closed her eyes tightly, fighting tears that rested at the edges of her lids, fighting the urge to touch the scales on her face and neck.

She was human!

She must be human!

How could she be anything else? How could this be happening? But worse, how could she be attracted to this gron?

"I hate to see you in pain," he said softly. "Is there anything I can do?"

"Let me go home."

"I can't. And besides, you don't want to go any longer."

She felt him in her mind, felt his jealousy of her feelings for Paul. She sensed it. He was thankful he hadn't killed Paul, though.

"Yes. Killing him would have sealed my fate with you."

He stood and stared down at her.

Paul wasn't here now. She needed him! She needed someone!

Cacin came to her side. "It's alright to love me back if you can." He kneeled beside her, so boyishly, his massive body lowering slowly, almost tentatively.

She couldn't identify which of the emotions that ran wildly through her brain drove her most toward the brink of tears. Confusion reigned in her mind. She would have to proceed on instinct. She hadn't known that his loving her would have such an impact. Her Achilles' Heel, that one small sentence unhinged her. Holding her head as though it would explode, she moaned.

Cacin sat down on the edge of the bed and gently moved her hands away from her head. "I hate to see you in so much pain." He touched her shoulder. That touch she had come to love so much; that gentle touch was there again. She breathed rapidly.

"Hill'carn," he said, "I'm sorry this is the way we must continue our species." He drew in a deep breath and collected himself before continuing. "I'm also sorry you've been a victim of our need to reproduce." Relinquishing the breath he'd taken in one long tired sigh, he continued. "I recognize that this capture is enslavement. I don't pretend not to be able to see your point of view. I do." He released her shoulder and stood again.

Tears threatened to explode from her. But a scream also hung there, it hung just the other side of reality in the dark regions of sanity.

"I wish you could understand our predicament."

He took a few steps away from her, his back to her now when he spoke again. The sound of his voice soothed her. "I will not force myself on you. I've decided to remain celibate if you will not allow me to bed you," he crossed his arms and turned to look at her again.

"This doesn't mean you can leave Colony. You'll have to remain in my company." He snorted, a nuance that Hill'carn believed expressed disappointment. "For your own protection," he continued, "if for no other reason."

She had never before seen him in Colony without the silver cape of his ancestry. On Earth, when he stood in the basement doorway looking so fierce, dressed in armor, he'd presented one image. Later, on the lawn, naked, he'd presented another. But since then, while assessing her, he always presented himself formally. Now, for the first time she saw how this massive gron dressed when he relaxed at home; if he could be said to be at ease now.

She knew nothing about him really. Dressed in casual beige slacks and a dark green, short sleeved shirt, he looked very strange indeed. And he needed glasses to read, imagine that.

He sat down beside her again. The scream that begged for release ebbed away.

"You're no longer Human, all the less so for your voyage inside my body."

It was true. Hill'carn looked down at the scales that had spread down her arms to the backs of her hands. She had them around her ankles in delicate wisps and around her navel. The backs of her shoulders had an oblong of emerald green and mahogany that feathered out from her shoulder blades.

He continued to speak. "You're genetically altered, Hill'carn, completely changed. You would be incapable now of bearing Human children. Even by a Human male you would bear Gron'dalin offspring, since our genetic make-up is dominant. IF you could conceive by a Human male at all," he added.

A long empty pause drifted between them before he spoke again. When he did, his voice fell on her like the summer wind that had rushed past her small Toyota as she sped from Toronto and Kagoule, soft and warm but unlike that wind, this one was inviting.

"I love you," he said. "But I can't let you go. And the Humans wouldn't accept you now anyway. There's no way of reversing the changes in you. I won't hurt you by raping you. I can't let them hurt you either. I'm sorry you'll have to spend the rest of your life with someone you don't want to be around."

"You're pleasant to be with, Cacin. I enjoy your company." The steadiness of her voice startled her. "But I must be free. My complaint is no longer that I'm with you, exactly, but how I came to be with you."

"Would you have accepted me if I had come calling, asking for your hand in marriage?" he asked cynically.

"No. Not the way I was. But I must be free! Let me go," she implored.

"I can't," Cacin answered. "They'd kill you eventually, these Humans you love so well."

"With MY mind? I doubt they could."

"Am I so terrible to be with that you'd prefer solitude to my love?"

Hill'carn finally succumbed to the tears that had been pressing for liberation. Why this statement should have brought them she wasn't sure. Perhaps the confusion over her emotions had simply pulled the ripcord. They were tears of frustration, anger, sorrow, pain, that had been waiting for disclosure longer than she'd been exposed to the Gron'dalin tyranny.

Stooping, Cacin kneeled by the bedside, stroking her facial scales. "Don't cry," he said gently. "I can't stand to see you in pain." He bent forward and softly kissed her cheek. "Life can be hard, that's just the way it is. There are worse fates you could have fallen on, my love. One of them would have been to wed Kagoule. As much as I respected him, he was brutal. That was his nature. You would not have been allowed any freedom in his company."

"I'm not crying because of my fate. I'm crying because..." She hesitated, not knowing why she was crying.

"Because I love you?" Cacin asked. "I'm not able to understand your emotions."

"How could you love me?" she asked accusingly.

"I just do."

"You are the first person who has stopped doing what they wanted to do with me, because of ME," she blurted through a flood of tears. "Because of loving me. Caring what I thought or wanted." With this declaration he gathered her into his massive arms.

"I'm so confused," she wailed. "God! I have to be free. Let me go home." She didn't break their embrace.

"What are your feelings for me?" he asked, pushing her away to look into her eyes.

"I love you," she whispered as tears continued to fall like summer rain. "I love you and I feel ashamed of it. I feel like a traitor to my people and I feel that I'm giving up my freedom."

He pulled her close again. The sound of his hearts pounded in her ears. "They aren't your people any longer. We are your people now," he said emphatically. "And, if you can, show me a relationship - any relationship - in which freedom isn't relinquished."

"Never like this." She sobbed.

"I love you so much," he stated holding her close.

"I love you too."

"It's going to be a long and painful healing process but we'll make it, Hill'carn. I know if I were capable of letting you go, you'd come back to me now. I never dreamed that possible. This wonderful woman from the most unlikely place in the universe loves me." He laughed aloud like a schoolboy. "You can't possibly know how it feels to hear you say you love me, to have your love. Someone loves a Gron'dalin!" he announced in a booming voice, throwing his head back and laughing. Then more quietly, gathering her back into his arms, he added, "Love's a concept I never dreamed possible, Hill'carn. It feels marvelous. By my word," Cacin whispered. "I love you more than life itself."

Chapter 21
War

Cruchton Visad Sentry, commander of the Elite force attacking Earth, stood in the center of a large brown field. Directly opposite, an underground bunker containing ten females consumed his attention. Poorly constructed and very visible, it bulged like an ant hill in the parched land.

"The King should be heading this attack," his comrade, Bon, said in a whisper.

"Because of the unusual events leading up to his cousin's death," Cruchton said, "and the resulting complications, the King is procreating right now," Cruchton finished in his usual flat, apparently disinterested, tone.

"I know that, Cruchton. I'm not an idiot."

"Convention prohibits him from leading the attack until he impregnates the female."

Bon shrugged. "I know. But you shouldn't be stuck with this."

"Who then?" Cruchton challenged.

"I just think it's too bad that you're left with this war and HIS obligations, while he has a good time."

"I doubt he's having a good time with THAT female," Cruchton retorted, looking up at Bon, who towered a full foot over him. "He's doing what he must. Obligations are what life is all about." A breeze ruffled the brown ringlets that hung from his head.

Bon shrugged again.

"I only wish I had his advice," Cruchton said, brushing away flies that buzzed around his face away with one determined swat.

"Orgone tells me the substitution of the Chief of Sentry in the place of the King has only been necessary once in Gron'dalin history," Bon said.

"Orgone is an irritant." Cruchton crossed his arms, then brushed at some more flies and re-crossed his arms. He spread his legs.

Bon nodded. "True. But he knows his history. That King never sired an offspring and so never led a Bride Quest for his entire reign."

"Really? Well, it will be someone else's problem next time if our King doesn't sire any offspring. I'll have my bride and won't be in the next Quest at all. This attack on Earth is unusual in other, more important ways than that, Bon. I don't suppose Orgone will bother to tell you that we've never had an adversary so well prepared for battle before."

"Nothing so pertinent," Bon said contemptuously.

"That's correct. His head is in the clouds and in history." Cruchton adjusted the instrument he had laid at his feet and resumed his stance. "Where is that Zad? I've got a good mind to go in without him and just present the female to him when he arrives."

"Can't do that. No honor for him in that."

"I doubt he cares about taking her himself." Cruchton adjusted the instrument again and sighed. "I find it hard to believe Orgone worries about honor." He cleared his throat. "Most of the females aren't as easy to find as these ones," he said, changing the topic. "Most of them are surrounded by concrete and even our instruments can't detect them. Orgone is lucky."

"Following their evacuation movements, we've at least located a great many of their underground shelters," Bon protested. He looked at the timepiece on his large wrist. "Where is he?"

"Dawdling as usual," Cruchton said in his matter-of-fact tone. There was no animosity in his voice. "I don't see why I have to hold his hand on this capture, though," Cruchton complained. "Especially if he's going to be late like this."

"King's orders."

"There aren't any males in the bunker anyway. He's under no threat of death if he wears armor."

"Should we just go and let him fend for himself?"

"No, orders are orders."

Bon nodded.

"Those soldiers in the underground bastions in the north complicate the process," Cruchton said. "But down here in the dry lands there are no soldiers." He laughed. "I haven't detected any males at all."

"Yes I know. What's Orgone's choice doing down here anyway? Is she from this primitive culture?"

"No. She works to improve the lives of these ones."

"Do you think they know we're here?"

"Oh they know it." Cruchton crossed to a large rock and sat down. "See that telescope over there?" He pointed to the ant hill. Bon guffawed. "Did you influence your choice?" Cruchton asked Bon.

"Of course."

"Giving the Elite permission to scan for females should have been a bonus. The stupid Zad of course didn't establish influence over the females of their choice."

"You're kidding?"

"No. None of the Sentry I've spoken to failed to establish influence over them. Why can't the Zad do what they're supposed to do, just once?"

"And we're all held up in the mating because we have to locate their females?"

"Ya. Not only Orgone's, either."

"While OUR females are held on Mars?" Bon snapped with indignation. He brushed flies away from his face and continued, "in holding areas to become more agitated daily? We have to help the stupid Zad who didn't influence their females?"

"You got it."

Bon shook his head. "Outlandish. I only wish the King would suspend custom and allow us to mate as we catch them. This is a special battle."

"Yes. Going into the worst part of the battle I'd like the gron'ie to be fresh."

"Where is that Zad?"

"He's always late," Cruchton remarked. "Why don't you sit down?" The form of a gron started taking shape in front of them just as Cruchton finished speaking.

"Here at last," Bon whispered.

"Orgone. Nice of you to finally honor us with your presence," Cruchton said, rising. "So, now we can finally help you catch the female you should have influenced?"

"I apologize. I was unavoidably detained. Is she in this field?"

"She's been watching us for half an hour through that telescope over there," Bon stated, pointing at the telescope. "I think the females built the shelter themselves. What IS a desirable female doing in a primitive rural area like this," Bon asked.

"Her work brings her here. She's a sociologist. Are there any males in the bunker?" Orgone asked.

"No."

"Why did you stand around waiting for me then? I can do this alone."

"Orders are orders. I hope you're wearing your armor, Orgone. These females have been known to defend themselves."

"In the north yes. Down here they have no weapons to speak of. But of course I'm wearing armor. I'm not stupid, Cruchton."

"Oh ya?" Bon muttered contemptuously under his breath.

Hearing him, Cruchton raised his eyebrows. "Let's take all the females in the shelter. We can hold the rest for the Nationals and that will at least make our half-hour wait worth something," he said. "The ship is hidden just over there." He pointed to a grove of trees in the distance where a group of large gray creatures with giant ears and elongated snouts grazed on foliage.

* * * *

Having tried every measure at his disposal, Paul still couldn't locate Hillary. It was as though she had vanished from the universe or evaporated into mist. Her mind pattern was simply gone. He had located her once, briefly. He'd tried to communicate, but it was as if she vanished. One moment she was there, surprised at his contact. The next she was gone.

It had been two weeks since he'd first found her. He had no idea where she was now or even if she was still alive.

As the Gron'dalin began pillaging Earth of its women, Paul had abandoned his search for the woman he loved and threw his substantial powers and his altered mind behind Earth's resistance. Four others had been altered with Hillary's blood and they were working together as a team.

Chapter 22
Adjustments

Hill'carn leaned forward, staring at her reflection in the mirror. It was an odd feeling, looking at someone you didn't know in the mirror. Twenty-three years of seeing the same likeness, or an aging variation on the same theme, was hard to let go of overnight.

"How well would THEY adjust?" she whispered to her image, rubbing the shell-shaped motif on her neck. "They think they're brave for reconciling themselves to the Bride Quest." She guffawed. "At least they're active participants in that. No. They're more than that. They hold the power. They can force their will on others. THEY are in control."

Still feeling she could wash it off, she picked at the pattern again and thought of the times she'd caught sight of her reflection in the banit'ye barrier and done a double take. It startled her to see the delicate green and mahogany scale reflecting back from the window where she expected to see her familiar plain face.

She touched the pattern on her face again. It felt odd, cool. She pulled her hair away from her neck and assessed the width of the scale there, noting the tiny wisps that feathered out on either side.

Hill'carn straightened and opened her robe. Stepping back she examined the backs of her hands, then the reflection of her navel and breasts in the mirror. She looked down, flattening her small breasts with both hands. Carefully scrutinizing her body scale, she noticed an area not previously noted, feathering out from her pubic hair. It was spreading! Would she soon be entirely covered with this stuff?

A feeling of panic swept through her. Unable to control it, she shuddered violently in the attempt, since it inevitably brought Cacin to her side, concerned and apologetic. She closed her eyes.

Today proved no exception.

"You're unhappy again. I'm sorry," he said as the door slid open behind her. Hill'carn opened her eyes and watched his reflection approach her in the mirror. "You look beautiful, Hill'carn. I wish you could know how beautiful you look to me."

Hill'carn closed her robe and loosely fastened it. She dropped her arms to her sides. "You should stop reading my mind. Wherever I am, Cacin, I want my privacy. You promised you would not read my mind."

"As long as there is a chance you will harm yourself I must continue reading your mind."

She sighed and turned to look at him. "There are a lot of feelings I don't want you to know about."

"Why not. I want to help." He was beside her now.

"You can't. There's nothing you can do about this feeling of desperation I get from time to time, so…"

"I disagree," Cacin said softly, taking her in his arms. "I can comfort you." He embraced her.

Hill'carn sighed again. "Yes, you can do that. And you do."

"I love you, Hill'carn. If things were different. If we weren't required to seek mates outside our species and I'd met you…" he turned her toward him and looked down tenderly into her eyes. "I would woo you relentlessly. I would beg you to wed me." He laughed good-naturedly, throwing his head back.

She smiled. He was such a boy. The Boy King.

"I would have given up anything to spend my life with you," he said as his laughing subsided.

Smiling she rested her head against his massive chest.

He kissed the top of her head.

"You wouldn't have accepted me without the Marking. Even though it would have been futile and you would have thought me ugly without the Marking, I would have courted you."

Hill'carn's smile broadened. "You're right. I would never have accepted you," she admitted. "Besides, we would never have met. Without the Bride Quest you would never have come into this part of the universe."

"That's right," Cacin admitted. "I'm grateful then for the Bride Quest." He laughed and stepped back, gazing into her eyes. "That's a statement I never thought I would make."

He pulled her to him again. He hadn't left her alone for longer than a few hours since her arrival on Mars. His presence reassured her now. It was as though he were nursing her through a difficult illness. He was kind and considerate, always attentive to her needs.

What a difference from the treatment I would have received at Kagoule's hand, she thought.

"Why don't you get dressed and we'll go to a favorite spot of mine?" Cacin said. "Earth Garden One. I think you'll like it there."

Hill'carn nodded and he stooped to kiss her lips briefly before moving toward the door. Turning, he said jovially, "Shall we walk or should I show off my talents to you?"

Hill'carn chuckled. "Show off to me," she said. Was this the same gron who had killed the soldiers in Paul's basement such a short time ago?

"Yes it is," Cacin replied to her unasked question. "You'll have to accept that side of my nature too. Anyone is capable of killing, Hill'carn. I would gladly kill for you again."

"You should stop reading my mind, Cacin. I prefer my privacy in some things."

He smiled and winked. "Hurry now. Don't keep me waiting." His smile, warm and broad, lit his face. It reminded her of Paul's smile and that made her wonder why Paul hadn't tried to contact her again. But she knew in her heart of hearts why there was no more contact with Paul. Cacin was blocking him.

The doors closed behind him as he stepped through.

Turning to the mirror, Hill'carn opened her robe and looked at her body again. Then, disrobing quickly she dressed in the long flowing silver gown of the Zi ancestry. Anxious to see what Cacin would do to impress her, anxious to be out of these rooms for the first time in more than three weeks, she hurried.

The door swished open at her mental command and Cacin rose from where he'd been waiting at his desk.

"Come here my love," he motioned her forward. "You look lovely." Taking her by one shoulder he smiled broadly. "Close your eyes." She closed them tightly. "Now open them."

On opening her eyes Hill'carn found herself in a tropical garden. "How did you do that?" she breathed.

"Just one of our little tricks," Cacin smiled like an adolescent who'd just pulled a prank.

The thought crossed Hill'carn's mind that Earth didn't have a chance.

"I'm sorry it has to be that way," Cacin replied in response to her unspoken thought. "Come on. Let's not spoil our walk. The Quest will soon be over and we'll be able to start building our lives together."

Chapter 23
Soft Underbelly

Two months gone and the battle went badly. Worse than any of the Elite cared to admit.

Cacin drew a hand through his coarse black mane and, throwing his head back for no other reason than he felt like doing it, transported to Beau'nad's quarters.

The foyer he materialized in was decorated in bold splashes of color from the Lation era. Broad brush strokes kissed the white walls playfully in bright slashes of red, rust and electric blue.

"Beau'nad, as chief physician I would like you to attend the Queen," he said, straightening.

"You look worried," the doctor said, closing the door to his rooms behind him.

Cacin sighed. "It goes badly. The sooner I'm in the fray, the better."

"Well, let's get you into it then. I was with Hill'carn when she arrived. I feel like I delivered her in a way. I'm pleased you've asked me to attend. Is it for what I think it's for?"

"Yes."

"At last," Beau'nad said, not meaning any disrespect. He gathered some instruments into a leather satchel as he spoke. He looked tired, haggard really.

"Cruchton and I have decided on an ambush plan that I'll be able to implement personally now. Things will improve, Beau'nad."

"I hope so." He snapped the case shut and turned toward the King. "The Nationals are more than impatient and Orgone isn't making it any better by taunting them. If it weren't for the fact that the Elite aren't allowed to mate until all their brides are captured, there would be an uprising on the Armada, I'm sure."

Cacin shook his head. "There'll be no such thing."

"Well, Orgone had better stop teasing them. Orgone!" Beau'nad repeated the name with disgust.

"I don't know what his problem is lately," Cacin confided.

"He needs to mate." Beau'nad shook his head. "Funny, the most intellectual of us is, in the end, so physical."

"That's his problem?"

"It is. We aren't kidding when we say Gron'dalin males must mate. If there were any Gron'dalin females they would have to mate too. That's just the way our species evolved."

"Practices may have to be changed on this Quest, Beau'nad. We may have to allow the gron'ie to mate as they capture their brides."

"I doubt Orgone would bed his bride anyway. He is trying to WIN her." He pinched the bridge of his nose. "He spends the entire day with her, brings her whatever she desires." The leather satchel dangled from one hand.

"You look tired, Beau'nad."

"I just returned from battle." He sighed and continued to pinch the bridge of his nose. "I have no stomach for war but I'll do what I must." He sat the satchel down on the floor and rubbed his eyes with his knuckles.

"Have you secured your bride?" Cacin asked.

"Yes. She's been in holding for almost three weeks."

Cacin sighed. "I have to get into combat. That's not good for the women either. Come on, Beau'nad. The sooner the Queen is pregnant the better."

"Well, that is up to you, Lord." He smiled mischievously despite his fatigue. "I can only say if she is or is not." With a groan he hoisted the case off the floor where he'd placed it.

"Beau'nad." Cacin smirked. "I do believe this Bride Quest is giving you a sense of humor." They both laughed.

"Well, it's that or become nasty like Orgone has chosen to be."

"He'll get over it. Let's walk there. What difference will another ten minutes make one way or another? And I need to talk to you about something." Cacin motioned toward the door.

As the doors swished open, Cacin continued. "Beau'nad, there's something you should know about the Queen. You haven't seen her since the mating celebration, and then she was drugged."

Beau'nad looked over at his companion. "I'm listening, Lord."

"The Queen is now able to enter your mind. She is inexperienced at it, and may insult you with the quality of that entry," he paused, sighing loudly. Beau'nad stopped abruptly. The long red reclining gown of the Zad heritage, which had been flowing out around him as he walked, now settled against his legs.

"Although she advances daily in the skill, she's terrible at it," Cacin continued. "You must tolerate her indiscretions," the younger gron instructed. "She's like a child. Frankly, I'm weary of her constant mind probing but I can't bring myself to tell her to stop. She's learning to communicate. Halting her learning would be inappropriate."

Whether battle fatigue or the sheer shock of the topic influenced his demeanor, Cacin couldn't know because he was in the habit of requesting admission to a Zad's mind. He wasn't reading Beau'nad who now looked like he'd been struck.

"How can this be?" he blurted. "Females we've captured in the past have never developed this ability."

Cacin shrugged. "They're a very intelligent species. And don't call them females if you want them to respect you."

"I see," Beau'nad replied.

"Call them women, Beau'nad. They don't like being called females." They resumed walking.

"Alright, I will," the older gron said. "Does this mean that my bride will be able to read my mind?"

"I believe she will."

"Oh great! No privacy."

"A little of our own medicine," Cacin replied, smirking.

* * * *

"The Queen is pregnant," Beau'nad announced as he snapped off the gloves he'd worn to examine her. The door closed behind him.

"I can't believe it," Cacin replied beaming from ear-to-ear. He leaned on the metal examination table by the sinks and continued to smile. Beau'nad crossed to the sink.

"Believe it. And to my great relief, she didn't commit any improprieties in my mind." He turned on the tap and water streamed out over his huge patterned hands. "She's quite shy isn't she?" He scrubbed his hands with soap and a bristle brush.

"Yes, she is."

"Well, she was very pleasant and amicable."

"You sound surprised."

"I am. Because of the drugging." The sound of the brush scraping his hands filled the small anti-chamber, "And all that went on before it. I expected her to be hostile."

"She's adjusting," Cacin said nervously.

"I can see that. There's hope for the rest of us then."

"It's a difficult adjustment, Beau'nad." Cacin crossed the floor to the viewing platform with his hands behind his back.

"Lord, these females are extremely arduous. May I ask how you won the Queen's trust?" He dropped the soap back into the dish beside the sink for the second time and continued scrubbing with the brush. A mountain of lather consumed his hands.

"You're going to scrape the pattern off if you keep that up," Cacin remarked looking back at him from the platform.

Beau'nad shrugged. "Always do this."

"I've won her love, Beau'nad. And I won it by not raping her with Xingat."

A look of shock crossed Beau'nad's face. He dropped the brush into the dish beside the soap. Placing his hands under the running water he rinsed them thoroughly. He picked up a clean towel and started drying them before speaking.

"You broke with tradition?"

"In a big way. And I misled the Elite."

Beau'nad nodded.

"I would appreciate it if you didn't discuss this fact with anyone for the moment." Cacin looked out the banit'ye barrier at the blowing sand.

Rolling the towel into a ball, Beau'nad dropped it into a basket by the sink, then joined the King on the platform. The older gron pursed his lips together contemplatively. "I won't tell anyone. Perhaps you should keep it to yourself and never let the rest of the Elite know. It's none of our business anyway."

"Do you think so?"

"I do."

"Where is your bride being held?" Cacin asked, changing the subject. Both gron'ie had their hands clasped behind their backs now as they watched the sand shift beyond the barrier.

"Cruchton has arranged a holding area for the females."

"Women."

"Women. At Hanger Three, Lord. She's in that area."

"I suggest you take her to your quarters, confine her securely there at all times and TALK with her."

"TALK with her?"

"Talk. She must get to know you. Don't force her to do anything against her will outside of confining her. Is she Marked?"

"Not yet." He yawned.

"Do that before you sleep. It will begin the process of alteration. You should have done that already, Beau'nad."

"I'm too tired to think of these things."

Cacin clapped him on the shoulder. "I know. This Quest has been awful hasn't it?"

"Yes."

"Remain gentle at all times and monitor her mind continually. If you want to win her and not just dominate her, you'll have to be patient. Be prepared to give her time to accept you. Try to imagine how you would feel in a similar situation."

"I'd hate us," Beau'nad stated, looking into Cacin's eyes.

Cacin just nodded.

"I'll Mark her immediately Lord," he replied. "You should go to the Queen." Stepping from the platform, without being dismissed he transported from the room.

* * * *

The sound of the doors opening drew her attention. Hill'carn looked up from an examination of her hands which she'd been idly engaged in for several minutes.

"Don't read my mind," she said.

"Why not?" Cacin said as he crossed the floor. He was smiling broadly.

"I don't want you to." Sitting on the edge of the elevated examination bed in a pale blue silk gown that was open at the back, she looked defiantly into his green eyes.

"If I know how you're feeling I can help."

"I don't even know how I'm feeling so how can you?"

"Are you upset you're pregnant?"

"NO. Yes. OH, I don't know." She started crying and covered her face.

"Hill'carn, you're being so brave." He attempted to raise her face to look into it. She resisted.

"I know how hard this is for you. I couldn't endure what you're enduring. He pulled her close and hugged her. "Now you have to adjust to a massive hormonal change in your body."

She buried her face in his chest. He bent and kissed the top of her head.

"Now you'll go down to the Bride Quest and leave me alone," Hill'carn whined. She couldn't believe she'd said that. She sounded like a spoiled child. She wanted to scream and cry and throw herself on the floor.

"Not today, my love. I promise I'll stay with you today."

Hill'carn tried to regain control. She'd never experienced so many emotions all at once. She didn't know which one to hang onto for dear life.

Beyond the banit'ye barrier, the sand swirled on the planet's surface, touching silently against the thick transparent barrier.

* * * *

"Bopack, I want you to stay with her constantly, unless she orders you away." Cacin sat behind the massive desk in the outer room, toying with a pen. The light from a reading lamp spilled over his shoulder. Across the desk, papers sprawled at various levels of completion. He dropped the pen to the hard wooden surface and tidied some pages.

"Yes, Lord."

"I don't want her alone for long periods," he said, placing the papers in a wooden basket. "Being alone might cause her to sink into depression. She's very delicate right now. Her body is full of hormones she's never had before, or at least not at these levels. She's stuck on this miserable planet." He gestured to the blowing sand beyond the barrier and picked up the pen.

"May I make an observation, Lord?"

"You always may, Bopack."

"That's right. I'm always allowed to talk with you, to say what I really feel, aren't I? Although until this Bride Quest I didn't have access to you except at official functions."

"Has it been that bad for you?"

Bopack looked down at her hands, clasped in front of her. "I have managed."

"You women always do."

"What I wanted to say was this. You are becoming very casual lately."

He smiled and turned the pen in his massive hands. "Casual. Is that bad?"

"No." She smiled. "It's wonderful. I hope the other women who have been taken will affect the rest of the gron'ie like this. It is much easier to live with you when you are relaxed."

Cacin smiled. "We're always changed by the women we take, Bopack."

"My race didn't change you."

"You're mistaken. We learned patience from your race. That was no small feat for a Gron'dalin."

She smiled and a look of contentment crossed her face. "Thank you. That's a very kind thing to say."

"It's been patience that's won Hill'carn for me."

The old woman raised her eyebrows.

"It's true," Cacin said, dropping the pen on the desk with a clunk. "And you've affected us in other ways. Look around you. This is from your culture." He pointed to the coffee cup that sat at the edge of the desk. "And this." He touched a pen holder that sat beside it.

"Perhaps we HAVE affected you. I wish you'd been my son. I would have had something to be proud of then, in my old age."

"You have yourself to be proud of. You've always conducted yourself with dignity. You were a well-loved queen and you are still revered, Bopack."

"I am so glad my son did not bed Hill'carn." The old woman smiled again. "Is that treason to his memory?"

"No. You have always been forthright."

She nodded. "I understand you will be taking up your post shortly. Have you told your wife?"

"My wife. Yes. That has a nice sound to it. I've told her I'm going to be away. I haven't told her why, although she's capable now of taking that information from my mind. I don't think she has, though. It would only upset her to know. Please don't tell her that I'm attending to the Bride Quest unless she specifically asks. I'm going to Level Four immediately after the Arena."

"The Arena?"

"Cruchton has assembled the Elite in the Bay Arena. After I speak with them, Gradspin and I will go to Level Four for an indefinite period of time."

"You must be there for her, Bopack."

Chapter 24
Taking a Stand

"Why can't we go to Level Four?"

Bopack cleared her throat and raised thin gray eyebrows. Her huge eyes looked all the larger for the exercise. "Why don't you just take the information from my mind?" she said in a challenging tone, an offended tone.

"I know you don't want me doing that. And I know how awful it is to have your mind probed when you can't do anything to stop it."

"Well, thank you, Hill'carn," Bopack bowed slightly. "I appreciate the gesture. Frankly it was getting tedious having my mind violated every day."

"Violated. That's how I used to think of it," Hill'carn replied. "How many months ago did I feel like that? It seems like a lifetime has passed." Standing, she crossed the floor to look out the banit'ye barrier. She smoothed a wrinkle in the blue slacks she wore. "I'm sorry I was violating your privacy. Why didn't you say something?"

"The King said I mustn't stop you. You were learning to read minds."

Hill'carn glanced back at her. "I see. That is like him. You still haven't told me why we aren't allowed on Level Four."

"I don't wish to tell you." Bopack straightened defiantly.

"It has something to do with the Bride Quest, doesn't it? Is Cacin on Level Four?"

"You can't get information from me like that. I said I don't want to tell you."

"I don't really want the information. Not if it has to do with the Bride Quest." She frowned, her gaze locking with the Old One's

"You're wise Hill'carn." The old woman softened. "It's best to leave some things alone."

"Things I can't have any impact on I will certainly leave alone; at least for the time being." She looked back out the window. "There will come a time when there won't be anything I can't have an impact on," she promised.

The sand piled against the barrier in a small drift that came up as far as Hill'carn's waist. Behind her, Bopack stood silently watching her. If the old woman thought Hill'carn's last remark an odd one she made no indication of it.

"The Sentry will have to clear this away soon," Hill'carn said, pointing at the drift.

"Yes, they will likely attend to it soon."

"They've left it a long time. Where is everyone? The halls seem quieter than usual."

Bopack hesitated. "Perhaps it would be better to leave that question unanswered too."

"He's ordered them to start mating hasn't he?"

"Yes. How did you know?"

"I don't know. You don't have to read minds to know some things, Bopack." Hill'carn drew in a deep breath and exhaled through her nostrils. "Will it never be over?"

"No. Not as long as you live. Because you're Queen, you will be expected to see it happen every time it happens. You see, the King is expected to lead not only his own Bride Quest but ALL Quests. And, as each new group comes of age..."

"Well, the sooner this one is over the better," Hill'carn replied, cutting her new friend off while turning away from the barrier.

The room she stood in – her private room – was furnished in what Cacin called "Human" decor. Odd that she too would now think of it as Human decor. Always she had thought of things as 'Scandinavian' or 'Japanese' or 'British'. She looked around the room. Across the floor sat a beige couch and chair with delicate sandy colored pastel flowers in the background of the material. On either side of the long couch, an oak coffee table stood with small gold figurines of sailing men in raincoats with fish in hand. Above the couch, an oil painting of a ship on the ocean, tossing in a gale, drew her gaze.

Yes. She loved Earth still. Whatever humanness remained in her called out to her as she looked at this oil painting. How often had she wandered down to the ocean on a windy day when she was visiting friends in Sydney to watch waves crash on the beach? Gone. It was all gone now.

But something was in its place; a new life that she was going to shape to fit.

"Come on Bopack. Since I'm allowed to go anywhere except Level Four, take me to the holding areas," Hill'carn announced.

"Hill'carn!"

"Has he told you not to take me there too?"

"No but..."

"I can go alone if you have an aversion to going."

"Are you looking to quarrel with the King?"

"He hasn't said I shouldn't go there. He's said he wants to give me as much freedom as possible. He'll have nothing to be angry about."

"I don't think he wants you going to the holding areas."

"Sometimes what he wants and what I want will differ, Bopack."

"You don't know how unpleasant it is there. Women are crying, some are screaming, and the children..."

"Children? Children are being kept in these holding areas too?"

"They're not held there any longer. The King has ordered them taken to play areas during the day but they aren't separated from their mothers afterward unless the mothers are being mated."

"Oh my God!" Hill'carn clutched at her throat. "I think I could easily hate my new race."

"Don't put yourself through this. Let's go to Earth Garden Four."

"No. I'm going to the holding areas. Are you coming?"

Chapter 25
Taking the Bait

Hillary was lost to him. Had he succeeded in accepting that? No matter how hard he tried, Paul hadn't been able to locate her. But hope never completely died, did it? That was a human trait, if there was anything human left in him.

He thought he'd given up finding her a dozen times and found himself scanning for her the next day. He dreamed about her. Sometimes a woman would remind him of her with the turn of her head or a smile and he would feel that old familiar ache in his heart.

At those times a tremendous sense of guilt consumed him. He had failed her. He drew in a deep breath and shook his head in disgust. It was just that simple. He had failed her. Slamming the periscope shut he stiffened and rubbed the back of his neck.

"God I hate them."

"Boy, that's news," Duncan Stock replied, coming up behind him in the stark outer room. Tripping over a metal stacking chair, he lunged toward the wall Paul stood beside. Stopping himself from falling with the power of his mind, he steadied himself.

"I miss her so much, Duncan. You can't imagine how much I miss her," Paul said, ignoring Duncan's clumsy entry. Duncan's clumsiness was becoming legendary.

Duncan adjusted his coat and looked back at the offending chair with irritation. "You haven't been scanning for her again, I hope. You know how dangerous that is. They'll be looking for us now."

"No. I haven't scanned for three weeks. Not since Simon suggested they must have figured out that something funny was happening with Earth's defense. I haven't been above ground."

Duncan nodded approvingly.

"And now I'm afraid they're gone and I'll never see her again." He looked into Duncan's eyes, searching for something there, an answer perhaps.

Duncan raised his eyebrows then frowned slightly. Paul knew without reading his mind that Duncan understood. He had lost two sisters. That's why they'd chosen him for the program. He had no other family but the two sisters the Gron'dalins had taken, right out from under his nose. He was lucky he'd lived through the capture of his sisters. Many did not.

"Well, what do you think?" Duncan finally said, his breath hanging on the frigid air like smoke.

"About what?"

"Have they called it off? Have they left?"

The Gron'dalin attack had ceased days earlier. No one had been taken for almost a week.

"Not likely. I don't know what they're up to. Maybe they're waiting for reinforcements."

"Maybe they've got all the women they need. It's been six days since anyone was taken."

"What? You think they have enough with a few hundred thousand?" Paul patted his arms briskly in the cold room. "I doubt that's all they want. Hillary said they were going to take all the women."

"Maybe she was mistaken."

Paul shrugged and turned away from the periscope. "Well, there's only one way to find out, I suppose."

"I'll go," Duncan volunteered. Sincerity peppered his voice. He was brave. Paul avoided calling him a brave MAN because he wasn't that any longer. The bravery stayed intact but not the manhood. Paul scanned the other Alterin's scaled face.

"No you won't. If anyone is going to get it in the neck it's going to be me." He sighed.

"You just want to scan for Hillary again." Duncan smiled mischievously at Paul.

"No. I just want to get out in the sunlight again." He gestured to the gray concrete walls around him. They both laughed.

"I knew you were going up the minute I saw you come in here."

"You were right."

Paul swung the door of the cellar open. Behind him, past the closed door to the interior Duncan had just come through, the recently excavated rooms were packed with soldiers and anywhere up to four hundred frightened women.

A cold blast of air entered the small outer room Paul and Duncan stood in, hit them with a force that only winter in New England could summon.

"What day is it?" he asked Duncan.

Duncan shrugged, shivering. "I don't know. Sometime in early December? I'm not the best person to ask."

"There'll be snow on the ground."

"Possibly. Christmas is coming."

"It would be nice to go home for Christmas, wouldn't it?"

"Ya, for some of us," Duncan replied, sighing.

"I'm alone too," Paul remarked. "If they've gone, why don't you come home with me and we'll wallow in self-pity together over the holiday?"

Duncan laughed. "Sounds good."

"If this is a trap..." Paul continued more seriously. He let the sentence dangle there without an ending.

Duncan nodded and slapped Paul on one shoulder. Then he said, "This is the deepest Underground in the Eastern Grid. I'll bet that's why it hasn't been located. There's one large one on the west coast that has never been discovered either," Duncan added, building up to his point. "Don't give us away."

Paul sighed. "I'll take the High Road out to Hooligan's. That's a good mile away. Then I'll come up through that empty shelter out there."

Duncan nodded approval. "It's as empty as a shelter full of corpses can be."

"Ya. It's going to be fun going through there," he remarked sarcastically. "But we can't stay down here forever, Duncan."

With that he started down the steps that lead to the underground tunnel they called the High Road.

* * * *

Winter pressed the Eastern seaboard with cold crisp air as he stepped out into daylight again. Like waking from a nightmare where he'd been sealed in a tomb or fallen into a well or mine shaft, he welcomed the wind brushing against his face. Light touched him gently. Paul turned his eyes toward the sun, closing them, feeling the warmth on his lids. Thank God it wasn't cloudy!

The ground – bare except for a few corpses that littered the entrance to the shelter and sprawled along the path – crunched beneath his feet. Behind him, the stench of rotting corpses lingered on the frozen earth. Despite the warmth of the sun, the wind came in from the north, nipping with the threat of snow.

Ordinarily it would have snowed already in New Hampshire. Perhaps it had snowed and melted. Paul stepped out into the field that fell away in front of him.

Tired and dirty, he immediately scanned for Hillary's mind.

Nothing. Finding no trace of her, he sighed, fighting disappointment.

"No one – no creature, no man, no alien, will ever force me below ground again," he stated with resolve. "No one is ever going to take the sun away from me again. If they come back," he said like a man in a dream, like reading lines in a school play, "We'll board a transport portraying images of human females." His words echoed in his mind. "There are five of us! We can do it," he whispered to the frozen field. A feeling of foreboding raked over him. He pushed it away, or something did.

"We can blow the hell out of wherever the Gron'dalins have taken the women. We can destroy their base." A cold wind rustled his shoulder length hair. He stared across the field to the horizon.

"Why didn't we think of concealing ourselves on a shuttle earlier, before the loss of so many lives?" He looked back at the entrance to the shelter. "And the kidnapping of so many women. Why?" Paul shuddered and fought to get a grip on a thought that teased at the corner of his consciousness. It flitted through his mind like a small sparrow through the branches of a maple tree. Failing to catch it he aborted the effort and continued to look out across the field.

* * * *

"Good work, Gradspin," Cacin said clapping the Elder on the back as he sent a message to Orgone and Cruchton by mind transfer.

"The fact that this Alterin possesses superior mind powers to our Nationals worries me, My Lord," the old gron confided as he rose from the comfortable couch in the recreation room. He stretched his old bones. Light played on the wrinkled scales around his eyes.

"Why?" Cacin asked, rising from the high back chair he'd been sitting in for six hours straight.

"I don't know exactly. The Nationals can't portray images or decipher them. Never in our history has any species possessed mind powers that could threaten our race."

"You think they could threaten our race?"

"I know it."

"There are only five of them. They aren't a threat yet. And we'll soon find out if they're able to mate with Human women and what the outcome of that kind of union would be." He stretched the way Gradspin was stretching, trying to work out the kinks. "If they aren't able, as Beau'nad hopes, we have no worries. These five will live out their lives and die."

Cacin stretched. "Lord Elder, we've been closed in Far End too long. Let's go down to Colony." He rubbed his tired eyes. "I'm exhausted," he said.

"So am I," the old gron confided.

"I think I'll sleep for a week," Cacin remarked, laughing as he started toward the door."

Gradspin chuckled. "I haven't gone on a marathon like this in over two hundred years." He started following the King out of the comfortable room.

"I've never gone on one. I hope I don't have to go on one again."

"I can almost guarantee you'll have to do it again. And it will probably be on a Bride Quest."

"Well, I'll worry about that when I come to it. But congratulations. Placing a thought smoothly in an Alterin mind without their knowledge is a difficult task."

"Without guidance in finding that one particular Alterin mind, I couldn't have done it. And without your linkup," Gradspin commented as they walked toward the huge metal doors, "it would have been impossible." The old gron coughed. "You cleared his mind beautifully, My Lord. Artfully."

Cacin threw an arm around the Gradspin's shoulders. "Thank you. We'll leave the rest to Cruchton now. Let's go and sleep."

"Aw. Glorious sleep," the old gron said, smiling broadly.

Cacin released the old gron's shoulders and physically opened the door rather than using his tired mind on it. The door swung shut behind them as they walked down the hall.

"The battle will also proceed more smoothly with relieved Elite," Cacin said as they walked along together.

"You were wise to allow the mating."

"Women should be immediately bedded as we take them from now on," Cacin said. Gradspin staggered and Cacin steadied him. "Are you alright?"

Gradspin nodded.

"Can I be of assistance?" Orgone asked this as he approached from the bank of elevators.

"No. Thank you Orgone, I'm fine," Gradspin said. "Just a little tired. I'm getting too old for marathons. If we need any more on this Quest, you'll have to do it. You're up to it."

Orgone just nodded at the old gron. "The situation among the Elite without mates is pressing," he said to Cacin, coming right to the point.

"You don't look well yourself, Orgone. Have you mated?"

"No. As I told you I am waiting for her to accept me. But I'm fine."

"I don't think so. If Beau'nad gives me a poor report about you, I'll demand that you mate."

"Give me a chance to win her, Lord."

Cacin nodded. "I've given you almost a week. If Beau'nad says you are fit, okay." They continued down the hall to the elevators.

"The Nationals are complaining."

"Is it urgent?"

"They are apparently becoming ill from holding back."

"This should put an end to debates over whether or not we must mate," Cacin asserted. "Do I need to contact them before I sleep?"

"No. It's not that important."

"You contact them then, Orgone."

"Me?"

"Yes you. It's time you learned some diplomacy," Cacin said sternly. "Tell them the bait has been taken and we will resume the Quest shortly. The Elite will be finished sooner than I had anticipated."

"I trust you will be leading the Quest?" Gradspin asked.

"I will. With the help of a new and invigorated Cruchton," Cacin replied, stepping into the lift.

"Then the Queen IS pregnant," Orgone said, smiling broadly. "There was speculation she was; that you were beginning this endeavor after learning of her pregnancy."

"It was confirmed the day before I pulled the Elite back from battle," Cacin admitted.

Orgone embraced him warmly. "Congratulations!"

Cacin smiled weakly. "How many females are left to capture, Orgone?"

"A hundred thousand or so for the Elite," Orgone replied. "All of them are located in the advanced nations on the planet. All of them are hidden below ground or they would be in our possession already." The lift stopped on the ground level. Cruchton was waiting to greet them.

"Congratulations on contacting the Alterin." He bowed as the King stepped from the lift.

"Thank you, Cruchton."

"And the Queen is pregnant, Cruchton," Orgone announced.

Cruchton brightened visibly. "Congratulations!" He slapped the King on the shoulder warmly. Then a look of shock crossed his face at his indiscretion in touching the King. "Sorry, Lord."

Cacin smiled and nodded. "No harm done. Walk with us," he said to Cruchton. "I'm told by Orgone you've mated."

"That's correct.

"Did all go well?"

"I was forced to use Xingat."

"I'm sorry to hear that." Cacin acknowledged several gron'ie that were passing in the hall.

"I'm prepared to launch at dawn, Lord, to capture the Alterin."

"Good. I won't be ready for the capture. I expect to sleep all day. I will join you in battle the following day," he said.

"The Quest will be far easier with the removal of Paul Muntz and the Alterin," Cruchton confided. "It will be far easier with you leading."

"Wait until the Alterin meet in the same location. They'll do that soon. We've planted that seed too. Then, set down in the area nearest them. They will come to you. Perhaps to make it look more legitimate, you should capture some women. These Alterin aren't stupid."

They walked down the broad corridor on Level One, all four abreast. Shoulder to shoulder they made a formidable wall. Gron'ie passed on either side and nodded.

Cacin turned to Orgone and spoke in a low tone. "Orgone I'll sleep in your quarters. I'm in a poor humor and I don't want to see Hill'carn like this. How is Hill'carn?"

"There is something you should know."

"What?"

"Hill'carn has been visiting some of the holding areas in your absence."

"What? How could you let her go there? Where was Bopack while this was going on?"

Cruchton and Gradspin looked away uneasily.

"Bopack was with her."

"I beg your pardon?"

"She had no choice. You didn't tell Hill'carn not to go there and she asked Bopack to accompany her."

"I hope you managed the children properly while the mothers were being taken for mating. That would upset her terribly."

"As best we could."

"I'm glad I've decided to sleep in your quarters before seeing Hill'carn. I can imagine how upset she will be about this."

On reaching Orgone's chambers, Cacin and Orgone stepped through the door and the King bowed to Gradspin and Cruchton.

"Until tomorrow, Gradspin, Cruchton."

They bowed back. "Until then, Lord."

The door swished closed behind them. "San'dare'a is confined in these rooms, Lord." Orgone indicated rooms on his right.

"Call me Cacin when we are in private."

"Yes, Lord."

Cacin scowled at him for forgetting so soon. "That is your wife's name?"

"It is."

"I've heard her name before but I'd forgotten it. These have been difficult times."

"That they have. Would you be comfortable in here?" Orgone indicated the large room at the back of his chambers furnished with a huge bed and sitting area. Intended as the master bedroom it spread the whole length of Orgone's suites.

"That will be fine, Orgone."

"So," Orgone said. "We are finally finished with that interfering Paul Muntz."

Cacin glanced at his friend. "Orgone, Gradspin has informed me that his study of Human expressions reveals a wide variety of useful terms and I think one of those is applicable here. It's never over until it's over. Until I have Paul Muntz and the others securely stored away in detention, I won't believe we're finished with them."

Soft lighting illuminated the huge bed. Fully clothed, Cacin fell onto it without even turning the lights off.

* * * *

Paul and the four other men who had been injected with Hillary's blood crossed the wide expanse between the aircraft and the bunker where Cahill and a team of high-ranked military currently coordinated the North American defense. Simon affectionately called their defense location The Travelling Road Show. The underground roads constructed on an ongoing basis at Paul's instruction supplied them with a secure and clandestine method of travel. They were never in one place longer than a few days.

Paul walked over frost-covered brown grass that would have been knee high if the rain and wind hadn't knocked most of it flat. No farmers had gathered the hay this year; no cows were waiting patiently in their stalls to be milked or fed.

"This should have been cut for hay," Paul said to Duncan.

"How will the cattle survive the winter?" Duncan replied.

"Are there any left to survive it? I haven't seen any."

Duncan grimaced and shrugged at him. "We're in deep shit. How will we survive the winter without food?"

Scattered clumps of grass still defied the elements, standing erect in the first rays of sunlight that crept over the horizon.

The grass crunched beneath his feet. Everywhere, life quietly anticipated winter. So did Paul. He could smell it. He could smell the cold. December's grass had no odor from beneath the frost cover as it waited for the snows to come. The cold wind smelled of snow. Every breath released from his lungs hovered on the frigid air expectantly as he walked toward the bunker with Duncan at his side.

Nothing in the field moved but the large alien-looking men who walked across the frozen ground in steady progression. Paul spearheaded the line of Alterin with Duncan at his side. The others followed in a group of three behind them.

He glanced across the flat terrain at one of Earth's famous aboveground battle sites. The first of the ground battles had taken place here. The remains of bodies still cluttered the ground amid tanks and artillery. Partially decomposed; partially eaten by scavengers, the corpses were horrible in their defeat. Mercifully, the wind carried any smell off the bodies and away from them. At times like these it was merciful to be upwind.

"What is so compelling that we travelled here by air?" Duncan asked. "Why did we abandon the underground roads?"

Paul shrugged. "Something's wrong here, Duncan." He glanced over his shoulder.

"What?"

"We shouldn't be feeling so cocky."

"Relax, you two. They're gone," Peter admonished jovially from behind.

Paul looked back at the battlefield, suspended in the pre-dawn light like a bad dream. The face of the Earth, as scarred as its guts, cried out for justice.

The Gron'dalin, accustomed to laying down the ground rules in these battles, had called all the shots. Thrown off when the rules of engagement changed at this battle site; when the humans went on the offensive; they hadn't fared as well.

Humans had killed hundreds of the giant aliens since going "aggressive" as Duncan called it. But too many humans died in these first melees, killing too few Gron'dalins.

"We took out close to two hundred of the bastards in that battle," Pete remarked proudly, seeing where Paul was looking.

"Ya," Paul replied quietly. "But how many did we lose?" He nodded toward a pile of frozen bodies.

A kind of trench warfare, fed by the underground roads, had been crafted by the five Alterin. They located a transport as it landed and travelled as near as possible accompanied by seasoned soldiers who had engaged the enemy dozens, if not hundreds of times. Using the underground road system they dug themselves out and laid in wait.

Ambush. A simple concept used by defending armies throughout history was embraced once again on Earth.

They hid their thoughts by staying just below ground. There was an art to staying out of mind-scan reach. They learned it; studied it with resolve; committed to memory the need to keep the deadening earth between them and the aliens who searched for them daily.

Then, as the aliens approached their target, a group of Earth's women who had not yet been cloistered away in the underground cities that were springing up all over the United States, the ambushers attacked the Gron'dalins.

Now in the distance, Paul could see the charred remains of a farm house, burned out trees and a number of heavy weapons left abandoned on the surface. No one dared reclaim them, yet here he was walking across a field, above ground for any Gron'dalin to probe. He frowned at Duncan.

"I don't like this. Something's wrong. Something I can't get my mind around."

"We've got a fallback position," Duncan said reassuringly. "We can't stay below ground forever." A pilot, he more than any of the others suffered from claustrophobia.

"Yes. I know. So here we are as bold as brass."

Paul looked at the scene of the old battle, remembering what Simon Cahill had said. Eight hundred soldiers died here. The women were freed. They all saw that as a huge victory.

They fled across the fields.

In his mind, Paul could practically see them running, stumbling, some crying, others too determined to get away over the flat land with its green grass swaying in the breeze. The grass hadn't been brown when it happened. This battle happened on the last day of September with the sun shining and full of promise.

Paul remembered the battle well. This confrontation had claimed the life of one of their own, an Alterin nicknamed Big Red for his height and hair color.

The women had run in all directions, flattening the grass as they ran. He could see areas ahead where the grass, trampled smooth, lay entirely level. The women had been told to scatter if they were freed at a transport and these women had done that. Some of those women were still free. Some had been captured later in other, less successful fights.

On the odd occasion now, like this one, a group of women did escape. More frequently, women and girls were caught in the crossfire. Occasionally whole transports were accidentally destroyed. Once, a transport was deliberately destroyed by the women who'd been captured. Those women would live on in human history forever, if the race continued. Yes, Paul thought looking at the old battle scene, if the race continued.

Apparently the Gron'dalins hadn't thought it was important to search the women's minds before abducting them. Paul guessed they searched them after that for plots. They searched them physically now to find hidden weapons after one woman who had been taken hid her mind successfully from their mind probe until it was too late. She'd killed three aliens before escaping. She was later captured through a concerted effort on the part of about fifteen Gron'dalins.

"I smell an ambush," Paul whispered.

Duncan darted a glance over one shoulder. "How? How do you smell it?"

"I don't know. Some part of my subconscious mind I guess. You know how some women have a sixth sense?"

"Ya." Duncan cast a quick glance this way and that. "We can't hide out forever waiting for them to come back though, hiding like scared rabbits. It's been a week."

"Better scared rabbits than dead fools."

"I hope you're wrong."

"Me too."

Chapter 26
Altercations

Hill'carn waited impatiently for Cacin's arrival, pacing the floor from the desk to the banit'ye barrier with her arms folded. The blue cotton blouse she wore fell loosely around her slim body, concealing small shapely breasts and a tiny waist that had expanded an inch or two in past weeks. The blouse trailed out over her slacks and the tiny bulge that pushed out her abdomen.

At the steps to the viewing platform she halted, turned around angrily, and returned to the desk. Her shoes clacked out a steady rhythm on the tiled floor. Fury raged behind her brown eyes like a violent prairie thunderstorm as she leaned back toward the banit'ye barrier.

"Animals!" she said with disgust.

"Animals!"

* * * *

On rising, Cacin stripped off his clothes. Sleeping in them for twelve hours hadn't improved their condition much, he noticed, dropping them in a heap on the floor at the foot of the bed. Quickly crossing the bedroom he slipped into the shower and lathered up.

Stepping from the bathroom with a towel wrapped around his waist, he greeted Orgone, who came in as the water turned off.

"She's in a very bad mood," Orgone said.

"Hill'carn?" Cacin asked, a slight irritation in his voice. Orgone nodded. "HOW bad is VERY bad?"

"She's in a fury."

"Hill'carn? In a rage?"

"Yes."

"I know she has a temper but..."

"Lord, this is more than a temper. You'd better prepare yourself for the worst."

Cacin strode from the bathroom. He sighed and set his jaw then threw the towel on the unmade bed and stood naked before

Orgone. His broad scaled chest reflected the overhead light. "And what precisely has brought this on?" he asked, slipping into undergarments and pulling on black slacks that Orgone had laid out for him. He hitched them up at the waist and zipped them. "The children?"

"The mating."

"What do you mean, the mating? She knew we were taking these women for that purpose."

"She's upset that most of them were drugged and raped."

"Oh damn!"

Orgone looked at him in shock.

"That's an Earth expression, Orgone," Cacin explained.

"I know. I've studied the language too," the young gron replied. Dark circles highlighted his green eyes.

"I gave you instructions to protect the Queen in my absence. You should have interfered with her plans to go to the holding area. That's what has done this!"

"The holding area isn't what spawned this anger. She's been reading minds and has learned about the drugging.

"Great! I told everyone to guard information from her." He pulled on the shirt Orgone handed him, buttoning it quickly.

"She's able to read guarded thoughts now, it appears."

Cacin glared at him with disbelief. "This can't be. We can't even read guarded thoughts most of the time."

"Well, SHE can. Besides, even if she didn't obtain the information that way, and I'm almost certain she did, you gave her permission to go anywhere in Colony. I couldn't stop her from going to the holding areas."

"You take me too literally, Orgone."

"How else am I supposed to take you? You are the King." Orgone crossed the floor to open the curtains that were drawn over the banit'ye barrier. Light spilled into the room, falling across the unmade bed. "Although there's no real danger in Colony, I accessed her mind. That's my privilege as protector, but I can't make rules for her, Lord."

"Never mind, Orgone. You did your best."

"I asked her not to go back a second time but Hill'carn has been visiting the females on a daily basis. When the mating began, females were dragged from the holding area. When the Queen went there, of course she witnessed one of them being dragged away. That prompted her to scan the minds of the Elite and since you told me never to stop her from reading minds..."

"I don't want to hear any more." Cacin was hurriedly tucking his shirt into his pants. "You did your best." He slipped the belt through the loops and fastened it. "Her ability to read minds has complicated the matter hasn't it?"

"That is an understatement. She also learned about the emotional turmoil these women are facing, by reading their minds."

"She's reading their minds too?"

"Yes. Easily."

"I shouldn't be angry with her."

"But you are?" Orgone asked, looking out the barrier at the moving tide of sand. Outside, several gron'ie shoveled sand away from the base of the banit'ye barrier.

"Yes. I don't know why exactly. I just am. I'm glad I stopped here for sleep before going home. I'm sure we would have fought about this. What are those gron'ie doing out there?" Surrounded by reflective barriers put up by their minds, four huge Sentry shoveled sand relentlessly. "They could as easily move that sand with their minds from this side of the barrier. It's only sand." Cacin frowned at them.

"They're trying to get away from their wives."

"Oh Gods! What have we got ourselves into?"

"What indeed," Orgone complained. "Are you going to fight with Hill'carn?"

"I'll try not to." He drew in a deep breath. "Well, I guess I should get this over with." Looking away from the four Sentry he walked toward the door.

* * * *

The crowded hall resonated with conversation as he closed on his rooms, not far from Orgone's. Gron'ie greeted him as he passed, congratulating him on the Queen's pregnancy, on his success with the Alterin. A hum of activity outside the bank of elevators greeted him. He passed, nodding and hailing the group assembled there.

Outside his rooms he paused to collect his thoughts. Clearing his throat he commanded the door to open. As it slid open he stepped through, calling to his wife.

"I'm back," he said to Hill'carn who remained staring out the banit'ye barrier at the planet that lay beyond.

She spun around, arms stiff across her chest, her jaw set as thoroughly as his. Without greeting him she spoke in an accusatory tone. "Where have you been for the past week?"

"Coordinating the Bride Quest," he answered, "As I told you I must."

"I know you've been coordinating the Bride Quest. I also know you've been doing it from Level Four. That isn't what I meant. Cacin, in your absence..." she began.

"They were acting on my orders." Cacin stated coldly as he stepped further into the room. The doors closed behind him.

Hill'carn glared at him. "You ordered them to rape those women?"

"I ordered them to commence copulation. If force was necessary..."

"Rape is never necessary!"

"We are fighting a war! There's no time for civility, even when there's the possibility of acceptance by these females."

"Females? Are we females again?"

"Women. I'm sorry." He sighed. "You've been the lucky one, Hill'carn."

"You would have eventually raped me too, wouldn't you?"

Cacin's eyes flashed menacingly. He stepped forward and towered over her, looking straight into her eyes. She saw him gather himself. Suddenly he moved away from her to the banit'ye barrier. Outside, the red sand moved relentlessly. At the far corner of his vision he saw the Sentry team rounding the dome toward him. For no explicable reason this angered him further.

"I can't lie to you. After seeing the state my gron'ie were in, I don't believe I would have been able to remain celibate. I didn't know that at the time, though," he added, turning to point a finger at her. Lowering his hand he added, "That's the truth, Hill'carn."

He was more composed as he turned back to face her. "I didn't know the effects celibacy would have on us when I made that promise to you. I don't believe I would have allowed myself to die. And that would eventually have happened if I hadn't mated." Cacin sighed audibly and continued more quietly. His voice had been raised slightly but now it rang with calm as it usually did. "I would have tried my best, Hill'carn."

She looked down at the floor, away from his penetrating eyes.

"I wish it weren't this way. The Elders are right. The Zad are right. We die if we don't mate. I may have to force Orgone to mate before long if his bride will not agree. He's just stubborn enough to refuse."

"Well, they didn't need to..."

Cacin cut off her complaint. "We are in the midst of a very difficult campaign!" He spoke forcefully but without yelling. "This is the most difficult campaign we have ever waged. They were under instruction to mate before my return. If they chose to drug their brides then that was their choice."

"I'm glad someone has a choice in this society," Hill'carn said bitterly.

"I'm sorry it has to be this way."

"I don't believe it does. If you can develop ways to drug women so they remember nothing of a rape, you can develop ways to medically treat the gron'ie experiencing discomfort at not mating." She shook her head in disgust. "You just haven't felt that was necessary."

"This is more than discomfort I'm speaking of Hill'carn. And I'm not a scientist. I don't know what's been tried and what hasn't. We spend most of our time and energy on securing brides. As I told you, there have been few scientific breakthroughs since this curse began."

"Oh that's convenient."

He ignored the sarcasm. "All I know is that these gron'ie were aware that the war would resume at anytime and as many of them as possible should be mated before that happened. They had to make the choice on how to proceed under those circumstances." Cacin turned to the huge window again to look out at Xanthe, where the red sands of Mars still danced unceasingly.

"This sight affects me the same way the winds of Ranat do in storm season." He gestured to the blowing sand. "It's tiring. At least Ranat's winds don't always blow. Damn Orgone anyway for making this colony entirely banit'ye. There's nowhere I can escape it."

Hill'carn looked away from him. How had she thought to have any influence over him? How could she approach him about returning the girl children to Earth now?

"Did you order Zadanin to rape Fra'non without the drug?"

Cacin spun to look at her. "Is that what he did?"

"Yes."

"I will deal with Zadanin. I'm sorry he chose to do that," he said quietly. "But as for the others, there's nothing more important to any race than the preservation of the species, Hill'carn. That's what this Quest is all about. I won't apologize for their actions. We do what we must to survive. They were acting under orders."

Chapter 27
The Snare is Sprung

Only hours after Paul's arrival at the command bunker, the first Gron'dalin transport in over a week , touched down lightly on Earth's frozen soil. Landing only a few miles from where Paul and the others conferred with Simon Cahill, huge doors slid open to release twelve Gron'dalin invaders. Reports flashed in from all over the Eastern seaboard. The battle had resumed.

"Something's wrong, Duncan. That's what I'm saying," Paul said, sitting back in his chair. He threw the pencil he was writing with onto the long wooden table.

"Look, we have a fallback plan, Paul."

"I don't know, Duncan. I think Paul's right. It's just too convenient that all of you are in the same place at the same time when it starts up again," Simon Cahill said. "And look at where they've landed. In your backyard."

"Look, Simon, it makes perfect sense for us to go," Duncan argued. "We project images of women and board the shuttle. They won't know we're there. If they do there's always plan-B." He smiled mischievously before continuing. "But we'll make it to Mars. I know we will. Once on Mars we blow the hell out of them. We aren't coming back. We all know that." He looked around at the other Alterin who sat around the table in silence. "But that's the price we have to pay to get rid of these bastards."

"I don't like it," Paul re-iterated.

"Neither do I," Duncan said, misinterpreting Paul's statement.

"There's something I'm missing, Duncan," Paul insisted, not clarifying what the meaning of his statement was. "Something I can't get my mind around. It feels like walking into an ambush."

"Oh come on, Paul," Duncan said with exasperation.

"Duncan, we wouldn't have a chance without you," Cahill pointed out.

"You don't have a chance with us," the Alterin replied.

"Duncan is right," Pete conceded. Having remained silent throughout the discussion he added his opinion now. "We have to go. Ambush or no, we have to go. It might backfire in their faces if it is an ambush, but we have to try something different. It's only a matter of time before they get all of Earth's women."

"I don't like it," Cahill said. Losing the support of yet another Alterin weakened his resolve.

Duncan nodded and smiled at his victory.

Paul nodded agreement reluctantly. "They're going to win if we don't go, Simon. Duncan is right. It IS just a matter of time."

"Wake up and smell the roses," Duncan interjected.

"These guys are playing for keeps and it's Earth's women they're keeping," Paul continued. "By fighting the way we are, all we're doing is delaying the inevitable."

Pete started jabbing the air with a finger as he spoke. "I say Duncan's right. We have to take this chance, ambush or no ambush. If it's an ambush you're no worse off than you were before. It may happen faster, that's all. If we can't affect some change in events from up there, that is."

"If you live to get up there," Cahill replied.

"We've given you everything we have to offer," Paul continued. "And it hasn't been good enough. There isn't anything more we can do down here. There are too many of them. If this is a trap maybe we can turn it back on them."

"Paul's right," Peter said. "Let's go. Let's do it."

"Now, Duncan added, "instead of taking a few women from each compound they enter, they take them all. They've changed their tactics to accommodate ours. If this is an ambush, if they've planted something in our brains, it might just blow up in their faces. We've been developing our mental abilities." He shrugged. "Who knows? They have no idea how well we use our minds and maybe we use them well enough to beat them."

"What do you mean, beat them? Cahill asked "You've already said there are too many of them. You're going to tell me it's going to make a difference if you're on Mars? What if they just kill you right here on Earth? What if you never make it to Mars?" He threw down the pen he'd been tapping on the long table the way Paul had abandoned his pencil earlier.

"That's a chance we have to take," Paul replied. "Besides these aliens are duty bound. Hillary told us months ago before they arrived that she wasn't raped by the thing that came for her because it was duty bound. Maybe something will keep them from killing us outright." He shrugged. "I'm willing to take the chance. We aren't doing any good here."

"I don't know," Simon said.

"And if it's not an ambush," Duncan continued, "We'll finish the bastards once and for all." He patted the ammunition pouch filled with high explosives slung over his shoulder. A hum of agreement went up among the other Alterin.

"Alright. Go ahead," Cahill said with resignation.

"Simon, as soon as we leave, move your command centre just in case," Paul said.

"Okay, good precautionary move. I hope you're right about doing this Paul."

"We're right," Paul answered. "It's Earth's only hope. We have to be right."

* * * *

Guarding their minds, Paul Muntz and the other four Alterin joined the women being corralled and forced aboard the transport. Everywhere, women cried, screamed, begged not to be taken. General pandemonium at the doors of the shuttle where the Gron'dalin invaders finally released the grip they had on the minds of the captured women enabled Paul and the others to slip aboard unnoticed.

The five Alterin, portraying images of women, sat silently watching the bedlam, interlopers in a world of pain.

Paul cautiously held the MP5 rifle hidden behind the projected vision. Beads of sweat dotted his forehead, drenched his hands as he sat ramrod straight in the transport chaos. Precariously held in those sweaty palms, the gun threatened to slip to the transport's deck. He adjusted his hold on the weapon and ran his tongue over his lips. As terrified as he'd been when he attacked Kagoule, Paul struggled to control trembling hands. Glancing at the smallest of the Gron'dalins who stood by the transport door in an authoritative manner, he sized it up. That one was in charge, no question of it.

"Cruchton, you may throw the latch, we are secure for lift," one of the Gron'dalins suddenly called from the door that lead to what Paul thought must be the control room.

The screaming rose to an unbearable pitch with this announcement given in English. Some women threw themselves to the floor, some rushed the Gron'dalin at the door, only to be thrown back by the power of its mind.

The one addressed as Cruchton yelled back over the bedlam. "Thank you, Fa'pal." It turned to close the doors.

Polite. What a contradictory bunch, Duncan thought to Paul.

Why are they talking? They don't need to talk. And why in English? Everything they need to say could be said through mind transfer more easily than bellowing across the transport with the kind of mayhem that's going on in here, Paul thought back, looking around at the screaming women.

Paul's heart sank as he suddenly knew the Gron'dalins were speaking for their benefit. Duncan! Can you read any of their minds?

NO.

I've been trying to read their minds since we joined the women. I can't pick up anything.

Me neither.

They're guarding their thoughts. Why would they do that unless they knew we were here?

The smallest Gron'dalin sealed the compartment and Paul knew their fate was sealed with it. General pandemonium continued around him. Women cried and clung to each other now that the doors were closed. Some shrieked in terror. Others screamed and tore their hair now that the mind control that forced them to walk to the transport had been lifted. A few women continued to attack the invaders. One in particular flew through the air at Cruchton a second time, striking it on the face. Finally, gripped by the arm and forced back to her seat, she swore repeatedly at it.

On letting go of the woman, the alien glanced at Paul.

Oh Shit, Duncan, Paul thought. We've been had. Guard your mind more carefully.

How do they know we're here? How for Christ's sake?

I don't know, but it knows we're here. Alert the others. We're attacking on my order, he said. Sweat dripped off his chin. Around him the women were slowly falling silent. Whimpers of fear replaced the screaming but the crying continued.

Cruchton moved slowly in Paul's direction, examining women as it went. Was it trying to conceal its advance? Lifting their faces up towards its own face, as though inspecting them, it worked its way over to Paul.

It's coming, Duncan.

Ya. I see what you mean. Duncan thought back with resignation.

Are you ready? Paul asked.

As ready as I'll ever be.

Paul launched himself from the bench with a scream, the MP5 coming up to point at the large Gron'dalin chest that closed on him. He heard similar shrieks from the other Alterin scattered among the women.

The barrel of his weapon thrust up toward the ceiling by the creature's mind, Paul struggled to keep the rifle in his grasp.

"Get down!" he screamed to the women, dropping his disguise. "Ambush!"

Bullets from Paul's weapon sprayed the roof of the transport. The women began screaming, but not as they had previously. Some women held their heads; some fell to the floor as instructed. The sound of gunfire mingled with the screams of terrified women to rip through the compartment. Slammed with a mind blow, Paul crashed against the wall with enough force to stun him. The gun flew from his hands, sailed through the air and crashed with a clatter on the back row of empty metal seats.

Bastard! He thought, gasping for air.

You would do the same, it thought back to him, gripping his mind.

The battle was over!

Four gron'ie and six women lay dead. The Alterin were all alive.

Rising, the creature called Cruchton pushed off a woman who decided to assist in the attack. She had thrown herself on it as soon as it hit the floor and bit it repeatedly. Now as she fell to the metal floor in a heap, the creature rose. She attacked its legs. Suddenly her head jerked back involuntarily, her features locked in a grip of agony. Paul grimaced, guessing at her suffering as pain raked her mind.

"You will come this way," the creature said to Paul. "We have arranged special accommodations for your trip to Mars."

Fuck you, Paul thought.

Lifting Paul from the floor with the power of its mind, it motioned to one of the other Gron'dalins to open the door between the compartments.

* * * *

Cacin waited behind the barrier as the shuttle arrived from Earth. As the huge outer cargo bay doors closed, he stepped around the banit'ye. The floor-length silver cape of the Zi ancestry swept out around him as the doors to the transport opened. The women immediately began their trek to the holding areas, herded by the gron'ie.

Cacin stood to one side as they passed. Some cried, other's were silent and staring. When the brides and two small children that had been brought with them disappeared out of sight, the five Alterin emerged from the transport.

Instructed to deal with them physically as much as possible to avoid teaching the Alterin any further use of their minds, Cruchton descended the ramp, closely following the leader.

On seeing Cacin, Paul immediately attacked with his mind. The King went crashing backwards into a transport docked behind it. Using the same technique that had been used on him inside the craft, Paul lifted the creature again and slammed it on its back.

You learn fast, Cacin thought.

"My Lord!" Cruchton yelled in astonishment, moving to protect the King.

Paul felt the lead creature trying to grip his mind. He fought it.

The rest of the Alterin lashed out with their minds, almost as skillfully as the Gron'dalins, shattering equipment, overturning small craft, destroying everything in their path.

Paul focused his attack on the creature he remembered from the one short contact they'd had in his basement the night Hillary was abducted.

Don't interfere, Cacin instructed Cruchton, I'll handle this one myself. You attend to the others.

Cacin skillfully slammed Paul against a shuttle, deflecting the mind surge that Paul directed at him, then pulled himself up with obvious pain to a standing position as Paul collected himself from his own prone position.

You are greatly disadvantaged in this fight because this form of combat is new to you, Cacin thought.

Paul directed a stream of mind energy at his opponent. Cacin deflected it again. Standing near the ship they had travelled in, Paul tried again. Cacin deflected and attacked him again.

As the alien struck, Paul was lifted off the ground and flew across the room, landing in a pile of crates. His crumpled body crashed to the floor. On trying to rise he found he couldn't. Held in a mind grip so powerful he could barely breathe, Paul fell into unconsciousness.

* * * *

Cacin released Paul's mind and looked around. All five Alterin lay unconscious. He stepped over to Paul. His huge form hovered above the Alterin's. The silver cape of the Zi ancestry brushed against Paul's feet.

"Cruchton, remove the others to cells. This one will walk there shortly."

"Yes, Lord."

* * * *

Paul opened his eyes. His head pounded. He reached up to touch it and groaned. Then his eyes focused on the creature that stooped beside him.

"I'm not a creature. My name is Cacin. You may call me that in private. When others are around, if you wish to be allowed to speak at all, you must call me Lord."

"Fat bloody chance I'll do that," Paul answered as he sat up, still holding his head.

"Then call me nothing at all or have the privilege of speaking removed." Cacin stood. "You're a formidable foe, Paul Muntz. I'm not surprised you killed Kagoule, even in your former state." He called to a Sentry who stood at some distance, "Help him to his feet."

"I can get up without your help," Paul snapped defensively.

Cacin held his hand out to prevent the Sentry from coming closer. The Sentry stepped back to his post.

When Paul finally gained his feet, Cacin continued. "What would you do, Paul Muntz, if you found yourself in the same predicament we're in?" Even with Paul standing, Cacin looked down on the Alterin. "If your race was facing annihilation and you possessed the ability to mate successfully with," he gestured with one hand "many other races without altering your own significantly? If you possessed the ability to travel through space, would you evaporate into oblivion as a species? Or would you take the females of another race?"

Blood ran down the King's face as he spoke. Pleased he had done some damage, Paul smiled but said nothing in reply to the question.

"Yes, you would do as we have done." Cacin walked around Paul slowly.

"I didn't say that."

"You thought it."

"Get out of my mind and stay out!"

"You realize of course, that by injecting Hill'carn's blood you've altered your own genetic make-up so much that you're no longer Human. You're a Gron'dalin now or something pretty close to it."

"You're lying!" Paul swirled on him.

"No. One thing you'll learn about us is that Gron'dalins don't lie." He thought of his change of heart during Xingat and corrected himself. "Well, seldom. We've never had a reason to lie. We're both physically and mentally superior to every race we've ever encountered. We have no need to lie."

"You're Hill'carn's brother, for want of another term that would more accurately describe what injecting her altered blood makes you. She was Marked. You took her blood, and your DNA has been altered as a result."

He continued to walk around Paul. "Ten Zi accompanied Cruchton on this mission. You have killed four. They were all related to Kagoule, whom you are also related to."

"I don't believe you."

"You're related to Kagoule through Hill'carn, who was Marked by him at the time you injected her blood. Oddly," he laughed, "that puts you in line for the Gron'dalin throne." Cacin dismissed this thought with the brush of one massive hand. "You're related to all Gron'dalins who performed this mission, except Cruchton and Fa'pal who are Sentry. Happy little family we have here," Cacin said sarcastically. "They were particularly anxious you not be left on Earth to betray your race again and tarnish the Zi house."

"This is not my race!" Paul spat in Cacin's face.

"This spitting thing is a cultural adaptation," Cacin said snidely, remembering Hill'carn's attack on Gradspin. "Take him to the retaining vault." He made no attempt to wipe the spittle from his face.

The Sentry who'd been standing by the door stepped forward.

"In case you're wondering," Cacin said, spittle still on his face, "Fa'pal here is a Sentry. Our Elite is divided into three classes. The Zi or ruling class, the Zad or scientific class and the Sentry or military class. If you think I can grip your mind effectively, try Fa'pal."

"Let's go," Fa'pal said.

Paul turned and walked in the direction Fa'pal indicated. He stumbled along the corridor toward imprisonment, knowing the Gron'dalin told the truth about his lost humanity, but knowing he couldn't let them destroy the Humans either.

Chapter 28
One's Duty

Bopack spoke softly to San'dare'a as she sat near her on a sofa. Beside them, the parrot Orgone had brought to keep San'dare'a company cleaned its bill on the large perch within its cage. The pale-haired woman watched it intently with sad eyes. "It's trapped too," she said in a calm voice.

"There is no way to resist him, San'dare'a," Bopack continued, in a serene voice.

"My name is SANDRA!" San'dare'a said emphatically.

Bopack ignored her, choosing to continue her appeal instead. "He will give you time to accept him, but he won't wait forever. They can't. He would die if he did. And although he's willing to, he won't be allowed. Don't put yourself in the position of being raped, San'dare'a."

"Quite frankly, I'd respect myself better with that eventuality. I can't let it touch me, Bopack. It revolts me."

"You're not doing yourself any favors with that decision."

"You talk about it as though it's just something unpleasant I have to do and get over with. This creature is utterly revolting to me." San'dare'a looked into Bopack's eyes. "Do you understand what I'm saying? This creature is absolutely repugnant. I'm not suggesting it looks a little ugly. It is utterly nauseating to think of having intercourse with it. I will die first. I WILL kill myself." She spoke calmly. Her decision had been well thought out. It was final.

Bopack recalled her own first impressions, now so far removed from the life she lived. "He won't allow you to kill yourself. He'll remain in constant contact with your mind for as long as you live to prevent you from doing that." She snorted. "I mean every day of your life. Every waking second he will be tuned to you. You'll never have a private thought again."

With this declaration, San'dare'a finally broke down. After weeks of nervous confinement with the other women, weeks more held in solitude by this odd disgusting creature, Orgone, she lowered her head and began softly weeping into her hands.

Her shoulder-length blond hair fell forward toward her lap. "Oh God, is there no way out?" she sobbed in desperation.

"No. There is no way out. Don't cry San'dare'a," Bopack cooed softly, squeezing the other woman's shoulder.

"SANDRA!" San'dare'a snapped, breaking the contact.

"It won't be all that bad," Bopack said, ignoring San'dare'a's assertion that her name was Sandra. Bopack always ignored it. "Orgone loves you." The parrot squawked and plucked a grape off the vine hanging in its cage; the grapes San'dare'a had put in its cage. "He isn't able to express it like Cacin does, but I can see it in his eyes every time he looks at you."

San'dare'a looked into Bopack's large eyes. "Maybe I'm not being clear. I don't want anything to do with this thing. If I don't love it how can I let it touch me?" She cringed, looking as though she would vomit. "What has happened to you? You were captured once. They are going to destroy my people! How can you ask me to just accept it?" She glared accusingly at the little alien woman.

Bopack said nothing.

"I don't want to be here," San'dare'a said. "I don't want to sleep with that creature. And I won't!"

"You must stop calling Orgone a creature. He's not."

"Boy you could have fooled me," San'dare'a dried her tears.

"You're no longer entirely Human, San'dare'a, look at your face."

San'dare'a's face, very lightly laced with a smooth, pale green and yellow shell-shaped motif, reddened at the accusation.

"It can have these scales back," she answered defiantly, touching her facial scale. "I don't want them."

"They can't be taken back. The gene has altered you. It has changed your DNA."

"Well, I'll never let that thing touch me. A few scales don't mean I'm one of the gang."

"You will never be free of him."

This only started the other woman crying again. Exasperated, Bopack snorted. "There's no point in resisting. You'll never go back.

You aren't Sandra any longer. And he loves you. Doesn't that mean anything to you?"

"If it loves me, it will keep its scaly big hands off me!" she cried.

"San'dare'a, I can't think what is to become of you. They will drug you soon if you don't acquiesce." She paused and shook her head. "Is he so repugnant to you?"

"That's what I've been saying all along. I'm glad you're finally hearing me. Yes! I can't conceive of life with a thing like Orgone," she yelled, drying her eyes again.

"Well, get used to it," Bopack yelled back as she rose. So out of character for her the statement and tone of voice shocked even her. "This is your life, San'dare'a."

The parrot squawked a word of protest beside her.

"Why do you have this bird in here?" Bopack asked resentfully, startled by the big bird who's cage hung from the ceiling on a thick chain.

"I like parrots. Your friend Orgone knows that. I hate caged parrots. But perhaps its love for captured things outweighs its common sense."

"There are worse fates that could befall you, San'dare'a. One of them would be to be bedded to Zadanin!" Again Bopack surprised herself with her outspokenness. But the inflection in her voice alarmed her more.

San'dare'a shook her head at the other woman, wondering why suddenly she was short tempered with her.

"At least Orgone will drug you. Zadanin didn't do that."

"Oh, big consolation! And you think that's fine I suppose?" she challenged.

"No, I think it's awful," Bopack blurted, controlling a sudden unexpected urge to cry. Where had this emotion come from? How long had it been lurking in the recesses of her heart?

Continuing, she added, "But it's better than what Zadanin did. Look around you, San'dare'a. We are far from your planet." Bopack gestured past the parrot's huge cage, out the observation deck window. Around them in the pleasant rooms, flowers from Earth bloomed in stark contrast to the blowing Martian sands.

"Do you think anyone is going to save you here? They can't even get here. And even if they could, do you think they would want you looking like that?" The declaration made the other woman cringe. "Or perhaps you want to go out there," she pointed back toward the blowing sand.

"I would go if I could get past your friend, Orgone," San'dare'a whispered.

Something had been bothering Bopack during her conversation with San'dare'a, tickling at her mind like annoying feathers. Now, burning with rage as she stood looking down at the other woman, she realized that her anger was not aimed at San'dare'a at all. Someone was in her mind!

Hill'carn spoke to her with words so soft they barely registered.

* * * *

Bopack stormed through the huge entrance with her head held high, her back stiffened by temper. The long silver gown she wore swished aggressively against the floor tiles, highlighting her indignation. Striding forcefully across the green ceramic leaves that kissed the tile so gently they hardly appeared there at all, she set her jaw defiantly.

"You have violated my mind, Hill'carn!" she snapped. "To get me here you have done what I hate most. What you know I abhor! Well, here I am," she said tersely. "Do with me as you will. You certainly do with my mind as you will."

"I'm sorry, Bopack. I had no other means of contacting you without Cacin knowing I wanted to speak with you," Hill'carn said meekly. "It is imperative he not know I contacted you."

Bopack's manner softened. She relaxed slightly. The anger that had sculpted her lips into a tight slit fell away. She sighed with resignation.

Hill'carn continued to inspect her from the viewing platform. Towering over the small woman who stood at the bottom of the steps to the platform, she gauged the other woman's mood carefully without re-entering her mind.

Hill'carn's hand rested on the smooth brass railing beside her.

Yes, diplomacy was needed. She knew she had offended the Old One, could see it in her eyes, the tight curve of her mouth, her stiff back. More than Bopack's words screamed at Hill'carn from the tile floor below.

"I'm sorry," Hill'carn repeated softly, letting the words drift down like the feathers that had brushed Bopack's mind minutes earlier. "I'm sometimes reckless with these new skills."

She tested her approach carefully, watching the other woman for signs that these were the right words; words that would mend the tear between them.

Bopack grunted and her outrage softened further. She drew in a deep breath and released it in a loud sigh of submissiveness and long suffering.

"I'll try to be more careful."

The old woman shifted feet and looked up at Hill'carn with her large soft eyes less full of vexation. She folded her arms in front of her, pressing them against her small breasts.

"Why have you called me here?"

"For a very important reason," Hill'carn began.

The Old One raised her eyebrows and shrugged. "Knowing how much I hate any interference with my mind, I hope it would be for a very important reason," the old woman said pointedly. "Incidentally, Hill'carn, as I've told you before, no one is permitted to enter my mind except the King. And he respects my privacy," she added.

"I'm sorry about entering your mind." Hill'carn stepped down the first stair. "I know you hate it as much as I did."

"More," Bopack stated flatly. A stern quality had entered her voice that Hill'carn had never heard before. "I have never been able to learn the skill of reading minds, not even a little bit. Your hatred of it faded fast. Mine has endured a lifetime, hundreds of your years. My hatred of it is still intact."

"There was no other way to get you here without Cacin knowing. I apologize for offending you," she said, trying to win back Bopack's trust.

Bopack shrugged and looked hurt. "Very well," she said. So much of her life had been lived in one state of resignation or another that resignation had become her closest companion. There was no point in fighting these Gron'dalins. They would win. How often had she given up her own needs and wants in place of someone else's? And now a small wrinkled old woman with very little left of life stood before the new Queen. Yes, she would give up her own needs again for Hill'carn's.

Hill'carn stepped off the last step and quickly embraced her. "Thank you for not staying angry with me. I could think of no other way to contact you without Cacin knowing. Please forgive me?" The Old One grunted and gently removed herself from Hill'carn's embrace.

"What is so important, my dear?" she asked. Was there a little triumph in her voice, perhaps the knowledge that she was important to the Queen, that she was loved and respected? She was significant enough to warrant an apology, after all.

"Did anyone see you enter?" Hill'carn asked, stepping back.

"No. I came as you asked, without telling anyone." A sad sort of compliance crept into her voice, as though she always did what she was told.

"Good," Hill'carn replied, turning as Cacin so often did to gaze at the swirling sands of Mars. The long silver gown of the Zi ancestry swished out around her and glistened in the overhead light, the same light that twinkled along the scales on her face.

"You are one with them," the old woman said softly. "How easily you fit in. If any King deserves a real wife, it is Cacin."

Hill'carn turned and looked at her, her eyes wide with disbelief.

"You object to me speaking my mind?" Bopack asked.

"No. I just hadn't thought I was 'fitting in'," Hill'carn replied clutching at her throat. "Bopack, that thought frightens me."

"And well it should. You are adopting the most powerful species in the universe. And you will probably be a better Gron'dalin than they are. The way you are developing your mind, I suspect you will have better mindreading powers than they do before long." She looked almost proud as she spoke, as though Hill'carn were her daughter.

"Oh, I doubt that."

"Orgone can read a mind without a person's knowledge of it when he tries," the old woman muttered, more to herself than to Hill'carn.

"Well, I doubt I will ever be able to do that," Hill'carn said. A shiver ran through her. "I resent your thinking I'm one of them," she admitted.

"No you don't," Bopack challenged. "Fear and resentment aren't the same thing. But look how you've changed. You were determined not to accept your fate when I first set eyes on you. Now, of all the Earth women who have been captured, you are the most accepting, and the happiest. There's nothing wrong with that. I'm not accusing you of anything."

"I've been in Colony longer. Perhaps the passage of time has affected the way I look at things. I don't know," Hill'carn said desperately, turning back to the banit'ye barrier.

"Time never eased my loss of freedom," Bopack stated. "Of course, freedom stayed lost to me. It won't be that way for you. I still long for freedom, although I'll never have it."

"Bopack?"

"Yes, you're startled at this news aren't you? I can't ever go back but I still long to see my family, my brothers, my father. They're all dead now, dust long ago. They were not genetically altered. I thought of them as time passed and I aged so slowly. They've been gone now for hundreds of years. Don't tell Cacin I told you this."

"I won't."

The Old One crossed the tiled floor to a comfortable high-backed chair. "You've had a wonderful affect on him," she said, sitting down. The chair seemed to swallow up her tiny body. "He is happy and he acts more casual now than he ever did. He is more relaxed."

Hill'carn smiled. "Wasn't he casual before?"

"Never in public. He was very formal. In private he relaxed a little."

Hill'carn drew in a deep breath and turned back to the view outside the barrier. "What I am about to tell you must never voluntarily be revealed, Bopack."

"My goodness! That sounds ominous," the old woman answered, adjusting herself in the chair. Her small feet dangled above the green tile like a child's. Hill'carn continued to stand.

"Cacin is very unlikely to read your mind so I feel you are the only one who can do this. Promise me you'll never reveal any of this to Cacin?"

Bopack's curiosity was pricked. She smiled and looked puzzled. "You have my word."

"Two days ago..." Hill'carn turned fully around to look at the old woman. "A very good friend of mine was brought here."

"Is she in the holding area?"

"My friend is a man. An Alterin." Hill'carn stated. "Have you heard of the Alterin?"

"Yes," Bopack answered cautiously.

Hill'carn searched the old woman's face for a reaction but did not read her mind. Bopack nodded knowingly. Did she know what Hill'carn was going to ask? "He is being held in the detention vault on Level One. He was apparently the reason Cacin went to Level Four for so long. He was laying a trap to catch him."

"There was nothing you could have done to prevent it," Bopack stated.

"I know. Orgone would have blocked me, but Orgone can't block me now. What he doesn't know he can't interfere with, and he has no right to read my mind now that Cacin is in Colony daily. Do you know where the detention area is, Bopack?"

"I know the area," she answered warily.

Hill'carn was tempted to ask if the old woman knew what she was going to ask of her but didn't. "His name is Paul Muntz. I want him released, but I can't get near him."

Bopack gasped. "You've tried, haven't you?"

"I have but the corridors leading to him are well guarded." She paced for a moment. "Cacin didn't tell me Paul was in Colony. I learned that by accident from Cruchton's mind. Cruchton is very easy to read." She stopped in front of Bopack's chair.

"I'm told all the Sentry are easy to read."

Hill'carn nodded. "They are. Most of them aren't worth reading though. Cruchton is. He is a great wealth of information." Then she returned to the issue dearest to her heart. "They've been guarding this secret from me, Bopack. All the Zi have been guarding this secret. I knew they were guarding something and I know now what they were hiding from me."

Bopack inhaled deeply and shook her head. "They may have taken on more than they expected by stealing your race, Hill'carn," she remarked, marveling at Hill'carn's ability to read minds." Then she sat forward in her seat. "Releasing him will do nothing, Hill'carn. He's on Mars. Surely you don't want him to destroy Colony?"

"No!" Hill'carn turned away and looked back out through the window in a melancholy way. "I don't want him to do that. I love Cacin." She walked to the barrier that protected her from the unfriendly Martian environment. "I wouldn't bring any harm to him."

"Then what do you expect to accomplish by releasing this man," Bopack asked, silently shocked at Hill'carn's admission of love for the young King as she gazed at the young woman's back.

"He is no longer a man, really." She turned abruptly from the window and the shifting red sand. "Like me, he is something else. He was altered by my blood."

"This is the one they talk of," Bopack remarked, more to herself than to Hill'carn. "There are five of them," she added, looking up into her friend's brown eyes.

"Yes, but I want you to release only one. Paul Muntz. He will escape," Hill'carn answered, staring back out at the ceaseless motion beyond the banit'ye barrier. "He has the sort of mind," she said, still facing the barrier, "that can learn how to pilot a transport. He's very adaptable." She sighed. "I want to give him his freedom as he once wanted to give me mine."

A feeling of melancholy swept over her. The sand piled against the barrier outside. Behind her, the old woman sat pensively, considering her request while Hill'carn thought about her old life; the life that was so far away in time now that it hardly seemed a reality; a dream perhaps; a daydream that rode the gossamer realm of fantasy.

"This is the man you once loved," Bopack stated to Hill'carn's back.

"He is my brother, Bopack," Hill'carn answered without hesitation spinning to look at the Old One.

"Your brother?" Bopack tried the words on slowly. "It sounds like you've rehearsed that answer."

"Perhaps I have." Hill'carn drew in a deep breath. She nodded. "Yes. But he is my brother, never-the-less. That is what Cacin and the others are calling him. That is what prevents them from killing him." She paused to look at the old woman with the saddest eyes Bopack had ever seen. "And the others are also related to me although I've never met them."

"Yes. And the others. But you aren't asking me to release the others. You are asking me to release the man you loved, this Alterin who has caused your husband so much grief. You are asking me to release him, and him alone," Bopack said.

"You're shrewd, my friend. Very little escapes you. Yes, I was in love with him once." Hill'carn turned back to the old woman before continuing. "But I love Cacin now. I want the release of this Alterin because..." She glanced down at the floor with a look of despondency. "He loves his freedom so much. I know what it is to love freedom."

"We all know what it is to love our freedom," Bopack stated, crossing her arms over her small chest. She leaned against the chair, resting her head against the back.

"If I agree to do this for you, you must promise not to tell Cacin."

This was the first time since her capture that the Old One had made a demand on anyone. The words almost stuck in her throat.

"You must guard this in your mind and I will hope he doesn't break that barrier. I will hope he doesn't instruct Orgone to protect you in his absence again."

"Don't worry about Orgone. He's not as good at reading minds as he thinks he is."

"What you're asking me to do is considered treason."

"I give you my word. He will never know."

"Even if things turn out a little differently than you might expect?" Bopack asked.

"What do you mean by that?" Hill'carn stared into the old eyes that sparkled mischievously back at her. She was tempted to search Bopack's mind for the answer to the question – only tempted.

"I mean I have a plan that might see a few more than just your friend leaving."

Immediately thinking of the other Alterin, Hill'carn chuckled. "If it doesn't damage Colony in any way," Hill'carn stated, "then by all means do it."

"It won't damage Colony," she replied. "I promise you that. But two of the Alterin cannot be released. Two cannot guard their minds sufficiently to escape notice. Orgone has told the Elders this in my presence."

"Bopack?" Hill'carn began. "There is one more thing."

"Yes?"

"I don't want you to tell Paul Muntz any news of me." She turned her face away from her friend, knowing the old woman knew the reason for her request.

Chapter 29
Bopack

Bopack scuttled across the room, attending to the needs of the new arrivals, soothing them, consoling them, counseling, biding her time as she had bided her time so often over the centuries. She had done a lot of biding her time over the course of this lifetime of imprisonment. Eight hundred years of living, the so-called 'gift' the Gron'dalin gene change gave her, had not dampened her resentment. Better five free years than a million in sexual slavery. She sighed and turned back to the crying female.

"There is no point in resisting," she said. "There is no use for tears. Partinon," she called to the Opan woman behind the front desk, "bring me a glass of water for this one." She patted the young Human on the back.

"Yes, My Lady," the middle-aged woman replied. Her floor-length hair touched the tiles as she bowed.

"You Human females need a lot of tending," Bopack remarked, more to herself than the Human she consoled. "More than most. You are all extremely high strung."

"You would be, too," the woman snapped.

"I've been there, dear," Bopack said calmly. "Thank you, Partinon," she said, turning to take the glass of water from the Opan's hand.

"My Lady," the woman replied, bowing again.

"Don't they have lovely hair?" Bopack remarked as the woman retreated.

"Maybe, but I don't care for the ridges in her forehead," the Human replied snidely, taking the glass extended to her.

Bopack laughed. "Such racism!" she said. "Perhaps she could learn to dislike the shape of your eyes. Her own are very round while yours are very slanted. Shall we try to teach her to think of you differently than other women?" she asked in the woman's tongue, one different than the dominant Earth language and one she'd had particular difficulty learning. The Human looked shocked. "Do you also think ill of other varieties of Humans?"

The young woman shrugged and looked away from Bopack.

"So you do. Very interesting. And what of me? Do you hate me for being Zantinean?"

"No." The Human drank from the glass Bopack handed her.

"Well, it doesn't matter if you do. You will learn there is only one thing that is important. We all live, feel pain and die."

"Why does everyone call you Lady?" the Human asked, trying to change the topic.

"I was once Queen," Bopack remarked.

"And you are here? Looking after us?" the young woman asked, wiping the last trace of tears from her cheeks.

"We all live, feel pain and die," Bopack repeated, taking the empty glass from the Human's hand. She placed the glass on the bench beside her.

Regularly pressed into service from the time of her own capture because of her calm, gentle manner and persuading tone, and because of her station, she was well acquainted with misery.

One of the Zad came to the door as she finished speaking and the room went into an uproar again. He swept in rapidly and snatched his chosen female with the power of his mind.

"I am sorry," he repeated over and over as he forced her from the room amid the screams from the other women.

The young Human Bopack comforted broke into uncontrollable sobs.

"Good sense should tell you, my dear, that a male of his size, to say nothing of his mental capacity, will prevail." She hugged her charge but the woman wailed even louder. "That's it. Get it all out, my sweet." Bopack rocked her back and forth, cooing as she performed the task.

She smiled to herself at the thought that they were fighters, these Humans. She would give them that. High strung but fighters to the last. Not one of them failed to attack the gron'ie as they came for them. She liked that in them. They were such lovely creatures with their small eyes, round or slanted, and their variety of heights and colors.

None was prettier than Orgone's bride, or more trouble. Bopack looked at the far wall, sympathizing with San'dare'a in her mind. Until today there had been no hope for San'dare'a – until today. Today everything changed with one word from the new Queen and the arrival of the altered Humans.

"I didn't resist when I was captured," she said to the woman she was holding. The woman clung to her like a small frightened child. "None of the other Zantinean women did either," she said, her voice a soothing elixir. "We saw no possibility of escape."

"I'll never let it touch me!"

"We were a practical race. A patient race," Bopack cooed. The woman continued to cry, rocking back and forth in Bopack's arms. "And you must be practical too."

"Never!" the woman roared. But she continued to cling to the old woman.

"You must be strong. This is going to be your life."

"Never! I will die first!" the woman blurted through tears.

Bopack had thought at the time of her capture that she would await retribution. Eight hundred years of waiting had stretched out from that day!

"Life is too sweet for an early death," Bopack said.

The woman in her arms groaned and propelled herself into a louder crying fit.

"Perhaps you will find something to bring you joy," Bopack called over the general bedlam in the room and her charge's din in particular. Along the long benches that filled the waiting area, women sat in various degrees of agitation.

"Don't be foolhardy," her voice droned on in the woman's ear. "To resist these gron'ie is foolishness."

"Nothing is impossible," the woman cried. "Maybe I can get away."

"My mate would have killed me for the behavior you're exhibiting," Bopack said sadly. "You are lucky. These are different times. A different age with a softer King. They could kill you with their minds if they wanted. They have the power to easily do that with their minds. But he will not allow it."

"Let them kill me," the woman challenged.

"Palin, will you take over here please," she said to another small woman who was passing.

"Yes, My Lady."

"I have things to attend to," Bopack said to the Zantinean woman as she rose from the bench. "Palin will help you now," she said to the woman she'd been holding.

"I don't want help. I want to go home!" the woman cried as she quickly slipped into the embrace of the other helper.

"We all did," Bopack said. She walked to the door with her back straight. The long silver cape of the Zi ancestry that she had worn to the holding chamber, hung on a hook by the door. She slipped it off the hook, looked at it and put it back. Better to be seen for what she was – rather than what she wasn't – at this first meeting.

"How many women are chosen for the Elite in this group?" she asked of the small Opan at the desk, her hand still touching her cape.

"Only four more."

"Are they to be mated soon, Partinon?"

"Yes. Within the hour, My Lady."

"She is one of those four isn't she?" Bopack pointed to the woman she'd been comforting.

"Yes. Huang is her name."

"Huang was her name. She is now Hu'anin." Turning to look at the small woman again, she added, "I'm taking a break. Can you handle things here until my return?"

"Yes, My Lady."

"Good. I won't be long, an hour or so. Remember, the King has stressed that we attend to their emotional needs. Don't leave any of them crying if you can avoid it."

"I won't, My Lady."

"That's an odd request on a Bride Quest isn't it," Bopack said.

"What? Attending to their emotional needs?"

"Yes."

"I hope the trend continues," the Opan said. They nodded at each other and Bopack turned toward the door.

It slid open before her and she gasped. The four Zad who were going to mate, entered to claim their mates all at once. The room went into chaos behind her. Women started screaming; holding their heads as though their brains would spill out through their ears; some moaned softly; some fell to the floor. Bopack looked back at Hu'anin, sitting silently now, as though by sitting silently she would go unnoticed. Not able to bear seeing her dragged from the room, Bopack turned and fled.

Bopack's secret pleasure, indulged as she walked from the holding area, caused a smile to crease her lips. She heard a woman fly at Cran. His startled cries rose behind her, drifting only momentarily on the air. Was it Hu'anin who'd attacked? Or one of the others? Bopack sighed and hurried down the corridor. It was an exercise in futility, really, but it pleased the Old One that they fought so hard just the same. She couldn't think why it pleased her as her feet scurried over the smooth tile, but it did.

Bopack thought of the 'champion' as her feet flew over the delicate leaf pattern in the tile. One female in particular, noted for this attack tendency, had pleased Bopack greatly. Gra'lin she was called. Linda, she still insisted her name was. She had been mated early on, as she was Cruchton's bride and his continuing services were required on the planet. But while in the containment area she had been formidable, sometimes inflicting real damage. Laying in wait behind objects, she lashed out with precision.

As if that held any real hope, though. This far from her world, on a strange planet that could not, outside these gron-made structures, support life, what did her protest accomplish? Like the others, Gra'lin was trapped.

Bopack shook her head sadly as she rushed toward the cells. Gra'lin had caused untold disruption in the holding area but Bopack was sorry she was gone. She was sorry she couldn't have helped her.

Well, there was one woman Bopack might be able to help. "We will see," she said aloud as she sped toward the detention cells.

"And now I get to reward you, Paul Muntz, for killing that abomination for me," she whispered. "There IS some justice in the universe, albeit slow in coming."

* * * *

Bopack wound her way slowly to Paul's prison cell, not wanting to attract attention. She had never seen him, but had overheard - as she overheard so much when she listened for nuggets of information - that he was very like a Gron'dalin. Praying his heart remained Human, she nodded and smiled at two gron'ie. She turned into the corridor that led to the confinement areas.

If his heart wasn't Human, her plans were in vain and her life would be forfeited pointlessly. Hill'carn would be punished and, realizing he was unable to penetrate all her thoughts, Cacin would probably instruct Orgone to monitor the Queen's mind. She might even be put to death – but no – not now that she was pregnant. Bopack glanced over one shoulder toward the busy main corridor she had left behind.

With the guards gone, the door to the confinement area opened without notice. Tests showed the Alterin unable to manipulate complex objects within their immediate vicinities. The guards were withdrawn. While a Gron'dalin could unlock any device they came across from a distance of twenty yards with their minds, an Alterin could not. Outside their range of abilities, or at least until now outside their range. The removal of the guards paved the way for Bopack's involvement. The door swished open on an unguarded prisoner.

She smiled. No one thought about the Old One coming to free him. Her smile broadened. The harmless Zantinean woman who always did as she was told, never a threat to anyone, would never release a prisoner. Bopack shook her head slightly at what she was about to do. Perhaps the wait had paid off.

The door to the cell area slid back silently and Bopack looked on the Alterin for the first time. He sat quietly, reading, his large scaled hands holding one of the translations firmly aloft. As the door fully opened he looked up at her inquiringly.

"Don't think about me being here or they may read your thoughts and I will die!" she said briskly, her old heart fluttering at the proposition. "I have come to help."

She walked into the room and the door closed automatically behind her.

Paul emptied his mind, erecting an obstruction through which he knew no one but the ugly green and yellow thing could penetrate. Unlike the Gron'dalin mind, where whole areas of the mind could be blanketed at once, each subject in Paul's mind had to be protected separately and that took concentration.

Paul rose, placing the pen he'd been holding in his teeth in the book to mark his spot. The book snapped shut and he set it on the table beside him.

"Alright you're safe," he said, eyeing the small, odd-looking woman that stood before him. Being very like a human, only smaller and with huge eyes, she reminded him of a peculiar-looking child. Her eyes protruded slightly, like someone with gout. While this gave her an odd appearance, she looked unremarkable otherwise.

"I've come to tell you of a way to stop the rest of Earth's women from being captured. A way to save your race," she declared. A thrill rushed through her. Yes, she was doing this! She was striking a blow at the nation that had imprisoned her!

"Why would you risk it?"

"A millennium of repression," Bopack responded. "I've lived more than eight hundred of your Earth years with these people."

She gingerly walked toward the force field that contained him as she spoke.

"My spouse was the most brutal of the Zi. That's not to say the Zi are all brutal, they aren't. Cacin is a decent gron. But some are brutal. Cacin is the one who took your lover." Paul straightened and took a step toward the force field, stopping short of it.

"What do you know of Hillary?" he demanded.

"She is fine," Bopack remarked with a flip of one hand to dismiss the topic. Her promise to Hill'carn stayed uppermost in her mind. Not wanting to trample on her friend's wishes, she continued.

"And there are others, like Gradspin," she shook her head slowly. "Who are decent types. But for the most part, the Gron'dalins only take what they want, have done for thousands of years. And if they must use force..." She shrugged and bit her lip. "Well, you know all too well about that. Granted, they've been under a rare curse." She placed her hands on her hips. "But it doesn't justify their attitudes or behavior," she said in a preaching manner.

Paul smiled at her, thinking her fanciful. How could an old woman strike a blow at these creatures? "I want to know about Hillary," he said, grasping for something tangible in what she could give him.

"She has asked me not to talk to you about her."

"Then she knows I'm here?"

"She does indeed." Bopack folded her arms over her small breasts. "She sent me. My name is Bopack." Bopack stopped talking and looked around the enclosure for a chair.

"To set me free?"

"Yes, she sent me to release you."

"CAN you?" Paul asked.

"The closure," she pointed to the force field that surrounded him, "Can be lowered easily. But not yet. Trust me. These people don't have the right to destroy races the way they do. I would like to see the Human race escape them," she confided in a loud whisper as she walked toward the corner to retrieve a chair. "And you are going to be the one that accomplishes that. But only three of you can leave the Colony. Two are incapable of guarding their minds as you have just done. You, Duncan and Peter are the only ones capable of high mind control. Will you trust me in this?"

"Okay."

"You will save the Human race, Paul Muntz."

Oh Sure, Paul thought.

"This Bride Quest will not be the last their race engages in." She shrugged as though that was of little consequence to her plans. "Even if you succeed with my plan they will destroy other races. But at least one race can be spared."

Pulling a large chair up to the force field with some difficulty, she placed it in front of where Paul stood.

"The Nationals have arrived and are waiting their turn to select brides," she said, circling the chair to sit down.

The huge warehouse-like area she occupied, packed with crates and boxes mysteriously labeled in a foreign script, awaited her revelations almost as expectantly as Paul did. Far above, metal catwalks zigzagged the ceiling.

On the other side of the force field, where Paul stood, the room was finished. Such a contrast to the area Bopack stood in. Behind him, a reading lamp winked above the comfortable reclining chair he'd been sitting in when the old woman arrived. A single bed stood at the back of the confinement area. Beside the bed, a washroom with no door for privacy gaped at the old woman. A false ceiling, only eight feet above Paul's head, with a force field running its length, completed the scene.

Fa'pal had clearly explained the parameters of his cell to Paul when it put him in it. "Don't try to escape through the ceiling, Alterin," Fa'pal had said. "You'll do yourself damage."

"They are taking all the women from each underground enclosure now," her voice droned on as she lowered herself into the chair, "to store them for the Nationals. Because Humans have given them so much trouble they wish to minimize the deaths among the Nationals. So many Elite have died. This is an unprecedented move on Cacin's part. Oh well," she shrugged. "What does that matter to you?"

"It matters. I want to learn as much about them as I can."

"They are a very proud and tradition-bound race. Always in the past, each gron'ie has fought for and won his mate."

Paul nodded and seemed to file the scrap of information away. "They started taking women weeks ago," Paul confided.

She sat down. "Yes. If you think Earth has seen bad times, just wait," she warned. "And those poor women left to be taken will be afforded none of the luxuries these women have be afforded." She gestured with her hands to indicate the women currently on Mars.

"Once the Nationals have begun, there is no hope for your race. Every woman on your planet will be removed," she said, folding her hands in her lap. "And if they have to kill every man to get them..." She shrugged and saw understanding in his eyes.

"The men are as good as dead without the women," Paul said.

Now it was Bopack's turn to nod. "I've been involved in eight Bride Quests," she said sadly. "One first hand. None have been so arduous. But..." She shrugged again. "They will prevail. And these are not all the Gron'dalins that live," Bopack continued. "It will happen many times again. I often wonder if, in the end, there will be only Gron'dalins left and no more races to pillage."

With that she folded her arms, waiting for her words to impact the strangely scaled alien that stood before her.

He didn't flinch. Standing with dignity, his face concealed his emotions from her. Determination and control surrounded him. She felt a flash of pride in him. This noble gron would carry out her plan.

"There are Gron'dalin in this Quest that are as young as a Human of thirteen years," she said quietly. "The King is very young."

"Thirteen?"

"No." She laughed. "He is the equivalent of about seventeen Earth years. And there are some that are as old as a male of thirty-two. Kagoule," she hesitated. "Do you remember Kagoule?"

"Yes." Paul stared at her with dead pan eyes, revealing nothing of what he thought.

"Kagoule was too young at the last Quest to mate. He was the equivalent of thirty-two Earth years at this mating. I am surprised he did not bed Hill'carn on Earth. He might have, had he not been killed. These older ones have less tolerance for waiting. Once they are allowed to mate, their bodies begin preparing. The bodies of the older ones prepare more rapidly than the younger ones."

She settled into the chair and looked up at Paul with large sad eyes. Paul sat on the edge of the wooden table he'd placed the book on.

"This isn't an isolated event here, Paul. It's a way of life for them," she continued. He nodded. "In another hundred of your Earth years," she snorted, then added in a fatalistic way, "Probably sooner. As their numbers increase the length of time between Bride Quests seems to decrease. They will be heading out to the stars again in search of more planets to plunder. If you succeed in your mission, if you drive them away as I am planning for you to drive them off, it would be wise to prepare for another attack before they come out again."

"They love Earth's women. Earth's women have, for the most part, taken the Marking well. They are impressed by your women."

"Bastards!" Paul replied through clenched teeth. He folded his arms over his broad chest.

"I believe they will return. But who knows," she shrugged again. "Cacin respects Humans."

"I bet!" Paul said. "What has become of Hillary? You said Cacin took her. What do you know of her? Please tell me, Bopack."

"She is called Hill'carn now. And she thinks of herself as Hill'carn."

Paul nodded. "Go on."

"They change the names of women at the Marking," she said. "Sometimes before, during the Assessment. Kagoule would have done it during the Assessment. That was his way. He would have reinforced it at the Marking. Giving them Gron'dalin names that are close to their Earth names helps with assimilation." The Old One looked sad. "My name before I was taken was Bocranin Pash." She sighed as she finished speaking.

"Yes, I understand the psychology behind changing their names." Paul drew in a deep breath. "You say she answers to that name now?"

"Yes. She is lost to you, Paul. She answers to that name and she is mated with the King. She carries his son. She is Gron'dalin now," Bopack said, disregarding Hill'carn's wish to keep knowledge of her from Paul.

His pain, too intense to leave questions unanswered, cried out to her. She saw it in his eyes, festering there like an open wound. If he didn't know, he would always fret for Hill'carn.

Paul looked down at the floor and drew in a long sharp breath. He released it slowly.

"She was special to you," Bopack said tenderly.

"Yes," he replied simply.

Bopack was moved. You love her still, she thought. He had not probed her mind and she knew her privacy was safe. She was free in his presence to think at will. "She's happy. She is trying to get Cacin to return the Human girls to Earth, if that makes you feel any better, Paul. She still loves the Humans."

"It does make me feel better," he said, blocking his thoughts of Hillary so Cacin would not have access to them. This mind thing was so new, so challenging. At any moment the Gron'dalin King could roll through his mind just as Hillary had said it could, with a feeling like cotton wool gently dabbing at him. He'd felt it too often now to forget what the feeling was like.

Bopack continued in an attempt to sooth him. Soothing others had become almost second nature to her, perfected over hundreds of years. Bopack comforted people now without even thinking. "She sent me here to deliver you, as I said. She wants you to be free."

Paul's face lit up. "I will take her with me."

"She's pregnant with the King's son," Bopack reminded patiently.

Paul shrugged. "I'll raise it. It will be partly hers."

"Don't be silly. Cacin would never allow her to be taken, let alone his son raised by someone else. And besides, she doesn't wish to go with you."

Paul looked down at the floor. "I want her back."

"You will have to accept that you can't have her back. You will have to find someone else. There will be someone else for you, Paul. I'm sure of it. Don't fret for her. She's loved by Cacin. And he's the most gentle of the Elite. He's the Gron'dalin King. Her life will be comfortable. She will have everything she needs and wants."

The old woman looked into Paul's eyes. "She loves him, Paul."

Paul swallowed hard, fighting to maintain his mind block, toiling to keep tears from spilling.

"She realized early in her captivity there was no use in struggling, no use resisting. There is none, they are too powerful."

The old woman looked down at the floor, too, as if there was something of interest down there. Then she shook her head. "Too powerful," she repeated.

"I know how powerful they are," Paul replied angrily, recalling his recent encounters. Removed from his cell by mind force only hours earlier, he remembered the incident with distaste. With no will to resist the command to follow, he placed one disloyal foot in front of the other and followed. "But they won't be the most powerful forever," he announced with determination.

Bopack looked up at him, deserting the scuff mark on the floor she had focused on. "Will you Alterin become more powerful than the Gron'dalin?"

"I plan to," he said through clenched teeth. A long angry silence filled the room. He stared at the old woman with eyes as cold as ice, through her really, to his own dark thoughts beyond. Blinking finally, he seemed to come alive again.

"How are you able to think what you think without detection? Do you have the ability to mind block?"

"Oh no!" Bopack laughed. "I'm harmless. That's why they don't read my mind. That and the fact that I was their Queen for many hundreds of years. No one is allowed to read the Queen's mind but the King. That's their custom.

And they talk freely in front of me now, have done for many hundreds of years. They do like to talk, you know. Even though they could think everything to each other, they more frequently talk. After eight hundred years of doing nothing, thinking no ill thought, they trust me."

"You were Queen?" Paul asked in amazement. "Then you were Kagoule's mother. You are Cacin's mother."

"The lineage is passed from cousin to cousin in this society if a King is childless. I am Kagoule's mother. I was widowed from Kagoule's father, who was King at the time of his death. I bore him three sons. Kagoule was Pajan's first born son. He inherited the throne. Zadanin is his second son and fourteenth in line to the throne. Cacin is their cousin, not my son, unfortunately. The throne passes to the first born of four Gron'dalin families, all Zi."

"Yes, now that you mention it," Paul said. "I think Cacin said something about Kagoule being his cousin. Do you know I killed Kagoule?"

"I applaud you. I carried Kagoule's life inside me for a span. Not that I had a choice. I know you killed him and I'm glad of it. I hated him. I wish you could kill the other two for me." She leaned forward, almost leaving the chair she sat in, almost touching the force field with her face, then jerked back when she realized how close she had come to getting a rude shock. The glow of the field returned to its usual red shimmer.

"I hope you will be able to sting the whole race, Paul Muntz. If you're able," she flopped back in the chair, "you will be my hero." Bopack sat up straighter as she said these last words. Raising her face to gaze admiringly into his eyes, she smiled broadly.

Paul chuckled at her comment. Did this old woman have some viable plan? Could she have a plan?

"YOU would be the hero in that case," he replied. "This will be your victory if it succeeds, not mine. What's your plan?" he asked.

"Before I go into the plan I must tell you certain things I have overheard, to ease your mind," she looked over her shoulder. "Or at least to inform you. It might not ease your mind to know these facts." She adjusted herself in the seat, settling in for as long a conversation as she could seize upon.

"They have learned that while you look Gron'dalin..." She interrupted her own train of thought. "They thought you were, you know."

Paul nodded impatiently at her. "Yes?"

"Unless you mate with a true Gron'dalin woman, of whom there are none, you will sire Alterin children."

"If I marry a human woman?"

"You will sire children with your advanced abilities, yes. You cannot alter Humans genetically as they can. You do not possess that ability. You can mate with altered women, too, women they have altered genetically."

Bopack blinked several times. Her pliant eyes filled with sadness as she spoke. "Paul Muntz." She smiled at the next statement. "They are afraid of you. The Nationals cannot project, or decipher an image. They can read minds but they do not possess the ability to create a false likeness around themselves. You are more clever than the Nationals are. Even the Sentry cannot, for the most part, project guises that will fool large audiences. You, Duncan and another Alterin named Peter can! Any image that has to be seen from different angles at the same time by different people is beyond most of the Sentry's abilities. You three Alterin have mastered it beautifully. But only you three. The other two can project but cannot guard their minds. You three are a wonderful hybrid."

"That's a nice way of putting it." Paul chuckled.

Despite the fact there was no one present to overhear their conversation, she continued speaking in hushed tones.

"The Elite have acquired all the females they chose for brides just this evening. With you and the other Alterin off planet the battle went well for them.

"I'm not surprised it went well. It would have gone well in any event. We'd exhausted all our tricks."

Bopack sighed and looked at him with empathy. Yes, she knew how easily the conquest came. How easily the tricks ran out. How many times had she seen it happen; how many races brought to their knees?

"It's customary now for a celebration," Bopack continued, her voice full of sorrow. "The Nationals will start descending to your planet to remove the rest of the women after the Elite celebrate their victory. But the Elite have removed all the women they encountered in the Undergrounds and have amassed several thousands. None of them are Marked as they are intended for the Nationals and it will take the Nationals only a very short time to divide up the prize before they go to Earth for more. Unlike the Elite, the Nationals mate as soon as they secure a bride."

Paul cringed.

Bopack noted his pain. Her voice droned on despite his obvious discomfort. "The extra women in Colony will be transferred after the Elite's celebration, to the fleet for bedding with National's."

"The fleet?"

Bopack leaned forward, again for emphasis, her face almost touching the force field. "There are six ships larger than the one we came in, carrying Nationals," she confided.

Paul gasped.

"Yes, now you see the gravity of it." She sat up slightly, staring into his blue eyes. In a whisper she continued. "These ships are joined at an axis. They are in orbit around Mars, awaiting the opportunity to take brides, to take the rest of the women from Earth.

Believe me, Paul, there will be no females left on your planet if you fail." She looked grim.

"If I fail?"

"That is where my plan comes in." She smiled broadly.

Bopack adjusted herself in the chair and brightened, her face almost glowing with pride. She glanced at the door warily now and then, and Paul became aware of her mounting urgency.

Chapter 30
The Die is Cast

Cacin threw his cape over one shoulder. Beau'nad had done an excellent job healing the broken bones of his rib cage, bones that Paul Muntz had crushed on his arrival. He felt no pain as his torso twisted with the movement.

"I have decided, Gradspin. They will be returned. Hill'carn is right. It doesn't benefit us to take children when they die on our planet."

"There are other possibilities."

"I will not entertain other possibilities. Containing these children on another planet until they are adults, farming females," he snapped in contempt. "We're warriors. At least there's some honor in fighting for our brides. Besides, they age much faster than we do. They would be past child-bearing age or even dead of old age before we came out to the stars again."

"We could Mark them."

"No." Cacin turned abruptly from the observation window. "I have made my decision. There will be no further discussion. They are to leave for Earth immediately after the celebration."

"If that is your will?"

"It is."

"May I speak openly on another matter?"

"You may always speak openly, Gradspin," Cacin said, hiding his displeasure with the Lord Elder.

He turned back to the window again. It was almost dark beyond the barrier. Stars were just erupting above the Martian landscape, tiny pinpoints of light, barely discernible.

"Zadanin is talking offensively about your views on returning the children. It might be wise to consider the Challenge."

"I was going to speak to you about him. I have already decided to issue the Challenge. His rape of Fra'non is intolerable. He defied me by not using Xingat. He will die for it. I will issue the Challenge immediately. Before the celebration."

"Before?" Gradspin said in amazement.

"Yes, I'll kill him tonight before we celebrate. He has caused me too much trouble. I should have issued the Challenge on Ranat." Cacin drew in a deep breath.

"I advised you against it on Ranat."

"Don't feel responsible, Gradspin. I wanted to believe it was possible to avoid it too."

Gradspin nodded and stared out at the growing darkness. "I wish you success against him."

"I will succeed. You may go, Gradspin. See to the arrangements."

The old gron turned without another word. Silence cloaked him as thoroughly as the long silver cape that draped from his stooped shoulders. With a heavy heart he crept carefully across the tiled floor, passing Orgone who was on his way into Cacin's Chambers. "We always meet this way, Orgone," the old gron said, bowing his head slightly and smiling.

Orgone bowed but did not smile back. He stumbled as he raised his head and Gradspin grasped his arm to prevent him from falling.

"I'm alright," Orgone whispered, trying to brush the old gron off. Gradspin quickly glanced at Cacin, who motioned him silently out of the room with a nod of his head.

"You sent for me, Zi?" Orgone asked as the door closed behind Gradspin.

"You know why I've called for you." Cacin walked to his desk and lowered himself into the comfortable chair.

"I do," Orgone sighed. His eyes were glazed. "I don't wish to force her."

"You have no alternative," Cacin snapped. "Look at yourself. You're ill. You're going to die if you do not mate." Cacin's face softened as he looked at Orgone. The Zad stood unsteadily where Gradspin had left him, fearful of moving lest he fall.

"You've lost weight. Your bearing has diminished. You stumble frequently. Beau'nad has approached me to say it can't go on any longer."

"Would you have raped Hill'carn?" Orgone asked, knowing his friend's intentions toward his wife, which had been conveyed by Cacin the day after the drugging. He stepped toward the desk unsteadily.

"We've easily come to accept this word rape, haven't we my friend," Cacin said as he rose from his seat, "and with it all the negative connotations."

"As thinking people it's impossible not to," Orgone replied. "But you haven't answered my question."

Cacin dropped the pen he had been holding onto the smooth wooden surface of the desk he now stood behind. It clattered on contact, dancing across the hard surface. Many of the furnishings in Colony had been taken from Earth and this desk was one of those objects.

"We are thieves of all sorts of things." He gestured to the desk.

"Don't browbeat yourself over it, Orgone. We do what we must to survive."

"You still haven't answered my question," Orgone insisted.

Cacin tolerated the tone of Orgone's inquiry because of his ill health. Drawing in a long slow breath, which he released suddenly, he answered the Zad.

"I probably would have 'raped' her Orgone." He paused for a moment. "The best intentions are sometimes not achievable."

Looking down at the pen that lay on the desk, Cacin pressed his lips together in contemplation and slowly crossed his arms over his huge chest.

"Yes," he said emphatically, raising his eyes to meet Orgone's gaze. "I would have. We're made the way we are made."

Orgone steadied himself by leaning against the edge of the desk. He broke eye contact and, casting his gaze downward in a trancelike manner, looked utterly miserable.

"Take heart," Cacin said compassionately as he walked around the desk that had been a barrier between them. "All things are sorted out in due course." He embraced the Zad briskly, slapping him on the shoulder.

"The way all things have worked out for Cruchton?"

"San'dare'a is not Gra'lin. She will not terrorize you the way Gra'lin does Cruchton. On a different topic, one that is also close to your heart, I am going to kill Zadanin tonight," he announced offhandedly, as though it were a commonplace thing to do.

"I won't say I'm sorry about that. He's been, like his brother, a ruthless and aggressive Zi. I wonder if the youngest one will prove a bully and a pig like his two elder brothers. Zadanin would continue to cause you difficulties if he lived. Wouldn't it be nice if their whole line disappeared? Kagoule is gone with no heirs. Zadanin will be gone with no heirs. That leaves only Hip-nat."

Cacin nodded. "The worst of them all from what I hear."

"NO! Really?"

"Really." Turning his back on his friend Cacin walked to the window where the sand still swirled in the darkness beyond.

"After I've killed Zadanin, I'll personally drug San'dare'a and you must mate. I will not watch you die."

"You will tarnish my honor," Orgone stated.

Cacin looked over his shoulder. "I'll tell her I am forcing you, if that will help."

"It won't," Orgone replied. "You're sealing my fate with her."

"It would be sealed less favorably otherwise." He returned his attention to Mars' eternally shifting sands, almost invisible to him now in the darkness that embraced the planet.

Chapter 31
The Challenge

The arena was well stocked. To one side physical weapons of destruction were amassed. Hill'carn shivered at the sight of them as she walked toward her seat beside Bopack.

"Dear God no," she said aloud, feeling guilty for having told Cacin about Zadanin's brutal rape of his bride.

A choice of eight lethal pieces, all of which took considerable strength and skill to use, lay in a line. Hill'carn looked at them with fear as she walked in front of Orgone to her ringside seat. Not expecting Cacin's announcement at supper, she walked in shock as she made her way to the seat reserved for her.

What if he died? What if Zadanin won the battle?

If Cacin died in this foolish contest, she would be maintained for the rest of her life, he had assured her. Maintained? What did 'maintained' mean? How dare he!

The argument over whether he should engage in combat with Zadanin or not had ended abruptly and unsuccessfully. Even though Zadanin had viciously raped his wife, - Hill'carn now differentiated between types of rape - she didn't want to risk Cacin's death. Her concern wasn't for her own safety or MAINTENANCE. Her concern went out to him. She loved him.

There would be no risk, he'd said. She couldn't believe that looking at the ranked weapons. She made her way to her seat with Orgone close behind.

It was true Cacin was larger.

She sat in the seat intended for her, lowering herself into it in an almost a trance-like state as she considered his words over supper.

Cacin was fitter and better trained. She had nothing to worry about.

Oh that was ridiculous, simply ridiculous. You could never be sure of something like that.

Again his words echoed through her mind. He should have done this before leaving Ranat. It was a Challenge that was long overdue.

Long overdue Challenges, like long overdue goodbyes, were better left unsaid. She sighed and adjusted the silver Zi gown she wore. Looking down at the weapons, she tried to determine the outcome of this 'long overdue' Challenge.

No, he should NOT be engaging in this Challenge. Why not just hang the gron for treason? She fidgeted in her seat. Why did the gron she loved have to risk his life? He was King wasn't he? Couldn't he decide how to deal with a traitor?

Again his words echoed through her mind. This was Gron'dalin custom. Their stupid customs! Cacin wasn't free either. He was bound by convention. He was as big a prisoner as she was in some ways.

Hill'carn cringed at the thought of seeing him die in front of her. Tradition would be the Gron'dalins' downfall.

The arena, a raised circular stage covered with sovan, a material not unlike fine sandpaper, spread in front of her. This was the same arena where Cacin had addressed the assembly when informing them of his plan to capture Paul. She knew that now. The Bay Arena. Why had they called it that? There was no bay here. She glanced around.

The surface covering was intentionally coarse to provide traction for the combatants. Traction! Good Lord what a barbaric ritual. She looked away from the arena floor, adjusting herself in the padded seat, the Queen's seat.

Around her in the massive arena, the spectators' seats were tiered, allowing maximum visibility for all in attendance. All were in attendance as Hill'carn gazed around the room. A hum of conversation rose on the tense air.

The Zi elders seated themselves in the graduated booths directly behind the Queen. As she turned to see who sat there, they all nodded to her respectfully as they took their seats. She smiled and nodded back. Where was Gradspin? She scanned their number looking for him. Orgone sat in his own seat.

The rest of the theater, filled with the Elite – Zi, Zad and Sentry – leaving no one to guard Colony against attack, filled with the gron'ie as she scanned.

Who was there to harm these Gron'dalins anyway? These Rulers of the Universe? They were accustomed to believing no one ever would. And probably that was true. Well, sometimes the tortoise wins the race, Hill'carn thought, guarding her mind closely as she stole a glance at Bopack.

Would Bopack choose this time to free Paul? She looked at the Old One suddenly and abruptly, wondering if she intended to make her move now. Then Hill'carn quickly looked away.

Hill'carn, Bopack and Fra'non, the only women present, were lined up in the front row. Hill'carn glanced over at Fra'non. She looked dazed.

"Don't worry," Orgone whispered, touching Hill'carn's shoulder, startling her. She glanced back at him resentfully, torn from her thoughts. "Cacin is by far the superior." He stepped back to his own seat directly behind Hill'carn's.

She had forgotten Orgone was with her, responsible for her as if she were a small child. She boiled with anger.

"You are all very flippant about death," Hill'carn said under her breath, closing her eyes as she spoke. "You have no way of knowing the outcome, Orgone."

"You must be braver, my Queen, if you are to live among your people," Orgone replied tersely, leaning forward but not getting up this time.

Hill'carn almost snapped a reply, but held back. She almost said they weren't her people, but caught herself. Perhaps they were her people now.

Instead she replied, "I didn't ask to be here, so perhaps you will just have to tolerate my cowardice."

Orgone was adjusting himself in his seat when the Queen's reply came. Something, possibly his deteriorating health, moved him to respond. Turning back he rebutted in an angry voice. "Well, you are here. Make the best of it as we all do."

Stunned by his cutting words, she made no reply. Instead she busied herself to hide her surprise and agitation by adjusting herself in her seat again.

With the long flowing silver gown, symbol of the Zi house to which Hill'carn now belonged, finally arranged to her satisfaction the battle could begin.

Unaware that the proceedings awaited her attention, she took an inordinate amount of time doing it. As she looked up from the activity of smoothing every crease, the combatants walked out toward the center of the arena.

Bopack, seated on the Queen's right, now appeared to be studying her. Hill'carn noticed the old woman's scrutiny. She glanced over at her absentmindedly then back out at the drama that was unfolding.

Cacin entered from one passage on the South. He stopped in center ring, his long silver cape swirled out around him. Zadanin entered opposite from the North and proceeded to the middle of the arena to stand beside him. Hill'carn could hear his cape scrape against the rough surface of the floor as he approached Cacin.

Her heart sank. What if Zadanin killed Cacin?

From the corner of her eye, Hill'carn saw Bopack sneer at her son. Was she thinking this a fitting end for him? Or was it just her deep hatred that would have been expressed at any sight of him?

Hill'carn shuddered as the two gron'ie stood beside each other in the arena, shoulders almost touching, as though this were a casual encounter, a dignified matter.

Cacin stood much taller than his cousin, perhaps by a foot. Would that have an impact on the outcome of the Challenge?

Bopack told her once that, over the duration of her captivity, she had witnessed a dozen Challenges. They were always dispassionate affairs. For Hill'carn, this attitude reinforced her belief that this new race of hers was nonchalant about death.

She took a deep breath, fearful of the outcome of the Challenge and already tired of their practices. Something would have to change. She could not, would not endure a lifetime of this.

"He will prevail, Hill'carn," Bopack whispered.

Hill'carn nodded to the Old One as Gradspin entered the arena and walked toward the two gron'ie. The assembly fell silent. Needing to be left alone with her thoughts, Hill'carn nodded to dissuade the old woman from attempting to comfort her further.

The cape sailed out around the old gron with a snap, and back, and another snap. Gradspin slowly made his way to center stage.

The cape somehow afforded him the dignity they all desired so much, despite the twisted posture age had imposed on him.

All eyes fixed on Gradspin as he closed the distance between himself and the combatants.

The contest would be entirely physical, as they easily possessed between them the mental power to destroy the arena and every inhabitant in it. Hill'carn remembered Bopack recounting one such devastation, witnessed when the old woman was first introduced to the Gron'dalin nation. The battle had been between two Sentry and had ended in the death of both gron'ie and many hundreds of spectators.

Gradspin's stooped posture showed his age more with each passing day. Ever since Hill'carn had joined the nation, he had deteriorated. He stood beside the two fighters now. Hill'carn watched as Cacin pulled the silver cape off his shoulders, glancing at her as he performed this task, and handed it to Gradspin. Zadanin followed suit. Gradspin took both capes in turn. Folding them, he handed each back to its owner.

Everything must be done exactly as custom dictated. Hill'carn sighed.

"Do you have something to say to kin?" Gradspin asked, loud enough for all to hear. The two gron'ie walked toward the women seated in the booth.

Hill'carn sat motionless, her face devoid of expression. The gron she loved prepared to engage in a battle to the death. She had been snatched from a life she wanted, forced to accept one she did not and now even that could be stolen from her.

As Cacin drew nearer, her heart raced. She knew she should say nothing when he arrived. Protocol dictated she remain mute. She wanted to tell him she loved him.

But then, what was love anyway? Was it just that living with Cacin was better than living with Kagoule would have been? Was that what love had become? Or was there something more?

Would she have loved him if she'd been given a choice? Would she miss him if he were killed tonight? Would she miss watching him sit at night with those silly spectacles balanced on the end of his nose while he read a book after searching in vain for his more practical mislaid glasses? Or, would she wish they could talk together while walking through Earth Garden One, as the brightly colored parrots squawked noisily around them. She fought to control the emotions these memories generated.

Cacin approached the kiosk, first to give Bopack his apology for what Hill'carn hoped would be the impending death of her son. Both combatants would speak with all women that would be affected by any outcome of their actions. The women had no say in whether they engaged in this madness or not, but their lives would ultimately be affected.

On Earth, men habitually went off to war without the approval of their wives and their deaths undoubtedly affected those women. Was that any different? Her head spun.

After Cacin gave his regrets to Bopack, he turned aside to Fra'non and, instead of an apology said in a private tone and without emotion, "I give you this kill."

Fra'non stared at him in disbelief. Hill'carn's heart went out to Cacin. He was honorable. He had really been troubled by the treatment Fra'non had received at Zadanin's hands. She knew that now.

Turning to Hill'carn, Cacin spoke in a whisper. "I love you." He said. "Don't worry."

Hill'carn didn't care that it wasn't acceptable to respond. "I love you too," she whispered back. Leaning over the edge of the kiosk she kissed him. Cacin smiled broadly and winked as a murmur went up from the assembly. He turned and walked away from the booth.

Yes, it was love she felt for him. She swallowed hard, trying to keep tears from her eyes. If he were killed tonight, she WOULD miss watching him read at night. She didn't want to love him – she never had – and that was never clearer than it was right now.

Now as he prepared to engage in this ruthless, mindless battle that this race should have outgrown hundreds of thousands of years ago, she reminded herself that she hadn't chosen this life. But she was in it. There was no alternative and she must make the best of it, as Orgone had said.

There would be the times in Earth Garden One when there couldn't be a better life, when she walked with this contradiction in his gentler state. She loved those walks. Surely there couldn't be a happier time, not even if she'd been allowed the life she'd chosen.

Hill'carn straightened her back, folding her hands in her lap as Zadanin approached to apologize for the death of her husband, the King. How many times would she have to conceal her emotions as she did now? She nodded politely at him, as was expected.

* * * *

Bopack received her son as convention dictated, but as he returned to center ring, she became distant, as though deep in thought. The contest began and Bopack shifted in her seat. Hill'carn became engrossed in the battle and did not see her slip from the arena.

Cacin landed a solid blow on Zadanin's face that sent him reeling. A murmur went up from the crowd. Zadanin recovered his footing and lashed out with his own fists, hitting Cacin in the chest and stomach. The King fell heavily.

Hill'carn started to stand but Fra'non pulled her down again.

"Don't do that," the young woman said in an Australian accent not unlike Hill'carn's own. "You'll get punished later."

Hill'carn sighed and swallowed hard. "Cacin isn't like that," she whispered.

The other woman removed her hand from Hill'carn's arm. "You're lucky then. I pray your man wins."

Hill'carn never noticed when Bopack slipped from her seat and left the arena.

Chapter 32
Good byes

Paul Muntz had just finished reading the operating manual Bopack had brought when he heard someone in the corridor outside his cell. He hurriedly concealed the handbook under four books about Gron'dalin engineering, including spacecraft design, which he wished to take with him on leaving. Two of them were in Gron'dalin and undecipherable to him. But any code could be broken. The Gron'dalins were confident of his continuing confinement. They allowed him access to any reading material he wished. Such conceit would be their undoing.

The door opened, revealing the old woman's form.

"Oh! It's only you," he breathed with relief.

"Paul Muntz," Bopack whispered hoarsely. Paul had heard her use this same hoarse whisper on their first encounter. "Now is the time!"

"You said we would go in the morning," Paul replied, jumping to his feet. "It's a good thing I read this now," he chastised in the same whisper, retrieving the manual and holding it up as he spoke.

"Cacin issued Challenge on Zadanin to the death. There will be no better time than the present. You'll have a much easier time getting away now." She spoke rapidly, keeping her voice low. Agitation clung like a second skin. "All the Elite are at the Challenge and their minds are occupied with their favorite sport. They've been kind enough to load the women aboard a vessel for an early morning departure." She snickered nervously, hugging herself as though warding off the cold.

As she spoke, the old woman crossed the floor to the controls that would free Paul. She lowered the force field and turned to face him. Her eyes, all the larger for the excitement that embraced her, focused on the books Paul now held.

"You can't take those books with you." She frowned, as Paul tucked the volumes under an arm anyway. "Do you want Cacin tracking you?"

"Won't it anyway?"

"I believe it's unlikely he will. You will be gone a long time when he discovers you missing, if we're lucky. If there's a reason to follow you he will pursue with a vengeance."

Bopack had entered the confinement area as she spoke, and gently touched Paul's arm, trying to influence his decision. She would never dare tell a Gron'dalin not to do something. She tried this new experience on for the first time like donning a new coat.

"He won't follow if there is nothing to gain from it, if you don't pose a significant threat to him. That is what Cacin is like."

"It spent a lot of energy capturing me. I doubt it will just let me go"

"Well, he certainly won't let you go if you have their technology. He'll be right after you as soon as he finds the books missing."

Paul threw the books on the table.

"Let's hurry, Paul," she said, wringing her hands. She started toward the door to freedom, Paul's freedom. He felt his heart leap.

"Gron'dalins are odd in this one respect," she continued, sweat forming in small beads on her forehead as she looked back at him. "They will admire you for your ingenuity."

"It's not my ingenuity."

"They won't know that. They must never know that."

She wrinkled her brow. "That's what Gron'dalins are like," she said. "They respect aggressiveness when it's preceded by a well thought out plan. And Cacin will think you've escaped entirely on your own." The old woman looked proud though nervous.

Paul followed her, glancing around anxiously in all directions.

"With you in possession of Gron'dalin technology, he would hunt you until your death. Believe me, Paul." She shuddered. "It would be your death if it had to be. Kinsman or not. It could even mean the destruction of your planet if he became convinced you had reproduced the materials contained in those volumes. They guard their technology almost as zealously as the females they steal. You are being very wise to leave the books. You can take with you what you have in your mind. It's my belief Cacin will give you that, at least for the time being."

"Oh," she whispered, stopping at the doorway, "Cacin has decided to liberate the children. This is unprecedented in Gron'dalin history and was in fact the reason for tonight's convenient Challenge. He would have issued Challenge tomorrow night, after the celebrations, because of Zadanin's rape of his bride. Zadanin started speaking poorly of the King's decision to send the children back and Cacin is Challenging tonight instead.

Cacin has made a compromise though. They will be sent back when all the females necessary have been taken. Since no more females will be taken after tonight, they will probably be returned within a few days."

"One more thing," Bopack held up a hand. "Take this." She handed Paul a cylindrical object the size of his fist. "Explosive. The red button is a ten-minute timer."

Bopack wiped her brow with the back of her hand and turned to press the door open button that would give them access to the rest of the vast warehouse. She continued to talk on another theme, one that was dear to her heart, as the door slid silently open.

"I have to speak to you about another matter," she began. "I've drugged a woman named San'dare'a into unconsciousness. Her intended mate can't read her mind that way. I want you to take her with you."

"Okay," Paul said halfheartedly. He owed Bopack that.

"You'll have to carry her to the ship and conceal her onboard before you leave. Don't place her among the other females, they will kill her. She is Marked."

"By whom?"

"She's the female Orgone chose as a bride."

"Orgone! Shit! Why him?" Paul grabbed her by the arm, halting her progress in the corridor.

"Are you fearful of him?"

"I would be stupid if I weren't."

"Get her underground as soon as you arrive on Earth. Keep her there."

Paul glanced quickly in either direction to ensure no one was coming, holding Bopack back firmly all the while.

"They are occupied with their favorite sport," she said to ease his mind. "They have no adversaries, so no guards are on duty tonight. Don't worry. There are none of them around."

"They're very smug," Paul remarked. "You're releasing me now and a few well-placed guards would prevent it."

"They can't conceive of this," Bopack whispered, dismissing the idea with the wave of her free hand, although the sweat continued to gather on her forehead. "They are all at the Challenge," she reiterated.

Despite her reassurance they both stood tensely outside Paul's former prison.

"I don't want to take this woman," Paul said.

"San'dare'a is heavily drugged. She will be in a coma for at least two, possibly three days," she whispered. "The mind is impossible to trace when in a coma," she whispered, anxious to get on with the escape. "This is an area that could cause you lasting trouble though, Paul," Bopack admitted, shaking a finger at him. He released her arm.

"I know. That's why I'm not taking her. First you insist I leave a few books behind so Cacin won't chase me tonight. Then you want me to take Orgone's bride! Are you mad? Better Cacin chasing me than Orgone."

"Orgone is the King's favorite friend and Orgone loves this female very much. He will want to recapture her. You are right in not wanting him after you."

"You bet I'm right. That's why I'm leaving her here." Paul whispered. "If I'm not going to have Cacin on my tail for what I'm about to do, why put Orgone there for taking one female? Although I'm not convinced they won't try to seek retribution."

"It's not in them. They aren't like that. Come on," Bopack urged. "I will explain everything as we go."

Paul looked unconvinced as she made to lead the way.

"Get behind me just in case we have trouble," Paul instructed, pulling her back.

"We won't have trouble," the Old One said as Paul jerked her back. They prowled the corridor quietly, their shoes gently tapping the tiled surface as they passed.

"You must take San'dare'a," Bopack asserted. "You can handle it, Paul."

"I doubt that. Orgone is a powerful mind reader."

"He's more than that," Bopack announced. "But you will prevail over him. Trust yourself."

Paul sighed and looked back at her. As they approached Peter Shaw's cell, Paul asked, "Did you speak to the others?"

"Yes."

The door opened on the Alterin's cell.

A sudden crash behind them startled them both.

Paul reeled, ducking into attack position ready to spring.

"Only a box falling from a stack. Whew!" He straightened, sweat running down his back, wetting his shirt.

Bopack let out her breath and drew a hand to her throat. Her old heart raced wildly.

"I don't want to risk everything for one woman!" Paul stated.

"She must go!" Bopack replied, panting as though she'd run a race. "Of all the females who have wanted to escape these gron'ie, this one must succeed. You can't imagine how much this woman wants to escape this fate. How much we all have."

"There's a whole spaceship full of women succeeding," Paul stated. "Jeopardizing everyone for one woman..."

Bopack stopped him, holding up her hand as she regained her composure. "She wants to leave more than all the women in that ship, Paul Muntz. Do this for her. Do this for me. I beg you. Her escaping with you now will not cause immediate trouble to the mission. Orgone will want to recapture her himself to satisfy his honor. But Orgone will not know of her escape for hours. And Orgone is sick because he has not mated. He is diminished. And you will be on Earth for a very long time before the Challenge is over. These things take hours!" She looked up into his blue eyes, with eyes that held compassion.

"Why does it have to be that woman?" Paul complained.

"Is he so much more of an opponent than the others?"

"You better believe it!"

"You will have two or possibly three days before her mind will start to function at any level that can be read even by him. You can get her underground before then."

"I have to get her underground before that. It will be able to locate my mind as soon as it knows what's happened."

"Can you get her below ground in three hours?"

"Maybe. It will be close."

"The mission won't be in danger because of her, then. You may be in danger eventually because of her, because Orgone will undoubtedly search for her. But this Challenge will take at least three hours and probably a lot more. If you can take her somewhere they have no knowledge of, you'll be safe. He will eventually give up."

They had stepped into Peter Shaw's cell. "If you don't take her she will be raped tonight," Bopack said.

"Okay, she goes," Paul said decisively, hearing this.

How could he deny so urgent an appeal? He thought hard. Was there any place he could take her that they didn't know of? Yes, in Washington State there was an Underground that had not been discovered. Duncan was always telling him about it. Duncan would know exactly where it was.

"Are we going into Orgone's quarters to get her?"

"Yes. Why? He is at the Challenge. You don't need to worry about discovery as long as you maintain your mind block."

"I'm not worried about being found out. I will need a pen and paper when we get there," Paul whispered.

Peter Shaw watched this exchange from behind the force field. Holding his hands up in supplication he now whispered in an exasperated tone. "Come on, will ya! We haven't got all night. Let's move it."

Paul continued to talk with the old woman as they turned off the force field, freeing the other Alterin.

"Lets go!" Peter urged impatiently, making for the door.

"I think I'm making a big mistake taking her," Paul remarked to Bopack, ignoring Peter.

"Will you move your asses!" Peter snapped.

"Relax, Peter. They're in some kind of duel. No one's around."

"Let's go," Peter reiterated.

They started down the corridor behind an anxious Peter Shaw.

"Bopack," Paul whispered. "There's something I've been meaning to ask."

"Yes?"

"Why are no female offspring ever born of these unions?"

"Oh who cares!" Peter snapped. "Let's just get the hell out of here. We have a mission to complete."

"They aren't sure. But I am," Bopack announced in a loud whisper as the procession neared the final detention cell. "The female fetus dies in the mother's womb immediately on landing at Ranat. They have always returned to Ranat with their brides within a very short time of capture. The virus that destroyed the Gron'dalin females so long ago continues alive there to this day," she said as she crept along. With her small stature crouching was hardly necessary. "They continue to feed this virus by bringing back female children of conquered races who die when they reach puberty. The fetus is not safe within the womb and dies as soon as they land. That is my theory."

"Can you guys hold this damn conversation later?" Peter hissed, sweat running down his face.

"Relax Pete," Paul whispered. "Nobody is on guard."

"I'll believe that when I bloody well see it," he answered. "And if you believe it, why are you creeping around like this?"

The three continued the rest of the way in silence. At the cell of the third cageling and the only other Alterin capable of sustaining a mind block and portraying an image for a large audience, they stopped.

Duncan Stock, rapidly rescued from behind the force field, charged from his prison cell out into the warehouse and embraced Paul briefly, slapping the other Alterin on the back. In the company of the small large-eyed woman, they left the warehouse and headed towards Orgone's chambers.

* * * *

The door to Orgone's rooms opened smoothly, without sound. Paul and the others entered, hearts pounding, sweat dotting their brows. He felt like a thief as he crossed the sitting area to the bedroom where San'dare'a lay. He was a thief. He was stealing the one thing Orgone treasured. Well, perhaps this would separate him from the nagging feeling that he had failed Hillary. Then again, perhaps it would mean his death.

His eyes scanned the dimly lit room. On his right, the weak light from Mars' moons spilled through the banit'ye barrier, illuminating a plush sandy pink floral carpet and casting fingers of radiance across a small writing table. The room was tastefully decorated in shades of dusty rose.

His gaze settled on a large bed against the far wall. She was there, unconscious on the bed as Bopack had said she would be. Her golden hair fanned out on the pink bedspread around her. Behind him, beside the banit'ye barrier in the living area, a large red and green parrot suddenly squawked. Paul and the others jumped.

"Get on with it!" Peter complained. Paul quickly crossed the bedroom floor and stooped over San'dare'a. Years of training motivated him to take her pulse and, as he did, the Old One silently glided to the other side of the bed. The long shimmering silver gown she wore gently brushed the carpet as she passed. Picking up a half empty mug from the night table, she replaced it with another empty but dirty mug concealed beneath her cape.

"That's how I drugged her," she whispered.

Paul glanced at the mug she held. He nodded.

"What did you use?"

"Xingat."

"Don't know it."

"It's a Gron'dalin special. They have lots of it around and it's harmless. Use it to drug the women before mating. They use a lot less than I used." She chuckled mischievously and calmly walked to the foot of the bed with the mug in her hand. "I'll drop this back in my rooms before we go."

Satisfying himself that San'dare'a was stable, Paul motioned for Duncan to pick her up. Crossing the floor quickly to the open door, he ran through the living area, sat down at the writing desk and wrote a brief message on a scrap of paper.

"Shit!" Peter complained from his post at the entrance to the bedroom. "Now we're writing bloody love letters I suppose? Can we get on with this?"

Folding the sheet of paper in half, Paul rose and, without a word of reply to Peter, returned to the bed where Duncan now stood with San'dare'a over his shoulder like a sack of potatoes.

Peter glanced nervously around as though any moment Orgone would spring out at them. Paul placed the note on the bed where Orgone would be sure to see it upon entry.

"I hope to hell you're not baiting him!" Peter warned. "The last bloody thing we need is to make this thing any madder at us than it's going to be. I think this is a big mistake!"

"Take it easy, Pete," Duncan said soothingly, turning with his little burden to gaze calmly into Peter's dark eyes. To Paul he added, "He gets this way sometimes."

"He sure does," Paul responded, raising his eyebrows. He gripped Bopack gently by one shoulder and guided her from the room. Duncan fell in behind them and Peter took the rear position with a disdainful grunt.

Slipping from the Zad's apartments undetected, the small clandestine group silently trod the tiled halls back past Bopack's room, then turned and retraced their steps toward the docking bays.

In a heightened state of anxiety, enhanced by the detour into enemy territory, they made their way stealthily without much conversation.

"Shit!" Peter finally said in a low whisper as the four passed a corridor leading off to the medical wing. "We're never going to get away with this."

Paul stopped. "Will you take it easy?" he snapped in a constrained whisper.

Bopack was now out in front, leading the three Alterin. Duncan passed Paul, knowing it was discipline time and Paul wanted words with Peter. He continued after Bopack with San'dare'a on his shoulder.

Pulling Peter roughly by the collar until he was face-to-face with him, Paul said in an angry whisper, "That old woman will lose her life if we're caught. You'll just be recaptured. Now bone up man! The real test is yet to come."

Peter looked ashamed.

Bopack and Duncan stopped some distance from them and waited, deliberately looking away to give them privacy. Paul released Peter, who straightened the collar of his shirt, his shame deepening. He stiffened and breathed deeply, steadying himself.

"Sorry," he said, chagrined.

"We need you to hold it together." Paul gazed steadily into Peter's eyes. The other man blinked but didn't flinch. "Can you do it?"

"Ya," Peter replied, nodding resolutely.

"Let's go," Paul said, slapping Peter on the shoulder. "Peter, you take the lead."

The procession moved quickly in single file down the corridor, the three Alterin scanning the silence. None among the party spoke again until Bopack whispered, "We are nearing the Arena where Cacin and Zadanin are in Challenge. Be very quiet. Guard your minds."

A moment later they reached a branch corridor leading from the one they fled through. Paul hesitated at the mouth of the passageway. Bopack motioned frantically for him to move on. He stood with his feet cemented to the floor, held there by some invisible but potent emotional force that he couldn't, or wouldn't, hold in check.

He sensed Hillary. She was there, just at the end of the hall. He closed his eyes briefly then motioned the others to continue on. They stared at him in disbelief. Duncan frowned and jerked his head, demanding that Paul accompany them.

Paul motioned more forcefully, threateningly. Peter rolled his eyes and shook his head in disgust but turned the corner and disappeared. Duncan turned abruptly and followed Peter with San'dare'a on his shoulder.

Looking down at the gray and green tiled floor, Paul's heart raced. How could he leave without her? He had fought to free her from this fate for weeks on Earth's surface. How could he walk away from her now on Mars without so much as an effort? Was he being given one last chance to free her? If the old woman could sneak away from the battle, so could Hillary.

From inside the arena he heard the sounds of fighting, mingled with sporadic cheering. He turned into the hall. The audience was engrossed in their entertainment. They wouldn't see him. What had Bopack said? This was their favorite sport.

Slipping down the corridor that led to the arena, he stopped in the darkness, just out of sight of those assembled. He could see the back of Hillary's head, her thick, dark hair spilling over her shoulders. He longed to touch it. Closing his eyes for a moment he wrestled with his feelings, knowing she wouldn't come with him.

Bopack stepped up behind him. He ignored her.

His senses were heightened. He could practically hear Bopack's heart pounding in her narrow chest almost as well as he heard the thrumming of his own.

He would accomplish nothing in this corridor but extend his own pain, or be caught. What was he doing here? How could he demand Peter hold it together and fall apart himself?

"It's only me," Bopack whispered softly, almost inaudibly.

"I know," Paul responded flatly.

"Paul?" she whispered. "Come away. They will sense you here. You're too close."

Paul remained rooted to the spot. He closed his eyes momentarily. Opening them, he fixed his sights on Hillary.

* * * *

Hill'carn watched the battle. Slowly she sensed Paul's presence. She drew in a deep slow breath and fought to control the shock she felt. What was he doing here? Anger rose in her throat like a hot ball of wax. How dare he come here! She had been so worried about the fate of her husband that she had forgotten her request to Bopack.

Of course, this was the ideal time to free him. Her admiration for the Old One grew. But how dare he come here and jeopardize everything!

Startled by his presence behind her, she almost turned to look at him. She caught herself just in time. Suddenly she didn't want him to see the changes in her. Her displeasure softened.

Go, Paul. Take your freedom while you can, she thought.

I love you, Paul thought back. I didn't fight to keep you free on Earth to leave you here.

I can't go with you.

You can. Slip away, Hillary, he implored. No one will notice.

Cacin will notice.

He's busy.

Go! Hill'carn thought again. I don't belong on Earth any longer. I belong here. I'm one of them now. Leave, Paul, while you can get away. Take your freedom.

I love you! Paul thought beseechingly.

Knowing she must shock him to force him to leave, she turned her head slightly, allowing him to see the extent to which the scales had spread.

I am changed, Paul. And I bear Cacin's child. I don't belong to Earth any longer. Go.

I'm changed too, Paul began. She cut him short.

I don't love you Paul. I love Cacin. I'm choosing to stay here with him. You must go and help the Humans or do whatever you must do in your new life. But I will stay here.

Bopack tugged gently on his arm. "Please come away," she whispered in that same soft, almost imperceptible whisper.

Goodbye then, Hillary, he thought. I will always love you. He received no reply as he turned in the darkness to leave.

Paul rushed from the corridor, concentrating on maintaining his mind block. His face twisted with pain and a few times along the corridor he stopped, leaning against the wall to gather his composure.

Bopack followed close on his heels, her heart finally returning to something like a normal beat.

"This is too much excitement for an old woman," she whispered jokingly as they turned into the main corridor.

* * * *

Duncan and Peter waited at the Bride Ship.

Paul turned to Bopack.

"What will happen to you?" he asked.

Smiling bravely, the Old One answered, "I have lived too long anyway, Paul. If they find me out I will die. But it is unlikely they will find out. I've concealed my activities quite well and as there is no reason to suspect me of wrongdoing, it is doubtful the King will read my thoughts." She smiled at him.

"I'm actually sorry that my chance to sting the Gron'dalin nation comes in the reign of one as gentle as Cacin," she said, trying to ease Paul's pain at leaving Hill'carn. "He is a very kind gron."

Paul looked down at the stone floor. Above him the Bride Ship loomed, huge and imposing. It waited for him with more patience than Peter had. Drawing a stiff breath in slowly through pinched nostrils, he said, "I'm glad to hear that."

"She will be happy with him," Bopack whispered, touching his arm. Paul nodded. "You must make a new life for yourself now, Paul. Hill'carn is. You have San'dare'a to make that new life with. Oh, she likes to be called by her Human name, Sandra," she added.

Paul nodded again, slowly straightening as he did. He had lost Hillary but perhaps the old woman was right. Perhaps life went on. Or at least it might if they accomplished their mission. As he stood at the loading ramp with two impatient Alterin standing to one side, the huge bulk of the Bride Ship behind him, he tried to accept his loss for the first time with hope.

* * * *

Hill'carn sat silently, once again absorbed with the battle that raged in front of her. She had forgotten that Paul was escaping as she sat there watching her husband fight. Her only concern was for Cacin.

The King received a violent blow to the side of the head that caused him to stumble. She cringed. The smell of blood and sweat permeated the theater. The battle had just begun. The thought that this custom MUST be changed crossed her mind as she straightened in the front row seat.

*\ *\ *\ *

"Go now. You must hurry," Bopack said. "The Challenge continues. But your work is best completed before its conclusion. If you aren't finished before the Challenge is settled, I doubt you'll succeed."

"Okay. Let's go, men," Paul said, gathering his resolve around him like a cloak.

"About bloody time," Peter hissed impatiently, continuing to look around nervously. He started up the ramp.

Paul stooped and kissed the old woman on the forehead. "Thank you, Bopack," he said. "You've been a good friend to us and the Humans."

She smiled at him. Turning quickly she disappeared back along the deserted corridor.

Chapter 33
The Armada

Paul maneuvered the enormous vessel from the dock without serious incident as Duncan and Peter hid San'dare'a's body beneath metal floor plates, among what served in Gron'dalin technology for electrical wiring.

"I hope she doesn't get fried in here," Peter remarked.

"She won't," Paul said as he guided the vast ship from the docking bay.

Rather an ignoble hiding place for one as lovely as her, Duncan thought to Paul. Paul made no reply.

They hovered just outside the Mars colony while he quickly searched the console he sat at. Behind him, Duncan and Peter replaced the floor plates over San'dare'a.

"She's quite a looker," Duncan said as he took his seat next to Paul.

"What? Oh, ya. She is." Paul remarked offhandedly. "Duncan, we have only six minutes to discuss our course of action once we dock at the Armada," Paul said, punching in a set of coordinates on a control panel.

"Here's what we're going to do." He leaned forward, concentrating on the controls.

"No!" he suddenly shouted, pounding the panel. "Wrong way!" The huge ship lurched violently as he quickly re-set the instructions. Once he satisfied himself they were heading in the right direction, he turned back to Duncan.

"I'm going to take the papers," he looked around the bridge. "Peter find those papers Bopack said we needed to give the commander! Look for something official-looking." Turning back to Duncan, he said, "I'm going to take the papers to the head honcho. They're expecting this ship tomorrow, but Bopack tells me they will be too ecstatic about getting the women early to reason things through."

"Let's hope she's right," Duncan muttered under his breath. "We're mincemeat if she isn't."

Paul punched in a few instructions on the strange-looking keyboard in front of him as a red light flashed on the control panel.

"Did Bopack tell you the general plan?"

"Some."

"I know the route to the air control module," he looked up at the Alterin again. "How much DID she tell you?"

"I've got the gist. We're going to plant a bomb on the Armada."

"And blow the bastards to kingdom come," Peter interjected. "No sweat! Then we're heading back to Earth."

"Oh that's real likely," Duncan stated, shaking his head in disgust at his comrade. "I think we'll be lucky to pull this off. Let alone get away with our lives."

"It's going to be hard," Paul said, ignoring Peter who was now cursing Duncan under his breath as he riffled through the papers he had found in a side panel of the huge command chair.

"More likely we're going to crash this boat or be blown out of the sky before we get there," Duncan remarked to Paul.

Paul smiled at him. "Lot of faith in me."

Duncan leaned forward and slapped him on the shoulder in response. "If anyone can do it, Paul, you can."

"I'm going to try to look like I'm headed where I should be when I disembark," Paul continued. "You both stay with the ship." Again he punched in some directions for ship's computer.

"How can you read that stuff?" Duncan asked, staring at the foreign looking symbols on the keyboard in front of Paul.

"I memorized it from the manual. The important thing for you to know is that you'll have to get the females and the ship away from the Armada if I'm not back in fifteen minutes."

"Women," Duncan corrected.

"Peter, are you getting this?" Peter continued to shuffle through the papers on the console beside them. His face was a mask of fear.

"Ya. I'll be there in a minute," he said with resignation.

Paul pulled out the thick operating manual from inside his shirt. "Read this," he said to Duncan. "And memorize enough to get you off the Armada." Duncan gaped at Paul in disbelief.

"Duncan you're going to have to cram enough info from this manual into your head to get you away from the Armada if I don't make it back," Paul insisted.

"Oh fat chance!" Peter protested. "I like the sound of this more and more," he complained. Duncan took the manual from Paul's hand and started flipping through pages.

"Why is it in English?" he asked.

Paul shrugged. "Compliments of Bopack. I never even thought of it."

"Wait a minute." Duncan held a page of the manual up to a light. "She's translated the words on each page. Look. There's another set of instructions underneath."

"Who cares?" Peter protested. "Just learn the damn thing!"

"Why would they have an operating handbook for one of these things anyway?" Duncan asked, ignoring Peter. "This ship is massive. There's no way a lay person could learn to operate this baby in a crisis."

"Duncan, shut up and learn how to fly this rig!" Peter snapped, spittle flying from his mouth. "Paul is a lay person. He learned how. I know there's no chance of surviving but we can go through the motions."

"Calm down, Peter," Paul said.

"Paul, I haven't got a clue which paper you're supposed to take. I can't read this damn stuff," Peter said, slamming a fist on top of the pile of papers. "Everything looks official," he complained, snapping the papers off the console and waving them at Paul. "Why can't these assholes speak English?"

"Sure would make our sabotage easier," Duncan said sarcastically.

"Oh shut up, Duncan!" Peter yelled, his fear turning to anger.

"Okay!" Paul yelled back, holding his hands up to prevent anymore discourse. "Simmer down. Both of you. Anything with a seal on it? Look for a red or gold colored seal."

Peter threw the papers on the console impatiently and went through them again, muttering to himself as he did.

Paul grabbed the book back from Duncan. "This will get you off the ground," he said, turning to the section on lift-off. "Memorize this control sequence. It's easy, really."

Duncan nodded at him as he spoke.

"Thrust-out will get you off the Armada. Power-up will move you forward. That's all you need to know."

"I bet!" Peter interrupted sarcastically, shaking his head in disgust.

"Look," Paul snapped, "I'm a doctor. If I can understand it, two pilots should be able to. You've got to get the females out of there if I'm not back in time."

"Women," Duncan reminded. "Here. Give it here," Duncan said calmly as he took the operating manual from Paul's hands.

"You're always calling them females," Peter muttered.

Paul sighed. "I'm starting to SOUND like them too." He wiped sweat from his forehead and pushed his hair from his eyes. He breathed rapidly. Suddenly the viewing screen glowed and Paul motioned urgently to the others to be quiet.

"Look calm!" he said between clenched teeth. "Peter sit down! Portray an image of a Sentry. Not Cruchton! Remember what Bo-pack said."

"Shit! Peter hissed, as he sat and tried to force the image he portrayed to look busy.

A Gron'dalin National appeared on the viewing screen.

"What is your mission, Shuttle *Conzar*?"

"We bring the females," Paul answered in a tone that said, you dumb klutz, what do you think we're coming for, our health?

"We will await your arrival," the National answered in a surly tone. The image faded from the screen.

"I bet you bloody will," Peter said hatefully. "It's not going to be quite what you're expecting though, boys," he added.

"That's more like it, Peter," Paul admonished.

"We're into it now. No going back." Duncan announced calmly as he settled down to read the manual.

"Let's give them the time of their lives," Peter said, grabbing a document off the top of the pile. "This'll be it," he said confidently.

* * * *

The Bride Ship docked at the center of the linked ships of the Armada with a bump. Paul threw Duncan a quick glance and wiped the stream of sweat from his forehead with the palm of one hand.

"This is it."

Duncan nodded. "Go for it!"

"Good luck," Peter barked from his post. "We'll be waiting here, boss. Projecting and studying this damn manual."

* * * *

Noticing the awkward landing of the *Conzar*, the National commander cleared his throat and smiled broadly.

"Clumsy landing," he commented to his next in command.

"They're a stupid lot," the officer replied.

"No skill in these matters." He donned his ceremonial jacket as he spoke in the observation area above the docking ring.

"I'm expected to be civil to these morons," he said as he opened the door and disappeared down the stairs, his massive body stiff in the starched uniform.

* * * *

On the bridge of the *Conzar*, in preparation for being accompanied, Paul held the sharp meat knife Peter had found in the ship's galley. Slipping the knife under his shirt he felt the cold steel against his flesh. He wore the image of a Sentry easily, like someone else might slip on a shirt.

"How do I look?"

"Like a Gron'dalin fighter," Duncan said, smirking at him in a conspiratorial way.

"Hand me those papers, Peter." He tucked them in his belt, adjusted his collar, took them out of his belt again. "Better carry these," Paul said.

Peter nodded. "Nothing casual about these sons-a-bitches."

"Okay. It's going to take me five minutes, tops, to get there. If I'm not back on board in say..." He looked at his watch. "Sixteen minutes?" Duncan nodded at him. "Clear out."

He held up the explosive Bopack had given him in the confinement area on Mars; the bomb Bopack had stolen from military supplies.

"This thing will go off ten minutes after I set it, so don't be sentimental, guys. Five minutes to get there. Another minute to set the bomb. Sixteen minutes and you have to get out of here; you have to be far enough away when she blows."

"Just be back before that," Duncan said, rising from his seat at the controls and slapping Paul on the back.

Paul took in a deep breath. "Okay. Here goes. Remember, you guys have to look like you're standing on ceremony at the gangway. Lucky we have enough men to pull this off."

Duncan nodded back at him and assumed his own image of a Sentry.

As Paul descended the loading ramp, Duncan and Peter marching stiffly behind him, his heart rose in his mouth. Fear gripped him. At the bottom of the ramp stood the first obstacle.

"Gae noda si van a patiie ha'lada fur hassie," the National commander said in its own tongue, bowing slightly as Paul stepped off the ramp.

"Speak Human English!" Paul snapped. "The females don't speak our tongue. Haven't you learned theirs?" He slammed the documents Peter had assured him were the transfer papers into the gron'ie's chest and hoped they were the right ones. Sweat formed in tiny droplets on his forehead but he dared not wipe it away. His guise looked fine. Too much movement might distort it somehow. He wasn't sure how this worked!

His heart pounded. He prayed it wouldn't read his mind. Nationals were not allowed to read a Sentry's mind, Bopack had told him earlier. Good God, let her be right!

"I apologize." The commander said in English. "Of course I have. I just thought..." it said, looking down at the papers that were thrust upon it.

"Never mind what you thought," Paul said sharply.

"We weren't expecting you until light dawned on the planet's surface," the commander said, glancing in an irritated manner at the officer that stood to its right.

"That's better," Paul responded, appearing appeased. "We have the time now," he said, brushing off further inquiry by jerking his head. A crude gesture, it fit well with the gron he addressed.

"I thought you were celebrating tonight."

"We've finished," Paul answered. "And we wanted to be rid of these females."

He almost called them women but caught himself in time.

"I have papers to be signed and a female to return to. Let's not tarry," he said as he, in the image he was portraying, pushed past the commander.

To Paul's amazement, this gron was bigger than any Gron'dalin he had ever laid eyes on. He gripped the knife in his belt, wondering if he could overpower it.

Sweat dripped off his chin. His heart raced! The cold steel of the blade had warmed with exposure to his flesh. The blade pressed reassuringly against his skin. Paul felt its sharp edge cut his stomach and stopped pushing on the knife.

The commander smiled a taut controlled smile as Paul pushed past.

"Of course," it said in the most condescending tone it could muster. "We will proceed expediently."

Turning abruptly, the creature followed the Sentry that its eyes deceived it into seeing.

"Vi Sentry, this way is shorter," the National asserted.

Paul wheeled on him. "Now you know my job better than I?" he thundered. Then reeling back, he strode off in the direction he had started in, the direction he must travel in if he were to find the passageway he needed.

"No, Vi," the National said with resignation. "I just thought I could be of help. The lounge is closer from this direction," it said, motioning. Paul did not turn to look. "The officers who must sign these papers are assembled there waiting. I am just trying to help."

"You can help by being silent," Paul snapped.

Duncan and Peter watched this show with poker faces from the loading ramp, projecting Sentry images like Paul's. Peter shot a nervous glance at Duncan as Paul's Sentry imprint disappeared through a set of doors. Duncan had already re-commenced his study of the manual behind the image he depicted.

Paul passed the exit point to the air modules. He said a silent curse. Perspiration rolled down his face. They walked briskly without speaking, past Nationals that were gathering to welcome their brides. His false replica held.

A full six minutes later, Paul found himself alone with the commander. Swinging around suddenly, his heart pounding loudly, Paul thrust the knife firmly in the National's chest and into its larger heart. Right up to the hilt the blade sank in.

The commander grunted, looking with disbelief at the knife handle that protruded from his chest, then back at Paul. His mouth fell open.

"Why?" he whispered.

Paul herded the commander's enormous frame into a small darkened chamber off the corridor before the gron could recover his senses. The commander grabbed for the handle of the knife. Paul wrenched its fingers away and yanked the knife out, pushing the gron against the wall at the same time. It would bleed to death more quickly with the knife withdrawn. There were advantages to being a physician. Knowing that fact was one of them.

Paul braced himself, expecting the gron to lash out with its mind as its large frame began to sway. To his amazement there was no struggle. The gron, too shocked to respond, only began moaning as blood trickled from its mouth.

"Why?" it whispered again.

Paul caught the commander's massive body as it fell, lowering it to the floor quietly. Sweat glistened on his face. His heart raced as he dragged the body to the far wall away from the door and hurried from the dark, closet-like room. Blood drenched his sweatshirt and jeans, sticking them to him as he re-traced his steps.

Paul's Sentry image remained clean and precise. He searched for the door that would lead to the air modules, heart pounding as he mopped sweat from his brow with a bloodied hand. At last the door loomed ahead of him! Opening it, he rushed through.

Paul could hear nothing above the sound of his own heart pounding in his ears. He had lost time! Ten minutes had evaporated like mist. Only six minutes were left to set the charge and get back. Sweat dampened his face. He ignored it, not even trying to rub it away.

He ripped a second door open and ran to the modules. Red symbols warned him not to tamper with the huge metal levers attached to each module, sixteen in total. Fumbling with the bomb, almost dropping it twice, he secured it as Bopack had instructed. He activated the timer and fled the chamber, glancing at his watch.

The Bride Ship would be leaving without him in four minutes.

* * * *

The Nationals coming to greet their brides clustered at the docking ring now.

Peter had never been good at staring matches. Now in full view of twenty National warriors he stood erect, confident in the knowledge they would see whatever he wanted them to see, whatever he portrayed. He was an excellent image illustrator. That was his forte in the area of mind control.

Where the hell is Paul? he thought to Duncan. He should be here by now! Behind the mask he portrayed, Peter was wired. His face was taut, his nostrils flared. Again he glanced at his watch without moving the arms of the image he portrayed.

Unable to move his own arms as freely as Peter when he was agitated and still leave the image arms at his sides, Duncan remained stiff.

Take it easy. How long have we got? Duncan thought, still holding the manual in one hand.

Two minutes.

Oh God! I can't reach him by mind transfer.

Probably because of the effort he's exerting to maintain the image, Peter thought back. We have to leave in about a minute.

I know. Duncan started panting. He clenched his free fist and bit his lip.

Let's go.

They were just turning when they received Paul's frantic burst.

Hold on. I'm coming. I've just set the charge. We have about five minutes.

Turning back, they caught sight of Paul racing toward the ship.

They reacted instantly to the appearance of their comrade. A sense of relief leaping in both minds. Then Duncan dropped his image.

Peter whispered a curse under his breath.

"Get inside, Duncan! You've lost your Sentry likeness!"

Both Alterin bolted up the gangway. They covered the distance in mere seconds, aware of a murmur rising from among the guards assembled at the base of the ramp. Not only had Duncan dropped his image – what was worse – Paul ran toward the ship in the most outlandish and unbelievable fashion.

Still portraying the resemblance of a calm Sentry that he had donned on leaving the air module room, an image that should have been passable, he ran like a zombie. Because of the fear of being deserted on the Armada, he'd forgotten to make the Sentry's legs move.

As Duncan looked back over his shoulder, the image Paul projected floated, or perhaps flew, a couple of feet above the metal surface. As the guards looked on, murmurs of incredulity went up from among their ranks.

Paul himself practically sailed through their formation in his bid for freedom. Before they could react, he was already on the ramp, his lungs almost bursting from the effort.

The sound of the ramp closing filled the air and rallied the Nationals. Its metal bulk swung upward toward the ship's smooth hull with Paul on it. The murmur rose to a clamor as the ship's engines began to cycle up.

"Shhhhhit!" Paul screamed trying to keep his balance as the gangway rocked.

Several shocked gron'ie now grabbed for the ramp as it quickly closed. One was able to hold on, pulling itself partially inside. Paul kicked it in the face, lost his balance on the moving ramp and fell. He lashed out with his foot again, contacting the gron's face once more.

"Get off, you Bastard!" he yelled.

The stunned warrior struck out with its mind, shaking the ramp so much that Paul could not regain his footing. Paul hit it repeatedly in the face with the heel of his boot, forcing it back, all the while yelling between gasps for air.

The huge National clung, half on, half off of the ramp, attempting to pull itself through the opening. It struck out with its mind indiscriminately, slamming Paul against the entrance to the bridge, which swung open with the force of the impact.

"Come on for Christ's sake!" Peter called. "The ramp is closing. Get in!"

"We've got to get out of here!" Duncan called from the main console.

Paul picked himself up and struck back with his mind, slamming the National with all his force, almost dislodging it entirely from the ramp where it still clung. As the vessel lifted the National adhered by its fingertips Pulling itself partially back onto the ramp, it battered the Alterin again with its powerful mind.

Paul slammed into a readout panel. The bridge entry closed just as the ramp snapped shut, crushing the screaming gron. Paul slid down to the deck.

"Help him, Pete!"

Peter rushed to Paul and lifted him from the deck."

"Get me to the controls," Paul said, holding his ribs with both hands. "Good job, Duncan," he said through clenched teeth.

"It's a cinch," Duncan responded. "These guys make everything so simple this baby can almost fly itself."

Propped up in the oversized control chair, Paul helped Duncan guide the craft clumsily away from the Armada and out into space. Two heavy impacts rocked the ship.

"They're firing on us!" Peter announced.

"Gee. I wonder why?" Duncan asked sarcastically.

"Beats me," Peter answered jovially.

Duncan laughed nervously. "You jackass, Pete."

"Take 'er out, Duncan!" Paul screamed, pulling himself from the seat. "I need to get the shields up. Give me the manual!" Peter threw the manual at him.

Duncan punched commands into his keyboard. "Under control here. Just get those shields up. Hurry, Paul!" Duncan warned.

"We aren't gon'a make it for Christ's sake!" Peter warned, his eyes bulging. "So close to the bloody impossible and we aren't going to make it!"

"Oh yes we are," Paul responded, licking the sweat off his upper lip. He hit some buttons on the keyboard and the display showed a blue field enveloping an image of the ship. "Oh YES we ARE," he repeated with determination.

Duncan guided the vessel rapidly away from the Armada.

"We bloody well are!" Peter yelled, slamming his fist down on the console beside him.

As the Bride Ship moved out to the stars the blinding glare of an explosion lit up the control room windows. A star burst into life at the center of the linked ships and spread rapidly, consuming everything in its path..

"That wasn't ten minutes!" Paul screamed, as glowing chunks of debris pelted the ship. "I thought it was supposed to be ten minutes before the thing blew!" he said.

"Who cares," Peter responded, gasping. "We're out. The old girl probably didn't know what she was talking about, but we're out." He laughed hysterically, running his scaled hands through his hair.

Duncan let out a whoop of excitement. "Yes! We made it," he bellowed in disbelief.

"What else was she mistaken about?" Paul asked under his breath.

Unstrapping himself, Duncan crossed to where Paul sat. He clapped the other Alterin on the back. "What was that little drifting trick I saw you pull back there, Paul?" Duncan teased. Falling into the empty seat beside his friend with a laugh almost as hysterical as Peter's, Duncan continued to laugh.

"Ya," Peter piped in. "You know, your little ghost imitation."

"Oh shut up," Paul answered, smiling as he suppressed laughter to avoid the pain it would bring. He gripped his ribs.

Unable to contain feelings of elation any longer the three Alterin were consumed by hysterics. Paul moaned intermittently but couldn't stop himself despite the pain.

"Phantom of the Armada," Duncan guffawed. All three laughed heartily, letting the fear that had enveloped them slip away like steam.

"Come on, guys," Paul finally said as their levity faded. "We have to find me some clean clothes," he held the blood-stained shirt away from his body, "and get these ladies back home."

Chapter 34
End of Challenge

As the Bride Ship streaked towards Earth, the Challenge raged on in the arena on Mars. Cacin took several severe blows to the head. He bled profusely. The blood ran down his face and dripped onto the sovan. He staggered now, gripping the sandy surface with his bare toes. Regaining his balance he lashed out at Zadanin with a closed fist.

Zadanin fared no better than Cacin, worse in most respects. He bled from the mouth and nose. Along the right side of his head a deep gash oozed blood relentlessly. He stood back, panting, trying to collect his strength and finding none left to gather.

Zadanin dodged Cacin's advance, stalling for time. Unable to focus he squinted at the King. In desperation he reached for a weapon and an exclamation went up from the crowd. Gasping, Hill'carn almost rose from her seat. The first gron to reach for a weapon, saying had it, was always the one to die. A sign of weakness, the move warned of an end in sight.

Cacin ducked as Zadanin swept the heavy war hammer in an arc above his head, pummeling the air. A murmur of disapproval rose from the assembly as Zadanin refused the King access to a weapon of his choice.

"He has no weapon yet!" Hill'carn said to no one in particular.

Zadanin swung again, missing by a fraction of an inch. Hill'carn whimpered and, if it were possible, sat more rigidly in her seat. The hammer came down on the floor again, smashing through the sovan. Cacin lost his balance and fell as he dodged the blow. He rolled toward the selection of weapons. Again Zadanin blocked him from the arsenal. He slashed, bringing his own weapon down an inch from Cacin's head in a clumsy maneuver that bespoke fatigue. Hill'carn moaned and rose from her seat. Bopack pulled her down.

"You must not."

"It's not fair!"

"He will manage."

Cacin rolled away. Jumping to his feet, he glanced in his wife's direction as Zadanin, exhausted, was pulled of balance by the force of his swing and fell.

"I would have been punished for what you just did, Hill'carn," the Old One whispered. "You have disgraced him." She still held Hill'carn's arm tightly. "Be thankful he's not Kagoule."

Hill'carn hadn't removed her eyes from Cacin. Her breathing grew rapid. Her heart raced. Cacin winked at her and smiled before lunging past Zadanin to reach for a halberd. The weapon seemed to fly to his outstretched hand.

With a movement as swift and smooth as silk he launched the weapon like a spear. It sailed through the air, embedding itself in Zadanin's chest. Zadanin cried out in pain; rising from the floor with a scream of agony, then fell back in death.

The assembly rose and applauded as Cacin turned to leave the Bay Arena. The smell of blood and death hung on the sweat-soaked air.

Stooped and stiffened by age, with his own death drawing near at the hands of a slower and less kindly adversary, Gradspin threw the King's cape up and over the young gron's shoulders. With the King's help, smiling and nodding congratulations, he stretched to reach the Zi's shoulders.

"You will be a great leader," Gradspin whispered.

Cacin smiled, blood trickling down his face. He turned and walked slowly toward the exit and the clamor rose to a frenzy in the tiered seats above him. All the gron'ie applauded more ardently.

Looking straight ahead, somber and dignified as he passed Hill'carn, he struck her as a stranger. Who was this gron that could kill in the blink of an eye with no remorse?

Blood and sweat oozed from the tiny shimmering scales around his eyes, following a path down his handsome face to his chin. It dripped onto his heaving chest, soaking into the silver cape fastened around his neck with the diamond-studded clasp bearing the royal insignia.

She watched him walk past, his body bruised and slashed, the wounds of battle hidden now under his cape. Hill'carn didn't move for a moment, standing erect and still as she was expected to stand as he passed. She cast a glance around the arena at the cheering gron'ie.

"This will be the last Challenge I sit through," she said to Bopack in a determined voice. "Unlike you, Bopack, I will not endure this barbarism."

"You will have no choice," the Old One said coldly.

"Oh, I will! I will make my choices from now on."

"Protocol demands you attend. And the Gron'dalins love these battles too much to give them up. Don't think you'll influence them to give that up."

"Hang custom! And they can learn to love other things. I will have them abolished, Bopack. Mark my word."

Bopack laughed. "If anyone can do it," the old woman said under her breath, "you can. This is the only Challenge I've enjoyed," Bopack whispered at Hill'carn's side. "One son to go and the house of Simar will be terminated."

"What do you mean?"

"I have one nasty, disreputable, aggressive son left. The worst of the three. When he is dead that lineage will die with him."

Hill'carn nodded but made no reply. "You didn't see much of the Challenge," she confided under her breath. A clandestine smile passed between them, and applauding continued around them.

Although nauseated by what she'd seen, Hill'carn was happy. Overjoyed that Cacin was alive and walking toward the exit, that it wasn't his body lying on the arena floor, she wanted to run from the stadium and throw herself on him, kiss him all over his face and neck. But, expected to remain at her seat, she waited like all the others.

What power did these gron'ie have over her now that she obeyed their rites? Who could touch her? She smiled to herself. With no one present who could stop her from leaving her seat, not even Orgone because she was Queen, she turned to leave. Bopack grabbed her arm.

"You have to stay," the old woman whispered urgently. "It's tradition."

"It's time for change," Hill'carn replied, pulling her arm gently away as she strode after Cacin. A murmur of disbelief rose like the hum of bees around a hive as she ran from the arena. The happy sound of collective laughter, low and contained, rose from the waiting throngs.

Was it approval? So, she had gauged them right. Hadn't she? It was time for change.

She caught him in the corridor. "Cacin!" she called, happiness ringing in her voice. Behind her the din died down as the Sentry removed Zadanin's body from the floor of the arena. The other gron'ie slowly vacated their seats.

Cacin turned. A broad smile creased his lips at the sight of her. "And you didn't believe me," he said, holding his arms out to her.

Lifting her gown away from her legs she ran to him. His cape parted, revealing his battered body. She grimaced at the sight of the blood on him but threw herself into his arms anyway, kissing his bleeding face frantically.

Sweeping her up in his massive arms he started carrying her down the corridor.

"I thought you were disgusted by this barbarism?" he said, laughing as she plied his face with kisses.

"I am. That doesn't mean I'm not glad you're still alive."

"I told you not to worry," Cacin said, smiling at her. She continued to kiss him. He finally broke into peals of laughter at the spirited behavior, stumbling down the hall with her in his arms.

"You shouldn't have followed me out of the arena," he said when she finally stopped. "Custom holds that the victor leaves well before any of the spectators. Even his wife waits. You were supposed to stay until Gradspin dismissed the assembly."

"I think that rule is stupid," Hill'carn replied. "I wanted to be with you too much to wait."

"The reason for this exercise is simple."

"Most customs are based on simple reasoning," Hill'carn replied, an edge to her voice she hadn't intended to be there.

"Do you want to know the reason?"

"Okay," she conceded, clinging to him.

"The victor is not always the popular contestant. Passions run high and he could be killed by a spectator after the match, before those assembled have time to recover from their feelings."

She guffawed. "Couldn't someone just reach out with their mind and kill you? No one would even know for sure who did it then."

"Aw!" Cacin raised his curly eyebrows. "Protocol dictates that no mind power be used at a Challenge."

She nodded condescendingly. "Obviously some regulations get broken. You brought the weapon to you."

Cacin laughed. "That I did," he replied. "But the little cretin wasn't going to allow me to get one. That's not permitted either."

"Instead of having so much ritual surrounding this barbarism," Hill'carn said, adjusting her hold around Cacin's neck. "Wouldn't it be better to do away with this Challenge thing and institute a more humane and safer method of dealing with treason?"

"More humane?" Cacin asked. "I'm not Human, why would I be humane?" He smirked at her as they continued down the long corridor.

Hill'carn groaned at him. "You know what I mean," she said.

"More humane. Like hanging?" Cacin asked sarcastically. The long silver cape of the Zi lineage flowed out behind him, flapping intermittently against his ankles as he effortlessly carried Hill'carn.

They turned into an open area that fed into various corridors leading to the living quarters, medical areas, and lower level gardens. Four hundred miles of Colony stretched away before them. Cacin turned into the med passageway.

Hill'carn thought about his statement. She shrugged. "Well, hanging would be safer at least."

Cacin chuckled cynically. "I know what you're thinking my love. The Challenge appears to be a contradiction within our society. We're advanced in so many ways. Surely we must be able to find a better way of settling disputes than this. The fact is, like Humans, we're violent by nature. The difference between our races is that we are more honest about our savage tendencies. I enjoyed killing Zadanin tonight. I was mistaken when I told you I should have killed him sooner. I would not have enjoyed killing him on Ranat. I didn't hate him on Ranat."

Cacin had stopped walking to deliver this speech and Hill'carn stared at him in disbelief.

Cacin spoke again. "Do you despise me now? Now that I've been blunt about who I am?"

Hill'carn lowered herself from his arms. "No," she replied, releasing a breath she'd been holding while he spoke.

Cacin smiled and kissed her lips. "You are undisciplined for coming after me as you did," he said, changing the subject.

"And my lack of discipline will be your undoing," Hill'carn muttered, smiling playfully.

"Aw. Are you predicting that?" Cacin laughed and put his arm around her shoulders as he resumed walking. Hill'carn made no reply but smiled up into his face as she walked along beside him.

Releasing her, Cacin opened a door on his right and walked ahead of her into the medic center.

"Now I'm going to do something that's really going to anger you. I'm going to drug San'dare'a for Orgone," he stated flatly, pressing his mahogany lips together as he looked down at the syringe Beau'nad had prepared. "First I'm going to have a shower. Then I will do what must be done."

"I know how much this upsets you Hill'carn, but it must be done. I won't idly stand by while my friend dies."

Hill'carn looked down at the floor, her jubilation at Cacin's victory crushed beneath the knowledge of San'dare'a's fate.

Chapter 35
Discovery

Hill'carn could hear Cacin rushing through his shower. She stood quietly outside the cubicle, waiting for him to finish. The room had filled with steam, seeping around the top of the glass door. She knew he would dress quickly and leave, giving her no time to state her request. If she did not wait for him outside the cubicle. She would come out of the bedroom looking for him and he would be gone. As the shower turned off, she spoke.

"I would like to come with you," she said. "There's perhaps something I could say to San'dare'a to change her mind."

"Bopack has tried unsuccessfully for some time," he replied, stepping from the shower into the room. He snatched a towel from the rack and rapidly rubbed it over his massively bruised chest.

"That looks sore," she said tenderly.

"It will heal."

The small shell-like motifs that spread across his torso were lacerated and blackened. The cut above his left eye had swollen and the eye was almost shut.

"Beau'nad should see this," she remarked, touching the bruises on his chest and eye lightly.

"We don't go to a doctor with battle wounds unless we have broken bones."

"That's silly. But it's your choice. I would like a moment with San'dare'a," Hill'carn repeated. "Perhaps there is something I can say to console her, if that's all I can do."

"Very well. You'll have it," he said, pulling her into an embrace. He kissed her firmly on the lips and let her go. "But you mustn't interfere with the drugging." He pointed a finger at her as though she were a child then pulled his robe on.

"I won't," she conceded. "Bopack was right about one thing. You Gron'dalins are too big to argue with."

"I'm sorry it has to be this way, Hill'carn."

"I still don't believe it has to be. And there are going to be some changes there too," she said mostly to herself.

"Changes?"

"Bopack and I have been discussing changes that need to be made."

He chuckled. "You have, have you?" Then he sighed. "We will research a drug to dull the effects of the mating instinct as soon as we return to Ranat. I promise you that, Hill'carn. But now Orgone's life depends on him copulating."

As they left the bathroom, Hill'carn caught a glimpse of Orgone, waiting in the foyer, sullen but resolved to carry through with his coupling.

"Orgone looks unhappy," she said as they entered the dressing room together.

"Orgone will get over it," Cacin replied, dropping his robe to the floor and pulling on the sweater and slacks Palin had laid out for him.

"San'dare'a probably won't," Hill'carn responded as he dressed.

* * * *

Hill'carn stood in shock beside her husband. Cacin stood at Orgone's empty bed gazing down with his one good eye at the note left for his friend.

"Who could have written this?" he demanded, looking at Orgone.

Hill'carn stared first at the bed with disbelief, then at the note in Cacin's hand, trying not to look too shocked, yet wondering if she didn't have a right to look that way under the circumstances.

"If you love her, set her free?" Cacin read aloud again. "What does that mean? Who would leave a message like this, and in English?" he asked, still holding the syringe in one hand.

Hill'carn stared at the paper Cacin held, knowing the answer. More astounded by the Old One's treachery - a treachery she was now sworn to conceal - than she was at San'dare'a's absence, she stood blinking at Cacin and the note and the empty bed. She said nothing.

The words hadn't completely left Cacin's lips when a look of realization crept over his face. How much did he know, she wondered? Involuntarily she gasped.

"Paul Muntz!" he blurted, discarding the Xingat filled vial on the bed. "It could only have been Paul Muntz."

"Paul Muntz?" Hill'carn gasped, trying to sound surprised at the sound of his name.

"We captured him a few days ago," Cacin admitted.

"Oh." She nodded slightly. "Whatever for?"

Ignoring her in his rage, Orgone fixed Cacin with a look that made Hill'carn's blood run cold. "I will kill him," he stated. "I swear I will kill him!"

Hill'carn gasped again.

"Don't be hasty, Orgone," Cacin replied. "He doesn't know our practices. He doesn't know what he's violated with this theft."

"If it was Paul," Hill'carn said boldly in his defense, guarding her mind carefully from Orgone, "he was acting out of kindness only. San'dare'a did not want to be with you, Orgone."

"Hill'carn!" Cacin snapped, shocked by her outburst.

"That would be his only concern," Hill'carn continued.

"That is not MY only concern," Orgone snapped back. "No-one ever wants to be with us. Or have you failed to notice that glaring fact?"

"Orgone!" Cacin shouted in amazement.

"I'm quite aware of that," Hill'carn replied coldly. "And I'm glad she's gone," she said walking toward the door. "Perhaps now you'll have to find an alternative to your 'pressing need'," she said bitterly, turning to look at them.

"Hill'carn you should leave," Cacin stated, glaring at her with almost as much disdain as Orgone mustered.

"Perhaps now you will put Beau'nad to work right away on a medication that will..."

"You may leave!" Cacin bellowed, cutting her statement short. His posture threatened.

"You mean I MUST leave," Hill'carn replied coldly as she turned to go. She guarded her mind from both of them. The door slid open to her command. She turned back. Both gron'ie followed her exit in silence with their eyes, eyes that would rather have slapped her than looked at her. Cacin's nostrils flared. The look he wore was menacing.

"One day you will not be able to force me," Hill'carn stated. "That IS a prediction," she said.

Drawing in a deep breath, she swung around to leave, glad of what Bopack had done and pleased she could keep the knowledge of it from Cacin.

She could feel their eyes ablaze behind her, burning into her back. She rushed through the foyer, the door to the inner chamber slamming shut behind her. Out into the corridor she tore with a vengeance, her face set in stone.

Bopack waited in the hall, as she emerged with her granite mask. Hill'carn smiled wickedly at her and winked, adjusting her gown briskly around her neck.

"Will you join me for a cup of... hot chocolate?" Bopack asked, carefully returning the smile.

"I would love to, my friend," Hill'carn answered, understanding the message.

The two women walked arm-in-arm down the nearly deserted corridor to Bopack's quarters as they often did of late, Bopack's small frame almost hanging from Hill'carn as they proceeded. The door to her lavish suite opened with a swoosh. They stepped into the outer room.

A small wooden table sat against one wall with a vase of flowers on it, beside it a bench not unlike a deacon's bench. There was no window in this room. Beyond the doors, Bopack's inner rooms beckoned.

"You have outdone yourself," Hill'carn confided immediately when the doors closed behind them.

"There's another surprise coming," Bopack said, disengaging herself from Hill'carn. She quietly walked through the doors into the room beyond.

"What have you done?" Hill'carn asked in disbelief.

"Are you coming?" Bopack replied, looking back at the Queen. "I really would like a drink of chocolate. Orgone ordered one every night without fail, for San'dare'a. Did you know that?"

"What have you done?" Hill'carn repeated.

* * * *

"Don't worry, Orgone. He couldn't have taken her far. He's not a pilot, he's a doctor. He wouldn't be able to get a ship off the ground. He must be in Colony somewhere."

Orgone scanned Colony. "He's not on Mars, Lord Zi."

"He must be here," Cacin answered. "He's tricking us with his mind."

"Peter is a pilot," Orgone reminded his friend. "Duncan is a pilot. Neither of them is on Mars either." He dismissed the statement with the wave of a hand.

As if to confirm Cacin's worst fears, Gradspin rushed into the chamber unannounced, his old visage twisted from the effort of running.

"Zi," Gradspin blurted breathlessly. "Three Alterin have escaped! They've stolen the Bride Ship." He held his old gnarled hands out in disbelief. "With all the National's brides on board!"

"There'll be trouble over this," Orgone announced. The Nationals will revolt.

"How did he know which ship to take?" Cacin asked, spinning to gaze out the banit'ye barrier into the blackness that surrounded Mars.

"Accident perhaps," Gradspin answered.

"How did he know about San'dare'a?" Cacin asked. Gradspin looked puzzled.

"The dirty swine must have been able to read my mind after all," Orgone replied, anger boiling up to consume him. All these years his mind had been respected as the greatest of his generation.

"These are truly worthy opponents," Cacin stated, staring up at the stars that Paul and his motley crew had vanished into. He laughed cynically and shook his head. "I marvel at their ingenuity. Don't worry, Orgone, we will get San'dare'a back if that's your wish."

Gradspin looked down at the empty bed. "What has happened here?" he said, suddenly taking in the female's absence.

"Paul Muntz has taken San'dare'a," Orgone whined, looking for sympathy.

"Aw!" Gradspin nodded with admiration. "He is truly remarkable."

"Is that all the two of you can say?" Orgone snapped. Like a child he stamped his feet. "He is truly remarkable? To hell with him!" He stomped three more times, growling as he did it.

Gradspin cleared his throat but said nothing. Cruchton suddenly entered by mind transfer. Materializing rapidly, he bowed slightly to the King.

"NOW WHAT?" Orgone boomed, stamping again and glaring at the Sentry.

Cruchton looked at him with venom then back at the King. "Zi," he said to Cacin in his matter-of-fact tone, ignoring Orgone, "I bring bad news."

"That's a change!" Orgone said.

"Not more bad news!" Cacin replied, glancing at Orgone. "What more could have happened during the Challenge?"

"The Armada is destroyed and the Nationals have all perished," Cruchton replied, his face a composed mask that hid his anger and disbelief. "It appears their air module exploded."

"There!" Orgone yelled. "You see? Now are you going to admire this creature?"

Stupefied, Cacin gaped at Cruchton for a moment. "The Alterin?" he asked with the same skepticism Cruchton hid from them.

"Now are you so ready to commend him for his ingenuity?" Orgone snapped again.

"Orgone, get yourself in hand," Gradspin admonished.

Cruchton shrugged at Cacin, disregarding Orgone as he was wont to do on most occasions lately. "I don't know."

"Not only has he secured his own freedom, stolen the females, taken San'dare'a, but he has annihilated the fleet?" Cacin's voice was thick with incredulity. "Is this what you're telling me?"

Cruchton nodded. "Two Alterin remain. The two who were unable to guard their minds and project. Neither of them knows of the escape, apparently. Their minds have been scanned and they know nothing."

"I can't believe it!" Cacin said, lowering himself into a chair beside the barrier. "How did we underestimate Paul Muntz so badly?" he asked Cruchton, looking up into the gron's green-blue eyes.

Cruchton looked down at the empty bed, and then over at Orgone as he realized that San'dare'a was gone too. "I don't know," he answered quietly.

"We have perhaps met our match," Cacin stated. A shiver ran through him and a look of apprehension passed between the two gron'ie.

"We have created our match," Gradspin announced. With these words, a heavy silence fell over them.

Turning to Orgone, Cacin finally spoke very slowly. "We have truly underrated this adversary, my friend."

His brow knit, he slowly shook his head. "What is your will regarding San'dare'a, Orgone? Do we recapture her?"

Orgone inhaled and straightened "Yes," he answered resolutely, looking out at the shadows that engulfed that foreign world. "I will bed no other."

Gradspin raised his eyebrows. "Zadanin has left a widow, Orgone. She might be a fine match. Although she's quiet, and not beautiful, she's very intelligent."

"She is stupid."

"Don't misjudge her potential as we have underestimated Paul Muntz. She is a lovely female and she is not pregnant."

Turning to Gradspin, Cacin spoke. "This is Orgone's choice, Lord Elder," he said.

Gradspin shrugged. "What are we Elders here for, if not to advise?"

Turning to Cruchton, Cacin asked, "Have they taken anything with them other than the females?"

"They have the Bride transport, Zi," Cruchton answered.

"Locate it," he said, throwing Gradspin a quick glance. The old gron had folded his arms across his chest. He nodded at Cacin, knowing what the young King was going to say next. "Destroy it immediately if it's empty."

"If it's empty?" Orgone challenged.

"There is no need to kill wantonly," Cacin replied. "And don't forget, San'dare'a is on that ship too." To Cruchton he continued, "I am presuming they have landed on Earth already as everything else has gone so badly for us. If they are still in flight, let them live. Wait until the ship is empty and blast it to pieces."

"Why not just recover it?" Orgone asked.

"Show of force," Cruchton replied.

Cacin picked the syringe up off the bed where he'd thrown it. "We will put this away for the moment," he said, looking at Orgone with his one good eye. Orgone glared back at him with his anger more in check now.

Turning to the Chief Commander, Cacin said, "Cruchton, you're with me." He started toward the door. The Sentry stepped in beside him. Both gron'ie held their hands behind their backs contemplatively as they walked.

"As we planned, you will arrange for the return of the children in the morning, Gradspin," Cacin announced over his shoulder as they left. "This changes nothing."

"But Zi..." Gradspin began.

"No! We will not keep the children because of this. We will have San'dare'a back because she belongs to Orgone. But we will not retaliate over the destruction of the Armada in any way. This is war. In every war there are losses. There must also be honor. I made the decision this morning to send the girls back and we will do so."

His voice trailed off as he rounded the corner into the corridor, Cruchton striding along beside him.

"After you locate the ship, which I believe you will find empty already," Cacin addressed Cruchton in a private tone, "investigate this escape. Determine how they accomplished it." They walked quickly, as though bent on reaching some destination.

"I can't believe the Alterin were able to escape the force field," he continued. "Beau'nad's tests revealed they weren't advanced enough to manipulate the closure. Orgone confirmed that." He paused. "Unless they're able to conceal more than we know." Cacin stopped, turning around to face Cruchton at the door that led to Cacin's own apartments. The inevitable pending confrontation with Hill'carn awaited him on the other side.

"Do you suspect someone here of helping them, Lord?"

He shrugged. "No. The only one who might help them escape is Hill'carn and she did not know Paul Muntz was in Colony. At least, I don't think she did."

"Perhaps they are just smarter than we realize. They certainly have done the impossible where the Armada is concerned. Even if Hill'carn did release them, she would never be able to advise them about the armada. They've been very effective in halting the Bride Quest." He shook his head and snorted. "Paul Muntz knows me better than I like. It was a tactical error to capture them and bring them here. It was an error to give them access to our library."

"He knows you will not remove the rest of the females now," Cruchton observed.

"How could he know me so well?" He wrinkled his brow. "It is I," he hit his chest lightly with his fist, "who have been studying him."

It was Cruchton's turn to shrug. "It appears he has been returning the favor."

"These are indeed a worthy foe!" Cacin said, shaking his head in disbelief again. His anger at the bad news was tempered with respect. "You may go, Cruchton."

Cruchton nodded and strode down the hall as the King turned to enter the fray.

Chapter 36
Confrontation

Hill'carn had been monitoring Cacin's mind to know when he was returning to his chambers. This was a new talent she had been developing that Cacin was, as yet, unaware of. When she felt him leave Orgone's rooms, she left Bopack, not wanting to be found with the Old One in case Cacin should wonder at their companionship so late at night and on so momentous an occasion as this day had become.

She arrived at their rooms just moments before Cacin appeared, aware that he wanted to argue over her comments in Orgone's quarters. Resolved not to fight with him, she waited in silence. As the door slid open to admit him, she walked from the antechamber into the sitting rooms beyond.

"I want to talk with you," Cacin announced as he followed her.

"Perhaps tomorrow," Hill'carn replied.

Cacin stopped suddenly where he stood. "I beg your pardon?" he replied, not believing what he had heard.

"You are angry now and will say things we'll both regret. We should talk in the morning," Hill'carn retorted with determination. She unclasped the hook at the back of her gown as if making ready for bed.

Crossing the floor he grabbed her arm and whirled her to face him.

"Do you intend to be physical with me too?" she asked, her eyes wide with anger.

Cacin dropped her arm. "Of course not." He drew in a deep breath. "You know I would never harm you." His puffy eye was turning purple now and looked terrible. They continued to gaze at each other, he with his one good eye and his battered face.

"You've forced me in many things, Cacin. I don't know where you will stop."

Cacin drew in a deep breath, apparently considering this statement. "Do you wish your freedom?" he asked suddenly, after a moment of contemplation.

Hill'carn looked into his one open eye, the other almost closed with swelling. "Are you offering me my freedom?"

"I will give it to you, if it's that important," he answered bitterly, his eight-foot height reduced somewhat by fatigue.

"The freedom to choose is what is important to me," Hill'carn replied. Her back stiff, she held her head high.

"Then choose," he said, challenging her. "You'll have what you want."

Hill'carn looked intently at him, her nostrils flaring with anger at first. Then she felt the corners of her mouth turning up slightly as the anger subsided and she fought to conceal a smile.

How could she not love this young gron, so good-hearted in ways that mattered to her? She raised her hand, touching his face gently then buried her face in his massive chest in reply.

Chapter 37
Down to Earth

Paul and Duncan hurried away from the others, separating themselves and San'dare'a as quickly as possible from the women being loaded onto buses brought to the landing site at Paul's request.

Although Bopack had assured him Cacin would not recapture the rest of the women, she had been wrong about the timing on the bomb. Perhaps she would be wrong about Cacin's reaction to the destruction of the Armada too.

While Duncan carried the limp body of the drugged woman easily on his shoulder to the waiting car, Paul pressed a hand against the damaged ribs on the left side of his body.

"Lucky I got away so lightly. My body could be floating up there with those Nationals right now," Paul said.

"You see to that as soon as you get where you're going," Cahill muttered from beside him.

"I will," Paul answered.

"Will there be a doctor there?"

"I'm a doctor, Simon."

"Ya, but you can't treat yourself."

"The hell I can't."

They passed some moments in silence with Duncan lumbering ahead of them, his feet periodically dragging through the gravel.

"You shouldn't have brought her back with you," Cahill said as he shuffled awkwardly along beside the Alterin. "You put the whole mission in jeopardy."

"I know that," Paul answered.

"Then why did you do it?" Cahill asked, rushing forward to open the rear door of the vehicle for Duncan.

The Alterin lowered the woman's body onto the back seat effortlessly.

"Because the fuckers aren't going to get away with this one, too, that's why," Duncan replied for Paul, his jaw set with determination.

"She didn't want to stay, so we brought her back," Paul answered defiantly.

"Do any of them want to stay?" Cahill asked.

"I've got to go," Duncan said to Paul, slapping him on his good shoulder.

"See ya, Dunk. Thanks," Paul said, embracing the other Alterin quickly.

"Ya," Duncan answered. "Be careful," he called as he retreated toward the buses. "And good luck."

Paul stopped momentarily to watch his friend sprint back in the direction they had just come. He drew in a deep breath then turned to Cahill.

"Maybe," he answered, reflecting on Hillary's response to his offer to bring her back to Earth with him.

"Eh?"

"Maybe some of them are choosing to stay now. Perhaps it's too late for some of them. It isn't too late for her, though."

"It looks pretty late to me," Cahill remarked, looking down at San'dare'a's face.

Paul slammed the car door. "And what about me?" Paul asked. "Is it too late for me too?"

"Hell no!" Cahill said quickly, too quickly.

"I've got to get to the Undergrounds, Simon." He ignored Cahill's discomfiture. San'dare'a looked a lot more Human than Paul did. With a light scaling along the sides of her face she was not nearly as covered as Paul.

"They can't mind trace her right now," he continued, "But they can trail me easily enough."

He dove into the driver's seat, grimaced with pain, slammed the door and turned the ignition key. He lowered the driver's window.

"The one that wants her happens to be their best mind," he said. "I've got to keep one step ahead of it if I'm going to win this."

"Is that how you see it?" Cahill asked. "Win or lose?"

"Ya. That's precisely how I see it. They got Hillary but they aren't getting her," he motioned with his head to the back seat.

Cahill moaned. "You would have to steal the one woman wanted by the best mind in the bunch, wouldn't you?"

Paul signed. "Where's the challenge otherwise?" They both laughed.

"Get the rest of the women away from the ship as quickly as possible," Paul instructed. "They'll destroy it as soon as they find it's missing."

"Shame," Cahill responded, shaking his head. "Nice piece of technology."

"Don't even think about it, Simon. You'll die trying," Paul warned. He glanced down at the steering wheel momentarily, then back up at Cahill.

"You take care," Cahill said, grasping Paul affectionately by the shoulder.

Paul smiled weakly. Putting the car in gear he pulled away from the bedlam and headed out into darkness. The headlights of the buses spilled light to his right, illuminating the spacecraft that sat empty in the clearing. He beeped at Duncan who stood at the back of the last queue of women, barking orders. The Alterin waved back briefly then resumed directing the women aboard the buses.

Once on the main highway he accelerated, drawing on as much power as he could for his escape. His cracked ribs complained as he drove into the night, the headlights of the car the only light under a starless sky.

Duncan had landed the Bride Ship in a remote part of Washington State. There was an elaborate Underground only ten miles from the landing site that had never been entered by the aliens during the Bride Quest. Paul believed they didn't know its whereabouts.

He flipped open the arm rest and scanned through Cahill's CD collection.

"Classical."

That was okay but he didn't want classical music right now.

"Dream of the Blue Turtles?" He shrugged. "Maybe." Then he fell on the theme music from the Rocky Horror Picture Show.

"Cahill?" he said aloud as he loaded the disc, shaking his head. "Who would have guessed?"

The music boomed out into the car as he sped toward their destination, only eight miles away now. He watched the odometer as much as the road for the next few minutes.

Suddenly, the first scan started. Like cotton wool rolling over his mind it was hardly discernible at first. It was almost indistinguishable with the music blaring. He turned off the music.

"Orgone." He blanked areas of his mind. "Shit!" Could he feed him wrong information? Mislead him?

The probe gripped his mind brutally. He struggled to maintain control of the car, at the same time thinking San'dare'a was with Simon Cahill. It was the first thought he seized on. He knew at once it was a bad one. The probe vanished but he knew immediately that Cahill was in trouble.

While Orgone didn't know Cahill's exact mind pattern, he would easily find him through similarities in knowledge like searching a string of text in a book. Cahill knew a lot about this particular situation, having coordinated the buses that came to retrieve the women. Orgone would soon know that San'dare'a was with Paul.

If Orgone gripped Cahill's mind the way he'd gripped Paul's, Cahill might not have a mind left when he vacated.

"You're on your own, Buddy. Sorry. I can't take the chance that I could find you and get you below ground before Orgone finds you. Damn! Why did I think that?"

Paul floored it. He turned onto a gravel road now speckled with snow, barely maintaining control. Swinging into the gravel parking area he slammed on the brakes. The car spun like a top then finally came to an abrupt stop. San'dare'a's body slid off the back seat onto the floor with a thud.

"Shit!" he cursed, launching himself from the driver's seat. He screamed with pain as his ribs ground against each other. Ripping the back car door open he collected San'dare'a off the floor, throwing her unceremoniously over his right shoulder with considerable difficulty. He grunted and hobbled into the shelter opening. Grabbing the hand-railing for support, he stumbled down the stairs. Suddenly he was face-to-face with a guard holding a hunting rifle. Very young and barely out of his teens the man was clearly terrified.

"Freeze!" the guard yelled.

Paul held up his hands in supplication as best he could without dropping his burden.

"Sorry. Sorry," he said. "Didn't mean to startle you. I'm being followed by an alien."

"You look kind'a alien yourself," the young man answered cautiously.

"I'm Paul Muntz," Paul answered, wedging San'dare'a's body between the wall and his shoulder.

"That supposed to mean something to me?"

"I've just brought some women back from Mars," he said. "This one is special to one of the aliens up there and I'm determined he's not going to get her." San'dare'a was slung over his shoulder like a bag of potatoes. "Can I put her down?"

"Mars, eh?" the young man replied cynically. "I'll bet. All right. Put her down. But don't try anything stupid, buddy, or you're dead. I've got ya covered."

Paul looked around for a place to deposit San'dare'a's limp body. The room, lined with concrete, was open to the surface and entirely square. His breath hung on the frigid air as he assessed the best place to set his load down. On his immediate left, a small wooden table and three chairs, an ashtray with a burning butt and a steaming cup of coffee filled the space.

"Little cold to be sitting out this time of year?" Paul said. He had smelled cigarette smoke when he entered. On his right a long padded bench stood near a heavy metal door. "Can I put her over there?"

"Okay but don't try anything."

The young man kept him covered.

Walking toward the bench, he spoke to the guard. "Where is everybody? You aren't the only one here are you?"

"Inner rooms." The guard answered carefully, not wanting to give away any secrets.

He followed Paul with his eyes and the barrel of the rifle.

Paul dumped his cargo on the bench, being as gentle as he could. The action caused a sudden flash of pain. It overtook the dull ache that had been resident in his rib cage for several minutes. He moaned.

"You okay?" the guard asked, tightening his grip on the weapon he held at Paul's back.

"Yes," Paul answered, gasping for air. He lowered himself to the floor holding his chest firmly. "I'll be alright in a minute."

"What's the matter with you?"

"I have some cracked ribs," he answered as the pain subsided.

He relaxed the grip he had on his chest and added, "Got into a little altercation with one of them. I have to check her vital signs. Will you let me do that?"

"Okay, but don't try anything funny."

"You've already said that. I promise I won't." He pushed himself to his knees with the help of his right arm, grimacing as he performed the task. He took the woman's pulse, stooped and listened to her heart.

She was beautiful. He could see why Orgone was attracted to her. Or could he see? Orgone was a Gron'dalin. What would he see in a Human woman? Paul certainly wouldn't have been attracted to one of their women when he was Human. The thought 'when he was Human' frightened him.

He examined the decorative green and yellow scale that adorned the sides of her face. Behind him he could hear the guard stepping forward to see what he was doing.

"She's been Marked," Paul said as he gingerly rose from the squatting position he had worked his way into.

"Neither of you are human," the guard said nervously.

"I'm not a Gron'dalin. I'm part Human," Paul assured. "I'm altered but I'm still part Human."

"I know you're not a Gron'dalin or you'd be dead right now. What happened to you then? Did THEY do that to you? Did they change you?"

"Ugh, not exactly. I injected the blood of one of the women they had altered."

"Why?"

"Long story." He was standing upright now. The pain in his chest throbbed. He drew in a deep breath and flinched.

Paul chuckled. "I know what you're thinking," he smiled at the man because he really did know what he was thinking. It wasn't just a saying for him any longer. "Maybe you're right. Maybe I was crazy to do it."

The guard shrugged. His shoulder length dark hair bobbed slightly. "I never said that."

Never taking his eyes off Paul, he stepped around him to the metal door, still holding the gun on him. He pressed a button beside a speaker grille and a moment later a man's voice came on.

"Ya?"

"I've got a weird looking guy here that claims to be trying to hide a woman from the aliens; looks like an alien himself except he's got hair on his face and head. He doesn't have a mane. He says he's a human that injected some woman's blood." He withdrew his finger from the button and listened.

"Brent, if he was a Gron'dalin he would have killed you by now. I'll be right up," the older voice replied with exasperation.

Paul sat down on the edge of the couch and waited.

"Ya know if you thought I was an alien, you shouldn't have waited to blast me. They move fast. They use their minds and it's not as if they have to reach for a gun or anything," he said to the young man. "You'll get yourself killed if you don't fire the instant you see one of them."

"Ya? You should just be glad I didn't," Brent replied.

A loud click announced the opening of the entrance. The metal door swung outwards and three men emerged. Two men in their twenties holding assault rifles flanked a short black man with graying hair, middle aged, forty-eight perhaps.

"Brent, next time shoot first, ask questions later. I'm not leaving you up here alone again."

"He was carrying a woman over his shoulder. I couldn't shoot him!"

The black man looked down at Paul, who still sat.

"Well, what have we here?"

"I'm Paul Muntz," Paul began, "I'm not an alien, I'm an Alterin."

"Ya. I'd say that was pretty accurate. Your hair gives you away," the man replied. "I heard about the experiment. So, you're the product, eh?" He stepped forward.

Paul stood and extended the hand that wasn't clutching his broken ribs.

"My name is Joseph Grill," the man said, smiling as he took Paul's hand. "People just call me Joe."

"Nice to meet you, Joe."

"Why didn't they tell us you were coming?" Joe asked, looking down at San'dare'a briefly and back up at Paul.

"No one above ground can know where we are or THEY will know. This woman is wanted by one of their best minds."

"Well?" Joe pressed his lips together defiantly and drew in a deep breath through his nostrils, releasing it in a rush, "Then it won't bloody well have her, will it?"

Paul smiled and nodded. This was a man after his own heart.

"How did you come by her?" the older man asked.

"My colleagues and I escaped from their base on Mars, took her and some other women with us."

"Christ!" Joe replied in amazement then added, "You were on another planet?

"Wow!" Brent added, realizing Paul hadn't been lying earlier.

"If you'd said that to me a year ago I would a' thought you were crazy," Joe stated. "Ya know?"

"I know," Paul responded. "Me too. We took her and several thousand other women off Colony," Paul continued, "Destroyed their Armada."

"Hey! Way ta go," Brent piped in respectfully. Joe shot him a glance but didn't succeed in silencing him.

"I'd like to get my hands on some of those bastards," Brent added.

"No you wouldn't," Paul replied sitting back down on the couch. "You wouldn't have a chance against them."

Joe looked down at San'dare'a more carefully now. Stooping he rested a hand on one knee. "Why's she so still?"

"Drugged," Paul replied. "So they can't trace her mind pattern."

"That the only way to hide your mind from them?"

"Above ground."

"She's got scales," Joe announced, straightening. "Were the other women you brought back like that too?"

"No. She was the only one. They only Mark them when they claim them. The others were being held for transport to the Armada."

"And the Armada's gone now," Brent announced jubilantly. Flexing the substantial muscle in his arms, he looked defiant. The other two guards threw him an angry look this time, saving Joe the trouble.

"My wife and daughter were both taken," Joe said. "It was my second marriage. Why would they want a thirty-eight year old woman?"

"Age doesn't mean much to them. Once she's Marked," Paul paused realizing that this was painful for the man.

"No it's alright. I want to know."

"Once they're Marked they're changed genetically. She will live a long time."

"How long?"

"I don't know. Hundreds of years."

His face brightened. "Is there any chance my family was among the women you brought back?"

"When were they taken?"

"Right at the start. Before we really knew what was happening. Before we knew what we were up against. My daughter was visiting from Boston. She was a teacher there. Had a life ahead of her." He shook his head and cast his eyes down at the floor. "They wouldn't even come to the shelter. Said it was a big hoax. Nothing was going to happen. The whole time we built this place," he motioned around them. "They insisted it wasn't happening. Linda was supposed to be back in Boston for school starting. She didn't go. If she'd really believed nothing was happening she would have gone. Right?"

"She couldn't help it," Paul answered. "They influenced her."

Joe pressed on. "Then the day they were taken they just sat in the house crying and holding each other, rocking back and forth." He looked at Paul, pain plainly visible in his eyes. "These Undergrounds were close to finished by then and I tried to force them to come with me." His eyes clouded over. "They ran away!"

Paul nodded. "Sentry."

"What?" Joe asked.

"All the Sentry controlled the minds of the women they chose."

Joe looked baffled.

"There are three divisions in the Elite which is the group we've been fighting. Zi, Zad and Sentry. The Sentry are the military. They're the most organized for Bride Quests."

"That what they call this. A Bride Quest?"

"Ya. While I was on Mars I studied them. They were the only ones who controlled the minds of the women they chose so they wouldn't hide when they came for them."

"Oh God!"

"I'm sorry Joe," Paul said. "I don't think your wife and daughter were among the women we brought back."

Joe nodded, pressing his lips together. "I kind 'a thought that," he said. "They've been gone a long time."

"I lost someone too," Paul said, rising carefully so he wouldn't stress his ribs. Joe hung his head and a look of melancholy crept over his dark eyes. Paul squeezed the older man's shoulder. "I know how you feel."

Joe looked at San'dare'a, forcing the sadness away. "And this one got away," he said, trying to hide his own pain.

"That's right. She's a very sought-after woman," Paul answered, letting him leave the topic of his wife and daughter behind.

"You're welcome to hide her here."

"Thanks." It had never occurred to Paul that they could be turned away.

Joe drew in a deep breath. "Come in, Paul," he said, jerking his head toward the door that led into the main part of the shelter. "They'll get her over our dead bodies."

Joe started toward stairs that led further down.

Paul stooped to pick San'dare'a up, grimacing with pain. Brent stepped forward.

"I'll get her," he offered.

Paul thanked him and followed Joe down a further flight of stairs leading downward. "Being below ground doesn't require you to burrow down miles." Paul laughed as he descended the long staircase holding a railing. "All you have to do is be below the surface," he said as each step down sent pain jabbing through his side. "The distance below doesn't affect their ability to read your minds," he said.

"What is it about being underground that prevents them from finding you?" Joe asked over his shoulder.

"I don't know. Something about the earth. They can't scan for mind activity through soil."

"We wanted to be on the safe side," the older man assured him. "So we went deep. The more earth between us and them the better. Besides, we've never been invaded so maybe being far below is a bonus."

Joe turned to face him. Lined with concrete like the upper room where Paul had met Brent, this room was painted a pale yellow. At least twice the size of the first room, it stood empty except for a long heavy dining table and dozens of chairs.

"What's the matter?" Joe asked, nodding toward Paul who was again grimacing with pain.

"A few cracked ribs," Paul replied. "Little disagreement I got into."

A woman stepped out of the dark recesses of an adjacent room as the young guard lowered San'dare'a's body onto the table. She had been listening quietly in the distance.

"You're an Alterin," she said. "What's wrong with your friend here?" she asked, taking San'dare'a's pulse.

Paul watched her lift San'dare'a's eyelids and flash a light over her pupils.

"You a doctor?" he asked.

"That's right."

"She's been drugged so we could get her off Mars."

"Off Mars?"

Paul nodded.

"Okay! So they can't find you when you're drugged?" she asked.

"Not when you're in a coma," he answered.

"That's a dangerous state to put someone in," the woman said. She stared at Paul with steel-gray eyes.

"Frankly I would have hesitated to do it, but I had no say in it," Paul replied. "She was drugged by someone else before my escape."

"With or without her knowledge?"

"I don't know. I do know she wanted out of there pretty badly."

"Do they keep women heavily drugged up there?" the doctor asked, disgust evident in her voice.

"No. They don't drug them at all. She was drugged by..." he hesitated. Telling too many people about Bopack could endanger her life. "A friend of mine who wanted to see her go free. Another Alterin," he lied.

The young woman nodded then motioned to the young guard. "She's stable." She patted San'dare'a's shoulder. "Put her in the ward, Brent," she said, and then to Paul, "I'll have a look at those ribs you were talking about." She started toward a door at the back of the room, indicating Paul should follow.

Once inside he looked around the medical rooms. "Nice setup you have here," he said.

"Ya, whatever I need. It's probably the best underground facility of its kind." She smiled. "Love working here," she said sarcastically. "Take off your clothes."

"Nice bedside manner," Paul remarked. "You want everything off?"

"You're not shy are you?" the young doctor asked. Her long dark hair, held back on either side of her face with flowered ceramic clips, drooped across her shoulders. She was small and wiry.

"No. I'm not shy," Paul remarked, removing his shirt. She turned her back to him. "You might be a little surprised though."

He dropped his shirt and began unfastening his jeans. In the outer rooms he heard the hum of voices. Readying supplies and instruments she would need for the examination, she allowed him some measure of privacy.

"Just get under that sheet when you're ready," she said.

Paul was already sitting down on the examination table when she spoke. "I'm ready," he announced as he carefully laid down, pulling the sheet over his chest.

The doctor turned and crossed the floor with no expression, a tray of instruments in her hand.

Placing the tray on the bedside table, she folded the sheet back to his waist, making no comment about the extensive scale covering on his body.

"Did you expect me to be so altered?" Paul finally asked.

"Your skin, you mean?"

"Ya."

"I didn't have any expectations."

"Is it revolting?" Paul asked in a tone bordering confrontation.

"Quite pretty, actually. Almost glistens," she said.

Surprised by her reaction, Paul frowned. She pressed lightly on his ribs.

"We'll need X-rays but you're right about your ribs. There are definitely some fractures in here," she said, gently plying the area with cold fingers.

"Ya," Paul grunted.

"What do you do for a living?" she asked to take his attention away from her examination. A common tactic to get the patient talking and stop them from thinking about their ailment, hearing it used on him, amused Paul.

"I'm a physician," he answered, smug with having kept his secret as long as he had.

The young woman straightened and smiled. "Okay," she said, nodding. "Anything else I should know, Doctor?" The smile spread.

Paul laughed. "Nothing I can think of off the top of my head."

"My name is Beth Wallis."

She extended a hand for him to shake. In his prone state that proved awkward. "Nice to meet you, Beth," he replied, taking her hand, "Paul Muntz."

"THE Doctor Paul Muntz?" she asked in amazement.

Paul laughed at her tone. "The one and only," he replied.

"I've heard about you," she confided. "Last I heard, by word of mouth, you'd been captured by the aliens." Her voice rang with disbelief. "Didn't know they took you to Mars though.

Paul smiled.

"Unbelievable!" She shook her head. "What's it like there?"

"We were inside the structures they've constructed so I can't really comment on Mars, per se. A lot of their technologically is way ahead of ours or my stay there might have been unpleasant in the extreme. Not that it was a lot of fun."

"I bet. Technological advances are one thing. Too bad they're not civilized," Beth said.

"They are."

"Why are they taking the women from Earth then?"

"They have no women of their own."

"Oh, I heard that. What I'm saying is that, if they were civilized they wouldn't destroy our culture to facilitate the survival of their own."

"That's a subject for debate," Paul replied.

She scowled. "Is it?" She resumed her examination.

"Let me ask you a question," he said. "If there were no women in the United States, let's say some natural disaster killed you all off, do you think the United States government would just throw up its hands and accept the fact?"

She shrugged at him.

"Not on your life," he continued.

"There are plenty that would be happy to come here."

"Ya, but the Gron'dalins don't have that luxury. We'd wage war to get women if we had to. And you can bet we'd put everything we had into it, which is exactly what they've done. They were lucky enough to possess the ability to alter other species. They had the technology to travel through space and they have this extraordinary talent of mind control."

"Can you read minds in your altered state?" Beth asked. She stopped her examination momentarily to look at him.

If he told her the truth she might fear him. "Not like they can," he replied.

"But you can."

"A little," Paul admitted.

"Did you ever lose anyone to them?" Beth asked, resuming her examination. "Sit up," she said, helping him.

"Ya. I did," he said, swinging his legs over the side of the table. "Someone I loved and was trying to protect."

"So did I. My sister."

"Sorry to hear that."

"Who did you lose?

"A sweetheart."

"What was her name?"

"Hillary."

"And you can still see their side of it?"

"I didn't say I liked their side of it."

Chapter 38
Old Allegiances

Hill'carn slipped quietly into Bopack's rooms unnoticed. The Gron'dalins had surrounded the Old One with delicately carved objects from her own planet, much as they had done for Hill'carn. Strange proportions in articles of everyday use, new shapes and colors entered the Gron'dalin world every hundred or so years by way of the women they captured.

"Culturally they are a hodgepodge of every race they've assimilated," Hill'carn said, toying with a vase from Bopack's desk. "I wonder what the Gron'dalin culture was like before the Bride Quests began."

"The King said something to me once about how they have been changed by the women they take."

"Not all the women in Colony are Zantinean," Hill'carn stated, replacing the vase. She crossed the floor to the banit'ye barrier.

"No. There are six different races of women in Colony."

"I knew that by more than just the fact that some women are much taller than you are, or have much larger or smaller eyes or four fingers on their hands instead of your five." Hill'carn gestured with one hand as she looked out on swirling red sand. "You can clearly see the cultural heritage of the different women. The Gron'dalin rooms contain a mix of objects, some Zantinean, some Pocanish. What is truly Gron'dalin?"

"I don't know."

"I like the variations in the different rooms, Bopack. It's like stepping into another world each time a new door opens, but it leaves me feeling slightly uncomfortable too. There's a lack of order in a way I don't quite understand."

"Perhaps that's the reason for the Gron'dalins' strict adherence to tradition. Without it, they would be lost in the ever changing landscape HOME has become."

"Perhaps," Hill'carn replied, turning to look at the old woman. "What have you learned about Orgone?" she asked.

"Orgone located Paul Muntz almost immediately when he began scanning but Paul tricked him," the Old One said, positively ecstatic. "He tricked him into believing San'dare'a was with another Human named Cahill." She stood with her hands clasped together.

"I know him. Simon Cahill," Hill'carn said his name as she started pacing the room.

"When Orgone found this man named Cahill," Bopack continued. "He knew nothing of the whereabouts of San'dare'a, only that she was with Paul Muntz."

"Paul is cunning."

"Very lucky that he is."

"Cahill couldn't withstand the kind of mind probe Orgone would have sent out in his state of mind last night."

"Oh he did!" Bopack answered in a loud whisper, shaking a finger at Hill'carn who had turned to pace back towards her.

Hill'carn stopped abruptly.

"Orgone was quite impressed with Cahill's mental abilities. It appears that, even without any alteration by injecting your blood, Cahill was able to project a very loud thought into Orgone's mind. He apparently called Orgone a 'bastard.'"

Hill'carn smiled and shook her head. "Just like Simon. I'll bet Orgone was pleased about that!"

Bopack chuckled. "He was enraged. The King had to stop him from retaliating. Revengefulness isn't a characteristic the Gron'dalins possess ordinarily." Bopack glanced over her shoulder at the door as though worried they would be discovered, then continued in a whisper. "When he scanned for Paul Muntz again, after examining Cahill's mind, Paul was gone." The old woman literally beamed.

"Smart man," Hill'carn remarked, taking up her pacing again. "Paul has always been very clever." She smiled as she trod the tiled floor.

"Orgone knows the general whereabouts of his prize but she must be underground by now," Bopack announced triumphantly. "Paul is certainly underground or Orgone would have found him."

"I'm sure she's underground," Hill'carn confirmed. "Paul lost me. He won't lose San'dare'a." She rotated clockwise and started her return pace, slowly, methodically. "They have gone back to the United States, I'll bet," she said aloud to herself. "Where are they exactly?"

"They are on a 'west coast' of some continent or other. Does that mean anything to you?"

"Yes. It means a lot." Hill'carn stopped in mid stride. Still looking away from Bopack she brought her hands up to her mouth and sucked air through her fingers. Her brow tightly knit, the sadness in her eyes would have told Bopack of her emotional pain, had she been facing the old woman.

"I spent many vacations on the west coast of North America with my father. In Washington and Oregon."

"Oh my! That place sounds like Orgone's name," Bopack interrupted. "I hope he didn't take her there. That would anger the King and I'm sure he would personally intervene in the hunt. Paul wouldn't have a chance then. Of all the gron'ie, the King is the most determined. He is relentless." Bopack hesitated momentarily, then added, "As you know."

"Yes," Hill'carn replied absentmindedly.

The old woman continued. "Even if Orgone agreed to give up the search, the King would not allow it if he believed he were being mocked."

"Paul would never taunt Cacin. He's too smart for that," Hill'carn replied, still far away in thought.

"I hope not," Bopack remarked.

"Sometimes we'd go as far south as California," Hill'carn continued. "We used to camp all the time. Everywhere we went. My dad rented a Volkswagen Vanagon with a roof that we could put up when we stopped. I loved it." She smiled broadly, remembering the holidays.

"State campgrounds are wonderful in Oregon. They're full of little animals and they're so clean."

Her face had relaxed and she looked happy. A feeling of melancholy swept through her and passed. She stood quietly in contemplation for a moment.

Hill'carn spun around to face Bopack. "I'll bet he's in Washington State. I remember him saying once they were building extensive underground networks in Washington. He was impressed with them."

"I will listen again and perhaps find out exactly where he has gone with her."

"Do you think Orgone will get her back, Bopack?" Hill'carn strolled past the old woman, her arms hanging at her sides.

"I hope not, Hill'carn. She wants her freedom so much."

Hill'carn snorted. "We all did," she replied. "I will do everything in my power, whatever that might be, to hinder Orgone," Hill'carn stated. "Is he going to Earth to search for them?"

"I have heard nothing about it."

"I think he'll go, Bopack. It's their way isn't it?" Bopack nodded in agreement. "Keep me informed of any new developments. If I can hamper Orgone's recapture of San'dare'a in anyway, I will," Hill'carn said, crossing the room to the door.

"Your husband has put four of the best Gron'dalin minds to work in helping Orgone. Gradspin among them."

"Well, I'm no match for Orgone as it is." Hill'carn shrugged. "But I will do whatever I can, if the opportunity arises. You never know how things are going to develop. I do have the advantage of stealth." She smiled a cunning little smile at the older woman as the door swished open. The Old One nodded and smiled back.

* * * *

"I'll go with you," Cacin asserted.

"My honor demands I go alone," Orgone insisted.

"You're too weak to go alone."

"I didn't question your right to honor on the flagship many months ago."

"Yes you did. And I wasn't ill as I recall. You did dispute my going, Orgone."

"I'm fit enough with the tonic Beau'nad has supplied," Orgone insisted, shifting his weight onto his other foot.

Cacin considered this for a moment. Beau'nad had assured him the Zad would be restored for awhile. He turned his attention abruptly to the banit'ye viewing screen, his long cape swirling out around him as he rotated.

Gazing out the window at the drifting soil on Mars he finally spoke.

"Very well Orgone, satisfy your honor."

* * * *

Orgone had been on Earth several times during the Bride Quest and, while acquainted with the vegetation from those expeditions and from his walks through the various Earth gardens he had established in Colony, he'd never been in a forest quite like this. He gazed around at gigantic, stately trees. The forest floor, covered with ferns and shrubs, lay in silence. He paused for a moment to listen for the songs of birds. There were none. Winter gripped the region. Severe weather had descended and snow dotted the foliage at the edge of the road. A cold rain fell, washing the clean white covering away.

Transporting to a position near the location where he had probed Paul Muntz's mind, he stood in awe for some minutes, feeling the cold rain on his face. He knew an underground shelter existed near this location because he had been unable to locate the Alterin only minutes after his first probe.

Orgone walked along the dark road. Dusk was well advanced when he arrived. Night promised to follow. No lights brightened the road. No vehicles interrupted his journey. He had been walking for twenty minutes under an overcast sky when he came to a gravel road that turned off to his right.

Turning down the road he began to sprint as he closed on his quarry. His mouth was set and his eyes determined as he rounded a corner into a gravel expanse containing only one vehicle. Rain splashed the surface of the vehicle in a rhythmic pitter-patter.

* * * *

Hill'carn had been scanning the northern part of Washington State for almost half an hour. She had learned of Orgone's departure shortly after he left, from Bopack, who learned of preparations to ready the landing dock to receive San'dare'a through Gaylant. Beau'nad had requested two hospital beds and massive supplies and instruments be taken to Docking Bay One, a favorite landing place for body latch victims, it seemed.

Suddenly she had him! She withdrew and held her mind at a distance. A master of mind probe, Orgone would easily know if he were being studied. He stood in a forest approaching the entrance to an Underground. Hill'carn panicked. He was thinking of killing Paul.

She looked out the window into the darkness that engulfed Colony. Stars flickered above her and Mars' two moons lit the heavens, providing the only light outside the barrier.

Hill'carn pushed away from the window and crossed the floor of her private chamber, throwing on the light on with her mind as she passed the switch. The door swished open. Cacin sat at his desk in the outer area surrounded by Elders.

"I must speak with you," Hill'carn said abruptly, crossing the floor with her back rigid, hands and jaw tightly clenched.

Cacin frowned. "Can't it wait?" he asked. "I'm involved..."

"It can't wait," Hill'carn declared. Her heart pounded. Her breathing rapid though it was, her face revealed nothing. There was a stir among the Elders and Gradspin cleared his throat awkwardly.

"Very well," Cacin said. "Speak."

Hill'carn looked around at the Elders, her eyes settling for a moment on Gradspin, who appeared to be waiting to hear what she had to say. She looked back at Cacin.

"I need to speak with you alone."

Cacin gaped at her. "Alone?"

"Alone."

He dismissed the assembly to wait in the foyer.

"Now," he said once the room cleared out, "what is so pressing you must speak with me alone when I have matters of state to attend to?" His tone fell more on vexation than anger.

"Is finding San'dare'a a matter of state?" Hill'carn blurted, anger easily rising in her. Then remembering the urgency of the situation she waived the question away with the flip of a hand. "Never mind.

I'm sure Orgone is going to kill my brother," she said, referring to Paul deliberately in this fashion because she knew Cacin would be compelled to listen to any argument about a family member.

"Paul Muntz has violated a sacred precinct."

"He knew nothing of our practices," Hill'carn snapped. "It's not fair that my brother has to die for his lack of knowledge."

Cacin drew in a deep breath and sat back in his seat. "I can't interfere with Orgone's right..."

"Orgone's right! Is it Orgone's right to kill my brother because his honor has been marred?"

"In our culture..." Cacin began in defense of Orgone's actions, gesturing with his hands.

"My brother knows nothing of our culture!"

"He would have taken her even if he had, my love. You know that."

"Perhaps. But he didn't know. That's the point." Hill'carn could see she would get nowhere with Cacin. Tradition had outweighed his sense of fairness and his love for her both.

"I thought you liked him," she said, trying one last avenue.

"Your brother?"

"Yes."

"I do like him."

"Then do something to stop Orgone," she screamed.

"I can't." Cacin replied flatly. "It's conventional that a gron be allowed to decide how to handle situations of disgrace."

"Disgrace!" Hill'carn snapped. "To hell with your damn conventions."

"I can't," Cacin yelled. "It's custom! Listen Hill'carn, I would have done anything to protect Orgone from the soldiers I know he has to face down there. But tradition demands he be allowed to decide how to address a matter of disgrace himself. I cannot abandon our ways to protect Orgone or Paul.

"Then I will protect my brother," Hill'carn replied.

"Don't interfere in this dispute, Hill'carn," Cacin warned as she strode away from him. He had risen from the chair he'd been occupying.

Hill'carn knew he didn't believe she could interfere anyway. She turned abruptly at the door to look at him but said nothing. Storming from their rooms, she rushed past the Elders, erecting a mind block to conceal her destination from Cacin. Being in Earth Garden Four, the area most like the forest surrounding the Underground Orgone stood in, would help her concentrate.

* * * *

Orgone strode down the steps. The guard, unable to fire his weapon because of the speed of the attack, collapsed in agony. Orgone gripped his mind with a forceful probe that brought the Human to his knees. He cried out in pain. Orgone lifted him off the floor and slammed him against the concrete wall with ease. His young body crumbled to the floor in death.

Fading through the door, not attempting to open it, using his powerful mind to conquer the matter they expected would keep him out; he encountered three others climbing a set of stairs. They looked up to see, from nowhere, an eight-foot gron bearing down on them.

He gripped all three minds, simultaneously. Screams of pain filled the stairwell as they collapsed, writhing in agony. Their bodies tumbled down against the closed door below

* * * *

Paul heard the commotion from the outer rooms and knew immediately Orgone had found him. San'dare'a lay unconscious and well hidden within the structure.

"Get the hell out of here!" he called to Beth and Joe, not even attempting to reach for a weapon. "Go into the apartments!" He motioned toward the inner rooms where hundreds of women still hid."

Joe grabbed an automatic rifle and cycled its bolt. "I'm not deserting you!" he yelled.

"Then you'll die! Go NOW, Joe!" Paul ordered.

Joe ignored him.

Paul ran across the floor to the door as the screaming in the stairway stopped. Throwing open the heavy metal door he jumped over the body of a man he had been joking with minutes earlier. With his mind, he slammed Orgone against the door at the top of the stairs.

Orgone lashed out with his mind, still pinned against the door. Paul ducked the blow, turning to see it impact against the concrete wall of the bunker. A huge section of reinforced concrete crumbled to the ground and Paul knew he had to get the battle outside or risk having everyone at this end of the shelter buried alive.

Holding the gron against the door with the power of his mind, he dodged the bodies of the three men who had been going to play cards with Brent. He ascended the stairs by two's and was beside Orgone in seconds.

"I see you've come, you slime," he whispered, hitting the door open button. From below he heard Joe yelling for Paul to get out of the way. The door opened. Paul dropped his hold on Orgone and the gron collapsed on the floor in the upper room. Gunfire ripped through the cold air.

Reaching out with his mind Orgone clipped Paul in the head as the Alterin raced up the second flight of stairs.

"Come kill me, Asshole!" Paul taunted, trying to draw him away from Joe.

Orgone reached into Paul's mind, trying for a total grip. Paul resisted, putting up a block that even Orgone couldn't penetrate. Not allowing Orgone to destroy him by twisting his brain to bits, Paul called down the shaft. "Physical impact only, Orgone. Come and get me."

He burst out into the night, panting from the exertion and pain His cracked ribs, wrapped tightly in adhesive tape, ground painfully. The pain, while secondary to the hatred he felt for Orgone, tore at him with fingers of fire.

He stood in light drizzle, waiting for the Gron'dalin to emerge. The racket of an automatic rifle resounded in the stairwell.

"Shit!" Paul screamed, rushing to the top of the stairs again, arriving just in time to see Orgone grip Joe. The sound of Joe's screams filled the concrete cavity.

"Orgone!" Paul yelled. "I'm up here! I'm the one who took San'dare'a. Come and get me, you coward!"

Orgone dropped his attack on Joe. The black man fell to the ground in a heap, groaning in pain. Suddenly Orgone stood in front of Paul. Without effort he materialized face-to-face with him. He stood glaring at the Alterin with as much hatred as Paul had for him.

Paul backed away. "You'll never get her back," he said. "Can't you guys get it through your thick heads? These women don't like you!"

Orgone spoke through clenched teeth. "Can't YOU get it through YOUR thick heads? "Orgone replied. "Women never do!" Orgone struck out with his mind as he spoke. "San'dare'a is mine," he bellowed. "I WILL have her."

"San'dare'a is her own person," Paul replied, taking a blow squarely on the side of his head. He knocked Orgone off his feet with a mind blow to the stomach. "You've Marked her and she still doesn't want you. Let her go, Orgone," he said, striking Orgone in the mouth with another blow as the gron rose from the ground.

Suddenly Paul soared through the air and slammed down on his back, knocking the air from his lungs in a painful gush. Never having experienced Orgone's full mind strength before, Paul reeled. Pain shot through his chest, ripping at him. He screamed in agony.

"She's mine," Orgone shrieked.

"She belongs to herself," Paul sputtered, finally gasping in a short breath to quench the flame in his lungs. Pain shot through his chest as he spoke. The words whispered out into the cold rain and fell around him like shadows.

"She belongs to me. She always will. We mate for life. Once Marked, in time she cannot resist me."

* * * *

Hill'carn had waited patiently in the garden for some sign of Paul and Orgone. Paul had finally emerged on the surface followed by Orgone moments after. Hill'carn had her chance. Paul lay prone on his back, not a good sign. She leveled her mind against Orgone as he slashed out with his own mind to kill Paul, knocking his mind force aside and sending him sprawling.

Orgone rose in disbelief. Paul still laid flat on his back, struggling to rise. Again the mind attack came from elsewhere; hitting Orgone with such force he dropped like a stone.

* * * *

Paul gaped in amazement as Orgone was hurled around the parking lot like a rag doll. He staggered to his feet and looked around. No one else was there! How could this happen?

* * * *

Cacin searched for Hill'carn frantically. Unable to locate her through mind probe, he ran through Colony, checking areas she frequented, ripping open doors to people's quarters, throwing room dividers back to reveal startled occupants.

Finally it donned on him. "Earth garden! She must have gone to an Earth garden." Unsure of her intent when she left their rooms, he felt certain she would attempt to interfere in Orgone's affairs. He willed himself to the upper levels of Colony and burst into Earth Garden One, sweeping through the mile-and-a-half of tropical rainforest like a giant bird of prey.

He cursed as his effort brought no rewards. Coming to a halt, he tried to think it through. "Four!" he blurted. "Four is like the area Orgone has gone into. She must be in Four." He materialized in Earth Garden Four, sweeping into the center of the garden easily, his long silver cape trailing out behind him.

"Hill'carn!" he screamed as he closed the distance between them, running to her. "What are you doing?"

Hill'carn turned abruptly. "He's my brother!" she yelled. "I will kill Orgone before I allow him to harm Paul!"

Cacin stopped in mid-stride and stared at her in disbelief. "Have you developed the skills to reach out with your mind and kill someone?"

"Don't try me," she warned, her eyes blazing with rage.

"This has never been a possibility in the past." He stood silently staring at his wife, then, without a word he faded from the garden.

Standing in the rain beside the two combatants, Cacin spoke calmly to Orgone. "Take the woman and we'll go. Let him live."

Orgone rose quietly from the ground. "Hill'carn?" he asked.

"Yes," Cacin replied. "This is her brother."

Cacin felt a probe as soft as down touch his mind and knew she was checking his intent.

"My honor demands I kill him," Orgone stated.

"Your honor does not extend to my wife's brother," Cacin answered. Paul stood in the drizzle watching with amazement. Blood ran from his nose and a gash above his left eye. His chest ached mercilessly.

Cacin had never argued with his friend before. "You of all people, Orgone, should be able to let this go. He is alien to our ways."

Orgone cast his eyes down at the ground then back at Paul who still stood in silence to one side of them. "Very well." He spoke almost inaudibly.

"Come on," Cacin said, "I'll assist you in recapturing the woman."

"No." Orgone replied, drawing in a deep breath. "I won't take her," he stated like a spoiled child. "She may have her freedom. Perhaps the Alterin is right. She was Marked. If she is so opposed to having me so long after the Marking, perhaps its better I leave her. I don't want her under these circumstances. I will bed Fra'non. Gradspin is right. She is a fine specimen. Let the Alterin win."

"She's yours," he yelled at Paul as the cold rain continued to fall, drenching the snow at the edges of the parking lot, drenching the gron'ie and Paul. "And good luck with her. She will bring you only grief."

Paul made no reply as Cacin and Orgone faded from the parking lot. "Oh God!" he said under his breath when they were gone.

Joe burst above ground, his automatic rifle waving from side to side in search of the invaders, one eye swollen shut, blood running freely down his face.

The rain continued to fall on the majestic Douglas-firs as Paul sent a brief message of thanks to Hillary.

* * * *

Tears of relief slowly trickled down Hill'carn's face as she squatted in Earth Garden Four. She wrapped her long slender arms tightly around her knees as she'd seen her mother do so often. It was almost all she remembered about the woman who bore her, but it was enough to keep the memory of her mother alive.

She felt a thud in her womb as the child she carried kicked for the first time. It was an odd sensation that filled her with mixed emotions. She moaned softly under her breath. Rising, she rubbed her hands on her small round stomach and stared at her reflection in the banit'ye barrier that stood between her and the blowing red sands of Mars.

The woman who looked back seemed more familiar now, not the stranger she once was.

Available soon from Babora Books

C.A. Dawson

Alien Stalker

Because happiness is but a moment's glance
The spin inside the circle's charm
And I walked my line to have my chance
To lay my head on your blessed arm

Ferron - The Return*

*published by Nemesis Publishing 1984 and copywritten by Ferron, used with permission

Chapter 1
The Landing

Brandon sped along the deer trail crashing through the bush alongside the road. Pain shot through his left hip as the arthritis that had settled there a few years earlier complained at the unaccustomed effort.

Wet branches raked his face. Breathing hard, he frantically lashed out at them and raced up a small incline. The thing disappeared over the top.

Tripping on a tree root he sprawled face first in peat and twigs with a grunt of exhaled air. His father's old Winchester, clutched in one gnarled fist, came crashing through bushes at the side of the path with him. The undergrowth tore mercilessly at the backs of his hands, drawing blood. The antiquated weapon, barely grasped in one bleeding hand, pushed through overhanging branches.

"Shit!"

Brandon hauled himself up and ran on. The creature's passage through the forest sounded more distant.

Brandon's boots smashed unevenly through the underbrush as his good leg hit harder than the other. His and the ungodly creature's footfalls, muffled by the morning fog, were the only sounds disturbing the silent timberland.

Nothing moved. Nothing dared. Birds, speechless after the noise of the crash, flew to distant trees for safety. Small creatures crouched in their dens or hid in foliage deep within the forest.

Closing on the thing, Brandon dodged a branch that snapped back in its wake. The alien may have youth on its side but he had that old McKinley determination.

Fallen twigs cracked beneath his feet. Ducking another limb he tried to bring the rifle up to fire. He was no marksman, but he couldn't miss at this distance. The weapon caught in brush, unbalancing him, pulling him to one knee—luckily his good knee.

"Hell!" he hissed, his patience all but gone. Time had tricked him. Age had crept in like fog, sapping him of strength. Using Panting, he hoisted himself up.

Fog closed between them, hiding the godless thing. He heard its progress through the bush and listened for any change in direction. His breath came in short painful gasps but he pressed on, drawing closer.

He had to kill it. He was the only one who knew what had come to this world and, by God, he wasn't going to let a little age interfere with killing this thing.

The hip screamed. A branch, hidden in the fog, cruelly lashed his unshaven face, clawing his gaunt cheeks.

The fog broke. He raised the rifle and fired without aiming. A sharp crack split the air, the gun's recoil against his shoulder bruising the arthritic joint. Wood splintered at the side of the path. The alien broke stride but rallied and dashed on.

"God damn!"

He grimaced as pain burned a path through his shoulder to his wrist. As if the arthritis and the impact of the recoil weren't enough to contend with, stinging sweat ran into one eye. Fearing the fog would close in again, he swung the rifle to his other shoulder and fired. Another miss. More punishment from a weapon that wouldn't have made a difference to a healthy body.

Ignoring the pain as he ran, he worked the lever without stopping to chamber another round. Breaking into a clearing he fired again. Another miss! Rich topsoil at the side of the trail rained down on ferns. The beast screeched with fury and disappeared into the dark woods unharmed.

He looked resentfully at the old weapon as his boots beat an uneven rhythm on fallen leaves and needles. If only he had taken an interest in his father's life-long hobby and learned to use this antiquated thing!

"You can do it. Come on, Brandie," he coaxed. "You're not old yet."

His blue eyes scanned the entrance to the forest, assessing the trail his quarry had taken. "I'm gonna kill ya, ya bastard!" Brandon screamed.

One ragged sleeve of his red checkered coat flapped as he ran. Spider webs hung from branches, heavy with droplets condensed out of the fog. He raised the rifle once more.

"Come on!" he growled through clenched teeth, aiming for the first time. He fired. The thing roared with pain, stumbled, but kept running.

His heart hammered. "Yes!" he hissed between wheezes. "Next shot takes ya down!" he snarled. He felt in the pocket of his ruined jacket for more shells.

Ahead, the alien encountered a nurse log. Ferns, small saplings and moss protruded from the massive hulk that was slowly returning its substance to the forest floor. His quarry lunged this way and that, holding its thigh, trying to find a way over the obstruction.

Confusion. Here was Brandon's chance! He had it!

Breathing hard, Brandon closed for the kill, feeding shells into the rifle. His fingers trembled as he raised the Winchester to one aching shoulder.

Suddenly vaulting the log, the creature raced away. Hissing, it darted a look of pure contempt over one shoulder.

"Damn!" Brandon snarled, hesitating. He'd been too slow. The creature had slipped out of easy range. Lowering the gun he started after it.

He had to do better than this. In answer, the recluse hurled himself over the log like a young buck, the jarring impact of his landing sending pain from his ankles all the way up his spine.

He could do it when he had to. Ya see! He could do it when he had to! And he had to now, more than he'd ever had to in his life.

The rifle still smoked from the last attempt to bring down the unearthly beast that wore a face he knew. He'd seen that face in his own mirror just thirty years ago.

How had it done that?

One minute a blank slate, smooth flesh moving above him, wrestling him into the underbrush at the crash site; the next it wore Brandon's face imprinted over its vacant features. The burning red eyes—its only distinguishing feature—disappeared. Penetrating, black, human-like eyes looked out at the startled farmer.

Yes. That was the only thing this shape shifter couldn't duplicate, wasn't it? It couldn't copy his deep blue eyes.

* * * * * * *

Helen cranked up the music. This was a bit she loved! There was nothing better than listening to Ferron FULL BLAST. Why the hell not?

She brushed unruly strands of blonde hair from her eyes only to have them fall right back.

In the Highlands for her usual adrenaline fix, hell the only thing that kept her sane, a weekly event that stayed the boredom of a sedate, though moderately successful life . . . She chuckled at this. Imagine her, Helen McMaster, being successful. Yes she was and, thank you very kindly, she was going to stay on that path even if it meant coming out here once a week to work out some of the kinks.

She gunned the little hovercar.

Reaching speeds of up to one hundred and fifty on the open stretches she had just traversed was nothing compared to what lay ahead on the twists and turns of the narrow mountain road.

"Ohhhhh!" she screamed. "Let's go! We're in the pipe."

On a clear day, she only traveled at sixty or seventy on the upcoming stretch but the thrill of taking the switchbacks; the dips and peaks even at that speed . . .

"Invigorated." She laughed, tossing her head to get the hair out of her eyes.

In this fog she wouldn't get speedy on the switchbacks. Forty maybe fifty if she was lucky. But fog presented other challenges.

She cuffed the steering yoke with the palms of her hands and sang along to the old recording. The woman who sang her favorite song, long dead, still filled the cab with words Helen took to heart.

Thunder cracked in the woods. Puzzled, she peered up at the misty sky then quickly back at the winding road ahead.

Thunder? In a fog? The fleeting thought grazed her mind, easily pushed out by the music and the adrenaline rush of keeping the hover under control.

In the back of my mind I maintain
The thought of you, my heart's horizon line
They say love travels blind

How come I still see myself with you
whenever I look behind
I have to say I don't know . . .*

Helen had never traveled anywhere blind, let alone in the company of love. She'd never had anyone on her heart's horizon line. Melancholy rolled in, defying the adrenaline high as the song wound on. Imagine letting a song get to you, she thought as she brushed away another wisp of hair. Sentimentality was not a part of her adult life. She wouldn't allow it in.

The hovercar accelerated.

Helen took the turn leading onto the rarely used section of road too fast, nearly losing control.

"Whoa!" she yelled, spinning the yoke to stabilize the vehicle, the seat belt cutting sharply into her flesh. The little red toy veered from the asphalt, tilted dangerously as though going into a roll, then rocked back on its air cushion. Her heart pounded fiercely as she fought the controls.

Braking, the car steadied and her heart eased up as the songstress plied the rough waters of that long ago relationship.

We weren't untrue
It's more we just spent our love imagining
We were something else.
I have to say I don't know
Wouldn't say that I know
And as soon as I find my shoes I'm gone.

"Ya," she said aloud. "As soon as I find my shoes I'm gone, baby. Outta here! Whoa!" she cried, pressing harder on the accelerator.

Excitement dancing behind her eyes; smiling so hard it hurt, she turned into the roughest part of the road, cheeks ablaze. The bun atop her head, loosed by the jostling, released more blonde hair to tickle her face.

Fog clung more closely in the dense bush. Golden pine needles littered the road, thicker at the edges where the trees grew than in the center. Wind from the hover's passing scattered the damp needles, driving them further to the sides as she ran the center line of the narrow road.

She plunged into thick fog. As low-lying cloud closed around the car she slowed. "Aw come on!" she complained. Speed always comforted her, drove away her demons. Excitement! She craved excitement!

Suddenly a silver flash . . . A blur . . .

Without warning a man crashed onto the front of the vehicle. Helen gasped and braked abruptly.

"Aw SHIT!" The hard reverse thrust, combined with the weight of her unwanted passenger, pitched the craft forward, collapsing the air cushion.

He groped for a hand hold as the hover spun out of control.

"Oh my GOD!" she screeched, fear instantly gripping her.

The hover grounded hard, sliding in the pine needles. As it lost forward momentum, the craft's back and front ends tried to swap places. Helen spun the controls to the right, trying to counter the skid but overcorrecting badly.

The man on the lid toppled this way and that grasping at the lip of the windscreen.

Cranking the yoke to the left to prevent the hover from upending, she managed to stay on the road.

Managing barely to hold on, the rider's feet slid across the air intake and caught briefly on one of the nav-lights. Losing his grip at last he tumbled off before the vehicle came to a full stop.

"Oh my GOD!" she screeched. She slapped the music off and jumped from the vehicle almost in the same breath. "Are you all right?" she cried.

Running to the man's side, she bent to help him. The craft idled behind her, its lights piercing the gloom. With her assistance, the man struggled to his feet, gasping and moaning. Stunned. She supported him, holding one elbow, apologizing all the time.

"I didn't see you," she gasped. "I'm sorry! Oh God what have I done?" She brushed at his strange shiny coverall. What was he doing up here anyway? No one lived up here.

Then something big crashed out of the bush behind her.

"Get away from it!" a man's voice screamed hoarsely. "Get back for Chrissake! It's not human!"

She turned her head without letting go of the guy's arm, and gaped at a mountain man dressed in rags. Trying to understand what the wild-looking creature was saying, Helen gaped at him. Get away?

Unable to grasp what he was saying, she shouted back. "I didn't mean to hit him! Honestly. He just came out of nowhere."

"Move away!"

"I didn't see him 'til he was on top of me!"

The sound of Helen's heartbeat pounded in her brain, drowning out any sense she might otherwise make of the old man's command—and command it was. The victim leaned heavily on her, mumbling something incoherent.

She strained to see the fog-shrouded figure hugging the bush like a shy deer.

"Get away from it!" the man angrily shouted, his voice booming in the mist.

She mouthed his last words with incomprehension. 'Get away from it?'

Behind, the man who'd landed atop her hover babbled something unintelligible through clenched teeth. He'd been talking all along in a language she couldn't understand.

Anger seemed to cloak his words. Of course he was angry. He had a right to be. She had just hit him with her car. She looked at his strange tattered clothing, the sleeves hanging in rags, the silver coverall smudged with dirt, wet leaves clinging to it. He looked odd. 'Get away from it.'

Thank God she'd been forced to slow down. She most definitely would have killed him at the speed she'd been travelling only moments earlier.

"Alap ovkala gu zia!" the stranger yelled.

Although she couldn't make sense of his words, she knew he was telling her to do something. Then he grabbed her arm and began dragging her toward the hovercar.

Somewhere in the turmoil into which her mind had spun on hitting the stranger, this at least registered. Resisting she yelled, "Get off me! I didn't mean to hit you! I'm sorry I hit you but you have no right . . ."

Unfamiliar guttural words spilled around her like sawdust, suffocating her protest.

She stumbled under his aggression. On looking up, her gaze met the darkest most intense eyes she'd ever seen. Set in a handsome though strangely unexpressive face, they commanded her to act.

"Let go of me!" she demanded, jerking one arm away.

"Get down!" the mountain man ordered, urgency ringing in his voice.

Helen fell. Not intending to comply with the order but unbalanced by the man who was forcing her back toward her vehicle, her knee connected with broken asphalt. Abruptly, before she could gain her feet, the stranger's cold hands were on her, pulling her up.

At the same time a shot rang out and dirt beside her at the side of the road leapt skyward. Helen screamed and sprang to her feet.

The stranger released her.

"Shit!" she yelled, sprinting toward the open door of the hover. For the first time she realized the danger.

Gravel kicked up behind her as more shots rang out. She closed on the hovercar. The gravel splashed onto the broken asphalt on the road, a small landslide that punctuated her fear.

"No! For chrissake," the man with the gun screamed, running toward her vehicle, his weapon in full view.

It all made sense now. This maniac was trying to kill the guy she had hit. That's why he ran out in front of her. He was trying to escape a crazy man. And the poor s.o.b. was just trying to get her to take him out of harm's way.

Whimpering she dove inside the craft, she fumbled with the passenger hatch to admit the man she'd hit, while more shots struck the vehicle. The stranger lunged through the hatch, slamming it behind him, barking orders in a language she couldn't understand. Sealed inside with him she hit the accelerator and shot forward.

* * * * * * *

Brandon doubled back along the lane that passed for a road in these parts, limping badly on a twisted knee and his arthritic hip which was determined to punish him for the transgression of running full out.

He charged into his familiar farmyard just as the mist turned to rain. Jumping into the rarely used pickup that reclined like a dinosaur in the driveway, he swore while rummaging through the glove box. Finding a carton of shells for the old weapon, he reloaded, then set the rifle onto the seat beside him. He turned the key that always stayed in the ignition.

"Come on ya bloody shit bucket!" he cursed as the starter groaned. He'd done more swearing since eight o'clock this morning than he usually did in a week and Brandon was no stranger to colorful language.

In trouble throughout his senior years at school for his use for, among other things, his use of the Queen's English as his teachers put it, he'd given up on ever finishing. In fact, Brandon had given up on most things connected with life. The wreckage of three marriages was strewn out behind him as he set out after the beast this Saturday morning on the last day of October.

He couldn't give up on this, though. Shit! This was no game. He just knew this thing wasn't here for the fun of it. Whatever it had come to Earth to do would impact on Brandon too. Society could go to hell, for all Brandon cared, but he still needed an infrastructure of some sort out there beyond the limits of his little subsistence farm.

"Please baby? Please?" he coaxed. The engine caught. "All right!" he yelled, slapping the steering wheel. "Now I'm gonna nail your red-eyed ass!"

Peering over one shoulder, he hurled an arm across the seat as though anchoring himself and threw the transmission in reverse. The pickup lurched backwards toward the road. Then the truck shook violently, misfired, and a piercing clap split the air. Great blue clouds billowed from the exhaust, blocking his view of the lane.

Reaching the potholed pavement of Millstream Lake Road, he slammed the truck into first. Tires squealed with the abrupt change of direction. Brandon geared up and pressed down hard on the gas. The speedometer slowly climbed to forty.

"Come on! Come on!" he urged as the truck labored. Not daring to travel these roads any faster, and knowing he couldn't force the jalopy to do much more, he slapped on the windshield wipers and tried to see through the muddy mess they spread across his line of vision. Switchbacks and hairpin turns he knew by rote waited ahead.

He snatched the rifle off the seat and cradled it on his lap. In the distance the sound of the little red speed demon tickled at the edge of hearing. He rolled down the window. Rain pattered on his left shoulder. Taking a corner without slowing he closed the gap between them.

"I know this road better than you do, girlie," he whispered.

His breath came raggedly. The weapon almost slid off his lap as the old rust bucket dipped into a gully. Then her nose thrust suddenly into the air as the outmoded vehicle had to climb a steep hill, slowing with the effort.

With the gas pedal to the floor he jerked back and forth as though the motion would help the pickup overcome the incline. The gun leaned back against his gut reassuringly. The truck dropped again to follow the road and the firearm slid onto his legs. A switchback came on him from the right and without slowing he piloted the broken asphalt like winter run-off in a river bed, hugging the banks. The insect whine of the hovercar's turbine grew closer.

* * * * * * *

Helen leaned forward, gripping the yoke with both sweaty hands. The swoosh-flip of the wipers across the windshield distracted her from focusing on the road. Trees crowded at the edges of the asphalt, branches overhanging in places, scraping the little red hovercar as it passed.

"Gra flap a kap! Gra flap a kap!" the stranger yelled striking the control panel with a slap. He stared over his shoulder anxiously.

"I'm going as fast as I can in this fog!" Helen protested, taking his meaning if not his words. "And the rain isn't helping." The worst

Alien Stalker

switchback on the road loomed ahead and she slowed to negotiate the turn. The stranger gripped her arm painfully.

"Wina calbritron, Diasala!"

Helen snapped her arm away and yelled at him. "You can go to hell if you think I'm wrapping this thing around a tree!" Steering with one hand she almost did just that. "I'm going as fast as I can! Now back off!" The last words were spat like venom.

Now it was his turn to take her meaning, if not her words. He sat back in the bucket seat and regarded her with cold dark eyes.

Behind, the ancient truck poked its head through the mist. A shot rang out and something struck a fist-sized chip of bark from a tree at the edge of the road.

"No!" Helen breathed, stepping down hard on the accelerator as she came out of the turn. They pulled ahead and the truck disappeared in a bank of fog. A battered sign flashed past in the haze. Helen announced their locale. "Mount Work Regional Park," she stammered. "McKenzie Bight. Almost there!" The windshield wipers whooshed across the screen. "Come on baby!" she said to the little craft encouragingly. "You can do it!"

Another shot ripped past the speeding craft.

"Gra flap a KAP!" the stranger shrieked.

"Oh shut up!" Helen screamed back. She nevertheless stepped harder on the accelerator. Ahead, a fork in the road announced the start of a well maintained surface. She spun onto it without braking and the staunch little craft flew over the smooth blacktop, speeding them away from the maniac with the rifle.

* * * * * * *

Brandon negotiated the corner with a squeal of rubber on pavement and let up on the gas. He pulled the old green Ford to the shoulder and watched as technology crippled him. There was no way in hell he could catch the hover now, not on the roads it was built for. No way in hell. And hell was exactly where that fat blonde was headed.

* * * * * * *

Helen felt like a rabbit that had just outrun a fox. "Good grief! That guy is nuts!" she said looking wide-eyed at the man she'd rescued from the lunatic. If it was excitement she'd wanted, she had surely found it. Only this wasn't the sort of excitement she had been expecting.

"I'm going straight to the police with this." With immediate danger receding behind her, she was, of course, now trapped in the speeding car with this stranger.

The thought crossed her mind that she might be no better off than she had been a few minutes earlier with bullets whizzing past. She dismissed the thought nervously.

Her passenger's head lolled back against the seat. His eyes closed. He groaned loudly then opened his eyes. Without a word, he ran his right hand over his thigh and groaned again.

"You've been shot!" she exclaimed, suddenly realizing that the old idiot with the rifle had hit his mark after all. "Why didn't you say something?" Then it dawned on her that she wouldn't have understood him if he had. She jerked the vehicle to the side of the road and stopped. "Let me see," she said with authority, leaning over him to examine the wound.

"Casan innash nova it a-bray, DIASALA?" he snapped, pushing her away. "Gra flap!" He gestured to the steering yoke.

"Don't you speak any ENGLISH?" Helen asked, carefully enunciating the last word as though that would make a difference to his understanding it. She wrinkled her brow in puzzlement. He frowned hard, peering into her pale eyes. Without answering her question he shrugged toward the controls. "Gra flap," he repeated.

The wiper continued its whoosh, flip, whoosh, flip.

"Gra flap," Helen repeated. "Drive." She adjusted herself in her seat. Gripping the yoke she looked out at the empty road, eased away from the shoulder.

"Drive," the stranger said perfectly as if in complete command of the language. No hint of an accent clung to the word.

"Do you speak English?" she asked again cautiously, hopefully, glancing back at him.

"Drive," he parroted.

"Yes." She nodded with disappointment as trees sped past, realizing he couldn't speak English. "Yes. Drive," she said belligerently. "What am I here for but to rescue you from raging lunatics and ferry you around?"

"Yes," he said nodding.

"I have to get you to a hospital. I'M TAKING YOU TO A HOSPITAL," she said in a loud voice, carefully pronouncing each syllable. "You know. Where there are doctors and things like that?" Then to herself she added, "Then I'm going to report that psychopath to the police."

He frowned at her. "Drive," he said, jerking his head toward the road.

"I have to get HELP for you," she announced, knowing he didn't understand a word of what she said. The statement helped clarify what she must do. Leaning across his lap she tapped his injured leg in an effort to explain. Instantly, in a flash she didn't even see, he had her by the arm.

"Ouch!" she complained. "Let go!" She twisted in his grip. "Let go!" she repeated, unable to wrest her arm free. Her eyes darted from the road to his face and back. The hover swerved dangerously, hitting the gravel shoulder and veering back onto asphalt, rocking as she tried to steady it with only her left hand.

"Let go," he uttered, staring into her frightened eyes, releasing her arm with an exaggerated, almost contemptuous jerk.

"Never mind," Helen said angrily, gripping the yoke until her knuckles turned white, easing back onto the highway. Trying to control her temper, she said, "I'll just take you to the hospital. You don't need to know where I'm taking you. The doctors can deal with you." She sighed loudly. "I shouldn't have got involved. Should have left you back there to face that nut. You're two peas in a pod as my old grandmother would say."

He smiled with what looked like amusement. "Oh you think this is funny?" Her blonde brow shot up challengingly. She shook her head. "It's not funny, buddy." He shrugged and mumbled something that could have been an apology. After a moment Helen sighed again and the anger eased. He was a foreigner after all. "I'm just taking you to the hospital. They can worry about you."

"Drive, Diasala," he said.

"Diasala?" she asked, thumping her chest in a superior manner.

He looked over at her with mischievous dark eyes. "Yes," he replied, smirking. "Diasala." He nodded.

"Helen," she said, this time whacking her chest. Anger still lurked just under the surface. She repeated her name as though speaking to someone of an inferior mental capacity. "Hel-en."

He nodded and the smirk changed to a grin, melting whatever residual annoyance she still felt. "Jonflan," he said, rapping his own chest.

"John Flan?" she repeated, looking puzzled. "That's a good English name." She thought a moment. "Or maybe it's Irish. Whatever! You should be able to speak English. You look English enough. Actually you look just like that guy who was trying to kill you. Only younger. Is he your father or something?"

John just stared at her without comprehension.

"Never mind," she said. "We're almost to the hospital and they can deal with all this."

Taking a turn onto Wilkinson Road, she guided her little, now less than perfect, red, sports hovercar into the Victoria General Hospital parking lot nearest to the emergency entrance.

Anger rolled over her. It would cost a lot to repair the damage to her car. There would be a lot of inconvenience too, waiting on repair men, deadlines that would never be met. As the thought planted itself she wondered how she was going to explain what had happened to the police. Hell, she'd have to give the doctors some account of how her companion had been shot. She flipped off the wipers.

"OKAY," she said loudly and clearly in an attempt to be understood. "You." She enunciated the word carefully and gingerly and only tapped his shoulder, not wanting to lose a hand in the attempt to communicate. "And I . . ." She touched her chest. "Are going . . ." She pointed toward the hospital entrance and, staring steadily into his dark orbs, nodded. "Understand?"

To Helen's relief, the light of understanding did indeed don on John's face. "Ac innash ovkala zit," he said, motioning with his chin toward the towering gray building with its antiquated bright red, blue and yellow ventilation ducts running from the ground to the sixth floor making it look like anything but a modern hospital. "Vas in noval obra," he sputtered, lowering his head.

"Vas in what?" she asked. "Oh John," she said with compassion. "You're ill. Please let's just go inside."

"Vas in noval obra, Diasala."

"We have to go inside," she pleaded, opening her door. Her eyes spoke compassion. The sound of her words, almost cooing, seemed to soften him. He looked at her, puzzled. "Come with me," she coaxed.

She started disembarking. Swinging one leg out she began bringing the other after it. Suddenly, like soap bubbles, the mood broke. He grabbed her arm with familiar strength—strength she thought out of place in his present state—and pulled her back inside, whipping her around to face him.

"Drive!" he demanded.

"You have to get that WOUND seen to," she insisted, pointing to his injured leg.

He shook his head. "Wound," he said clearly. Then he patted his chest.

"Oh. The wound is John Flan's?" she asked, nodding and feeling stupid at expressing his thought in so simplistic a manner. "Macho man I suppose."

"Yes. Wound, Jonflan.

"No!" Helen shook her head and looked stern. Perhaps the injury had made him delirious. For his own good she had to get severe. "John must see doctor." She jabbed a finger toward the hospital. For comfort's sake she brought her leg back into the car though, intending once she'd straightened out his wrongful thinking to recommence departure.

"No. Vas in noval obra, Diasala."

"Vas in noval obra?"

"Yes. Drive." He tapped her on the chest. "Vas in noval obra, Helen. Gra flap, Jonflan in noval obra, Helen. Obra," he repeated, pointing down the road to a house that was barely visible from their position.

"Obra?" she said, trying to understand what he wanted of her.

He closed his eyes for a moment, swallowed hard and, on opening them, tapped her on the chest. "Nova - noval!" he said, exasperation scarcely controlled. "Nova innash, Helen. Nova innash, Diasala." He tapped her on the chest again. Never before today had a man tapped her on the chest for any reason. Now suddenly one was doing it repeatedly, like he owned her. In some sense it was quite a comfortable and familiar action. In another, it was threatening.

"Nova innash Helen," she repeated, concentrating on the words. "You are Helen!" she said. "You are Diasala." She smiled broadly at her accomplishment. "Nova innash! You are!"

"Yes. You are Helen," he said. He rubbed her face gently. "Helen, pi griezin op, Helen. Obra," he repeated pointing to the house he had earlier indicated. "Drive Jonflan in noval obra."

Suddenly she understood. "That's a house? You want me to take you to my house?" she stated with incredulity.

"House," he repeated. "House?" He pointed to the house off in the distance. "Obra?"

"Yes. That's a house," she said.

"Obra. Yes. House. Take Jonflan Helen house."

"OH no, buddy!" she said. "You just hold your horses," she pointed a finger at him. "You need medical help and the hospital is where you're going to get it."

He clenched her arm with authority and looked deeply into her pale blue eyes. Running his hand along her jaw he examined her face. Helen stretched her chin out to smooth a plump little ripple she knew hung there. Suddenly she realized she was attracted to this man. There was something compelling about his rugged good looks. He looked as though nothing could harm him. Strength. That was the first attribute she would ascribe to him.

"Listen," she said softly. "You need help. John Flan needs to see a doctor."

"Jonflan take Helen house," he said. "Helen gis sakin bray, Jonflan."

"I should look after you? Is that what you're saying?"

"Helen," he touched her arm and then tapped his wounded leg, "gis sakin bray, Jonflan."

"That IS what you're saying!"

"Sakin bray, Jonflan, Helen house."

"Oh Christ!" she said, inhaling deeply.

He rubbed her chin playfully, then grimaced with pain. "Helen, ovin griezin op." He smiled and touched her fair hair. The bun on top of her head had loosened and strands hung down in blonde and light brown wisps.

"What language is that?" she asked. "German? Russian? Spanish? It doesn't sound like anything I've ever heard before."

"Drive Jonflan Helen house?" he asked gently.

Drawn into his gaze she felt paralyzed. Like a doe in the lights of an oncoming car. Dizziness momentarily gripped her. When her head cleared she felt enormously calm.

"Okay. Drive John Flan Helen's house," she said. "I'm probably going to regret this," she told herself, shaking her head with incomprehension.

She started the car. "But what the hell."

"Nova zik ashley pi slitt vera."

"Well I hope that's a compliment," Helen said. "I hope you're not saying I'm the biggest boob that's ever lived."

"Apil zulis os gin fonnar noval griezin op taka slitt!"

A chill ran down Helen's spine as he finished the statement. Of course she didn't know what he said. It was the way he said it. Something in the way he said those words made her uneasy. The only word she could really comprehend was noval. Noval was 'your'. If nova was you, noval must be your. She suspected 'griezin op' meant pretty because he'd said that when rubbing her face the first time. Or maybe her vanity interfered with her comprehension. She had no idea what was meddling with her ability to reason, although something inside said the idea of taking him home was crazy, insane.

It wasn't often a man called her pretty. She was flattered. 'You're pretty', if that's what he'd said, sounded almost like a slur. And the word fonnar; he'd said fonnar like it was a weapon.

But why then . . . was she taking him home? Her vision blurred for a moment as she asked herself this. But then the self-doubt cleared out like morning fog and she stepped down firmly on the accelerator.

The words of that old song ran through her brain.

In the back of my mind I maintain
the thought of you, my heart's horizon line
They say love travels blind . . .